TUNE IN
TOMORROW

TUNE IN TOMORROW

THE CURIOUS, CALAMITOUS,
COCKAMAMIE STORY OF
STARR WEATHERBY
AND THE GREATEST MYTHIC
REALITY SHOW EVER

BY RANDEE DAWN

SOLARIS

First published 2022 by Solaris
an imprint of Rebellion Publishing Ltd,
Riverside House, Osney Mead,
Oxford, OX2 0ES, UK

www.solarisbooks.com

ISBN: 978-1-78618-630-0

A CIP catalogue record for this book is available from the
British Library.

Designed & typeset by Rebellion Publishing

REBELLION

Printed in Denmark

To my mother, who made everything possible.

"We do not live in this world alone, but in a thousand other worlds."

— Irna Phillips, *Another World*

When I think of soap operas
And what makes them so popular
The answer's posing in front of my eyes

— The Trashcan Sinatras, "Thrupenny Tears"

CHAPTER 1

Wish Upon a Starr

Fork. Knife. Spoon. Napkin. Ring.
Stack.
Knife. Fork. Spoon. Napkin. Ring.
Stack.
Variations on a theme, thought Starr Weatherby, her blue nail-polished fingers on autopilot as she crafted stainless-steel utensil rolls, yearning to be anywhere but here. She was forty-seven minutes into her shift at Mike's Diner, it was 6:32 a.m. on a summer Thursday and she had seventy-three more rolls to construct before Mike would even consider letting her have the privilege of waiting on tables again.

All around her, Mike's thrummed: grease pans sizzling, plates clattering, short-order cooks swearing in multiple tongues. Regulars flirted with waitresses, whose shoes made *smuck smuck* sounds on the linoleum as they negotiated the packed booths and tables. A fug of burned pancakes, buttery eggs, fatty bacon and defrosted juices lingered in the air, settling on Starr's thick blonde curls.

All the while, Mike and his manicured handlebar

mustache lurked behind the register. He rattled the pages of the *New York Post* while casting a gimlet eye around the room.

Starr stood to one side of the coffee-and-supplies station spinning her utensil packages, bored solid. The subway had stalled underground this morning, making her late; eleven minutes into her shift she'd sworn under her breath and a customer had overheard her—but really, was 'craptacular' a swear?—then delivered regular instead of Canadian bacon to table twelve. She was distracted for a good reason, but in Mike's, three strikes and you're doomed to make one hundred utensil rolls, plus miss getting tips until you've finished.

Dang Canadians, she grumbled to herself. *Who wants your dumb hammy bacon, anyway?*

Checking first to ensure Mike was deep into the sports section, Starr poked at the phone on the counter. The face lit up. She couldn't miss this call. It might be *the* call, if she intended to get out of here.

Nothing.

Back to the rolls, her eyes scanned the room to relieve the tedium. Theresa was still AWOL. Her shift partner had been green all morning, then after taking a few orders had beelined to the bathroom. Starr was counting the minutes: if Theresa's morning sickness kept her off the floor much longer, she'd take over whether Mike liked it or not.

An overly loud, exaggerated yawn startled her, and she glanced around. "How much longer, Valentine?"

"Patience, mi compadre." A second voice, different. Both seemed male, but the additional one had a lilt that conjured folk songs and rolling green grass in Starr's mind. "All will be made clear—indirectly."

Most of the diner's cacophony washed over Starr as white noise, but these words sliced through the tumult like a knife through butter. She lifted up on her toes, peering over the workstation divider to catch a glimpse of the curved booth to the right. Table five. One of Theresa's. It held three occupants, a single mug of coffee and a growing stack of shredded napkins.

"This is not a whim," said the man called Valentine. He was a rangy, incredibly pale thing with a sharp nose and angular face. His wavy brown hair pointed up with two pronounced cowlicks at the crown—yet on closer examination they did not quite appear to be hair.

"Events shall unfold at a speed that will dazzle even a jaded old pombero like yourself," he continued. "We only need wait for Fiona to arrive."

Starr had never heard of a pombero. It sounded like a hat with a tufted end.

"She's late as usual," the jaded old pombero growled, glancing around the room. His skin shone like obsidian. "Speaking of missing humans, are you certain the mortal we've come to see is even here today?"

"Cris, I have never steered you wrong in four hundred years." Valentine pinched his friend's cheek while giving him a saucy look. "Her schedule is unwaveringly consistent."

Paper bits fluttered like snow as the third occupant of the table finished shredding a napkin. She licked her fingers, smoothed down her short, lustrous hair and adjusted her polka-dotted dress. "I, for one, hope this hire proves both acceptable and durable," she spoke while examining her pointed nails. There was a feline aspect to her—languorous and narrow-eyed—and her clipped accent reminded Starr of the way actors in Jane

Austen movies sounded. "We writers require fresh meat for our... inspiration."

Starr hadn't blinked for a full minute and her eyes were as crispy as potato chips. Table five was damned difficult to turn away from. It was as if they existed in color, while Starr toiled away in black and white. Weirdos, even by the standards of New York City—but she had a sudden urge to slide into the booth, lean over the table, and beg them to let her join the group. Whatever they were up to, it was better than working at Mike's.

Of course, if she made any move, Mike would descend upon her with more punishments. Maybe a year's worth of utensil rolls. Sighing, she returned to the stack. Only sixty-nine to go. Fork. Knife. Spoon. Napkin. Ring—

"Did you say 'mango'?" Cris, that jaded old pombero, barked laughter. Again, Starr inched her eyes and the bridge of her nose over the divide, unable to resist. Valentine was nodding, chuckling. She envisioned them as theater weirdos, maybe even filmmakers. One had said she was a writer, and Valentine was obviously in costume with those little horny points on his head. Show business, no question.

"...has other talents as well," he was saying.

"One of which is acting," said the woman, tapping her claw-like fingernails on the table. "She is a thespian, is she not? A player? An artiste? A ham?"

Acting! Starr straightened as if a gun had been fired. She patted at her headscarf and adjusted her uniform to reveal just a bit of cleavage. They were talking her language.

"Where is that blasted bruja?" Cris growled, pulling a cigar from behind his ear that Starr was certain hadn't been there a moment ago. "Can't Bookender keep her on a schedule for once?"

Bruja. Spanish. A foul word, but the translation eluded Starr. *Is he talking about Theresa?* Maybe they were getting impatient for their order. Something had to be done.

"Do you suspect this one is ready? Able? Willing?" asked the Jane Austen woman. "At least, more so than our... last attempt?"

Valentine twisted his spoon so hard it made a knot in the handle. Starr's eyes widened. "That will never happen again, Emma."

"Kind of bad form to misplace a whole mortal, y'know." Cris craned over to admire the spoon handiwork. It unknotted at his touch. "TPTB thought—"

Starr raised an eyebrow. *TPTB*. In showbiz, that usually meant The Powers That Be, as in, the executives. Maybe they were with a TV show?

Noise from the kitchen blotted out whatever Cris said next. When it faded, Valentine was saying, "—protocols. And I fail to see either of you two solving our mutual problem. Eyeballs are being lost every day. Arachne reports our buzz is down sixty-eight points on her web."

"Is that bad?" Emma stopped drumming.

"'Down' is bad in general," Cris grumbled. "Up is the preferred direction."

"Radical steps are necessary," said Valentine. "This is why we are here today."

Starr's phone did a little dance on the workstation.

"A truly radical step would be to release Fiona back into the wild." Emma's voice rumbled like a tiny motor. "She bores the whiskers off me."

"Fiona Ballantine is the primary reason we have any eyeballs—or buzz," said Valentine.

"You let her get away with all kinds of caca," said Cris. "She takes advantage."

Valentine let out a low, irritated snort. "Releasing her is not an option. Besides, we need more actors, not fewer. Thirty years is too long between hires."

Starr's phone continued dancing.

"Well," Emma chose another napkin to rend. "I might explore the old scripts if Phil would grant me access. They are a wealth of—"

"Absolutely not!" Cris boomed. Six leaves on the philodendron hanging over his head shriveled and tumbled into the radiator. "Joseph's work is off-limits for eternity. Phil will roast anyone who tries to access them."

Starr's phone wouldn't stop vibrating, and she snapped to. *Casting director!* This was the call! Yesterday's audition for an underarm deodorant had ended on a positive note—she'd even get lines if they hired her. Sure, she needed the money—but more importantly, she had to get this acting career of hers on track.

"Starr Weatherby," she whispered into the phone. It wasn't her real name, but who would hire a *Samantha Wornicker*? That was a name destined to fail. *Starr Weatherby*, on the other hand, had a future. Maybe.

Table five fell silent.

"Ah, yes," said a distracted, nasal woman on the other end. "Malcolm Underwood's office calling. We're going in a different direction for the 'Smell Ya Later' campaign. Mr. Underwood thanks you for your time."

"Oh." A crushing, vanishing sensation descended. Apparently, no one would hire *Starr Weatherby*, either. "Are there any—"

The line was already dead.

She stared at the phone, blinking back tears. Hot waves of shame rolled through her body. *No crying at work*, she admonished herself, but she had to let loose somewhere.

She grabbed a spoon and tried giving it a twist, but it would not knot.

Mama was right, she thought. *She always said my real assets were on my chest.*

But Mama was wrong, Starr knew it. Being someone else on stage was all she'd ever dreamed of. At seven, she'd memorized a few lines from Shakespeare and felt strangely transformed—transported, really—into a whole other person's mind. It was like putting on a costume for your soul. And it was *fun*. Then Grandpa had applauded, and that sealed the deal: applause was like love made audible.

But passion had not translated into work. Nor had a degree in the dramatic arts from Gilliard—not, as advertised, a sister school to Juilliard. She'd discovered that to her dismay after relocating to New York from Maryland. Six years post-graduation, though, she was starting to despair. Jobs, when they happened, were small and scarce. The last one had been eight months ago: a second lead in a play so far off-Broadway it was held on a barge in the East River. Midway through a soliloquy in act two on opening night she'd tripped on a chair and tumbled headfirst into the drink—dragging every prop on a kitchen table with her.

Last week had been the capper: she'd had an in with a casting director for a role on a kids' show that shot in Los Angeles and in a burst of surprising nerves, had brought along her motorcycle-loving boyfriend Gerry for support.

And they'd hired *him*!

Gerry, whose sole ambition until that moment had been to repair engines, took off for the West Coast three days later and simultaneously forgot how to text, because Starr hadn't heard from him since.

On the whole, Starr feared she'd peaked in her final year of drama school. Her class had been required to try out their improv skills in front of a real audience in a hole-in-the-ground comedy venue for a final project. She'd taken the audience prompts to become a mango that sang and ran with it. In that moment, something clicked: the randomness, the sheer surreal nature of improv made her feel like she had with Grandpa and Shakespeare: like her soul had put on a new outfit. She could be anything. She could do anything. So she'd given that mango her all.

But nobody ever became an award-winning actor by playing warbling tropical fruit.

"Perhaps we should simply adjourn, depart, exit." Emma's smooth voice caught her ear. "I have eight scripts to complete."

"And I'm blocking scenes in an hour," Cris muttered. "Fiona is clearly not coming."

Scripts. Blocking. Despite her despair, the words rang in Starr's ears like the jangle of a door. Her heart raced. All theater words. Stage jargon. And they were about to walk out. Maybe forever.

They don't have to, she thought. One of them had mentioned mangoes.

It was a sign.

Starr peered over the edge a final time, and Valentine's gaze met hers.

"Miss?" he lifted his coffee cup. "I'm as parched as the Rub' al Khali, and our waitress seems to have tumbled down a bottomless pit."

"Eep," said Starr, heart thudding. He was gorgeous. He was strange. She forgot her own name for a moment.

Come home. Admit defeat. The image of Mama, one claw hooked around her 'medicine' mug and the other extended to drag Starr back home—that was what finally goosed her, as sure as if Mike had pinched her bottom himself.

"Sure," she whispered to Valentine, and cleared her throat. "Be right with ya."

No sign of Theresa. Starr strode to Mike, who was pretending to scan the Help Wanted ads. "Table five," she gasped. "They're ready to order."

Mike eyeballed the dining room. "Theresa'll be out in a second. Get back to your piles."

"Theresa's been upchucking in the can for almost twenty minutes. I'll handle her table."

Mike gave her a cool look. He hadn't liked her since she'd told him to quit 'accidentally' touching her ass, and today's failures had only made him surlier. "You like working here, Starr?"

"*Love* it, Mike."

"Then make me more utensil packages, or you're gone."

Starr narrowed her eyes and turned toward the workstation. Cris and Emma were scooting around the booth, preparing to exit.

Go big or go home. Starr grabbed a pot of hot joe and hurried to Table Five, thinking of Grandpa and murmuring, "She is the fairies' midwife, and she comes in shape no bigger than an agate stone on the forefinger of an alderman, drawn with a team of little atomies over men's noses as they lie asleep." This *Romeo and Juliet* speech in particular was a calming mantra to her.

Arriving at the booth, she tipped the carafe into Valentine's mug and asked, "Y'all want some food?"

Cris folded his arms, the unlit stogie dangling from a corner of his mouth. He nodded and turned to Valentine. "Not bad, for a mortal. Bit on the larger side, though."

"We *have* a narrow blonde back at the show already," Valentine told him.

Starr did not waver, still holding the coffee pot.

Emma twitched her nose at Starr. The trio's mutual gaze was so focused and bright Starr had to look at the injured philodendron. Valentine pressed Starr's free hand down on the table and held her in place. A shiver ran up her arm.

"We'll take a gallon of your fruit salad," he said, smacking fifty dollars onto the table. "But first—words. You were quoting something. Continue."

He removed his fingers from her hand and Starr glanced over her shoulder. Mike would fire her anyway—if not today, then tomorrow. She closed her eyes and invited Mercutio to speak again.

Do it, said a voice inside that was not her mother's. *Be the mango.*

Diving in, she started the speech again, the words cold and refreshing. Getting into the part she began waving the carafe of coffee around like a scepter, throwing her whole body into it, gesturing broadly as if the diner had become a Broadway stage. She was graceful, sliding around the tables, fully in the moment, booming out lines with full vigor to her audience of one: Valentine and his remarkable emerald eyes.

He was nodding.

Encouraged, Starr bumped it up a notch. "Of healths five-fathom deep; and then anon drums in his ear, at which he starts," she thrust her hands forward, "and wakes—"

"*Starr Weatherby!* Put that coffee down right *now!*"

Mike's voice was not like a knife through butter; it was more like a mace swung at her skull. Startled, Starr slammed the carafe on the table and winced at the sound of glass shattering. She squeezed her eyes shut, flinching from the disaster.

Dead silence.

Opening her eyes, she expected to find table five and its occupants covered in hot brown java and shattered glass—but saw nothing of the sort. Emma's pile of shredded napkins had been reconfigured to form a barrier around the wide, spreading spill... of water, which was dripping over the edge of the table.

The carafe was intact. And empty. Starr gaped. Emma had jumped up on the banquette, one hand covering her mouth. Cris chewed on his cigar, his face full of gleeful anticipation.

Valentine, who had never taken his eyes from Starr, whispered, "*Showtime.*"

A hand clapped against Starr's backside and she flinched. Mike shoved her away, fingers brushing against her chest and lingering there for an extended beat. "Pack up," he hissed. "You are done here." He turned to the table, apologizing and throwing a dirty rag over the water.

Panic spiraled. Her brio of a few minutes earlier had dissipated in the face of reality: she wouldn't make rent without a job. She'd be kicked out of her apartment. She didn't even have Gerry's basement pit as a backup. There were student loans. And worst: she'd screwed up while *acting*, the one thing she thought she knew how to do well.

Cris and Emma slid around their seats. "Going back now," he said. "Fiona was right, skipping this mess,"

"Hold on." Valentine held up a hand. His gaze had remained steady. It was like he was waiting for something.

Every bit of Starr demanded that she flee. She wanted to throw her headscarf and cheap apron on the stove and set them ablaze. She wanted to run home, for as long as she had one, and settle in with a pint of Ample Hills ice cream and a bottle of wine and see where they took her.

But if she gave up, there was only one road to take—the one that ended in Mama's home, with Mama's claws.

Valentine raised an eyebrow and tilted his head. His hair shifted. Those were definitely horns.

Starr punted.

"Do *not* touch me, you pervert!" She jumped away from Mike, clutching at her chest. Or most of her chest.

Mike whirled, fists on hips. "Are you still here? Being crazy? I never touched you."

"You saw that!" Starr cried, pointing at a nearby table's customers, harnessing the panic and riding it like a wild horse. "And you saw it!" she turned to Valentine. "He grabbed my—my—" She burst into tears. "And then he *fired* me!"

The cigar fell from Cris' mouth.

Valentine's gemlike eyes lit up and he grinned. "Why, yes," he nodded broadly. "Harassment! Maybe assault! Possibly other seasonings, too. Miss, you should call the constables. Also, a judge! At least an attorney."

Starr turned on the waterworks, and they weren't entirely invented. She needed a job, even this crappy one. She needed a life.

Take me with you, she thought at this total stranger named Valentine.

Mike blustered and flailed, sputtering denials while every table gawked and a few hissed. Then he read the room and glowered. "Fine!" He tossed his rag onto the tabletop. "Not fired. You get to stay and make utensil pyramids forever!"

Starr gulped air, dramatically batting her eyes. She rested the back of her hand on her forehead. "I... don't know," she stage-whispered, loud enough for everyone to hear.

She'd never fainted in her life, she wasn't that type, but she could put it on when needed. "I might need to… lie down."

"Then lie down!" said Mike. "Lie down forever and come back never. You're crazy, completely nuts."

Valentine picked up his fifty dollars and slipped around Mike, who suddenly became solicitous. "Sir, please, stay. This restaurant—she's a little funny but this is a fine place to eat."

Valentine ignored him, passing behind Starr. He leaned over her shoulder, and she caught a musky scent reminiscent of sweet hay and almost—but not quite—forgot her name again.

"Quite a performance, darling," that sing-song voice crooned, and a business card slipped into her hand. Valentine raised his head and addressed the room. "Do phone sometime, Starr Weatherby. I know all kinds of great 'lawyers' who will help you advance your… case."

With that, Valentine headed to the door where his friends waited. He half-turned and winked. Starr's heart paused. A long, narrow tail tipped in fur darted out from his overcoat.

The weirdo trio from table five disappeared through the doorway.

Tail? Starr thought, head whirling. *Horns? Seriously?* She'd heard of the devil in the details—but never in the diner.

The corners of the business card bit into her hand and she turned her palm up.

JASON VALENTINE, it read, with a local phone number beneath in curiously pulsing, scripted numerals.

EXECUTIVE PRODUCER
TUNE IN TOMORROW

CHAPTER 2

Starr Gate

"WELL, SHIT."

Starr stood on a footpath just below the Verrazzano Bridge, facing a loosely locked set of bent, rusting gates abutting low concrete walls. Paint had long ago flaked from these nominal barriers, and tufts of weedy green pushed through the neglected, cracked path beyond. And what was beyond? Nothing. The asphalt continued to the other side, leading to a broader green patch and then—water. Either Upper Bay or Gravesend Bay, Starr couldn't be sure. But very definitely water. Over it all, the bridge towered above her and sang with the music of morning traffic just starting to jam.

The gates all but telegraphed: *Keep moving. Nothing to see here, folks.*

She checked the scrap of paper with coordinates scrawled on it—she'd never have found it without her phone's GPS—then paced back and forth on the path, dodging a lone jogger with a dog and a single cyclist. Could she have gotten it wrong? She probably wrote it down wrong. Everything had happened so fast. And now, here she was—alone, at five in the morning on a quiet cycle path in Brooklyn, nowhere near a studio, staring at the wrong location.

Starr swore again, louder this time.

Loser, Mama's voice groused again. *Can't even write down some numbers. Who would want you on their show? What makes you so special, missy?*

Her watch was accurate. She was on time.

On time to be the butt of someone's joke, that was.

YESTERDAY, SHE'D COLLAPSED at home after being fired from Mike's. After waking, she'd confirmed the bad news with her bank account: $287.25, then decanted wine from a bottle in the refrigerator into a mug. None of her roommates would be home at this hour, so she could get drunk in silence. It was five o'clock somewhere.

After a few swigs, she'd dialed the number on the business card.

"Starr!" Jason Valentine had shouted into the phone after barely half a ring. He sounded fuzzy and distant, as if she'd reached him all the way around the world.

"Aah!" she'd cried, spilling wine down her blouse. "You scared me."

Crackle, fizz. "You're the one who called me."

"Can't argue with that." She'd swiped at the wet patch, then began tugging the shirt off, trying to maneuver the phone and her sleeves at the same time.

"Delightful," he'd said. "One sec."

His voice had muffled, and the bubbling white noise surged. She heard him scolding someone, which gave her time to pull the blouse up over her head. She'd forgotten to unbutton it, though, and it stuck over her eyes.

"Starr?"

"Mmph." She'd pasted the phone to her ear, wearing her shirt like a hat. One arm remained trapped.

Jason had begun giving her a series of numbers, and she used a free hand to blindly scribble them down. "Is this a math test?" she garbled beneath the fabric.

"A location. I understand it helps fix humans onto a point on the map on your side of the Veil."

They were words, and they were in English, but she had no idea what some of them meant. But Starr couldn't focus on that: she was starting to get claustrophobic from the blouse.

"Be there tomorrow at 5:02."

"In the *morning*?"

Zzzzt crackle bsss. "Gate appears at 5:03."

"But—" She gave the blouse a great yank. A button went flying into her mug and sank to the bottom.

"No need to thank me. You'll love it here—hold on."

Starr had twisted the blouse from her head with one final jerk, hearing it tear. With a quick switch of hands, she wriggled the sleeve until it fell to the ground. The air in the apartment had been cool and goosebumps prickled her skin.

"Everything will be made clear tomorrow," Jason said when he returned. "Well, most things. OK, some things."

"Should I bring—"

"Only yourself. Maybe a change of clothes. You could be here for some time."

"How long—"

"Fine, you dragged it out of me: sometimes the Gate is persnickety." Again, faint noises distracted him, and Starr heard the tick-tick of heels nearing. "It's only open for a few seconds, so *be on time.*"

The noises had resolved into a robust, insistent female

voice. "There is a *watercooler* outside my dressing room, Mr. Valentine!"

"I know, Fiona—" Jason's voice muffled, as if he'd put a hand over the receiver. "Wait just one moment—"

"The last one spilled molten maple syrup everywhere and I will *not* ruin my wardrobe again!" The voice continued to rise in volume.

Starr had raised her eyebrows. Was someone particularly into pancakes at the studio? Also, this Fiona sounded like a nightmare.

Jason made a nervous laugh, then coughed. "That wasn't supposed to happen."

"Hmph," said Fiona. "I hear that a *lot* from you these days. In any case, you may place this new watercooler anywhere you like—including up your mythic little *ass*— but not outside my dressing room! Are we clear?"

"Pan's pipes," Jason had sworn. "Gotta gallop. See you tomorrow." The connection severed.

Starr had stared at the phone so long it went to sleep. Her head rang. She needed a drink.

Taking a fresh swig from the wine, she'd nearly choked on her errant button.

So here she was: 5:01. The map insisted she was in the right place. And there *was* a gate, though not one she saw any way to pass through. It was the first weekday morning in years where she didn't smell like grease or coffee. Today, she smelled more like Dove soap, Herbal Essences Lily of the Valley shampoo and Grape-Nuts cereal. She felt game and ready for anything.

Anything except a trick. Was this a trick? Table five had been full of weirdos. And she still couldn't understand how the coffee had become water. Still, much of the business of show was comprised of odd folks—and the oddest ones were often in charge. They could wield dagger thrusts to the ego. This might be the latest in a long line of missteps in her life.

But—Jason hadn't laughed at her. He hadn't asked for her measurements. He hadn't even wanted a resume. He'd appeared like a light in the darkness, a life preserver thrown to a woman treading water. He'd also been a man walking around the city with horns glued to his head and a tail tied to his waist.

Nobody Starr had consulted had heard of casting for a show called *Tune in Tomorrow*. The name Jason Valentine was agreed to be fantastical by all accounts, but there was no known producer who called himself that. She had briefly considered not showing up; the whole situation reeked of bad news. The industry was rife with people who had no sense of boundaries, in part because the industry thrived on crafting worlds that *had* no boundaries, often featuring the most physically striking specimens that humanity had to offer. There was always someone there to exploit that beauty and the fragile ego that usually came with it. She had crossed paths with more than one so-called industry mogul who glided through the world as if they were starring in their own personal movie, and Starr was merely a bit player.

She thought of Jason again. He was incredibly handsome. What if he wanted her to sit on his casting couch? To 'massage' him? Her palms felt sweaty at the thought and her brain felt as fuzzy as the connection on their call. She didn't want to think he was *that* kind of producer. He'd seen her. Seen something in her.

Starr could wait. But for how long?

"Shit!" she shouted for a third time, kicking the low concrete wall. It thudded against the toe of her sensible pump. The impact rippled up her leg.

"Hey!" shouted a high, clear voice. "What'd that fence ever do to you?"

Starr whirled. A young man with long, twisting hair—neither braids nor locks—slouched against a tree a few feet away, holding a book. He was thin and intense, dark eyes like ink spots. A fat backpack festooned with iron-on patches rested on the ground in front of his Doc Martens. One patch read: 'Impeach Everybody.' Another featured a rose in a circle and the words, 'Do no harm but take no shit.' A third: 'Respect Pronouns.'

"I was supposed to meet somebody."

"Sure 'bout that?" He shifted the book under one arm of a long, leather duster. His twisting hair seemed alive, bouncing despite his stillness. "Just us chickens here."

"I might be in the wrong place."

"We might all be in the wrong place, metaphorically speaking."

A long silence. Starr thought about leaving. "I'm not actually meeting someone," she admitted. "I was told there would be—gates."

"I see," he nodded. "Well, there are gates."

"Gates *to* somewhere." She gestured. "I'm not planning to swim."

"Well, I might've seen some beautiful gates about a quarter mile thataway." He pointed west, toward Bay Ridge. "Big black things. Glorious iron scrollwork. Popped out of nowhere."

Starr gulped. She *had* gotten the address wrong. Could she still get there in time? Hefting up her overnight bag, she nearly ran off as his mouth curled into a smirk.

"You lie like a rug," she snapped.

He glanced at his watch. "Well, we'll know for sure in a few more seconds." Leaning down, he slipped the book into his pack—*The Motorcycle Diaries* by Che Guevara. Gerry had owned it but tossed it away in disgust after learning it had nothing to do with fixing bikes.

"A little light reading?"

"When not assisting the writer's room, sure." He held up a fist. "Power to the people, my friend. Power to the mythics."

A strong breeze swirled up the path and Starr's carefully arranged, lily of the valley scented curls whipped at her face. "Mythics?"

His smirk morphed into a slow, lazy smile as the wind increased in velocity. "I love the smell of newbies in the morning!" he shouted over the increasing din. "I'm Janus. Call me Jan. They. Them."

"Oh!" Starr nodded. She'd been making assumptions. "Right. Got it!" But her voice disappeared in the cyclonic spin of wind that seemed to be touching down in the middle of the path. She grabbed at Jan's coat to keep from being blown away. The wind whistled a high, signaling whine as if coming to a climax—then cut out.

Starr's ears rang.

She turned to the rusting old gates and wondered if she'd been hit in the head with a flying branch. The lock on the gates had swung open. Dark swirling mist covered the water on the other side, a vortex roiling at its center. A puff of cool, moist air brushed against her ankles. Jan advanced toward the mist, but Starr had a death grip on their coat.

"Hey!" they cried. "Don't make me late. Emma'll scratch my eyes out."

Emma. That was the tissue-shredder from table five. That meant they were going where Starr was headed. "You—you know her? And Jason? And Cris? And—"

"'Course I know them! We work together!"

Terror locked Starr's legs. She could no more let go of Jan than take a single step. This was not happening. Then again, if it was happening, the job might be real. And if the job was real—she had a chance.

If I don't screw it up.

"Stay or go, lady, but release the threads!" Jan shouted.

She'd run out of time. *Go big. No going home. Be the mango.*

In that instant, Jan darted forward, yanking with godlike strength on the coat. Starr's hands opened wide as her feet lifted from the ground and she flew into the center of the deep, misty vortex, her bag sailing along behind her.

Then the gates clanked shut.

CHAPTER 3
Catch a Falling Starr

JASON VALENTINE CHECKED his watch again, then tapped one custom-fit boot on the linoleum. From inside the hollowed-out, clear plastic heel came a soft sloshing sound.

Only a few minutes more.

His name wasn't actually 'Jason' or 'Valentine,' but his True Name could turn a mortal's nostrils inside out. Over millennia he'd learned to be a polite faun among humans, respectful of their frailties. He'd shared those sensitivities with the rest of the show's crew, insisting everyone wear some form of clothing, use pseudonyms while in the presence of actors, and comprehend the concept of time.

Over those same millennia, Jason had come to very much like bespoke clothes and footwear (hoofwear in his case), watches and hats, earrings and sashes, belts and cravats, waistcoats and cummerbunds and all the other accoutrements mortals regularly decorated themselves with. His sequoia wood wardrobe was packed with items culled from the leprecostumers' department, and he spent an hour every night determining what combination of items he would wear the following day. His outfit always needed to fit the occasion.

Last night, he'd spent *three* hours picking out his clothes for today.

Starr's arrival today was the culmination of six years of patience, observation and—yes, fine, maybe some gentle tinkering. Certain mythics cultivated mortals the way humans worked with bonsai trees, but Jason's touch on Starr's life had always been light. A gentle nudge here, and there, to position her correctly.

Starr had been his personal project from the moment he'd laid eyes on her. One evening, while roaming the city on the human side of the Veil, Jason had caught her mid-performance in a comedy club's basement. A poster indicated the performers were all about-to-graduate seniors at some educational institution or other. As Jason settled on a stool against the wall, Starr had dazzled the room while pretending to be a karaoke-singing mango.

"Mango mango, mango mango," she'd sung with gusto, her eyes lighting up. Her body seemed electrified.

Jason had never seen *spark* lit before in a human. It was breathtaking—so much so that he did, in fact, stop breathing for several minutes. That night, he'd hunkered under a subway overpass and consumed a box of mangoes, seeds and all. Then he'd put Starr at the top of his observation list, attending every audition and performance she was involved in. Part of him wanted her to succeed; another part wanted her to fail—fail so that eventually he could bring her into the fold. And fail she had. She met rejection upon rejection, only to redouble her efforts each time.

Throughout it all she'd slogged through a dispiriting job at Mike's for paltry wages, while Jason kept to the shadows. Meanwhile, viewership on the show continued to decline a trickle away, the loss reflected in failures all around the studio: objects transformed randomly, floorboards began to scream, sets were vandalized, crew vanished for hours or days at a time. The thought of his show being canceled, of losing his access to all this excitement and those wonderful mortals, depressed Jason beyond understanding. Yet he couldn't rush things. While Starr did seem perfect for them, Jason had to be certain they weren't dealing with another... Amelia.

Now, six years of investment were about to come to fruition. Did he care if Starr's acting was a little... broad? Not a whit. This was a woman who could spontaneously invent songs for tropical fruit. Actors could be trained. Performers were born with it. *Tune in Tomorrow* had far too many of the former, not nearly enough of the latter. Starr Weatherby was precisely the mortal his show required.

Jason touched his horns. They were the correct length. The patches of hair that had fallen out of his legs during the last stressful disaster had grown back. He wasn't grinding his teeth as much when he slept. He had hope again. But until he saw Starr in their studio, he wouldn't be able to focus. So he'd left his forest-glamoured office, arriving five minutes early to the immense antechamber— or 'lobby,' as the humans insisted on calling it—that served as the entrance to the *Tune in Tomorrow* studio and stages. The 'lobby' had to be big: for one thing, it needed to accommodate their security guard Phil, along with his cave.

Jason tugged nervously on the sleeves of his grey-and-white pinstriped shirt, ensuring they were the correct distance from the cuffs of his blue velvet blazer, which itself was threaded with nearly indiscernible pure silver threads.

The blazer came to hip level over a pair of snug white cotton jeans, which almost but not quite hid the extensive hair on his legs. His tail gleamed with ointments he'd applied after giving it a thorough brushing-out that morning.

But the best expression of Jason's excitement could be seen on his feet. He was currently wearing his treasured soft chrome aquarium platform boots. It was only proper to greet his grand project in grand footwear; no considerate faun exposed random fetlock except among intimates. Within the water-filled heels of the boots swam miniature angelfish, tended to by downsized naiads. He sensed them swirling beneath him as he stared at the lobby's far wall—a grey, blank emptiness that would transform into a misty portal in a few more minutes.

"Oooo, hello there!" Nicodemus Reddy had taken a cross-legged seat on the floor next to Jason's boots, and he waved a finger at the transparent heels. Naiads blew him tiny water kisses. He blew them back, then leaped up and joined the faun staring at the grey wall. "Fresh meat on the way?"

"None of your beeswax," said Jason, smoothing down his hair. "And I dislike that particular... metaphor."

"Turn of phrase," said Nico, slapping him on the back. "Man, you're wound tight. Those horns never stand that high unless you're worked up about something."

A young woman with lustrous red hair sidled up against Nico and nuzzled his cheek. "I wondered where you went," she purred. "Why up so early?"

"Running an errand." He tousled her hair. "How about grabbing me some tea?"

"Don't you have *help* for that?" She planted her fists on her hips.

"I do... " He slid on a pair of sunglasses and beamed a

smile at her. "But you prepare it so beautifully, Madeline."

"That's *Martine*."

"Of course."

She narrowed her eyes and stalked off.

"Prince Charming strikes again," said Jason. "Who was that one?"

Nico shrugged. "One of the extras. Passing through. Tomorrow she'll have forgotten she was ever here."

"You are a credit to humanity." Jason examined the actor, who was still wearing yesterday's costume. "You know, there's nothing in your contract that says you have to be Roland one hundred percent of the time. I wouldn't mind a break from the whole—" he waved his hands, "package."

Nico straightened, then lowered the sunglasses onto his nose. "Trust me, Valentine—nobody wants to see the unvarnished Nico." He pushed the glasses up again and gave a small twist of his shoulders, like sliding back into an invisible cloak. "And that includes me. Besides, doesn't our newcomer deserve us at our most charming, princely selves?"

"So, you knew someone was coming."

"Valéncia—well, Fiona—tells me everything," Nico chirped. "You know that."

Jason did. Little remained under wraps in the studio for long, particularly if Fiona or Nico heard about it first. What one breathed out, the other breathed in. Nico always had his antennae up—not literal ones; he was a lovely human specimen of Indian-Greek descent, a dimpled Adonis Siddhartha whose sleek black curls were the envy of all breathing creatures, mortal and mythic, at the show.

Nico's problem was that he didn't trust himself to be himself. His history on the other side of the Veil was so dark and painful he'd long ago taken to disappearing into character as frequently as possible—and as Roland, he could be positively insufferable.

"*You just tell old furry legs that I will expect Starr Weatherby in time for breakfast.*" Nico spoke in a near-perfect imitation of Fiona's New England patrician accent, then raised an eyebrow and returned to his own smooth, low tones. "That's direct from the source. I assume she's not planning to *eat* Starr. No guarantees, though."

"I loathe when you do that voice thing," said Jason. "It's… wrong."

Nico waved his hand. "You just hate it when we use a little dime store magic."

Jason narrowed his eyes. Mortals couldn't do magic, not exactly. But they were awarded certain limited talents for outstanding achievement on the show at each year's Endless Awards, along with an intricate, color-shifting statuette that resembled a fiber-optic table lamp straight out of the 1970s. Nico had thirty-four such awards; one of those was Thrown Voice Mimicry. Fiona, meanwhile, had one hundred and twenty-eight awards—more powers than any other human on the show. They might be small, 'dime store' level powers, but they added up and over the decades she'd become almost as formidable as Jason himself.

"Anyway…" Nico blinked. "That's one of my favorites. I have so few that come in handy."

"Take it up with management. Or the *WaterWorlds* editors."

"I know, I know. The Powers That Be choose the prizes, the magazine picks who wins. But has anyone in the Seelie or Unseelie courts even visited this show? How do you appeal to a higher authority that doesn't even deign to stop by?"

Jason glanced at his watch again. Two minutes. "Believe me. You don't want them here. It's never good news. I go to *them*, and it's bad enough." His brow furrowed. "Also, it's hair. I have hair on my legs, not fur."

Nico chuckled. "Spill, faun. What do I need to know about our imminent arrival? All I have is a name. Enquiring minds and all that."

Whatever Jason told Nico would end up as a flea in Fiona's ear, of course. Two of the show's most veteran stars, they were close pals in real life and comrades-in-arms on the show: Roland and Valéncia, lothario rogue and wealthy Grand Dame. Yet so far as Jason could determine—not that he paid a whole lot of attention—they'd never been *that* kind of couple. Between them lay a weird history, something outside of sex yet beyond friendship. It was incredibly, deeply human, which meant Jason would never get to the bottom of it.

All for the best. Officially, as stated in the Guide, intra-show relationships were off-limits. Violations could get an actor fired, or a mythic removed. And while a mythic would be shunted to another production, firing a human was deeply unpleasant. Particularly for the human. Unofficially, though, what went on in an actor's dressing room or a mythic's office or elsewhere in the vast Veil territories was their own business.

"You don't need to know a thing," said Jason. "Not yet. She's going to have to pass muster with our Grand Dame, and only then will she really matter to the show. But when she does, and she will"—he waggled a finger in front of Nico's nose—"you leave her be."

Nico wilted against the security desk, his Roland character in full bloom. He clasped a hand to his chest, wounded. Behind him, a wisp of smoke drifted from Phil's bowling ball-sized left nostril, and then the guard flipped the page of his magazine, *Dragon Drawn and Quarterly*.

"How dare you assume," Nico huffed, "that I would press unwanted attentions on the newest sheep in our flock?"

One minute. Jason reluctantly averted his attention from the wall. "Do I need to spell this out?"

"It is not my fault the ladies can't resist," he grinned wickedly, "this whole *package*, as you put it moments ago." His hazel eyes sparkled. "I mean, could you?"

"I have thus far." Yet, Jason wasn't unaware of Nico's charms. When Fiona had hauled one Nicodemus Reddy through the portal over half a century ago, Jason had actually caught his breath. Then he'd held it: Nico had smelled like he'd been marinating in a wine barrel. He was tidier now, at least on the exterior. His interior was still an unknown country. But what was known was how he homed in on anyone female they brought on board, mortal or not, rules or not.

Except for Fiona.

"Nico, listen," said Jason. He had perhaps thirty seconds to make this clear.

"All ears." Nico fluttered his lashes.

"Give Roland a breather and be serious for once. This is important."

Nico nodded slowly and made a tiny shrug. Instantly, he seemed somehow... smaller.

"You must have noticed that the Gate's faulty. And the coffee in the break room sometimes comes out as bubble bath."

"And the bathroom urinals sometimes vanish mid-stream?" Nico nodded along. "Bah, it's a little wear and tear on the old joint."

"Mav is not here, in case you haven't noticed."

"Thought he was just on vacation. Mahroba, right?"

Jason clenched his fists. "He was supposed to be back last week, but apparently, he can't get his MARBLE to work! We're holding up story for him!"

Nico tsked. "What's the fairy world coming to, if you can't rely on a return MARBLE?"

Jason craned his face to the ceiling, willing calm, daring his hair to consider dropping out again. "Everything is going wrong, one piece at a time, Nico. And that's because we are losing viewers. If we don't have those eyeballs, we start coming apart at the seams. I develop mange. And over the long term, if we don't get the audience back, we disappear."

Nico's natural golden-brown hue paled. "Cancellation?" he whispered.

"It's not impossible. And you know what happens then. You land on your behind on the sidewalk. On your side of the Veil. Your prizes stay behind. You leave with nothing."

"Not even Temporal Arrest...?"

"Naturally. You start aging again."

"Even—"

"Yes. Even Fiona's little gift goes."

Nico chewed his lip.

"I need this one to work. We don't have a lot of time. Starr Weatherby must work. So, are you on the team, or are you in the way?"

Nico saluted. "Count on me. Besides, you know I only trouble with the temporary ones."

"Of course you do. We haven't had any fresh long-termers in thirty years."

Nico straightened, and Jason despaired at seeing Roland already returning. The actor backed toward the grey wall just as it began to soften. A gentle breeze rolled into the lobby like dry ice at a rock concert, and he looked as if he might be about to begin an opening number. Spreading his arms wide, Nico gave a small bow. "I vow not to lay a finger on our newest acquisition, as a favor to you."

A figure spun through the nothingness, missing Nico by inches, and landed hard on the linoleum floor. The actor stumbled backward.

"—off my jacket!" Jan finished shouting, then scrambled to their feet. They glared into the mist, then grinned at Jason. "Better late than never, boss!" They hoisted their backpack high on a shoulder, then dashed through the antechamber.

"Jan!" Jason cried. "Someone else is coming through with you, right?"

Jan slowed, shrugging. "Maybe." They disappeared around a corner.

Nothing happened. The mist would exist for only fifteen seconds, and not return until much later in the afternoon, unless it was glitchy again. Jason's face fell.

"Too bad." Nico clucked. "You made me promise all for noth—"

A woman fell out of the mist and slammed into Nico, who was still half-turned. Instinctively the actor caught what had been thrown at him, wrapping his arms around her. They tumbled to the ground, rolling on the floor, and when they came to a stop, Starr Weatherby was on top of him, her curls flopped across his face. Straightening, she flipped her hair to one side as Nico ogled her impressive décolletage.

An overnight bag arced over everyone's heads, landing with a soft *whoomp* on the floor next to the antechamber's sofa.

Jason clasped his hands together in delight, then jogged over. "Starr!" he cried, a tsunami raging in his heels. "So many happy landings!"

CHAPTER 4

Hitch Your Wagon to a Starr

STARR SCRABBLED BACKWARD, disoriented, head swirling. One minute she'd been standing on a windy jogging path; the next, she'd landed like a meteor on top of some random guy.

"Well, that's a thing that's never happened before," said the man, whose sunglasses hung askew. "It's raining women."

Jason stepped over Mr. Sunglasses and helped Starr to her feet. He seemed taller than she remembered—though no less dashing. His angular face was different today, framed by a pair of rimless glasses. A pen rested behind one ear. His hair was still pointy. "Feeling OK?"

"I'm... great," said Starr, momentarily distracted by Jason's footwear: a pair of giant shiny boots that would make Elton John envious. Were *fish* swimming in the heels?

"I'm super," Mr. Sunglasses grunted, squiggling around Jason's boots. "Thanks for your concern."

"Ignore Nico." Jason clasped Starr's hand between both of his own. "The important thing is you showed up. That's ninety-nine cents of success."

"Percent," said Nico. "Ninety-nine percent."

Starr felt like rubbing her eyes. She hadn't landed in the bay under the Verrazzano Bridge. She wasn't wet at all. But she did feel like she was treading water: she had landed in a cavernous lobby that seemed to have been designed by the same architects behind hospital wards and police interrogation rooms. The walls were grey, the floor a scratched, yellowish linoleum.

"Gosh," she said. "I'm in the DMV."

Nico chuckled. He was exceedingly handsome and appeared to have been spending a lot of time at the beach. *Smooth* was the first word that came to mind. "How very astute of you." He cocked his head. Even his voice sounded smooth, like a cool drink of water. "I'm Nicodemus Reddy, by the way."

Jason elbowed him. "Feeling frazzled? I promise, it gets easier to use the portal. You won't need to land on people every time."

"I volunteer." Nico twirled the sunglasses by one earpiece, waggling his eyebrows.

Starr squared her shoulders, glancing behind her at a solid grey wall. No door, not even a set of stairs. There was logic behind this, but damned if she could find it. The Halloween effects by the river had been some kind of diversion—a giant fan, a dry ice machine. That smartass socialist with the leather jacket probably knocked her on the head and dragged her here. But where was *here*? Had she been abducted?

"I could probably use some water," Starr said at last.

"Phil?" Jason glanced over his shoulder. "Mind snagging Ms. Weatherby a cool drink?"

Nico grinned wickedly.

"I don't do cool," said a voice like an eighteen-wheeler,

deep and rumbling and vast. The heat of a long-idling engine pressed against Starr's back and she completed her turn within the high school gymnasium-sized lobby to face the security desk. Behind it stood a fifteen-foot lizard the color of glowing embers, covered in feathery scales, with enormous hind legs and vastly smaller forepaws (each of which were still as large as Starr's head). A pair of folded wings rested neatly on his back, poking out of the button-down smoke-colored shirt he wore. An embroidered patch over the left breast read 'Phil.'

Oh! Is that real? Don't be silly. Her mind glitched, but didn't quite short-circuit. *Oh, oh, oh!* Now she got it. She was in a special effects production studio! That explained everything: Jason's pointy hair 'horns' and his 'tail,' the smoke and wind, and now this talking 'creature.' Her anxiety faded, replaced by awe as things came into focus. "Wow," she gasped at the 'dragon.' "What a fantastic... costume. How many guys fit in there?"

Nico made a soft noise.

Phil offered a talon. Starr wrapped her fingers around it, and they shook—or rather, Phil waggled her whole body. It was truly an impressive feat of puppetry.

"I have never consumed humans," Phil said. His steaming breath made her sweat. "I do security here. Or, perhaps, I *will* do security one of these years. Mostly I do reception."

"Phil mostly does deterrence," said Jason, tapping the tips of his fingers together.

Starr glanced between Jason, who seemed earnest, if a bit nervous, and Nico, who was biting his lip so hard he might draw blood at any moment. She shrugged. Fine. They weren't going to explain anything, not yet. Why should they? She was a visitor, not even an employee.

Still—the effect was tremendous; she could almost imagine Phil really was a dragon. Starr tapped her nose and winked at Phil. "Your secret's safe with me."

Phil narrowed his golden eyes, which were split down the center by lightning-bolt shaped pupils. "Excuse me," he huffed, lumbering down one of the anonymous hallways that branched out of the atrium, ridged tail slithering behind. The costume radiated power and muscle.

"We get two to three portal openings per day," Jason was saying. "That's 'day' as defined in here, by the way, and time has a way of shifting so—be prepared. The first opening comes at 5:03 a.m. on your side of the Veil; that'll be normal call time so don't miss it. Fifteen seconds for the opening. There's a final one late in the day so everyone who wants to can return to the other side of the Veil. Most of the time, you end up where you started, so it's a pretty good system. Though sometimes..." he shrugged.

"Sometimes you land somewhere totally unexpected," interrupted Nico, who was examining Starr closely. "And sometimes the afternoon one doesn't come at all. Not guaranteed."

Starr grinned, nodding as if she understood. "Well, it was a little windy on the way in."

"The Gates do love fanfare." Nico's eyes were bright and amused. "Sometimes it's weather. Sometimes trombones. They show off for newcomers."

"Of course they do," said Starr, wondering how he fit in here. There wasn't anything unusual about Nico, if you ignored his appearance. But people who were that level of good-looking—and there were plenty in the business— were to be steered clear of, she'd learned. They were their own biggest fans, and rarely made moves on someone of Starr's... shape. She'd taught herself to steel herself against their charms.

"Here y'go, miss." Phil returned, pinching a mug that seemed tiny between his talons but required both of Starr's hands to hold. He turned to Jason. "Looks like Ms. Ballantine got her way about that water cooler, Mr. V."

Jason rolled his eyes. "If Fiona had the final say it would have been stationed in the deep recesses of the prop and weaponry department."

Fiona. The name made Starr stand taller. She'd been the one ticked off by the watercooler placement.

"Nobody got the scales to stand up to that human," the guard muttered, picking up an oversized magazine called *WaterWorlds.* "Nobody."

Jason's jaw clenched. "Right," he told Starr. "Shall we?"

Starr slid the still-full mug on to Phil's countertop.

"Do not put that thing here!" Phil recoiled. Starr couldn't wait to meet the guys tasked with manipulating him; they were completely in the moment, totally in character. "I am not a fan of H☐O!" He cracked open his jaw to reveal enough razor-sharp rows of teeth to give a great white shark an inferiority complex, and the low-banked furnace she'd been feeling ramped up to full power. Starr felt her eyebrows singeing. "I gotta keep that lit!"

"Sorry!" Starr held up her hands in surrender. "I didn't realize dragons were sensitive."

Jason picked up the mug and tossed the contents into a nearby plant, which straightened.

"Aaah," sighed the plant, transforming into an olive-green colored woman with weeping willow-branch hair and clothes made of finely woven climbing vines. She unfurled her branches and leaves popped from her arms.

"That's one way to wake the roots. Is it time?"

Animatronics, too! Starr clapped her hands together, dollar signs popping in her head. This was a well-funded outfit, even if nobody had heard of them before. They could probably afford higher-than-basic union rates here, if she could land the job.

"Not yet, Celtis." Jason caressed one of the plant's outer leaves. "Cris is blocking in an hour or so."

The robot lifted a long branch and a stream of water rolled down its arm. It dangled fingers over its mouth, sipping at the drops. Jason tilted toward the bot and it—she; Starr was having a hard time not thinking of it as female—ran damp fingers through his hair. "You are a love—oh!" she stopped when she saw Starr. "Well, you're fresh growth."

Starr raised an eyebrow. How did they get a device to recognize new people? "I'm Starr Weatherby," she said, touching her fingers to an outstretched branch. "And you are quite impressive tech."

Nico made that sound again and covered his mouth.

"No, no," said the plant woman—bot—thing. "I'm a cameradryad. I record what's on the set along with my grove-mates. You'll see me on the stage floor later, if Fiona—" she cut herself off.

If Fiona what? Starr wondered.

Jason curled an arm around Starr and led her down one of the halls. "What Celtis means is that you're not hired... yet. We have one more, um, stage."

"Oh, of course." Starr suspected as much. There would be a casting director and maybe Jason in the room, with a small camera capturing her audition. She'd be given a small portion of script called 'sides', and she'd play whatever character they wanted her to try out for in front of that camera. They'd stare at her, bored or rapt or distracted, and then swear to call her in a few days. Or sometimes they told her right out in the room: they wanted someone less 'athletic.' Less 'full-figured.' Just... less. "Who am I reading for?"

Jason chuckled. It was the friendliest, warmest sound she could think of. "Oh, you're not reading. Your audition was in the diner yesterday. You passed with the grace of a unicorn cantering across a rainbow."

Nico, following them, stifled a snicker.

Starr glared over her shoulder, wishing he'd go away. "What's the snag?" Then it landed. "Is this about Fiona... Ballantine?"

"Indeed," said Jason. "Well spotted. We are unable to hire as frequently as we might like. In fact, the last mortal we brought on full-time was—some years ago."

Years ago. This was a tight cast. Then something he'd said in the diner returned to Starr. "Not... thirty years ago?" Jason and Nico shared a glance, and Starr filed it away for another time. "OK, fine. I've got to impress Fiona. Who is she, anyway?"

"Only the greatest actor that ever lived," Nico pronounced grandly, sailing ahead of them in the hallway, arm outstretched. Starr couldn't tell if he was serious. "The heart and soul of this show."

"Also, the biggest pain in my hindquarters," Jason said behind his hand.

"I heard that," Nico shot back.

"And I have to get her approval before I'm hired?"

"Precisely." Nico dropped back to walk with them.

Starr halted. "Fiona, who stands you up for auditions, who bosses everyone around about where a watercooler goes—she's the final decision maker? Does she run the show or something?"

The points on Jason's head grew a half-inch, shoving his hair to the side, and his eyes darkened. "No, Ms. Weatherby. Fiona Ballantine does not run this show." Jason's tail slapped the wall, the report like a whip, and Starr flinched. "I do. We are stuck with letting her make some of the decisions. But know this: the only authority you heed around here is *mine*."

"Or Cris, when he's directing," offered Nico.

"Yes, Cris sometimes—"

"And Emma," Nico continued. "She'll write you out of the script if you don't interest her."

"Fine, yes, and—" Jason whirled. "Don't you have lines to learn?"

"All the best drama is here," said Nico. "We deal in—" he gave a soft cough, "reality here, do we not? This is pretty real to me." He winked at Starr. "You could consider asking me a few questions, Ms. Weatherby."

Smooth, smooth. Starr gave him a cool look, ignoring the way his attentions made her heart thud. She forced herself to appear unimpressed. "Well, I guess I'm caught up. He's Jason, and he's the boss. I'm Starr, and I'm trying to get a job. You're Nico, and you're kind of a busybody. What do you actually do around here?"

Nico dropped his sunglasses. A lens cracked in half.

Jason nibbled his lip in delight, then lifted Starr as if she weighed nothing, spinning her around. "I knew you would be a fast learner, my little mango."

This group really likes mangoes, Starr thought.

Jason linked his arm with hers. "Now, let us see if Ms. Ballantine is receiving."

CHAPTER 5
Starr System

Nico made a hasty exit, claiming he had to get his sunglasses repaired. That left Starr and Jason alone, wandering through anonymous Hallways of No Personality—blank spaces free of wall hangings, doorplates, electric sockets or even light switches. "This is a dressing room," he said, holding open one doorway. "Winston's rehearsing right now, so he's not in."

Starr barely got a peek before he shut it again.

"And this is a—" Jason opened another door to reveal a tiny room that smelled like fresh paint. A small, wizened person in overalls was applying a hot pink shade over a light blue one, and tipped his hat at Starr. "Coat closet."

"I see it's getting a new coat," Starr quipped.

Jason grinned. "Precisely! We add a new one each week." He paused in front of another door, opened it and slammed it shut instantly. "Moving on."

The muffled sound of lightning crackling filtered through the door.

"You all use foley?" Starr wanted to show off her grasp of industry lingo: the sound effects folks tickled her with their creativity.

"Uh, sure." Jason's anxious face was back. "Well.

Not exactly. Just a misplaced thunderstorm. Happens sometimes. This way."

They twisted and turned so much Starr lost track of where she was, and Jason's strange mixture of delight and nervousness was starting to make *her* feel anxious. At last, she came to a hard halt in the middle of a hallway.

Jason tilted his head.

"Look, I get it. You're like a big VFX warehouse or something. I'm guessing *Tune in Tomorrow* is some kind of space opera on the web. But you showing me every nook and cranny and door hinge doesn't give me a clue about what's going on. What is this place?"

Jason took a dramatic pause and his green eyes shone. "*Tune in Tomorrow* is many things to so many mythics. We are the longest-running, most-viewed reality TV show ever made in any dimension. We are made by mythics, for mythics—but starring humans."

"*Reality?*" Starr twitched. "With dragon puppets and robots?"

Jason started to speak, took a breath and paced up and down. Raised a finger, lowered it, then stopped in front of her. Cleared his throat. "It's been some time since I had to explain this to a human. Bear with me." He pushed open another door and gestured inside.

Starr planted her feet in the doorway. "Jason, this is a toilet."

"Yes, well, needs must. I don't have any other handy water."

He was speaking in riddles—and disappearing into a bathroom with a near-stranger was awkward at best, creepy at worst. Still, she didn't sense Jason was up to no good. He practically vibrated with excitement, or nerves, or both. Swallowing, Starr took the risk and stepped inside. The bathroom door swung closed behind them.

Jason turned on all four sinks in the room. Water cascaded from three; butterflies burst from the fourth. Starr gaped. Jason quickly shut that one off with a sheepish grin and turned his back on the sink. The butterflies disintegrated. Starr blinked.

"You see," he raised his sing-song voice over the noise of the remaining water, "we adore human to'ings and fro'ings. We are the original fans of stories-without-end. Some hundreds of years ago when the Seelie came up with the idea of telling stories to mythics, they were known as Stories of All Purpose, or for short –"

"SOAP," Starr realized. The room was starting to heat up and the mirrors fogged; Jason had apparently turned on only the hot water. She wondered where he was going with all this; the fantastical elements of his story were fanciful and charming, but silly. Maybe he was just being very method about the show. "You're making a soap opera?"

"Shh!" he quietened her, glancing around. "Yes—and no. That's how we started. But most mythics are self-cleaning. Bathing is a hobby, not a practice. SOAPs fell a bit out of fashion. Mythics wanted *real* human stories. Finally, once humans on your side of the Veil began writing their own TV shows, one of us—me, in fact— infiltrated a few writing rooms and discovered that *you* were doing what we'd been doing for years and calling it 'reality TV.' That fit us perfectly. Our viewers tune in because they believe we are telling real stories, and that's what keeps us going."

"But reality shows—" Starr caught herself. It was no secret in the business that many so-called reality shows were scripted. That they were the soap operas of the modern age—even if few would admit to it publicly. Reality shows that weren't about some weird competition were packed with melodrama, family feuds, bed-hopping antics, people being underhanded or bitchy, sometimes all of those things combined. They weren't much different from *Days of Our Lives*, which Starr had often watched while being babysat by her grandmother.

None of which answered her real questions, like why was she here? And why was Jason letting all that water go to waste? And if he was the producer, why was *he* acting like he was in character? "Remind me how long the show has been airing again?"

"In various incarnations, four hundred and thirty-nine years and six months and three days and—"

"Got it." He was funny, this Jason. Adorkable and funny, even in a steamed-up bathroom. She could play along. "Last I checked, TV didn't even exist before the twentieth century."

"Human TV didn't. We have many ways to tell story on this side of the Veil that you do not. You've heard of Philo Farnsworth, yes? The so-called television inventor? Well, you don't imagine that's a mortal name, do you? The old rascal is one of ours, exiled on your side of the Veil for several dozen rotations. Always was a Promethean fanboy. Thought he'd gift mortals with a new kind of campfire, and so now you share your own tales in a more... mundane fashion."

Starr wondered if Jason ever knew how to be serious. Did they have to stand here in a humid room, her curls wilting, discussing a made-up history? Wasn't she supposed to be vetted by the troublesome Fiona? And then—she got it. Jason was warming her up for that meeting. He wasn't being method; this was a classic improvisational exercise, like her singing mango.

"Yes, and—" she tossed out the cue for the improv game, which was to support whatever outlandish idea your partner offered, then add on to it. "So let me guess: *Tune in Tomorrow* comes through an antenna. Or a cable box?"

Jason grinned. "Now you're getting it! We have in the past transmitted to mythics living among you through rabbits—their ears are useful for capturing signal—and on your mechanical boxes, our programming can be found on channel *W90&∞.3."

"Right." She nodded broadly. "I never subscribed to that one."

"These days," he continued, "we prefer to send and receive story via water sources." Jason waved at the steam now fogging the bathroom and the water in the sinks shot straight up into the air, folding back down over itself and into the sink again, creating not a waterfall, but a water wall. "Heated, actively moving water is best for story reception. There is a clarity and quality to the image that rabbits and boxes can't convey. Observe."

Starr's jaw dropped as the constantly rotating water calmed, then smoothed over until all three sinks joined into a near-glass panel. She inched closer: it was an effect she'd never seen done before. Practically a magic trick. Her nose nearly touched the water flow, and Jason eased her back. "Not good for your eyes to be quite so close," he said.

His warm hand on her shoulder made her straighten and lean into the touch. Then the water flickered, and an image appeared. Figures in a kitchen. One was throwing a dish, the other ducking. "Ah, yes," nodded Jason. "This is on right now. We created it yesterday. You see Nora—

she plays Beatrice—" he gestured at the dish-thrower, a thin blonde woman with a severe face, "and you may recognize—"

A handsome man with curly black hair ducked a platter. "Nico!"

"In this case he is Roland, but you are correct."

"But if it's about reality, how come they use different names? Aren't they playing themselves?"

Jason ran a hand through his hair. "Well. They didn't start off playing themselves, you see. But after so many years there is a bit of a tangle between where the show begins... and they leave off." His gaze drifted into the distance, then he snapped to. "Ah, well. Questions best posed to your fellow humans."

"Gotcha."

"So now you see how mythics watch a show—on whatever available water source they have. We call it—"

The penny dropped. "Streaming."

Jason beamed at her. "So you do understand!"

Starr understood nothing. Maybe half of a percent of something. And what she did understand was unnerving. This was beyond improv. Beyond visual effects. Her words emerged like treacle. "So, every 'mythic,' as you call them, watches your show."

"Not precisely. If everyone did our ratings would be much higher. You are here because we need new blood. Not literally—at least, not this week. But we have had difficulties obtaining and retaining anyone who was suitable. The rigors of the production are truly not for everyone, and Fiona is uniquely... qualified to weed out the undesirables."

He waved his hand and the image disappeared. The water collapsed into the sinks with a splash, and he turned the faucets off. "All clear?"

No. But she worried about asking too many questions. She could figure things out as she went. "Sure. I'll do whatever's needed. I'm a hard worker."

"You are!" he grinned, as they stepped back into the hallway. Starr shivered in the relatively cool air. "I've been observing that for many years."

The improv shattered. "You have?"

"Indeed, ever since I caught you at a comedy club years ago, singing about being a fruit."

Starr covered her mouth for a second. "A mango! You've been watching me since I was in college?"

He sighed. "Cherished memories. But we, and you, have had to wait. Much as a mango must ripen, you were not ready to be here back then. Now I believe you are. And we are in real need. This last bit will be up to you."

Starr glanced down the nondescript hallway, back in the direction they had come. She wondered where the exit was. What had seemed weird and fun a moment ago had turned weird all the way through. But she had few options. She had no job and no prospects, unless you counted finding another diner to bind up utensils in. Practically no money in the bank. Rent was due. And beyond all those mundane elements, she was going to be twenty-seven later this year and was spending her life pounding on the door of an industry that didn't seem to want to let her in. Lately, she'd begun her wine-ding down time after a long diner shift earlier and earlier. It wouldn't be long until the off-ramp reading 'Mama's Life' would come up to greet her.

You need this, she thought, the image of a red-feathered dragon handing her water jumping to mind. Behind that, a plant speaking. She unclenched her fists and glanced up to find a sweet, if slightly off-kilter guy in glasses telling her he was a fan of her work.

"Why me?" she asked in a small voice.

"Oh, Starr Weatherby," said Jason. "You are an incredible performer! You are going to help us save this show!"

She thought for a moment. "That's not the same as calling me a great actor."

"Well," he admitted. "Nobody's perfect."

CHAPTER 6
Reach for the Starrs

BEING FIONA BALLANTINE was no easy task.

Fortunately, she had a great deal of assistance.

Reclining in her zero-gravity chair—rendered as such because five silent brownie helpers were holding it aloft—Fiona focused on her first, most difficult task of any morning: complete relaxation. It took concentration to summon the energy of one Lady Valéncia Marlborough, and she required absolute serenity.

Come, Valéncia, she urged in her mind. *Let us be one again.*

Valéncia, the bitch, was being elusive.

One of the five brownies—Fiona thought of them as Who, What, Where, Why and I Don't Know—twitched its nose and stifled a sneeze.

"Do that again, Who, and I'll volunteer you to be my tea this afternoon," Fiona hissed.

The brownie stood bolt upright. 'Who' wasn't its name, of course; Fiona rarely kept track of the brownies' absurd names. That was a job for her beloved Bookender Riverbend.

Speaking of which: "Bookender! Bookender!"

Another brownie, perched on a stack of books piled on an office chair, hopped away from the Underwood typewriter on Fiona's roll top desk. He was nattily attired in a tweed vest that discreetly covered the gentle mound of his belly, short flannel trousers and a white dress shirt with French cuffs.

"Morning, Ms. Fiona." Bookender slid a pair of reading glasses to the top of his nearly hairless head. "Do you wish tea?"

"I wish to hear my schedule. I feel a headache coming on and I must understand how to best make use of it."

"Astute planning, Ms. Fiona," he nodded. "You were due to block scenes sixteen minutes ago."

"Let me guess: blocking hasn't actually started." Walking through scenes before shooting was expected in traditional productions, but Fiona found it a colossal waste of time. So many aspects of this show were creaky and old-fashioned. This was a *reality show*. Spontaneity was critical. Bad enough that they had to follow scripts. Besides, the cameradryads were trained to stay on the action no matter what happened, so why was blocking still part of the routine?

"No, indeed," Bookender was assuring her. "Mr. Cris has not yet appeared in his directing chair."

Bookender was always well-informed, which was one reason Fiona was always on top of things. But she didn't need Bookender to understand what was delaying their director; it came with a pair of long, gazelle-like legs, shining auburn hair and was called Dakota Gardener: the human reporter assigned to cover *Tune in Tomorrow* for *WaterWorlds* magazine. As a pombero, Cris was naturally incorrigible with the ladies, and he and Dakota had been an item for several months. It was against Seelie executive policy, but the Seelie never visited the set, so they carried on as if it wasn't a firing (in Dakota's case), exiling (in Cris') offense. The whole matter was something of an open secret around set, but no one discussed it. No one wanted to risk the wrath of a pombero.

In any case, Fiona knew to be fashionably late on the days Cris directed. She closed her eyes and opened her mind to Valéncia as another brownie—Because, she'd named it—applied cucumber slices marinated in the tearful remains of dissolved squonk to her lids. The brownie then hurried to the opposite end of Fiona's lean body and lotioned up his hands for her daily foot massage. Meanwhile, a seventh brownie—I Don't Give A Darn— put the finishing touches of Nightshade Purple polish on her extended, pointed nails. Once dry, the color would swirl and shift like a living Van Gogh painting.

Valéncia was still not responding. This was doubly irritating because Fiona *knew* Valéncia wasn't real. The character she had been playing for so many decades had become an alter ego, then her primary ego, and now she had a hard time distinguishing between Fiona, the idealistic 'it' girl model from over a century ago, and the high-handed, diamond-hard snob she'd been playing all this time. Perhaps they simply had become one another and summoning her was no longer necessary.

But Fiona wanted to think there was still some divide between them. In any case, her alter ego behaved like a muse who had to be coaxed awake for Fiona to do her best work. Giving up for the moment, she waved a not-yet-dry hand. "Continue, Bookender."

"Yes, miss."

Fiona didn't care for many of the mythics on the show,

but she treasured Bookender. He kept her in line and organized. He held her secrets. He'd been indispensable for nearly a century, one of her earliest and best Endless Awards. In a moment of weakness thirteen years ago she'd sworn to release him from his position when they reached their centennial together. Now that it was nearing, Fiona had regrets.

"The schedule has been re-adjusted as such, due to delays," he continued in a scratchy, officious tone. "Hairies and makeup fairies at eight. Breakfast at half past eight. Blocking immediately afterward. Filming, theoretically, from eleven to one. Lunch, then further filming—"

"Ach!" Fiona twitched, lifting a cucumber from one eye. "Your hands are freezing, Because!"

The brownie released Fiona's bare foot and stared at the floor. Fiona rolled her eyes. Brownies were so much effort sometimes. They were the biggest fans of the show, which made them so easily pushed around. For God's sake, they accepted wages in glitter. They'd probably have accepted wages in leftover table scraps, but crafting glitter was one of Fiona's award talents, so glitter it was. Alas, few had two brain cells to rub together. But Fiona had a hard time holding a grudge with creatures who had mastered the use of puppy-dog eyes. "I forgive you," she said at last. "Try again when you are prepared."

She leaned back and replaced the cucumbers.

"Filming will continue until suppertime, and the Gate is expected at 7:03 this evening," Bookender continued.

Bookender always informed Fiona about this last bit, though she never needed reminding of Gate times. F. Ballantine, LLC, had owned an apartment on East 65th Street and Lexington for half a century, but its owner had spent only two nights there. She would, as per usual, be sleeping on her dressing room's grey Chesterfield couch. It was the only place she could get quality sleep these days.

The Chesterfield was the most magnificent piece in Fiona's dressing room, a space that expanded two square feet with each additional year she appeared on the show. Sixty-five years ago, she had received the additional Endless prize of a room glamour, and with the flip of a switch her drab windowless box could transform into a proper Gilded Age lady's parlor. But she liked having real items that required no glamour. Along with the Chesterfield the room had a permanent cherrywood rolltop desk with the typewriter—largely employed for Bookender's transcriptions—balloon-backed chairs, deep cushioned seats and a round glass coffee table. The showpiece, however, stood against the far wall: an illuminated awards case, containing all one hundred and twenty-eight of her Endless Statues.

Warmed, lotioned hands kneaded the balls of her feet and she sighed deeply. At last, she could return to finding Valéncia. It should have been easy: she'd been playing Lady Marlborough for going on one hundred and eighteen years, ever since she'd been hired at *Tune in Tomorrow*. She knew Valéncia like a twin—or rather, a twin that had consumed its weaker sister while in utero. Nobody understood Valéncia like she did, including that logorrheic wordcat Emma, and anyone who suggested otherwise got the blunt end of Fiona's lion's head cane.

Valéncia, thought Fiona, but nothing came. She was swimming in her empty mind, a hole in which there was no light, as the character who was essentially herself receded. What would happen if she didn't come back? Who was Fiona *then*? Would she be as adrift as poor Nico? As sour and secretive as Nora? Only Charlie seemed to have mastered the tightrope of both being, and not becoming, his own character.

"Ms. Fiona?"

"What is it now, Bookender?"

"There is one more thing."

Fiona did not answer.

"I am most abjectly sorry to inform you that we will be having a visitor."

"Yes, yes," she sighed. "Over breakfast."

"Er," said Bookender.

FIONA HAD BROUGHT this situation on herself, but that did not make her any less cranky about it. She'd been invited to an audition yesterday, but Fiona Ballantine did not attend auditions. Certainly, she did not attend them on the other side of the Veil. Those who desired entry on *Tune in Tomorrow* would come to her—and she had a proud record of sending them scampering. The best time she had achieved between greeting and their terrified departure was six minutes, forty-two seconds.

For thirty years, she'd held new hires at bay in this fashion. It was the only way to avoid admitting another… thief. Yet Jason felt it necessary to keep trying. He'd dropped by her dressing room yesterday, peering over his glasses. "You are going to have to carve out time to meet this new one," he'd said. "Furthermore, you must give her your OK."

"I beg your pardon?" Fiona had gestured with her hairbrush. "Last I checked, I still have the right to say 'no.'"

His horns had grown an inch and his tail had twitched. "That you do. But you might learn that we do, too."

Fiona had gulped air like a fish thrown on land. "You

wouldn't dare."

"Try me." She'd never seen Jason so severe. He was almost worth listening to. "One stomp of these hooves and you lose brownie privileges."

"Hmph. Even you don't have the power to take away my Bookender."

Jason had shaken his head. "No, I suppose not. But we can reassign all the others. And the extras you enjoy that have nothing to do with your prizes can be... withheld." His fine features had drooped with unhappiness. "I adore you, darling, but we are out of options. I have curated this one especially. We must expand our ranks. You cannot hold a grudge forever."

Fiona's chin had wobbled and her eyes filled but did not spill over. In her most imperious, Valéncia-sized voice, she had nodded. "I will try. For you, my funny faun."

Jason had rocked back and forth on his oversized heels, embarrassed. "There's a good mortal. I knew we could come to an accommodation."

As soon as the door had closed behind him, Fiona summoned Nico. "Wicked creatures," she'd spat. "Look at what they're making me do!"

"There, there." He'd patted her shoulder. "We'll find another way."

"Er," said Bookender again now. Fiona had her eyes closed beneath the squonk-soaked cucumbers, but she knew he was tugging at the collar of his crisp white shirt.

"Spit it out, Bookender."

"That timetable has... shifted, I have only now learned."

"To when?" A rumble began in the back of Fiona's throat like warning vibrations before an earthquake.

"To now, Ms. Fiona."

Fiona sat up so fast her cucumber slices went flying. They smacked wetly against the wall and hung there a moment, then slid to the ground. "Now?"

Someone knocked at the door.

Fiona turned her Expression of Deepest Ire on Bookender for the first time in eight years and two months, and the brownie gulped. "Crimson alert!" he shouted, panicking.

Chaos ensued.

Spurred by the emergency cry, Because and I Don't Give A Darn fled. Who, What, Where, Why and I Don't Know released the chair they'd been holding up, which landed hard on the ground and dumped Fiona out onto the tiled floor. They scuttled through the brownie door at the back of the room.

Furious, Fiona tried righting herself, slipping on her lotioned feet, and careened toward the Chesterfield couch with an outraged screech. She nearly arrested her fall by latching on to a glowing arc lamp—but it wobbled, then bowed beneath her weight. Fiona flailed with the lamp in an awkward tango for a full second before it resisted and clocked her in the side of her head. Then she was falling for real this time, expecting to break her neck on the floor. It was all this newcomer's fault. And Jason's, that pointy-headed, feral—

She jerked in mid-air, inches from the floor. Bookender was standing on her Chesterfield, holding her aloft by the stretchy waistband of her pants, which now pinched abominably in her posterior. Bookender always knew the right thing to do. And like all brownies, he was much stronger than he looked.

She could never let him go.

"Set me down!" she glared. He released her into the

cushions. "Get me a towel. Delay the intruders. And get your shoes off my Chesterfield!"

Bookender leaped to the floor, straightening his shirt and adjusting the red-hair cufflinks. He bowed once and Fiona would have sworn he wore a small, satisfied smile on that wonderfully gruesome face. "Anything for Ms. Fiona."

A SECOND, FIRMER knock came a moment later. While Fiona ducked behind a privacy screen, Bookender opened the door.

"Gosh," Fiona heard a bright, quavering voice. "I'd thought Fiona would be... taller."

Behind the screen, Fiona rolled her eyes while toweling off her face and feet.

"I am not Herself," said her assistant. "I am Bookender Riverbend. Ms. Fiona has been expecting you."

"Go ahead," Jason urged. "I'll wait outside. She won't bite."

No promises, Fiona gritted her teeth.

The door closed.

Throughout the years, she had endured a parade of ingénues. Callow so-called adults who thought 'stage left' meant the theatrical troupe had left town. Whose training consisted of a high school musical about Peter Rabbit in which they had played Supporting Carrot. Who had amassed none of the experience needed to inhabit a character. Some newcomer being handed a spotlight she did not deserve left a metallic taste in Fiona's mouth.

But since the *thief's* abrupt exit, newcomers had become intolerable to Fiona. She had taken care of the potential scandalous mess uprooted by the thief and in return The Powers That Be rewarded her with the ability to control the acquisition of newcomers. Holding that line for thirty years had not been easy—though occasionally, it had been fun.

And, in the end, self-defeating. Fiona was not delusional: a small crumbling here, walls disappearing there, spells failing, infrastructure malfunctioning—the show was in decline. *Tune in Tomorrow* was literally buoyed by its viewers—'eyeballs' in mythic-speak—like a champion hoisted above a crowd. Without that crowd, the show would collapse. It might even be cancelled. If that happened, Fiona would truly be in dire straits.

Nevertheless, newcomers must match her exacting standards and she would not let the less-than-worthy through that Gate. Clearly, Jason had sent in another dummy. So how to mollify him while still keeping the show on course? Nico was already in play, but she couldn't rely on a single-fronted attack.

"Entrez s'il vous plait, darling," Fiona called out, still hidden. As intended, her voice sounded like a knife drawn across whetstone. "Are we just girls in here now?"

"Well—ah—" A pause.

"Speak up, child!" Fiona peered through a crack in the screen. The girl was gesturing at Bookender, who had returned to his paperwork at the desk. "He does not count." Fiona fitted on a pair of wide-legged white silk pants and a flowing, kitsune-fur trimmed robe, knotting it at the waist. "Are we alone?"

"Yes, ma'am!" The voice was beautifully projected, an ideal blend of terror and assertiveness. "I'm honored to meet the Grand Dame of the show, ma'am!"

That was fit and proper. Perhaps there was hope for this one yet. Fiona swanned around the privacy screen and patted her jet-black hair. There wasn't a hint of grey in it. She adored this hairstyle and had worn it since the 1970s:

cropped at the nape, thickening toward the crown, a few gentle curls sent over her head like a wave.

"I am Fiona Ballantine." She gave the girl a long, studied look. On the short side, plump. Top pulled tightly over her chest, skirt an unfortunate shade of maroon. Seemed like a teenager yet was likely in her twenties. They had no one on the show younger than age eighteen by design, but pinpointing age was a challenge for Fiona after all these years. "I believe you are honored to meet me."

The young woman met Fiona's gaze with a steady, unblinking blue-eyed reply and introduced herself. "I've heard a lot about you," she said.

"Oh?"

An awkward pause. "Just that—you're the—" Starr was clearly choosing her words carefully, which told Fiona everything she needed to know about what others had been pouring in her ear. "The heart and soul of this production. And I've also heard you're the greatest actor that ever lived."

Fiona warmed a few degrees. "Ah, dear Nico. The best PR agent ever." Fiona extended an arm, gold jewelry jangling. "Take a seat, girl. You seem both pale and flushed."

Starr touched her cheeks as she sat on the Chesterfield and leaned back. She almost sank into its overstuffed depths, feet barely touching the floor. "I'm fine, Ms.—"

"I see Jason has brought me another flower from the roadside," Fiona interrupted. "Are you of the hothouse variety, or are you a weed, Starr Weatherby?"

Starr dug herself out of the cushions and perched on the edge of the couch as if prepared for flight. "I'm not a plant, Ms. Ballantine." A small bead of sweat had appeared on her forehead. "But they say weeds are hardest to uproot."

"Which is why one should be cautious to permit them in the garden in the first place." Fiona raised an eyebrow.

"Foxglove is a weed." Starr's jaw was fixed, her eyes bright.

Fiona appreciated a good parry. "Foxglove is also poisonous."

"But its extract saves people from heart attacks."

The two women stared at each other for a moment. Fiona had to give Starr credit: she was quick. Time to go beneath the surface, like a scalpel.

"Jason, Cris, Emma—they bring me so-called actors rarely these days," she began. "I am bored with the process. So much ineptitude, so many fragile egos. Why are you here?"

"I want to act."

Fiona made a dismissive noise. "Acting isn't something one does. An actor is something one *becomes*. Try again."

"Well—I need a job and I got fired—"

Fiona waved her hand. Starr froze. "Bookender!" she cried. "Ms. Weatherby will be leaving now."

Bookender jumped from the desk, holding the dressing room door wide. Harsh artificial light spilled in from the hallway.

Starr was on her feet. "Wait, I wasn't done—"

Fiona snatched up her wrist, squeezing. "You never began, Ms. Weatherby. This must come from your heart, you simpering child. Clearly, you are unworthy of a position on my show." She gave Starr a push toward the door. "Out with you. If you require a 'job,' perhaps Jason can have you dust old props. Or tote water to the cameras. We require one hundred percent devotion on this show. It is not a mere job. It is your life." She glanced quickly at her watch: six minutes, eighteen seconds. Almost a new record. Now, to get this child out of the room.

Suddenly, Starr wrested her wrist from Fiona's grip. She took in a deep breath and pulled a clip from her hair, unleashing curls that billowed out like sails. Her pink face was set and determined, her eyes now flashing an unnatural shade of blue.

"I am not finished," she huffed and puffed like a small security dragon.

Good morning! a voice inside perked up. Valéncia's voice, one hundred percent. Fiona's heart thumped.

"There are things you don't know about me," Starr boomed, striding around the dressing room, filling the space with her presence. "I was born an orphan. I did unspeakable things to get this far in my career."

Honey, she is like a runaway horse, Valéncia piped up again. *Magnificent*.

Fiona trembled, thrilled to have her alter ego speaking again.

"See, there was nobody in my whole life who gave a crap about me—except my grandpa." Starr waved her arms around and nearly collided with the arc lamp. "He raised me on the greats: Shakespeare, Ibsen, Albee, Williams, Pinter. But I got sent to the School of Hard Knocks, 'cause we didn't have any money. Summers, I pickpocketed people all over town and ran scams in the shopping mall so people'd give me stuff. I put out my dirty little hand and people responded, soon as I pretended I needed anything."

The runaway horse took a deep breath and glanced around the room. "At school I ran long cons on my teachers. Blackmailed my principal once—he was stealing the milk money and I held it over his head so he'd let me graduate early. I faked my transcripts so I could get into acting school." She paused, giving Fiona a long, steady stare.

Fiona stared right back. She didn't even know what she was looking at.

Starr's lip quivered. Everything she'd said was almost certainly a lie, but the sudden, stupendous nature of her overacting gave Fiona a new idea.

You must allow her in, whispered Valéncia. *We can do so much with her. She's like wet clay. So deliciously... unfettered.*

And if I refuse? Fiona wondered.

I could always return to hibernation ...

That was unthinkable. Fiona tapped her nails on the arm of her chair. She did have to placate Jason. Starr had always been a done deal. But as Valéncia so wisely noted, she didn't have to use a blunt instrument to crowbar Starr out of here. She might create a situation where Starr would leave of her own accord.

Precisely, Valéncia murmured. *The death of a thousand cuts. So much more satisfying.*

A snake smile wound its way onto Fiona's face. *Valéncia, I have missed you.*

Of course you have. Without me, you are nothing.

It was true: after one hundred and eighteen years, Fiona and her character were virtually indistinguishable. When Fiona had first begun with *Tune in Tomorrow* as part of a radio broadcast, she hadn't quite been a soft, naïve innocent like Starr—but she'd had scruples. She believed the world was still, at heart, good. But associating with Valéncia for all these years had given her a different worldview. The steely Lady Marlborough, who'd been adored by dozens of husbands (including multiple Loves of Her Life), run business empires, won and lost fortunes, went on adventures, experienced near deaths and actual deaths (plus resurrections) and at least one entombment—was, for all intents and purposes, a more interesting version of Fiona Ballantine. The merge had happened dozens of years ago and fit perfectly with this so-called 'reality show' they were making every day. She didn't really have to act anymore. She just had to dial in to Valéncia.

Valéncia, who had been woken by a little nobody called Starr Weatherby.

Starr was still emoting but had calmed down. "That was when I learned the truth." Her face shone. Were those tears? "At acting school. Acting made me feel like a whole person. Like I mattered and had a right to *be*. When I get on stage, with those people in the audience, that is my whole world. Anything that lets me feel that way is worth whatever price I have to pay. I would kill for a job at *Tune in Tomorrow*." She took a long, deep breath. "I would kill... you."

Brava, thought Fiona and Valéncia together. *She's perfect. And perfectly disposable.*

Fiona had not considered this tack before. The newcomers they sent her had never seemed so malleable. Starr seemed clownish on the exterior, but she had sharp edges beneath the greasepaint. Fiona could hardly make out the lies from the truths in her tall tale declarations. She could do so much with her, yet still come out as the hero in the end.

I will be the one to save the show, she thought. *And Starr Weatherby will be my instrument.*

Out of steam, chest heaving, Starr planted her fists on her hips like an avenging superhero.

"Well, then," said Fiona as Valéncia retreated. "How much of that was complete bull hockey?"

Starr toed the ground. Without fire pouring from her, she was diminished and girlish. "I did have a grandpa who taught me about acting. We did read Shakespeare and some of those other guys. I did go to acting school." She folded her arms. "Also, everything about the way acting makes me feel."

"You invented the rest."

"I'm pretty good on the fly, or so I'm told." She raised an eyebrow. "Not that I'm sure how much any of it matters on a reality show."

"Oh," said Fiona, "you would be surprised how much acting we all do here, in the end. I'm just not sure how I feel about someone who lies to my face."

Starr threw up her hands. "That's what we do, Ms. Ballantine!"

Bingo. Fiona narrowed her eyes. "Bookender!"

"Ms. Ballantine, I wish you'd reconsider—"

"Shut up, Starr." Fiona clamped a hand on her shoulder. "Tea," she told her brownie. Gesturing with her cane, she pointed to the sofa. "Sit. We have much to discuss."

I hope we know what we're doing, Fiona mused, but Valéncia was long gone.

CHAPTER 7
Starr Struck

HEAD WHIRLING, MUSCLES aching, nerves mere spaghetti, Starr wondered if she'd blown a gasket. She gripped the edge of the largest, most plush couch she'd ever seen so hard she risked ripping out its insides. Flight crossed her mind, as it had in the diner. And as in the diner, she stayed.

Starr felt like she'd passed some sort of test, but wasn't sure whether it was a pop quiz or a final exam.

Why act? It was a simple question, yet not something she'd been asked since her Gilliard days. *Why do this thing you'll risk everything for?*

The complicated answer involved her mother, her sense of self-worth, the joy of finding something she truly loved and could disappear into, and—if she was being honest—the applause. The simple answer was: *because I have to.*

None of which had come out in her over-the-top explanation to Fiona just now. When the diva had seemed on the verge of dismissing her from the dressing room a few minutes ago, Starr's brain had gone into overdrive. Her bones had screamed *no* and she'd turned on the same vigor that had captivated Jason in the diner. *Go big or go home,* and all that. And it had worked, damnit. For now.

The wizened little person named Bookender wheeled a tea cart from a darkened back corner. "Please see that Jason Valentine joins us. Promptly." Fiona spoke in a lofty tone that reminded Starr of the great actors of the twentieth century—Katharine Hepburn, Bette Davis. As if they'd all gone to finishing school in the same New England town. Fiona fluttered her long, thin fingers at her assistant. "Hurry along."

Bookender vanished into the back of the room, and a door closed.

Starr took a long, slow breath and faced Fiona. She'd met types like her over her years in theater, actors who never took off the mask. Fiona wore hers well; she was poised and regal, with cheekbones that could cut glass and burgundy lips that echoed the *Snow White* queen. When Starr shook her hand, the touch had been as chilly as the inside of a refrigerator.

But what Starr had learned about Fiona types was this: beneath the bark wasn't often bite, but insecurity and fear—two things Starr understood without any experience as a diva. She could work with that. Fiona maybe just needed someone to listen to her.

The Grand Dame lifted the lid from the teapot and breathed deeply. A dark scent of earth and pepper filled the room. She decanted the liquid into two delicate, rose-shaped porcelain cups, then gestured at four small bowls filled with cream, sugar, cinnamon sticks and— improbably—sprinkles.

"Aah," Fiona sighed, taking a delicate first sip. "Nothing like the taste of freshly embered brownie first thing in the morning."

The tea didn't look much like chocolate. Starr took a

tentative drink. "I've never heard of brownie tea before, Ms. Ballantine."

"Fiona, please. Now that we are to be colleagues."

Starr flushed with happiness. She'd done it. She was in.

"Brownies volunteer for the service," she said. "They are rendered into tea and steeped; tomorrow, they reconstitute without any ill effects. It is considered an honor."

The words were English, but they didn't compute for Starr. Most of what she'd seen this morning hadn't fully snapped into place. Everything was happening so fast. "Well, it sure is different."

"Of course, silly girl. It's a brownie."

A bell went off distantly in Starr's memory. Brownies were, of course, desserts, and neophyte Girl Scouts. But before all that, they were small, helpful, mythical creatures. She cast a glance at Bookender sitting at the desk and the bell began jangling.

Mythics.

Couldn't be.

Starr shook her head. "Ms. Ball—Fiona? Why do you get to choose who is hired?"

Fiona laughed. "You haven't been informed about the award system?" She gestured at her crowded, illuminated cabinet. Thousands of multicolored filaments waved gently despite the lack of breeze in the room. "I have over a hundred in there. They are lovely, no?"

Starr sipped and nodded.

"Each comes with a 'prize' along with the statue. It is a small piece of magic. My first—everyone's first—freezes your age at the time you win it, for so long as you are employed by the show." She gestured to a center shelf. "This one permits me to vanish smallish spaces for short periods of time." She raised her arm another level, bracelets clanging like chains. "This one is quite unusual: it is a special award given to me for my service to the show, after I helped rid it of an undesirable element. Thanks to that award, I am permitted final say on any new long-term hire. I've had it for nearly thirty years, and I earned it the hard way."

Fiona might be a little off-the-beam, but she wasn't crazy. She'd used the word 'magic.' The jangle was growing louder inside Starr. "I see," she said. "Freeze your age. Vanish small spaces. Do you also saw ladies in half in your spare time?"

More laughter from Fiona. "Spare time? I barely know what that is, child." She caught herself mid-cackle and tilted her head. "I must say, you are very reasonable about all of this."

"No—I'm excited." *And trying not to embarrass myself anymore.*

"What I mean is, most... aspirants who make it to my doorway are more... rattled. But here you are, acting as if I'm the most frightening creature you've come across today. While I am laden with more awards than I can ever know what to do with, I promise you I am still only human."

"Aren't we all?" Starr was trying to match Fiona's airiness, but the alarm was starting to shriek. Jason had used that word, too. *Mythics. Humans.* So had Phil. *Mortal. Mythics.* Her eye twitched.

A knock came at the door, and Starr jumped, spilling some tea.

"Jason?" Fiona asked, but a woman peered inside. She was wholesomely beautiful, like the ad for a bar of soap, with an oval-shaped face and perfectly straight, auburn hair. Her lipstick was smudged, and the top of her cream-colored blouse was misbuttoned.

"Heading back to the office," she began, then spotted Starr. "Oh, hello there."

"Dakota Gardener, meet Starr Weatherby." Fiona rose to search her desk. "Starr, Ms. Gardener is our liaison with *WaterWorlds* magazine."

That was a new one to Starr. "Do you cover the pool industry?"

"We only publish on this side of the Gate," explained Dakota.

"Indeed," said Fiona. "And Dakota is extremely... hands-on with her reportage. Have you been keeping our Cris busy this morning?"

Dakota flushed to her neckline but held her gaze on Starr. "Are you good news?"

"Starr's presence is off the record, Ms. Gardener; you have seen and heard nothing today. Things are still in flux." Fiona returned from her desk with a manila envelope and handed it over. "Give Helena my best. I hope she enjoys this month's column—it's about how to incorporate bees into your wardrobe—and of course the same rules as always apply."

Dakota sighed. "Her eyes only. I know. I never look, but you remind me every month." She gave Starr a quick grin. "Hope to see *you* again soon." And she slipped away.

Starr offered a half-wave, but the door had closed. Her thoughts raced. They had been talking about tea a moment ago—and humans, and missing rooms—and then Dakota had interrupted. "You... write?" she managed, nodding at the desk.

Fiona waved her hand. "A bit. A minor column each month. *WaterWorlds*, like the show, is geared for mythics, but they seem to find my bits of advice amusing. Dear Dakota is happy to messenger my scribblings to her editor. There are faster ways, I'm told, but I prefer a personal touch."

You can't email them? Starr wondered, but immediately knew the answer, because she'd checked her phone shortly after arriving. There was no internet service here; it was a total dead zone. "And *WaterWorlds* has something to do with your awards?"

"Indeed. They choose the winners, though the prizes are assigned by The Powers That Be. As you see, we are all cozy here—though some are cozier than others."

"Are there other shows like this one? I never heard of it until yesterday."

"Of course you haven't, Starr. There are three of these so-called reality shows in all. Mythics do not require as much variety as humans in their entertainment. After all, *we* are their entertainment, even when not being filmed." She set down her teacup, the sound rattling in Starr's bones. There was something she was still not getting about being here, and it was winding her up tighter and tighter.

"All right," said Fiona, and the warmth drained from her voice, revealing the knife blade again. "I did enjoy your little performance earlier. You seem to have a special spark. However, there is something you should understand."

Starr's blood sank into her toes. Fiona leaned closer like a cobra about to strike, or a dragon ready to unleash hell—

And suddenly, Starr got it.

Boy, did she get it.

A knock came at the door. "It's me," said Jason, turning

the knob. And Starr understood at long last that what was about to walk into Fiona's dressing room was not a man who wore horns and a tail for kicks, or who liked devilish cosplay. On the other side of that door was a mythical being. Only, not a myth after all. A living, breathing impossibility.

Fiona clamped the talons of one hand around Starr's cheeks and squeezed hard. Starr couldn't move. "Listen well to me now," she said. "I am the star of this show. I am the sun and the moon, and you are but a distant gaseous blob whose light will take generations to reach us. You should do well here. I will assist with your weaker areas. But mind that you never do too well. Never upstage me. Never contradict me. Do I make myself clear?"

Jason's voice filtered through the door. "Fiona? Mind if I come in? I'm looking for Starr."

"Fisadgn," Starr gasped through her squashed cheeks and lips.

Fiona blinked and withdrew. "What did you just babble?"

"Phil's a dragon!" Starr burst out. Oh, she'd heard Fiona. But now, having fully grasped where she was and what she'd been seeing, she had a different priority. "A real live fire-breathing dragon!"

"Of course he is, you nitwit," said Fiona. "Did you think he was an elephant?"

"And the camera operators are—dryads exist?" Starr dropped her teacup and her fingers assaulted the Chesterfield sofa again. "And I drank—*real* pulverized brownie?"

Fiona bit her lip, suppressing laughter. "Jason! She's right here. Do come in."

"No!" cried Starr.

But Jason did come in and scanned their faces. "Oh, dear. Fiona, we spoke about this." His tail whisked up and he toyed with it. "I am heartily sorry—"

Fiona extended an arm and jangled her bracelets. "Au contraire, my dear faun. I accept Starr Weatherby with a whole heart. But you may wish to stand back a few paces. She's having a—moment."

Starr jumped to her feet, shaking. "Your horns are—real?"

"As is Mr. Jason's tail," said Bookender, who was preparing to remove the tea cart. "All fauns have horns and a tail."

"Wanna see my legs?" Jason asked.

Starr's head went from whirling to swimming, and the room blurred. Nearly toppling over the side of the Chesterfield, she jostled past Jason, escaping down the blank, empty hallways. Everything was confused. Nothing made sense. Fiona's cackling laughter rang in her ears. She ran blindly, not knowing where she was going, hearing the sound of galloping platform boots—or were they *hooves*?—behind her. Then she was off her feet, flying and kicking as strong arms swept her up.

"Hey," said Jason. "You just got here. Don't leave yet."

"You're a faun," she gasped.

"You bet I am." His tail, tipped with hair like a horse's mane, flicked around and slipped into her hand, giving it a shake. "Nice to meet you."

Starr had never been the fainting type.

But she was now.

CHAPTER 8

Starr Sign

"WELL?" JASON SLID his glasses on, pulled them off, then slid them on again, peering over Starr's prone form, now laid across his desk. "Is she *breathing*?"

"Why must I always check if humans are in a respiratory state?" Emma twitched her nose, prodding Starr's chest. "That is a terrible feline stereotype."

Jason snorted and stared into the distance of the moving, glamoured walls of his office, considering going for another extended bolt over the hills—but the naiads in his platform heels had communicated they were queasy after his last two gallops. He had to concentrate. Starr wasn't dead. That was a good first step.

But she wasn't with them. Not in a conscious sense.

Emma cocked an ear over the actor's mouth. Soft, even breath stirred her furry hair. "Mmm," she murmured. "Coffee... with hazelnut creamer and... lily of the valley?" She waved a handpaw at the faun. "She's attracted to you; I can smell the pheromones."

Off came the glasses again. "Be serious—" Jason spoke Emma's True Name, which created a tickle beneath Starr's left armpit. He cringed: one did not speak True Names in front of mortals, even ones that were not wakeful. But his concern had made him careless.

"No, she does! And if the stories are correct then you can wake her up by—"

Jason threw up his hands. "Stop believing everything you read. Also, that's *humans* kissing humans. Thirdly, I am not a prince. Eighthly, it's completely the wrong interpretation of what happened in that forest—"

Starr's eyelids fluttered. She blinked sleepily into dappled sunlight filtering through spreading green leaves.

"And she's back." Emma curled her tail around her legs, resting on the edge of the long, uneven wooden slab that was Jason's desk. She licked at a handpaw, murmuring about hazelnut cream.

"Zeus' handcuffs, that's over with," sighed Jason, peering at Starr's face. She appeared… softer than before. "I never saw a human actually pass out."

That was only partly true. Jason had seen humans faint, but at the time he had no idea why they'd collapsed at the mere sight of him. This was before he'd discovered pants. Later, when those same humans came after him with torches, he hadn't found time to ask.

"Central Park?" Starr asked, woozy. "Have I been dumped in Central Park?"

"Hmph," said Emma. "As if your level of Central Park ever smelled this good."

Starr sat up on her elbows and gaped at Jason's forest glade of an office. A breeze riffled through the leaves, revealing a plum-colored sky. "Whoa," she breathed. "I didn't dream it all."

"Whoops." Jason reached under his desk and pressed a button. The glamour faded to reveal cracked grey walls lined in bookshelves and filing cabinets, and no windows.

Starr sighed. "The office is magic, too?"

"'Tis," he said, heart beginning to return to its usual rhythm. "We've learned it's best to keep things... familiar for mortals."

"What, our little brains would overload if we saw the real deal?"

"If the boot fits," Emma purred.

"That was *so* dramatic." Jason clapped his hands together. "You went 'aah!' and then you went *zoom*—" he made a slicing motion with his arm. "And then you went *splat*. I thought you were dead."

"You're pretty chipper about it." Jason's tail was touching the desk and Starr reached out a tentative hand to give it a pet.

"He wasn't for a spell there," said Emma. "He was positively distraught. Agitated. Distressed." She crossed her hind legs behind a Peter Pan-collared, black-and-white striped dress and turned her amber eyes on Starr, offering a handpaw. "Emma Crawford. Head writer. Do not touch the fur."

Starr pulled her hand back from Jason's tail, but he gave her a nod to continue her ministrations. She swiveled her gaze between him and Emma and back again, and he suppressed a smile. After years of observing her from afar, having her up close had a heady effect. It was as if he'd breathed life into a dream constructed out of sticks and cloth and a little magical goo.

"I'm confused," said Starr. "Am I hired or what?"

Emma shook her head. "She's not caught up one bit, is she?"

"This all happened very quickly, furkins," he said. "I'll give her the Guide in a moment."

Emma pressed a handpaw to her chest. "All right, in brief: werepanther, primarily. Yes, we exist. The stories are all true."

"I don't know of any stories—"

Emma barreled on. "Head writer, secondarily. Also, wordcat. Words need chasing. Pinning down. Consuming. I always have more than I need, so I spill them into the scripts. I am the writer's room."

"That's crazy," said Starr. "That's not—"

"Human? Indeed not. Being able to write with four paws and my tail simultaneously makes me several times more efficient than humans."

"But reality shows don't need… scripts." Starr frowned, trailing off. "Well, I suppose they need some scripts. Only—how does a reality show work when you've got actors who play characters and read scripts and I *guess* you have a set around here someplace but… you know, that's not exactly reality. You two aren't exactly reality, either."

Jason sat next to Starr on the desk, helping her to a seated position. "You have discovered a bit of a… bump under the rug with us. And well spotted! Things are complicated. As I told you in the toilet room, actual soaps were our model for many years, but they are now out of fashion. So, we have—what is the word, furkins? Pirouetted?"

"Pivoted," noted Emma.

"Yes!" cried Jason. "Easy as pie crust."

"No, it's needlessly complicated," said Starr. "What is the actual 'reality' in your show?"

Jason grinned. "The fact that our audience believes it is actually happening. Or most of our audience. Or some of our audience. The stronger their belief, the better our ratings."

Starr's mouth opened a bit. "So you're lying to every person—every mythic—who watches the show?"

"Mythics are not above lying to themselves," said Emma.

"Our audience believes in us," said Jason. "I know this because we are still a functioning show. The more they believe, the more they invest in our show, and the stronger we become. Their belief in us keeps our stories chugging along. Therefore, we are duty-bound to support the notion that what they are seeing is actually happening."

"It's fan service," said Starr.

"It's a feedback loop," nodded Jason. "Call it what you will. Think of it like that toy human children play with." He flattened his arm and tilted it up and down. "The sawsee."

"A seesaw?"

Jason pointed.

"But that doesn't address the fact that you two... that dragons, that dryads and whatever else you've got here working on your show—I want to say none of you exist." Starr looked at her hands, then back up at Jason. "I want to say I'm having a vivid hallucination. That I got kidnapped on the street and am actually tied up in a basement about to be subject to horrible torments."

Emma leaned forward, chin in her paw. "Kidnapped! Stashed in a basement! What delicious ideas." She made a quick note by pulling a pencil from behind her ear and scribbling in the air. "Tell me more."

"You most certainly are not kidnapped," said Jason. "We would never do that. Well, almost never."

Starr's neck flushed. "But even if I agree to believe that you are all real—"

Jason clicked his tongue and took her hand. It was so warm; he loved how humans always had such a high body temperature. He curled her fingers around one of his horns, which had risen a couple of inches above his hairline. "Hold on tight."

He stood, and Starr dangled from his left horn. He let it shrink, and she slid off, stumbling against the desk. "Whether you believe in us or not makes no difference. What matters is what our audience believes. We are here. We have a show to create. We can use someone like you, and you've somehow passed muster with Fiona. But there are a few basic conditions—like your acceptance that every so-called 'mythical creature' you've ever read about exists. Certainly, you know about what you call the 'Loch Ness Monster.' Or the 'Abominable Snowman.' We practically live among you."

"But it's not like anyone ever sees you." Starr hesitated. "Well, hardly ever sees you."

"That's because you keep calling them 'abominable' and 'monster.' Or suggest their only important characteristic is to have big feet! Those are not encouraging descriptions. They have actual names. Take a trip to Scotland and call for 'Gertrude' over by the lake and see what happens. Or hang out in the Himalayas with some bananas and shout for 'Mi-go.' You'll see." Jason took a deep breath. "In any case, mythics work here, and you will have to get along with them. If you can do that, everything else is easy."

Emma coughed, as if trying to bring up a hairball. "That's an exaggeration. Magnification. Overstatement. Things are not easy here. But they are often... amusing."

Starr stared at her hand. A small bead of blood had welled up on the pad of her thumb where she'd brushed the tip of Jason's horn. She shivered. "OK."

"OK?" Jason pressed his fists on his hips. "That's it? Aren't you going to marvel before us?"

"Trust me, I marveled so hard a few minutes ago I passed out." She grinned. "Now I can say I've even bled for this job." She held up the thumb. "I just thought you were all... special effects."

"I rather like that," said Emma. "Special and effectual."

Jason leaned on the desk next to Starr, his tail wrapping around her hips. "I would much rather have a mortal who figured things out for herself than one who came in here like a... brownie. Brownies are all the super fans we need. We've had guest actors who couldn't stop petting everybody—"

"Oops," said Starr, but Jason waved the concern away.

"As if we were in a zoo," hissed Emma. "Short-termers all. Gone and forgotten."

"What happened to them?"

Jason swirled his palm in the air. "A little selective memory erasure. A spell we deploy as necessary." He cleared his throat. "Now, to business." With a leap behind his desk, he began rooting around in the drawers.

"So, this is a soap opera—I mean, reality show, and it stars... only humans?"

Jason nodded, digging deeper. His entire arm disappeared into a drawer, which was much deeper than it looked. He knew there was a copy of the Guide in there; the last one had come home after Amelia's... vanishing. He didn't want to revisit that dark time, but it was hard not to: it was the one time they'd actually lost track of an actor. No one knew what had happened; she simply stopped coming into work and fell off the radar. Jason had pushed hard to have her tracked down—they couldn't let humans roam the world with knowledge of what went on behind the Veil, that was both tradition and common sense—but TPTB had been unusually disinterested.

Jason pushed aside rocks and twigs, pencils and unmelted ice cubes and old copies of *Water Worlds* folded into origami. And then, at last—the Guide slid into his hands. "Aha!" he cried.

"But why us?" Starr asked. "People are boring. Our reality is particularly dull. We're the ones who spend billions making movies about you types."

Emma leaped from the desk to the top of a nearby filing cabinet. "Oh, my sweet, your super heroic comic book tales and fables about magic rings and flying sneetches—"

"Golden snitches, she called them," Starr corrected gently.

"We have all those things. We are endlessly entertained by weddings! Divorces! Lies! Cheating! Mail fraud! Conspiracy theories! *Embezzlement*, what a terrific word. Humans die, and we love it—no, not because we're all bloodthirsty, though some of us …" She shook her head. "The point is, we don't die. It's true, we do avoid the whole *babies* nonsense in this show for reasons best not gotten into now. But *Tune in Tomorrow* serves as both entertainment and education for our viewers. Hence, reality!"

Jason sat up, shaking the Guide hard enough to wake it up, then handed the book to Starr. It vibrated as it touched her fingers and bonded to her. She scanned the title: *Year One: A Compleat Guide to Show Survival, Assimilation Beyond the Veil, and Tea Brewing Techniques.*

"There's not much to know about brewing tea," Jason pointed out.

Starr gulped. "Survival?"

"Metaphor!" Emma cried.

Jason's grin felt pasted on. He couldn't tell her about Amelia. That might be the last straw.

Starr flipped through the pages, and he leaned over her shoulder as chapter titles whizzed by: 'Not Fairy Gold: Payment by Magic Deposit,' 'Health and Safety Procedures for Delicate Human Bodies,' 'Distant Future Retirement Options' and then, toward the end, 'Home Brew: Overcoming Revulsion to Brownie Tea Preparation.' Starr closed the Guide, smoothing her hand over the top. "It's an employee handbook."

"All yours, new employee," Jason said. "No one but you will see anything other than a Swedish-Paakantyi translation dictionary. If the Guide remains in your possession for more than one solar day, it will serve as your signed and bound contract, and will regularly update itself during your tenure with the show. But if you choose not to work with us, leave it on your open windowsill tonight. It will wing its way back home and we will not contact you again."

Starr paled. "No—" she began. "I mean, of course I'm coming back—"

"But you have more questions."

"I have so many questions. Like, salary? Vacation? Sick days?"

"All in the book. Take some time tonight and start reading."

Starr closed the Guide and rested her hands on it, beaming. "I accept."

Knots in Jason's stomach unfurled. He had so many things to be grateful for today: Fiona hadn't killed Starr, and she'd not only recovered from a sudden, terrifying faint but seemed to have no inclination to come after him with a torch. Jason tilted his head in admiration. They had hired a tough one.

She'd need to be.

He thrust out his hand and Starr fitted hers into it. They shook. He stared at the small smear of blood on her thumb. That wasn't insignificant: she trusted him. This job required trust from everyone, but for the first time in many, many years—maybe ever—he wondered about being worthy of that trust. The sensation writhed in him like snakes, or too many noodles. "Any other questions?"

"Oh, yes," she said. "Would you please turn the sky back on?"

Jason reached under the desk and the forest glade returned. The plum sky now had a bright orange moon in its center. Starr flattened against the desk again, and after a moment, Jason joined her. Emma made a giant leap directly over them and curled up at their heads.

"You're going to save this show," he whispered.

"No pressure," Starr whispered back.

"Oh." He nodded. "I think you know precisely how to handle pressure."

CHAPTER 9
Starr Light

"AND HERE WE are!" Jason rested a warm hand on Starr's shoulder blade, five days later. "Stage entrance!"

"At long, *long*, last." Fiona set icy cold fingertips on Starr's upper arm.

The two show veterans now flanked her like—prison guards? No, that was wrong. Starr *wanted* to be here. It had been tough, these past several days of preparation, but at least they were supporting her. Jason, like the angel on one side, Fiona like the... well, Starr didn't want to think of her that way. Fiona knew what she was doing. Jason wouldn't have put Starr into his most senior actor's hands if she didn't.

Starr clutched her sides, holding the small, stapled packet of pages from the scene they'd be blocking shortly, and swallowed. It was all down to this: a pair of giant double doors, over which a bare red bulb protruded.

A yellow-lettered sign on door one proclaimed:

WORLD ENTRANCE

A red-lettered sign on door two pronounced:

*DO NOT ENTER WHEN THE RED LIGHT IS ON
UNDER PAIN OF BANISHMENT*

The bulb was currently dark.

"*World* entrance," she murmured, thinking of the finicky Gates, which over the past five days had scooped her up and deposited her at the stages every morning. Some days it was more like 6:10, once it had been 4:59 and she'd missed the entrance and had to stand around until they returned at 9:12.

"These doors work fine," Jason said now, clearly reading Starr's mind. "Nothing to fear."

"Please, Jason. Don't give her false reassurances." Fiona turned to Starr and gave her a final scan. She twisted Starr's face this way and that. "Well," she said in that knife-edge voice Starr had come to equate with nails on a chalkboard, "it'll have to do. We have run out of time."

Starr's eyes widened as Jason opened the doors. There was a rush of air not unlike when the Gates arrived, but it immediately subsided. Faint sounds drifted her way, like a party in the distance. Several parties, in fact. But soundstages were usually cool, silent chambers, cavernous and packed with sets—not soirees.

Jason cocked an eyebrow. "Time to jump in, Starr. Or should I say—*Sam?*"

"Wait!" said Starr, scanning Jason's face, hoping for some last-minute advice. Something tugged at her, drawing her into the stage. She pulled back but felt a tear beginning on her dress. She stumbled backward, unable to keep her balance. "What don't I know?"

Fiona cackled. "Everything!"

And the doors slammed shut behind Starr.

FIVE DAYS EARLIER, Starr had walked—not flown—back through the Gate at precisely 7:03 p.m. Studio time. It had been a day of miracles and wonders: she'd been hired, she'd met a dragon, she had a crush on a man with horns and a tail.

Then she'd wondered: why was it so darn dark for 7:03? In July?

Walking to the subway, Starr had pulled out her phone for the first time since arriving through the Gates. She'd had no coverage while on the other side of the Veil. The screen flashed at her—and she realized it wasn't even Friday anymore. It was Saturday, 3:32 a.m. Somehow, she'd lost about eight hours.

"Time runs differently on this side of things," Jason had said airily while leading her through the studio's key departments. It was an explanation that hadn't really landed at the time—Starr was too busy being dazzled by the Hairies and Makeup Fairies Room, the Leprecostumer's Den, an incongruously mundane kitchenette, and then to her own tiny dressing room, which had been a tenth of the size of Fiona's and had the same bland appeal of Jason's dull, non-glamoured office.

Back through the Gate that evening, Starr had struggled to understand everything as messages flooded in on her newly connected phone: *Where are you? Is he cute? Rent due NOW!* Plus, a note from her dentist saying she owed twenty-five dollars for missing an appointment.

It had all been too much: Starr's stomach lurched and she'd vomited brownie tea into the street.

That night, she'd been unable to sleep, her brain both fried and electrified by her experiences. She'd tried writing some of it down for her roommates so they would understand if she vanished for an extended break but discovered the words on the paper instead told the history of the New York Knicks. She erased all that and tried again, ending up with a recipe for Apple Brown Betty.

"Today, I met a faun named Jason," she spoke aloud, and what came out was, "The new Ryan Reynolds movie looks hilarious."

The message came in clear: no talking, no explaining, no telling.

Again, it had been too much crazy for her. She'd brought the heavy Guide Jason had sent her home with to her windowsill, reasoning that a lifetime of wrapping utensils was tolerable, because it was understandable. Starr was game for a lot of shenanigans, but her day at the *Tune in Tomorrow* set had been like all of the shenanigans piled on top of each other and bound into a sandwich she had to eat in one bite.

But with each step, the Guide in her hands had grown heavier and heavier. As she tried to set the book on the ledge—she couldn't. And magic had nothing to do with it: it was because her heart refused to allow her to let go.

This is a weird situation, she'd thought inside. *But it's a special weird thing. It's your special weird thing. Be... the... mango.*

She'd taken the Guide from the windowsill, and it weighed almost nothing. Starr had slept with it under her pillow that night, and each night ever since.

Then there'd been the real hitch.

She showed up for work on Monday ready to rock and roll—only to find no one was ready for her, at least not in front of the camera. There were... preliminaries. First

Jan, who worked as Emma's assistant, dropped Starr off at the werepanther's pillow-strewn office, which led to Starr's morning hours being co-opted by brainstorming her character. Also, arguing about why they needed to give her a 'character' in the first place.

"I can be myself," said Starr. "You already told me the show's this workplace drama in a small town called Shadow Oak that centers around a detective agency that's secretly run by the town rich lady but fronted by Nico-Romeo and Nico-Romeo's girlfriend Beatrice but whose real name off the show is Nora. And they butt heads all the time with the town detective played by—"

"Maverick," Emma had nodded. "Played by Charlie. You'll meet him eventually."

"So just let me show up and be what I am, this newcomer in town who wants to help out." Starr grinned. "Easy as pie."

"What sort of pie?" Emma raised an eyebrow.

Starr had opened her mouth, then closed it. "Cherry pie?"

"I like that!" Emma had started writing. "So we will call you 'Jo.'"

"I *can* just be Starr."

"Starr is too ..." Emma had waved a handpaw. "Flashy. Extravagant. Over the top. Mythics prefer the things that are *not* flashy about humans. Your ordinariness is what makes you... exotic."

Starr began to think she was, at last, beginning to understand. "My real name's Samantha," she'd admitted in a small voice. "Sam, mostly."

All of Emma's fur had stood up at once. She'd reached for the catnip in the corner of her office and bit off a stem. "Spec-tacular, my pet!" All four hand- and feetpaws and her tail went flailing. "You shall be *Sam*!"

Starr wilted. "Really?"

"You wanted to be yourself, did you not?"

And so, after years of fighting to be called Starr she was back to being Sam. "Just—just don't tell anyone it's my real name," she said. "I want to be Starr... when we're not, um, filming."

Emma was too excited to inquire further. "Not a problem."

After a few hours of Emma drilling Shadow Oak history into Starr's head while fleshing out this 'Sam' person she was expected to play, Bookender picked up Starr and brought her to Fiona's dressing room. They'd sipped more brownie tea, and the diva tested the newcomer in the finer points of 'reality' acting for the mythic audience. "We are foreign to them, even to the ones who live among us in our world," Fiona had explained. "Think of Anglophiles, who sit up at the sound of an Anglo-Celtic or even Antipodean voice. Think of Europeans who believe America is one big parade or movie. Human nature has that kind of musicality to mythics. When we try to be like them, we sound— we seem—wrong. Be human. But be more human than human."

"I'm not sure I get it," Starr had admitted.

"Go over the top, as needed," Fiona said. "Embellish. These are big, melodramatic stories we are telling, even if they are ostensibly 'real.'"

"Reali-soap acting."

"That word gives me hives, but you have put your finger on it."

Starr left Fiona's dressing room with a roaring headache every day.

Meanwhile, Nico always found a way to be available to her for lunch. She found him at her dressing room door with extravagant offer upon offer to 'marble' someplace wonderful. She didn't know what that meant, and despite being flattered as hell that someone who looked like him was interested in her—she kept putting him off. He always wore those dang sunglasses, had his shirt half-open and acted like a combination of a 1970s swinger and his Roland character, which made him more sleazy than sweet. Yet the more she told him to buzz off, the more intent he seemed to be to win her over.

But after five days of this, she'd had enough and told Jason, Emma and Fiona—using different tones for each— "I don't know if you say this on your side of the Veil, but on my side we like this phrase: 'Shit or get off the pot.'" It was time to get her on that stage, to see if she could make this 'Sam' character work. The comment had produced a scandalized gasp from Fiona, a grin from Jason and a character description from Emma.

SAMANTHA 'SAM' DRAPER is a sweet, unschooled girl loaded with street smarts. She's fulsome and eager and new in town. She's taken a job she desperately needs as a maid in Valéncia Marlborough's mansion, but she keeps getting involved in the Eye 2 Eye Detective Agency. Sam may not be as wholesome or as unschooled as she appears, however. There's a stubborn, self-sufficient spark in her eye that says she will not be presumed upon.

Emma had handed her the blurb in her dressing room, then strolled away; Starr read it through and ran into the hallway. "It's me!" she burst out at the first person she saw—who happened to be Nico. "Read it!"

He peeled off the sunglasses and hung them on his open shirt, scanning the page. A small smile lifted, and his eyes sparkled. It was the first time she'd seen him look, well, like a normal person. Not Roland. "Well captured," he said. "I think she's done you justice."

"Oh," said Starr, her cheeks warming. "Well. I mean, not that my name's Sam or Draper. And I'm not too sure what 'fulsome' means—it kind of sounds—" *Fat*, she wanted to say, but bit it off.

"Generous." The word was a cool breath against her overheated skin. "It's lovely." He held out a hand. "Nice to meet you, 'Sam.'"

Starr hesitated, then joined her fingers against his. His touch was warm and welcoming. It was not Roland. This was Nico she was seeing, at long last. "Pleasure's all mine," she said, her voice a husky whisper.

All systems were go.

Now, Starr stumbled into a deep darkness that fell over her like a cowl. The stage doors had shut behind her, and though she reached out she couldn't even see where they were anymore. She'd asked for this. She was ready. She'd gotten them to get off the pot and send her in. But send her in—where?

The party noises in the distance seemed no louder than before. But there did seem to be more of them now. Then, cutting through that persistent buzz came an audible, comprehensible set of words: "*Thiswaythiswaythiswaythiswaythisway ...*"

The voices were a tiny chorus, accompanied by small lights that illuminated her feet and created a walkway that curved around a corner. In the near distance, a glow beckoned.

"Who are you?" she asked the darkness.

"We the Wills!" the chorus chorused.

Wills?

"Hark! Who goes there?" a voice boomed, seeming to

surround her. "Be that—Starr Weatherby?"

"No!" she cried. "It be Sam Draper!"

"Then step forward and be counted," the piratical voice continued. "Never tarry! Time's a'wastin'! Also, we're bored and need company."

"Who are you?" Starr slowed to a halt, folding her arms.

"Come forward... and find out!"

Starr put one foot in front of the other and followed the sparkling, lit pathway. Her eyes slowly adjusted to the darkness, and she began to make out squared-off structures filling the vast, dark soundstage. In a usual studio, these permanent sets—darkened rooms, patios, chambers, city streets, groceries, cafés and the like—would be held in stasis until needed for a script. She'd toured many TV show sets before and understood that when not in use it was like being in a ghost town.

But as she trod down the pathway, her heels making faint echoing sounds against the paved floor—something seemed off. For one thing, she couldn't make out the ceiling. The darkness above her head climbed and climbed into further darkness, so deep she expected to see the Milky Way... but there was nothing. For another, that soft buzzing, a gentle cacophony just beneath her ability to make out voices, persisted. Rounding a corner past an empty living room set, she approached a café that positively hummed. The coffee shop was lit from within and sounded as if it had been filled with bees. Starr neared an exterior window, blinking: there was movement inside. Too much movement. Too much, too fast—a blur of bodies and objects and sounds, as if someone was playing a movie on fast-forward. Voices inside all blended and looped together in a swooping mishmash that made her heart flutter. Queasy, she reached out a hand to touch the door frame and—*zap*.

Starr stumbled backward, cradling her hand. The frame of the set had sent out an electric shock. Her hand was unmarred, but the chill of the sharp jolt thrummed through her. She stood on the path again, shaking.

"*Thiswaythiswaythisway*"—the lights on the path flickered, the chorus urging her along.

"Don't be touching anything!" the piratical voice reached out again.

"I won't!" she shouted back. "Again," she added more quietly.

She hurried now, past more quiet, empty sets and strangely alive, thrumming ones. Inside each of the lit ones, figures raced around, some busier than others, each with their own song of voices within. She stayed true to the light-lined path and at last a new glow appeared, revealing a lit set with no unnatural movement or voices. A kitchen, in fact. Not like Mama's, strewn with mouse traps and unwashed dishes, but a throwback 1950s dream kitchen of streamlined, pastel appliances and chrome-rimmed Formica furniture. It was a classic three-walled set, the fourth sliced away and set off to one side so cameras—rather, cameradryads—could shoot from a variety of angles. It was both homey and alien and relief flooded through her to find something that felt normal.

At the kitchen table sat a slender, cream-colored blonde with a severe bob haircut, a jaw that could slice bread and too much makeup covering a suspicious expression. "Ugh," she said. "I guess you made it."

This was Nora D'Arbanville, whom Starr had seen in this very kitchen flinging plates on her first day, when Jason had explained to her in a steamy bathroom what "streaming" meant to them. She'd learned further from

Emma's discussions and Fiona's training that Nora played the airheaded, flighty, Beatrice—Roland's on-again, off-again girlfriend. "She's possibly even less excited that you're here than Fiona is," Emma had warned. "But we'll warm her up."

Starr ignored the non-greeting and held out a hand. "Nice to meet you! I'm—yikes!"

Nico's face had appeared abruptly in a false window above the sink, and her heart leaped into her throat. He waved. Starr rolled her eyes. She'd never met someone so effortlessly handsome who could also be as effortlessly obnoxious.

Nora leaned to one side, suppressing laughter.

"Ha and ha," said Starr, trying to be a good sport. "Way to put the new girl in her place."

"Aww," said Nico. "Well, ye be no coward, I see."

Starr narrowed her eyes. "That was *you* calling at me from all the way back there?"

He made a grandiose bow.

"Showing off, as per usual." Nora's tone was sultry and Southern. That put Starr on guard; some Southern belles were both honey and bee simultaneously.

"Just one of my little talents." He lifted Starr's hand to kiss the back of it. She jerked away, but not before feeling another shiver run up her—a lot like the jolt she'd received from the moving set. "Oh, right," he nodded. "You don't like me... yet."

"Take it down a notch, Nico, eh?" Nora finished filing a nail down and took a sip of water from a nearby glass. "Y'all are making me positively ill."

"That's a habit with you these days, doll face," he shot back. "Toilet's right through those doors, down the hall—"

Nora held up the flat of her hand.

Starr sighed. She knew she should turn up the charm and make nice with her new colleagues, but they weren't making it easy. She missed Jason.

Sure, go walk out, she heard Mama hiss inside. *Knew you couldn't hack it.*

Swallowing her annoyance, Starr settled into the description Emma had given her of 'Sam.' Of her old self. Who was now her new self. "Let's start over," she said. "I'm S—"

"I know who you are." Nora looked her up and down. "And I'm darned sure you know who I am. You should leave now. I don't know how much you paid Fiona to give you the go-ahead but take my word for it and scram."

Starr's hackles rose. She had a brother; she knew what goading felt like. But this was more complex than mere hazing. Fight? Flight? Was there a third option? She looked at Nico for help. He had on a half-smile of encouragement but said nothing. *Finesse,* she thought. That's another good F-word. Starr leaned across the table, close—but not too close—to Nora. "Sorry, darlin'," she drawled, imitating Nora. "Can't do that. I'm here for the long run. You're stuck with me."

Nora chuckled, her hazel eyes sharp and deadly. She rested a hand on Starr's forearm. "Aw, she thinks she's clever, Nico." Her hard, steady glance bored into Starr.

Without warning, the ground softened beneath Starr's feet. Every doubt she'd ever had about this job, about acting, about herself, about her future all boiled to the surface and washed through her. *Failure. Loser. No-talent. Hopeless.* Starr couldn't breathe. The words choked her. She pulled away from Nora's grip, her elbow knocking the glass of water right into her co-star's lap.

"Mother trucker!" Nora leaped up, the lower half of her white Capris soaked through. "You did that on purpose, you—"

"Stop it." Nico came between them. "Nora, put the claws back in. Starr, grab a dish towel."

Mechanically, Starr stumbled to the sink and returned with the cloth hanging next to it. Her head and neck cleared, the doubts ebbing like ocean waves, though their ripples lingered. She grabbed a director's chair and sat, grateful for Nico's intervention.

Nora dabbed at her lap. "Now I'll have to talk to the leprecostumers again before we shoot."

Starr's head still spun. "What happened?"

Nico scowled, shoving his sunglasses into a pocket. It was as if he shoved Roland in there, too—he reminded her of the man who'd called her 'generous' the other day. "That's one of Darby's little talents. What's it called, Emotional Blackmail or something? She plugs into your wavelength—whatever you're already thinking, deep down—and she can turn it up or down, like a radio volume. Fortunately, her range is extremely short."

Nora flashed daggers at him.

"Much like her temper."

"You are so not fun, Nico Reddy." Nora threw the dishrag into the sink.

"I am Mr. Fun. I only need someone to be fun with." He cut a glance at Starr.

Nora held up a finger. "That is just one of the reasons we were never gonna make it."

"You two were a—couple?"

Nora shrugged. "Longest three months of my life. They shoved us together on the show, so, you know, we played around with the idea. I mean, I was new here and he's, well—"

"Mr. Fun," said Nico and Starr simultaneously. They exchanged a glance. Starr felt it into her toes.

"That," Nora nodded. "And like all bad dreams it ended, a lifetime ago. Here's the thing—that charm he has? Not even one of the prizes. He's always had it. Like a birth defect."

Starr realized that they were always like this. Throwing dishes, throwing words. Bantering, bickering. If she hadn't shown up, they'd have found a way to argue without her. But Starr refused to be irrelevant in the room. She wanted to be a presence. And she was not going to be pushed around so easily. "Gosh," she shrugged languidly. "Guess it all makes sense now."

Nora raised an eyebrow.

"Older women are naturally jealous of young ones. I understand why you want me off the show, Ms. D'Arbanville. You feel threatened."

"That's 'Nora' to you!" She charged at Starr again. "And I am thirty-two, you insect!"

Starr darted around the table. "My Mama's forty," she lied. "Chew on that!"

Nora surged in one direction, Starr darted away, and they circled the table a few times until Nico again stood between them.

"I love watching ladies wrestle, but only when it's over me." He glanced at his watch. "Cris is officially late. Starr, how's about I give you a tour of the sets, so everybody can cool—or dry—off?" He gestured into the darkened innards of the stage area.

"That's a great idea. I have a thousand questions. But—" Starr reached into his pocket and set the sunglasses on the table. "Those stay here. All of the shtick stays here."

A glimmer of doubt crossed his face and then he shrugged.

"Sure. Why not? I mean, if you prefer."

"I do."

Nico started to say something, then pulled it back. "Darby, give us a shout when you get a whiff of cigar, eh?"

"Maybe." Nora dismissed them both with a wave, reading through her sides.

Nico reached behind Starr and guided her toward the dark again, but she sidled away. "You can show me around," she allowed. "But keep your hands where I can see them."

CHAPTER 10
North Starr

"WILLS," NICO CALLED out. "A little brighter, please?"

Above them, a swirl of dime-sized lights flickered on and took to the air, following Nico and Starr as they walked. Their luminescence increased until Nico held up a finger and nodded. They were the same lights that had given Starr a path to the kitchen set—but were now mobile. She squinted into the newfound brightness.

"Morning!" chimed the voices loosely. "Or is it night?"

"Right the first time." Nico gestured. "Meet Starr Weatherby, Wills."

The track lighting swirled, swooped and encircled Starr briefly, then returned to the air above them. "Ooooo," said the voices. "Aaaaah. We like stars."

"What are they?" she whispered.

"Will Twelve!" cried one. "Will Sixty-Five!" piped another. Multiple 'Will' names and their associated numbers piped up in the air, then the lights clustered together. "We's the o'Wisps."

Starr clapped a hand over her mouth in delight. She'd done a little internet research after work each evening—

thankfully, the Gate's time distortion was rarely as out of whack with her world than it had been on that first visit—and now she felt better informed. Will-o'-the-Wisps. In person. "My pleasure," she curtseyed. "Do you hang out in here all day?"

"Aye, aye," they chirped. "We come when called for the brights."

I think I just met the lighting department. "You'll try and make me look good?"

The Wills swirled and made a cartoonish face in the air that smiled at her. "Aye, miss, but 'tis not much work we need doin' there."

Nico scattered them with his hands. "I'll do the necessary flirting around here, guys." The lights returned to their silent, hovering position. "Now, that's pretty cool, eh?"

"It's like having a conversation with fireflies," she sighed. "I might never get used to that."

He smiled, and it was a genuine, warm thing. "Takes a little getting used to, this being around magic jazz. The fact that magic is, in fact, real."

"Even as they're trying to get us to be as unmagical as possible."

"We are most fascinated by the things that elude us." Nico paused. "You'll be surprised how fast you do get used to it. Give it a couple of decades. But what I meant wasn't just about the Wills. It's about—" He swept his arm outward. "This."

The Wills turned themselves onto full power and Starr gasped. The light revealed a boundless expanse of sets, reaching deeper and wider than she could perceive. It was a room without end, a world within a world. The sets were arranged like streets in a city, row upon row of empty rooms waiting for action. As select Wills followed along, providing illumination, Nico walked her through streets and alleys, revealing kitchens, bedrooms, living rooms, basements, fake parks, a swimming pool, storage facilities, garages, libraries. Viewed from space, he told her the room would be as large as Staten Island.

"Though it changes every day," he added. "Expands to fit what's needed. The edges are... tricky. Don't go wandering alone; it's too easy to get lost. And don't try to interact with the live sets."

So that's what that buzzing café had been, she realized. "Too late. But—why are some of the sets... live? The show's not shooting now, so—"

They paused in front of a pawn shop, which glowed with a grey, sickly cast and featured blurry movement beyond its closed-off fourth wall glass windows. "There's a saying one of our extras once told me, came from a TV show: 'We do not live in this world alone, but in a thousand other worlds,'" said Nico. "Those 'live' rooms—they're linked portals. They're connected to the *other* shows out there. There's only one *Tune in Tomorrow*, but mythics do more than make reality shows. They love movies and TV shows and plays and concerts and something they call High Art which, don't ask me because I've never understood it myself. We share certain sets so we can cross over between them. Have their characters in our show, or our characters in their show. Just for a bit. Just to provide that sense of... verisimilitude that The Powers That Be want." He gestured at the pawn shop. "This one links to a whole town called Second Chance. There's a bakery we have access to a few streets over that's part of a place called Swee'ton. Those places operate like real towns, and all their sets are always live. Not like here. We're a bit old-fashioned that way—we don't film outside. All of our 'outsides' are just glamours."

Starr peered into the shop, trying to wrap her head around that. "Real towns—with humans—but on this side of the Veil?"

"Yeah. Different rules, different parameters. Trust me, you'll have plenty of time to learn about all this stuff."

"Why don't we film outside, though?"

"The Powers That Be prefer it that way. *Tune in Tomorrow* wasn't the first ever mythic-run show but it sure was an early one. And it's the oldest one still in existence. You wouldn't think mythics could get nostalgic but"—he gestured—"they're not good with change. It was hard enough for Jason to convince them they needed to start letting viewers watch it through streaming. Too complicated, too risky. At least, that's what you'd hear if you heard it from TPTB."

"Who *are* TPTB?"

"Seelie. And Unseelie, depending on your show. You do not want to mess with those critters. Fortunately, they don't stop by often." He had folded his arms and was tapping a foot anxiously.

"You don't agree."

"I have thoughts. I am not in charge. Therefore, those thoughts are not useful to have."

"You could tell me."

She could almost feel him gearing up for some kind of witty rejoinder, but he swallowed it. "Maybe I could. But not today." He strode into the gloom again.

Starr, trying to process, felt the light leave her—except for one stray Will. "*Thiswaythis*—" it whispered.

"I get it, this way," said Starr. A feeling of overload was creeping into her brain again. Would she ever reach the bottom of all this new information? And what did he mean by 'a couple of decades'? She scurried to catch up to Nico.

"Remember, don't get lost!" he was calling to her, walking backwards. "There's hardly ever anyone back here!"

Starr came up behind him. "Hardly anyone?"

"Except for ol' Borborygmus. Better known as 'Griz.'" He pointed down a side alley. "Welcome to the Prop 'N' Weapons Emporium."

They paused in front of a caged-off area packed with shelves twenty feet high. Each shelf was also packed with labeled boxes revealing contents of every conceivable object of mayhem: battleaxes, wands, swords, whips, daggers. Mayonnaise.

"Mayonnaise?" Starr tilted her head.

"Surprisingly effective in the right circumstances." Nico rattled the fence. "Griz? You conscious?"

A thickset, bald ogre—though he looked more like a retired wrestler than like Shrek—emerged from between the shelves. He carried a slab of chain mail and tools, and wore a jeweler's loupe the size of Starr's head pressed against one eye. "Not open," he growled, pointing at a sign next to an oversized workbench that read:

I CAN ONLY KILL ONE PERSON A DAY. TODAY'S NOT YOUR DAY AND YOU BETTER HOPE TOMORROW ISN'T, EITHER.

Nico held up his hands and backed away. "All right then, here's something even better than Griz." They stepped onto a nearby set that was the exact opposite of some of the mundane, dated rooms Starr had seen thus far: it resembled a bridge from one of the *Star Trek* shows, though the panels were dim, and no vision of space appeared in the wide viewscreen.

"Wait," she said as Nico took a seat in the captain's chair. "There's a spaceship plot on this reality show?"

"Was. They're repurposing this for me in a week when I get—I mean, Roland gets—to go on a cruise with Beatrice. Naturally, there'll be a mystery they have to solve there. We'll get to put on tuxedos. At least I will." He raised an eyebrow. "Think that'll work for me?"

Starr dodged the bait, though a mental image of Nico looking like James Bond in a casino was worth holding on to. "Right, but when was there a spaceship story? I mean, if you're trying to do a reality show ..." She had a vision of Sam being sent on a voyage to Mars, but scrapped it quickly, pieces coming together. "No, let me guess—was it about thirty years ago?"

Nico flicked a glance at her, then at his watch. "C'mon. We've got one more place you should know about, and then we need to get back. Cris will be foul all day if we're late and he's already there." He quick-stepped back toward the kitchen set, just far enough ahead of Starr to keep her from pestering him with questions along the way. Then he stopped abruptly and turned right.

"Check this out," he said, and there was no teasing in his expression. "And watch your step."

A low burble reached Starr first. As she neared the new set, she thought Nico had brought her to a bathroom. But she was mistaken; the shining white tiles that covered the entire space were covered in water that originated from an unseen source, traveled to a sunken floor and bubbled over a slightly raised lip at the edge of a six-foot-wide gap. It was like an infinity pool to hell, the water disappearing into the deepest, darkest hole she'd ever seen. There was no bottom.

"That's not possible," Starr murmured, gut seizing up. To be real it would have to cut through the stage floor, through the foundation and into the earth below. It could never be relocated. It was utterly impractical as a set and terrifying to contemplate.

"And yet," said Nico. "I come out here every so often to stare at it. Reminds me I'm not in Kansas anymore. That we're among aliens. Nobody talks about the hole, you see. It just—exists. But you should be aware of it. Keeps you clear on how magic—and our overlords—are rarely comprehensible to human brains."

This was new. Starr had thought it would be all fun and games here with mythics—now that she'd come around to believing they were real—but the concept of them being not just physically but also mentally different from humans was like a gong to the head.

Something Nico had said a while ago filtered through just then. They were frozen in time, her co-stars. You win an award, you get to live... forever. She hadn't really faced that before; it was such a giant concept. But the hole, the abyss, and staring into it, gave her a new perspective. "It must be something to be immortal," she said.

"Not all it's cracked up to be." His smooth voice was low and tired.

The water gurgled. "You've got it, though, right? What do they call it?"

"Temporal Arrest." He nodded. "Everyone on the show has it—you'll get it eventually, I'm sure."

Starr stared at him, the next question on her tongue, but she couldn't let it out.

He smiled softly. "Fiona's been on the show for over a century. I've been here since the Korean conflict."

"'War,' they call it now." Starr's voice felt distant, as if it had fallen into the hole.

"Sure, fine. Not like I served. Anyway—everyone thinks they want to live forever. But it's kind of a trap. You'll see that, too."

Starr gave him a long look, something she hadn't allowed herself to do before, more pleased than ever that he'd left Roland behind. Nico was as old as her grandpa, if she did a little math. Strangely, that fact was harder to comprehend than the notion that Jason was likely older than Western civilization.

"You're kind of all right, when you're not trying so hard," she said.

"That's the nicest thing you've ever said to me."

They were quieter on the way back to where Nora waited, with Nico offering just the occasional tossed-off bit of information: this is Valéncia's bedroom, this is the jail cell and sheriff's office, this is the all-purpose room to create an outdoor glamour that somehow never really looks out of doors. "And this—" he cut himself off. They stopped walking.

Loud grunting sounds were coming from a set tucked down a side alley.

Breathy, whispered moans followed.

Starr swore she could smell cigar smoke.

"Well, that is Duncan Grouse's study," said Nico, hurrying along, "but we're going to pretend we were never here and scurry on back to that nice, bright kitchen."

He started to guide Starr away from the darkened alley, but she was riveted by the noises. Her eyes widened and she tilted her head; a glowing green-shaded lamp in a study provided just enough moving shadow to spell out exactly what was going on back there. She tilted her head.

"I didn't think people could bend that way."

Nico darted behind her, gulping. "Only one of them's a human."

Starr focused harder. Cris—that was obvious—was in there; the scent gave him away. But the other—she caught a flash of dark auburn hair. "Dakota?"

"Shh," Nico hushed her. "Yes, they're a thing. No, nobody's supposed to know but everybody except Jason does. And really—you do not want to see what happens if a pombero catches you spying on him. There are retribution ants involved."

"I read about pomberos," she said. "On the internet. They're South American"

"That's nice, sure, whatever the internet is, fine." Nico was starting to pull at her. "We really can't be here."

"It says they aren't known for being very... *nice* with women."

"Well, Cris is an evolved being. Come on, already."

"Are we sure she's all right?"

Just then, Dakota shrieked, then gasped. "Oh, Sugar Ears," she cooed. "Do that again."

Starr clapped her hands over her mouth.

"I'm gonna say she's A-OK," said Nico. "Remember: retribution ants."

Starr let him pull her away, tripping slightly. Nico caught her and they came face-to-face. It wasn't very bright, even with the trailing Wills, but she could swear there was a pinkness beneath his glowing skin.

The sounds behind them stopped. Then they resumed and joined together in a hair-raising chorus of—well, delight was one word for it. It echoed in the giant stage space. A second later came the clatter of furniture banging around, and more smoke.

"Ow," came Dakota's voice. "I'm stuck."

"Starr!" Nico hissed. He smelled like cardamom and coffee. She blinked back to her senses. "The retribution ants come *after* he fires you!"

Fired. That did it. Starr gulped and slipped her fingers into Nico's, then realized she did not need to do that at all to get the hell out of there. She let him go—and in a matter of seconds was outpacing Nico all the way back to the kitchen.

CHAPTER 11
Pop Starr

FIONA WAS HANGING upside down in her dressing room like a bat when Nico's special signal brought her out of meditation.

Knock-knock. Knock.

"Cookie?" he called through the door. "It's me."

Years ago, Fiona had read in a magazine—or perhaps she'd written it for a magazine—that ten minutes of inversion daily, suspended by one's ankles, was excellent for both skin and circulation.

"Entrez-vous," she sang out. "Door's unlocked."

Nico closed the door behind him and tilted his head upside down. "What's your poison?" he asked, offering a brilliant smile.

"Brownie tea, as per usual." Fiona waved at Whatsisname, the brownie perched on a shelf who'd been gripping her ankles for the last eight minutes, to lower her. Bookender caught her shoulders and maneuvered her to the ground. She gestured at the service cart. "Humblebrag Masonry was our volunteer today, but the taste is a bit... sour."

Nico flung himself lengthwise on the Chesterfield, folding his hands behind his head, and sighed. He seemed less than one hundred percent himself.

"Are you well, dear?"

"Unclear." He drew in a deep breath and released it slowly. "Were I still a drinking man, this'd be a reason to get blotto. Some things cannot be unseen."

Rapt, Fiona looped a towel around her neck and relaxed into an easy chair. Nico had taken to his Starr surveillance like a selkie to water, and she'd so enjoyed hearing back every little detail of his observations. He had been instructed to keep the newcomer simultaneously on her toes and off-balance, an idea straight from the Valéncia side of Fiona. If the show would insist that this ridiculous new hire become part of their clan, Fiona would simply have to make sure that the hire was as short-lived as possible. Step one: gather intelligence. Step two: undermine.

"I am yours completely."

Nico unraveled his morning to her in exquisite detail. All had gone well: Starr's quarrel with Nora, her chastening at the vastness of the stages, her primal terror of the bottomless pit. There had been speed bumps, though: Fiona was less than pleased that Nico hadn't contrived to 'accidentally' be in the rarely-seen character Duncan Grouse's office when Dakota and Cris arrived for their usual tryst. Instead, Nico and Starr had arrived late, after the couple were already deep into their throes.

"Made the most of it, though," he told her, smoothing down his hair. "And we now know Dakota calls him 'Sugar Ears.'"

"It'll have to do. And our little rookie?"

"Rattled like a snake."

"You are a love."

"That's another one you owe me."

"Nico, don't be tiresome. The balance sheets between us will forever be in my favor, and it is gauche of you to suggest otherwise." He knew full well that the prize she'd won all those decades ago—and then gifted to him—was what kept him from getting in trouble. She would never owe Nico anything.

He shrugged. "It has been a long time. Maybe I don't need it anymore."

This was alarming. Nico was usually so compliant. Nothing to do but call the bluff. "Any time you wish me to revoke it, you need only ask. It's a matter of a brief declaration and you can start enjoying your tipples as much as you did back in the day. Though when I last checked, you weren't really enjoying them at all anymore."

Nico tapped his fingers against his chest and stared at the ceiling. "You win. I'll keep it."

Fiona didn't need to say the words; her silence did it for her: *I always win.*

"There is one other thing," he ventured after a moment.

Fiona crossed her legs and sipped tea. This was the other shoe.

"Well—Starr—she dropped her sides when we scampered away from the... Dakota and Cris event. I tried to stop her, but she went back and I... followed."

Fiona leaned forward. This sounded delicious. "Please tell me she interrupted them."

"She ran into Dakota—sort of. Cris had, um, departed and left his main squeeze caught under a sofa. Starr was helping her out when I arrived, so I hid. Then I heard Dakota promising Starr a feature story in *Water Worlds* if she kept her mouth shut."

Fiona bolted upright and frowned.

"Sorry, Cookie. Circumstances beyond control and all that."

She considered this development, then fluttered her fingers. "What's done is done." Starr getting free publicity on that level for doing absolutely nothing might be a disaster. Or... it didn't have to be. This would require a fresh pot of tea. "Bookender!"

He was already at her elbow. "More hot water, miss. Right away."

"And make them scrub that pot before the next batch. Better yet, get a fresh pot."

Bookender bowed and slipped away.

Scrubbing. The answer came to her. "This... cover story," Fiona mused. "I believe we can make it work for us."

"Oh?" Nico turned on an elbow. "Do tell."

"Indeed. I have friends in all the right places."

He made a face. "Ugh, Helena. That scribbling harpy. Why you waste time on her I'll never know."

"Darling, one keeps one's friends close—"

"And one's enemies closer, I know. What does that make us?"

"Special."

Nico sighed again, closing his eyes. He hadn't told her everything, but she could be patient. It gave her a chance to admire his features in repose, something she didn't get to do much. Fiona knew how fortunate she'd been to have stumbled upon Nicodemus Reddy at the lowest point in his life. Back then, he'd been a radio personality-turned-conscientious objector, and when the press turned on him for not being patriotic enough, he'd lost his job. Then the racists wriggled out from under their rocks—he'd been white enough for them while he had a famous name, but when his tanned features began appearing in the papers, suddenly he couldn't get served in restaurants, couldn't use drinking fountains or public toilets. Blacklisted from work and his community, he'd become a drinker. Enter Fiona: she'd paused in a random bar for a packet of matches and discovered him doing a poor job of balancing on a barstool, being poked in the forehead by men asking where his turban was.

Fiona had scowled at one man holding a roll of toilet paper and put on every ounce of Valéncia she could summon. "I believe you can relieve yourself in the *rear*." She'd pointed at the men's room sign in the back. Then she met every one of the others' eyes. "Shame on you all. Your mothers should be embarrassed to call you sons."

Her tone had scattered them, but the moment she left Fiona had known they would start up again, so she'd slid onto the stool next to Nico. "What's your poison?"

"Abuse," he'd slurred. "With a garnish of my life swirling the drain."

Fiona had gotten a good look at him then. Her decision came faster than her drink. "I will fix both of those things," she'd promised.

And in time, she had. Now, he was her one true friend in the world. She loved and trusted him as far as she could love or trust anyone—and she also knew, on a deep level, that she owned him. He could never leave her. Fiona reached over and caressed his curls. "We are a perfect team."

Nico opened his eyes. "I gotta be honest with you, Fee. Doing this was not my favorite thing."

"Doing what, darling?"

He waved a hand. "Surveillance. Scheming."

Fiona silenced him with a haughty look. "Sacrifices are often painful, and necessary. It is for the good of the show."

"Are you sure that's what this is? I keep thinking it's really for the good of Fiona."

"Which is for the good of the show."

He shook his head slowly. "This show has seen better days. The other series—they've evolved. Grown. They have casts of dozens. We're trapped in some kind of amber." He blinked. "It wasn't always like this."

Nico's hesitations irritated her, and she set her jaw.

"Starr's not Amelia," he said.

Bringing up the thief! Fiona's eyes widened. *How dare he?*

"And Joseph's—he's not a factor anymore. You know that."

A poker of white-hot anger skewered Fiona, tears pricking at her eyes. *For goddess' sake, get a hold of yourself*, she admonished. The mere mention of Joseph, after all this time, should not tug at her insides like this. "I am never frightened by mice, Nicodemus. I only want them eradicated."

Nico sat up and patted her hand.

"I won't lose you," she muttered.

"I'm right here."

"Then don't betray me," she growled. Trying to smooth things over, she gave a small shrug and sat up straight. "There wouldn't happen to be a part three to this tale, would there?"

Nico half-smiled and recounted the actual blocking they'd done with Cris. Starr hadn't been able to meet the director's gaze: she kept blushing, stumbling over her lines, and swallowing unnecessarily. Nico hadn't been able to tell if she was suppressing hysterical laughter or nerves and declared it was probably both. All in all, she'd been a disaster, with her head anywhere but in the game. "As intended," he finished with a mumble, looking like he was developing a stomach ailment.

Fiona planted a kiss on Nico's forehead. "Darling, you do know how to make my day better."

"I'm well-trained." Having reported in, Nico made his goodbyes and left.

Moments later, Bookender returned with her teapot. "Phil sterilized it," he promised. "We started with a fresh volunteer, too. Enjoy Allsop Nattering."

The new tea had notes of peach, sage and leather that tingled in Fiona's nose as she sipped and thought about Nico. He hated conflict, so she supposed she might have given him the wrong task in her Starr project. In truth, she was startled he hadn't already bedded the newcomer. It had been almost a full week. Such actions were often the most direct way to deal with difficulties: get the heart involved—then break it. Fiona knew what that felt like, and how easily it could cripple even the most talented.

She wondered if Nico might be losing his touch.

Or that perhaps Starr required more knocking back. Even knocking down. She would have to explore fresh options.

"Bookender!" the Grand Dame shouted, but he was right at her elbow, awaiting instruction. "Fetch your notepad. I wish to brainstorm."

CHAPTER 12
Starr Studded

STARR STUMBLED FROM the stages, refusing to look anywhere but straight ahead. She held it together until she reached her dressing room. Once there, she flopped face-first into the ancient sofa in her un-glamoured, bare-walled, windowless cube. Stuffing a pillow under her mouth, she screamed.

Loud. Long. Fierce. It was a tantrum Mama would have watched appreciatively, sitting at the kitchen table without emotion, smoking down her latest Marlboro. *Just like a six-year-old,* she'd have said. *Like I always toldya, y'aint no good at this. Knockin' your head against a brick wall, Samantha.*

After this morning's blocking fiasco in front of Cris, Starr wondered if Mama didn't have a point.

"You totally tanked it," she told the fiber weaves of her pillow. "Cris thinks you're a moron."

Throat raw and aching, she lifted her head from the pillow to discover an unfamiliar wizened face lingering at her knees, smiling helpfully and blinking wide dark eyes.

"Eek!" she shrieked and hurled the pillow at it, startled.

The brownie caught the soft projectile with ease. It stood perhaps three feet high and wore a uniform of grey shirt and black jeans. "Starr Weatherby?" Its voice was thin and reedy. "I am Oleander Pinebough. Reporting for duties!" The creature held out a manila envelope. "Revisions."

Fingers shaking, Starr took it. Her heart began to calm. Her abject mood faded by twenty percent: *They assigned me a brownie! I'm not getting fired... today!* She swiped at her eyes. "So sorry, Oleander. I didn't know anyone was here. And I'm a little... broken at the moment."

Oleander set the envelope on the sofa and produced a box of tissues. "Does Ms. Weatherby require bandages? Needle and thread? Duct tape? Uisce beatha potion? Nail and hammer? Source code?"

Starr shook her head. "I'll self-repair, thanks. And call me Starr, please."

Oleander's smile warmed her heart. "As Ms. Starr wishes."

It would have to do for now. The Guide had explained that the brownie workforce at the show was a critical element to its survival, and that over the years, they'd become relied upon. The first brownie arrived when Fiona Ballantine had been awarded the indefinite, if paid, services of Bookender Riverbend. Once Bookender's happy fortune had leaked to his fellow brownies, they'd flooded the show in the hopes of also finding ways to be helpful. The Guide indicated that there was a long, involved process in finding the best possible brownie assistance, with emphasis on the ability to keep a secret: that while they were to work on the show, they were to share nothing about it outside the walls of *Tune in Tomorrow*—most especially the dubious nature of 'reality' that was going on. A small spell woven by Bookender kept them in line: should they try to reveal anything about the unreality of *Tune*'s makeup, they would begin to disintegrate. But it was an over-precaution. The brownies loved the show, even though they knew everything about it. And the actors loved them, or at least loved being waited upon by passionate fans. As many as a hundred brownies lived in the walls of the show at any given time; the most trustworthy and efficient ones received actor assignments.

Starr loved the concept but had raised an eyebrow about the whole idea of a creature being awarded indefinitely to anyone—especially Fiona. And she definitely had mixed feelings about the fact that they were paid in glitter. It sounded a lot like being paid in 'exposure,' something she'd been offered more than once while searching for her big break. Yet it seemed to work for all concerned.

"This is my best day!" cried the brownie. "So many years since my last actor."

Starr tilted her head. *Wonder if it's thirty years.* "How long?"

Oleander counted her fingers and toes and tapped her head once. "Years."

"Who was it?"

The hiss of a large cat and a deeper voice streamed through Starr's open door. She craned over the edge of her sofa and peered out. Down the hallway stood a man in jeans and a white T-shirt, arms crossed in annoyance. Pressed against the wall across from him, Emma stood with teeth bared, her fluffed-out tail swishing like a metronome.

Oleander peeked out, too. "That is Mr. Charles Forrest and Ms. Emma Crawley," said the brownie. "They are arguing."

"So helpful." Charles Forrest—she'd heard he was on vacation. He played the town sheriff and also Valéncia's son, Maverick. They called him 'Mav' on the show and in real life—but until now he'd only been a name in a script to her.

"I will ask about the substance of their disagreement!"

Starr caught the brownie by her collar and coaxed her back into the dressing room. "Maybe later. Where were we?"

"You asked Oleander who Oleander worked for last and—"

"And Oleander hasn't told me yet."

A long pause.

"Oleander? Are you not allowed to tell me who you worked for? Is this some kind of"—the word sounded odd on her tongue still—"spell?"

Oleander shook her head.

"I wouldn't bother," said a laconic, friendly voice. Starr glanced up to find Charles—Mav—leaning on her doorjamb, resting a hand on the half-opened door. "Didn't mean to butt in. But you'll never get a straight answer from a bro. Howdy."

"Mr. Forrest!" Oleander sounded scandalized.

"Howd—wait, what did you call her?"

"A bro. Collectively, they're bros. I'm Charlie, but I go by 'Mav.' Keeps things easy 'round here."

The laughter surprised Starr, bubbling up from a deep place in her. She had already been on an emotional edge from the episode with Cris a few minutes earlier; now, learning the collective noun for brownies sent her right over the edge. She started to titter, then giggle, then cackle and finally, out it came, a balloon burst of laughter that made her clutch her sides and roll against the sofa. Then she was crying a bit. Then she was laughing. Then she slid from the sofa right to the floor.

"I'm missin' something." Mav hadn't moved.

Starr sat up, legs splayed out, and hiccupped.

"Tea!" Oleander cried. "Mr. Forrest and Ms. Starr are missing tea!"

"Sure, I'll swig some." He shrugged his way into the room. "Assuming Madame Funnypants calms down for a second."

Sliding back onto the sofa, Starr dabbed at her eyes and shook his hand. His grip was as soft and warm as his nut-brown eyes. An image of him as a cowboy astride a horse named Ol' Paint, a Stetson cocked back on his head with a swatch of bark-colored hair dangling over one eye as he rode into the sunset, came to her like a scene from an old movie.

"Reckon I haven't made a lady laugh that hard from doin' nothing in some time," he gestured at the sofa. "Mind?"

"Go ahead." She sniffed once, a trickle of laughter escaping briefly. "It's just—well, 'bro' means something a little different where I come from. But anything's apt to make me laugh or cry today."

Mav rubbed the back of his neck. "Heard there was talk of bonfires during blocking today."

Starr sighed, the hiccups gone. So many things had been unsettling this morning that the discovery of a bottomless pit wasn't even number one on the list. But she'd always been certain of her ability to do the job, especially to do something as basic and simple as blocking. All you had to do was listen to the director explain where he wanted you to stand. To walk. To turn. All things an *actual* reality show wouldn't require, not really, but she was trying to go with the flow here.

But when it had been Starr's turn to show Cris she was competent and a good hire, all she could hear was Dakota's breathy 'Sugar Ears.' She'd bit her tongue so hard to avoid laughing that she nearly gnawed it off. The whole time he'd been directing her she'd been slow to respond and couldn't get her act together.

Then she'd made a real mistake.

"Turn to the window *after* Beatrice crosses!" Cris had shouted. "Not before!"

"Not what you said a minute ago," Starr had muttered to herself. "Maybe if you'd been on time …"

Sometimes, what was going on in her head slipped out of her mouth.

Cris had been in her face faster than she'd known anyone could move. Up close, he had a presence she hadn't felt with any other mythic, like he'd just filled the room and could squeeze her out with a puff of air. He was scarier precisely because he was more… well, *mythic*. They might have been standing on the biggest stage set she'd ever walked on to, but she'd begun to feel claustrophobic. "Instead of what," he'd breathed.

Starr had stared at the floor. Even 'Sugar Ears' had lost its hilarity. "Just that if we'd started on time we'd be… I'd be …" There was no good way to end that sentence.

"How long have you been on this show?" Cris had released smoke in her face. "One half of a hot second, last I checked. So, don't go telling me how to—"

Dinner dishes had clattered on the floor and Cris jerked away from Starr. Nico had stood near a small pile of broken chinaware. "Oops?" he'd said.

"TAKE FIVE!" Cris had bellowed, stalking off. "CLEAR THE SET OR I WILL TORCH EVERYONE'S

HAIR."

Now, as Mav slid onto the far end of the sofa, Starr shook her head. "All my fault. I lost focus."

"Cris is an acquired taste at the best of times."

"I haven't had much time to acquire."

Mav leaned forward, elbows on his legs. "I've been here seventy-five years, and I still don't know what 'normal' looks like with these mythics. Whole days go by I forget I fell into fairyland. But then Jan starts talkin' outta both sides of their head, or Phil smokes up the lobby again and I'll think, 'This place's crazier than a juke joint on free beer night.' And that's what reminds me why I'm here. Why it's the only job I ever really loved. Like the man said, 'Though this be madness,' and all."

"'Yet there is method in 't.'" Starr completed the phrase, loving that this cowboy-in-disguise kept Shakespeare in his back pocket. They shared a smile. His straightforward, earnest attitude was like drinking clear, fresh water. "That might be the first time I've heard Polonius in a Texan accent."

"Oklahoma, but I'll forgive ya." Mav's eyes twinkled. "Point is, you gotta remember what makes this place special. It's the same thing that makes it scary. I confess, I missed it."

"Where were you, anyway? I heard a vacation you couldn't escape?"

"Somethin' like that. My return ticket wasn't... uh, working right."

Oleander arrived with tea and biscuits on a tray that trembled like the San Andreas Fault. She set it on a small table between Mav and Starr, letting out a long, relieved breath.

Starr applauded lightly and the brownie bowed.

"Oleander wants to do right by Ms. Starr," she said. "There is milk and cream and three sugars and sparkles and cinnamon twigs. More can be fetched if these are not correct."

"I drink it black," Starr assured her. "This is terrific."

"Y'know"—Mav lifted his cup while the brownie poured—"seems like Oleander could do Starr right by tellin' her what was asked for earlier."

Oleander wilted a little. "Mr. Forrest? I don't think I'm supposed to... I mean, disintegration."

Mav shook his head. "Don't matter what you might've heard, Ole. Might be somethin' people don't talk about much, but it's not a spell-breaker. Anyhow, I'll save you the worry." He turned to Starr. "Your bro here—"

Starr coughed back a laugh.

"Used to work for a lil' gal named Amelia Beckenridge. She played Wilhelmina, who ran the local bookstore. And it's been a lotta years since she was seen in these parts." He shot a glance at Oleander. "An' that's all there is to say about that, isn't it?"

Oleander nodded.

Amelia. Again. Starr sat up straighter. "She quit?"

"She moseyed." Mav's tone indicated the conversation was over.

Starr raised her cup to him and took a long sip, feeling calmer already. Nobody wanted to talk about this Amelia person? Fine. There were more important things to worry about, like how she was shooting scenes in an hour that she'd already failed to properly block. Starr did not want to go back to the stage afraid. The only answer to falling off the horse—or, in this case, mouthing off to the director—was to get back on again.

Because Starr really wanted to keep this gig. It paid

rent, sure, and it made her feel at long last that she had exceeded her mother's expectations. But there was more to it than that: this place had gotten under her skin. She loved hearing Phil's morning greeting snorts, or brainstorming in the werepanther's pillow-strewn room, or feeling her heart race while hanging around with Jason. Even Nico lingering in the background felt right. He kept things pretty. As for Fiona's odd acting 'lessons,' well, she was the expert. Fiona thought Starr should project her voice and fling her limbs around? Fine. She could fit in.

This all spilled out in front of Mav, in a gush of words not unlike the suddenness of her tantrum earlier. He sat back and listened patiently, never averting his gaze, keeping his counsel until she'd finished.

"Well, then," he said, once she paused for breath. "Emma was right about somethin', at least: you are like a gust of fresh air here. You're also reminding me of a wild mustang, though, so that's somethin' to keep in mind. We'll find a way to make sure you stick around. I'll personally take a hand in that, 'cause it looks like we'll be in scenes together quite a bit. The writer of the feline persuasion moved all sorts of things around, which put a burr in my blanket—least, until I met ya." He nodded at Starr's manila folder. "Those'll be your updates, I reckon."

Starr drew the papers out of the envelope, shaking her head. She'd have to relearn everything. So much for making a good second impression with Cris. "Do you think they understand that this isn't really much of a reality show? I haven't shot a scene yet, but even I can tell them that."

Mav shook his head and chuckled. "Look, whatever y'all are calling 'reality TV' out there on your side of the

Veil... that don't matter too much to these mythics. You could call this the Super Bowl and it'd mean as much to 'em. They got their own definitions for everything. So—stop thinking so hard on it. Their world, their rules, their... reality."

That was the clearest explanation anyone had ever given her, and it made several puzzle pieces come together for Starr. Maybe, possibly, she was starting to get it. She scanned the new pages, which were yellow and smelled of lemon. "Mav? Any chance you'd be up for reading lines together?"

"I thought you'd never ask."

Starr grinned. "And what if we act them out, right here?"

He glanced around the dressing room. "Might be tight, but sure."

"And—maybe call in Nico and Nora? Assuming they're still in the scene?" She was starting to feel excited again.

Mav nodded at Oleander. "Send yer helper to fetch 'em. We'll get started."

The brownie was already at the door. "Right away, Ms. Starr!"

"Oleander," she called out, and the brownie stuck her head in the room. "Thank you."

Starr hadn't known brownies could blush. "I live to assist!" she cried and ran off down the hall.

Mav had his eye on Starr. "You're a nice lady, Starr Weatherby. That's a rarity around these halls. See you hold on to that, if you can."

"If we're going to be friends, Mav, know two things."

He tilted his head and a section of hair tumbled down over one eye. She had an unexpected urge to brush it back. "And what's that?"

"I'm neither nice, nor a lady."

Mav laughed, and it was exactly the sound she imagined a cowboy would make as he rode off into the sunset.

A FEW HOURS later, Starr was ready to rumble.

Form-fitting maid's uniform from the leprecostumers that looked and acted like a Halloween getup? Check.

Holding silver tray? Check.

Standing on her mark, ready to enter Lady Marlborough's parlor as soon as Cris and Emma finished conferring over the script changes? Check and check.

Now, all she had to do was stop shivering. Part of it was nerves about shooting her first scenes; part of it was that the vast cavern of the stages seemed to be just one degree above freezing.

Uniform, tray, maid. One week ago it had been uniform, tray, waitress. *Really moving up the career ladder there, Starr.*

Still, at least things were moving. The lemon-scented pages had revealed that the scene had been completely rewritten since the disastrous blocking, and 'Sam' was now being introduced not as a bumbling kitchen worker, but a member of the house staff who was proving to be nosy about her employer's business. Working the new pages out with Mav, Nico and Nora had been invaluable, and Starr promised she would not falter, or mouth off.

Back in her dressing room, she'd discovered that Emma's revisions altered Sam's role considerably: *Sam Draper has been sent to the estate by an employment agency. Lady Marlborough's home has a surprising amount of turnover in staff. Many quit, disappear or die.*

"Die?" She'd given Mav a worried look.

"Household help," he'd shrugged. "Holding cell for you rookies. 'Case things don't pan out."

Now, Starr rattled a piece of hard candy around her tongue to make sure her mouth didn't go dry and vowed once more: *I'm gonna take the reins on this pony ride.*

"Places!" Cris boomed on the other side of the oak door now. "I know we haven't had time to block out this new arrangement, but—" He glanced around, noting how his actors had already arrayed themselves in the Marlborough estate's lobby. Starr peeked through a small opening in the oak door that ostensibly led from the kitchen to the foyer, delighted at his astonishment. "Well," the director continued. "Looks like you mortals *can* learn a thing or two."

Fiona, only just now arriving to the stage, raised an eyebrow. Cris guided her to the front of the fireplace, then stood back and gave a nod to the tableau.

Adrenaline sang in Starr. She bounced up and down on the balls of her feet. Cold was no longer an issue. She flexed her hands, recalling Fiona's advice: *Think of your hair as a prop. Use it! They love flowing hair.* Also: *Your voice—make it soar. They should be able to hear you in the cheap seats.* Plus: *Big gestures. Wave those pudgy little arms of yours. Own that stage.*

It was all so different than what she'd been taught at Gilliard, but Fiona was the expert. This was a different world. As Mav had suggested, she should stop thinking so hard. Be Sam. Be the mango.

Still, as Starr peered through the crack in the door to the mansion's lobby, she wondered how anyone could believe this was human reality. The set had a cheap feel to it—high, ornately designed walls outfitted with antique wooden furniture, overstuffed and petrified chairs, and a round marble table whose sole purpose seemed to be to support a giant flower arrangement.

Why don't they just glamour the sets? Starr wondered. *If they can do the dressing rooms, they could make this place look amazing.*

No time to ask. Cameradryads perched around the room, camouflaged as plants on the interior and around Cris, beyond that missing fourth wall. Each wore a small water pack over a forked branch and took regular sips; Celtis had told Starr that if they worked too long without refreshment, they wilted.

"Kurupi!" Cris swore. "We're late again. Foxing time to get started!"

The slate snapped. Cameradryads rolled.

Fiona/Valéncia spoke to Mav about how another of her various offspring—his brother—was locked up in jail for 'grand theft assault.'

Starr was sure there wasn't any such thing. *Focus, idiot. Be Sam. Fling that hair around. Speak loudly and carry a big tray.*

Nora/Beatrice set down a cup of tea, wondering if they would ever get things tidy in this filthy house.

Cue! Starr straightened. All she had to do was push open the swinging door while holding her empty tray aloft, then circle the room while gathering up used teacups. She put her shoulder to the door.

It didn't budge.

She pushed harder.

"Oh, maid!" Beatrice called again, more insistently.

Starr took in a deep breath and accidentally sucked the hard candy into her throat. Choking, she stumbled. Seconds ticked by as she tried not to cough. The others bantered to fill in the space—and Cris let things roll on.

He hated having to edit a scene, and felt it was more realistic to do everything in one take.

But Starr couldn't breathe. The sweet melting candy wasn't shrinking fast enough. Hot blood filled her cheeks, and the room went from freezing to oppressive. Whirling around she backed hard into the oak door, which flew open, banged against the opposite wall and returned in an instant to smack hard against her back.

The candy dislodged and she spat it out.

Freed to breathe again, Starr turned and rammed her free hand into the door, stumbling into the parlor like a drunken trespasser. She gripped her tray like a shield and careened directly toward Fiona, who cringed and lifted her hands in defense—they would collide in a second...

Except Mav stepped into the breach. In one graceful move he relieved Starr of the tray and slid it onto the table, then made a half-turn and caught her in his arms, dipping Starr like a dancer. His hands were warm against her skin—it was a very skimpy outfit—and her heart raced like she'd been on a rollercoaster.

Still, no call of 'cut.'

Her head upside down, Starr glimpsed Jason off-stage. His eyes were huge.

Mango time, she thought, and grinned wickedly. "Well," she said loudly, holding position. "That's one way to make an entrance." Sam/Starr righted herself and straightened her apron, giving Valéncia a curtsey. "Evening, Madame."

"We appear to have an eavesdropper." Mav rescued the scene. "Are you going to give us trouble, Miss—"

"Draper," said Sam, giving her hair a mighty toss, the way she'd been taught. Her little maid's cap went sailing off-camera. "Samantha Draper. And I am absolutely *no trouble at all*." She placed heavy emphasis on her final words, again thinking of Fiona's lessons. "Unless you'd like me to be."

Nico/Roland snickered, and Beatrice stared off into space, attempting haughtiness. Fiona was unreadable, which worried Starr.

"I do enjoy a bit of trouble," Roland strode forward, and everything Starr had seen before of Nico was gone. He was precisely the person she'd landed on that first day in the lobby: slick as Teflon. He kissed the back of her hand. "As for ladies who know how to manufacture it, well ..." He winked.

A thrill ran through Starr. *Yes, and...* She was ready to take this ride wherever it went. What could she do next? Would Emma be angry if they didn't follow her script?

There was an opening here to get back to the original plan, but Fiona/Valéncia took an opportunity to sail in. Standing next to Sam, she announced, "Snooping can be dangerous to your health." She ran a sharp fingernail beneath Sam's chin, poking up at the last second. "But good help is so hard to find. Maverick, your decision. Shall we keep the interloper?"

Her subtext was as subtle as a hammer to the head. Starr gave it her all, batting her lashes at Mav. *Big gestures! Focus on you!*

Mav seemed to be choking on something, his shoulders heaving. Starr couldn't decide if Nora was somehow using her power on him or if he was choking back laughter. "S-sure," he said, voice strangled. He coughed. "I'm A-OK with that, Ma." He drew in a long breath and tried to restore his dignified demeanor. "Ms. Draper, what's your take on whether I can bust my wayward little brother Duncan out of jail tonight?"

And once again, the script was out the window.

Starr's heart raced. She didn't even feel like herself any more. She was Samantha, and not the old version. A new, improved one. She envisioned a door—different from the one she'd smashed through—and on the other side was this person she was crafting. Samantha would be 'Sam,' no question. And Sam, she sensed, was all about trouble. A street-smart chick with skills. "I believe you can, sir," she improvised, straightening her outfit and flipping those curls again. "With a bit of help."

Mav tilted his head.

"You see, I have a lot of practice busting through doors."

That did it; Mav's laughter broke through. Off-camera, Starr thought she saw Jason fall on the floor, but she couldn't break concentration long enough to be certain. Everyone was finding this a lot funnier than she'd expected. She tossed her hair again. Couldn't hurt.

"And—cut!" Cris shouted.

All laughter dried up. Equipment hummed and cameradryads sipped, but there was not a single other noise.

He hated me, she thought. *I'm totally dead.* But on top of that: *Actually, that was fun.*

Cris strolled around the set, eyeing them all. He gave Jason a hand up from the floor, and as the faun brushed clear his eyes, they huddled with Emma. As they spoke softly, Cris waved around his cigar, the tip turning blue, then emerald, then rose. Emma reached into the air with a pencil and scribbled. Jason glanced over their shoulders and caught Starr's eye.

She flushed to her roots.

At last, they broke formation. "Sold," said Cris. "Keep all of it. Emma, you're set?"

"On it!" the wordcat continued scribbling in the air. "Maid Samantha—now in scenes twelve and sixteen."

Starr's legs wobbled as she reached out for whatever was handy—Nico's shoulder. He patted her on the back while Fiona folded her arms over her beaded gown, face a mask.

Cris strolled over. "Two things." He waved the cigar at Starr. "Turn down that volume. Mythics are not deaf. And that thing with your hair, quit it."

"Aw," Nico murmured.

The director flashed a glance at Fiona. "Was *that* what you spent this past week teaching her?"

Fiona sniffed. "The student must be ready to receive the lesson."

Jason hugged Fiona from behind, and she stiffened. "Well, I liked it," he said. "There should be far more hair choreography on the show as a whole."

Starr met Fiona's eyes and caught a note of triumph: *she knew I'd look ridiculous.* Yet it had all worked out quite nicely. Starr gave her a small nod. *Well, now I know where we both stand.*

Mav clapped a hand on her back. "You did good, little lady. This may be the beginning of a beautiful friendship."

Starr hoped so. But based on the burning glance Fiona was giving her—as if all the Grande Dame's wheels and cogs were whirling at once—she suspected it was probably the beginning of something a great deal uglier.

CHAPTER 13

Swing on a Starr

SOMETHING HAD TAKEN a bite out of the jail cells.

Starr and Nora goggled at the wrecked sheriff's office, which intact had featured a long row of dank, musty cells that were more medieval dungeon than small-town holding facility. Now, fully half of the cells had been torn away, leaving a jagged, uneven set. There was no detritus.

Starr reached out to touch one of the chomped-away bars of a cell, wondering at the shiny interior encased in dark grey paint.

"This isn't... gold, is it?" she whispered at Nora.

Her co-star raised an eyebrow. "It sure ain't iron. Mythics are allergic, some of 'em, and you do not want to know what happens when they get hives."

Starr flicked her nails against the bar. One of these must weigh a ton, and even half of a bar could probably set her up for life on the other side of the Veil. Not that she was making any plans but... *gold*-barred cells. Really!

Jason, his horns thick and unabashedly sticking up out of tousled hair, gestured at Phil. The dragon had barely managed to make it through the double doors of the set, and now sat on his haunches, forearms folded. Starr turned from the marvel of the bars to stare at him: she'd never seen their security guard come out from behind the desk, and he was more glorious than the precious metal behind her. Heat came off him in waves, a blessing in the cold stage, and she held up her hands to warm them.

"Just look at it!" Jason pointed, exasperated.

"Pah!" Phil spat, his thrashing tail nearly knocking over several huddled cameradryads. "Just 'cause they're precious metal you think it was *me*? Dragons get iron from blood, not gold!" He lumbered back to his security desk in a puff of sulfur.

"Horse audits!" Jason swore, mumbling something about ratings. "Now we'll have to call in the poltergeists—"

Starr barely blinked at the concept: she knew by now the set decorators were all ghosts. Just a few weeks in and she'd completely adjusted to the idea of spirits in the sets, leprechauns in the costuming department and fairies—some of whom preferred to be called 'hairies'—in makeup. She'd looked forward to today: Jason's directing style was a welcome break from Cris. The pombero was locked in the underground edit lair, fiddling with tomorrow's show, and that meant a hundred percent less barking at actors and two hundred percent more fabulous outfits. And Jason always started on time.

"Can't we adjust the script?" she asked him. "Make like there was a tornado that ripped through—"

Jason, who'd been banging his head against one of the gold poles, opened an eye at her. "No, no, no, no." He thought for a moment. "Well, maybe, maybe, maybe."

"Or—glamour the whole thing? Like your office?" She'd been waiting for the right moment to lob this great idea at him.

Jason clapped his hands over his ears for a moment, then slid them down his face.

Nora was shaking her head. "Stop tryin' to run things, you. Glamour's *hard* to sustain. You need power and energy and focus and a mythic who can do all three and then the top brass can still tell when it's not the real deal. Like knowing couture from a knockoff. Why'd you think they still use all this?" She gestured around the stages, then tapped her head. "I swear, if you had a brain cell it'd die from loneliness."

"It's not just the set," Jason moaned. "It's—" He looked up at Starr. "We're still falling apart."

And finally, she understood. The ruined set was the latest indication that despite Starr's hire, the show was still not drawing enough eyeballs to arrest its slide. Sam's addition had some novelty value that helped, but the Gates were continuing to be erratic, and now a set had partially disappeared. Everyone knew it had nothing to do with a mineral-deficient dragon.

Jason kicked a fake lamppost, knocking it over.

Starr swallowed. Last in, first out. She'd have to step things up. But how? She already had more scenes than she could comfortably fit in her head—it turned out the wordcat loved writing for a street-smart tough gal—and the pace was challenging, to say the least.

"Wake up, Sheer Wannabe," Nora snapped, sagging into the sheriff's office swivel chair. Her normally pale complexion was so sallow that even magic makeup couldn't put it right, and she was pricklier than usual.

"Don't call me that, *Darby*," Starr muttered.

"Enough, ladies," Jason said. "Shoot the scene, not each other." He gestured for them to stand where the wrecked half of the set would be out of frame, then leaned in to adjust Starr's collar. A scent of burned cookies wafted from him, the smell of dashed dreams.

"I'll be good," she confided. "I'll be the best."

His horns shrank an inch, and he touched her nose briefly. Jason stepped back to check his staging, tilting his head as if arranging a painting. Mav, who'd been quietly going over his lines nearby, stuffed the sides into a desk drawer on the set and landed at his mark, giving the women a nod.

Starr resolved not to let Nora get to her and shrugged her shoulders, summoning Sam's mindset. It wasn't so hard, not really: Sam was in large part *her*, which she now understood was true for everyone's character. They got to be themselves, but a heightened version. She caught a glimpse of herself in a monitor and grinned: the new costume—blue jeans, a scoop-neck pink camisole and well-worn bomber jacket—was a vast improvement over the ill-fitting maid outfit. She gave Nora one last glance and was startled at how poorly she looked. *Green 'round the gills*, Mama would have called it.

Jason tumbled into his director's chair, pulling a licorice whip from a pocket. "Right," he tried in a bright, if quivery, voice. "Let's get moving."

The slate clapped, and Jason gestured. Cameradryads slithered on their roots to follow the action. Sam strolled over to Beatrice and launched into her scheme to break a dangerous criminal out of jail together. "Whaddya think, Bea?"

That was an ad-lib.

Nora hated 'Bea' as much as Starr hated 'Wannabe,' and glared, opening her mouth to deliver her line. Instead, what came out was a loud belch. Eyes wide, she raced off set and through the double doors without a glance back.

"Goat's teeth!" Jason slammed the script on the floor. "Now what?"

Wanting to be more useful than suggesting a glamoured set, Starr stood. "I'll get her."

Mav touched her shoulder and leaned in. "Try the powder room," he whispered.

Starr raised an eyebrow, wondering how he'd know, and raced away.

STARR SLID TO a stop outside the bathroom door. Sounds of retching echoed on the other side, which confirmed her suspicions. *Theresa, all over again.* Shoving open the door, she leaned on the sinks until Nora staggered out of a stall, looking ghostly. Starr handed her a roll of brown paper towels. Nora snatched them away and mopped her face, then swished some water in her mouth and spat.

"I hear the first three months are hell for morning sickness," Starr noted.

"You tell anyone about this, and I will make your life a living nightmare," Nora snapped.

Starr rolled her eyes. She couldn't figure Nora out. They should've bonded: they had a similar dark sense of humor, and after hearing her call Fiona a 'viper' Starr had decided they both had reasons to tiptoe around the Grande Dame. But Nora took every chance to undermine Starr, often comparing her to her cousin Bubba. Which, so far as Starr could determine, meant that Bubba was as wide as a house, wore a beard to his ankles and hadn't left his house since the Clinton administration.

But making friends wasn't Starr's agenda at this moment. There was a show to shoot and a faun to impress. "What's the big deal?"

"The big deal is I want to keep my job, Wannabe."

"Stop playing to the crowd," Starr sighed. "It's just you and me here. Nobody's going to fire you because you're, you know."

"What do you know?" Nora's voice turned shrill with panic. "They'll put her—I mean, me—into a coma or make me hide behind plants and furniture for the next six months or maybe even write me out."

"That's illegal." But even as Starr said it, she wondered if governmental agencies had jurisdiction beyond the Gate. "They can't just make her pregnant on the show, too?"

Nora honked her nose into a paper towel. "Nobody gets pregnant on this show. Nobody has kids. Best you get is a doll in a crib that vanishes. Real human babies—they're too... enticing for some of these Fae. They're known for taking the babies and replacing them with one of their own, and then the replacement dies and, honestly. No." She took big gulps of air.

Starr fanned her with her sides. "So, quit."

"You'd like that, wouldn't you!" Nora's panic receded. "Have Mav all to yourself. No thank you, missy. I am owed another Endless Award and I am going to get it. That prize means everything."

Starr shrugged. "Whatever you want. Nobody hears this from me. But—the mythics are going to catch on. You've been green since I met you. Can you take a vacation? A sabbatical?"

"Vacation? There's no vacation, you mooncalf." Nora patted her hair and ensured her makeup was unmarred, which of course it was. "The Guide says we can take as much as we want, but if Emma takes those cat eyes off you, y'all's story goes away in nothing flat. The Gate decides not to let you in. No way."

You mosey away, Starr thought. "Is that what happened to the actress before me?" Starr paused. "Amelia?"

Nora's color drained again. "Where did you hear that name?"

"She's in the air. My immediate predecessor, right? I heard she quit."

Nora chuckled, a grainy, dark sound. "That's one way of putting it."

"What's another way?"

The actor took a long, cleansing breath. "That nose of yours gets into a lot of business," she said evenly. "'Melia is gone. Don't ask about her. There's nothing to tell. Just know this: what happened to her can happen to you."

"But I don't know what happened to her!"

A ceiling speaker crackled to life above them. "Terrible to have lost both Starr and Nora on the same day," Jason's voice blared. "Guess we'll have to find replacements …"

Panic mode on full, Nora thrust herself through the bathroom door, shouting, "I'm on my way! All is well! I'm heeerrreee!"

Starr eyed herself in the mirror, more than a little shaken.

What happened to her can happen to you.

What had happened? It hadn't been firing. And it hadn't been moseying.

Starr had been composing a list of to-do items in her head: one, save the show. Two, get Jason to show her his arms and his legs. Three, find out what the hell happened to Amelia Beckenridge.

Not necessarily in that order.

CHAPTER 14
Starr Chamber

"Help!" Fiona swanned into the Hairies and Makeup Fairies Room some weeks later, waving her hands like a woman in the throes of religious ecstasy. Her white silk robe billowed behind her, and a green cashmere scarf held her hair back. She settled into the swivel chair and sighed to the Fae around her, "Darlings, darlings, save me! I look a fright."

Dozens of tiny hair and makeup Fae paused where they'd been hovering around Mav, Starr and four guest actors Fiona would never bother learning the names of. Tiny eyes fixed on her for a millisecond and—clearly understanding the show's hierarchy—the creatures swarmed over with spell brushes, enchanted combs and charmed paints.

Fiona closed her eyes and flung out her arms, delighting in the sensation of so many tiny hands and wings tickling, poking, plucking and massaging. "Aaah," she sighed. "Darlings, you are the most wonderful part of working here."

The Fae fluttered and twittered in appreciation.

"Remind you of anything?" she heard Starr ask under her breath.

"I reserve all comment on the matter," said Mav in reply, but he sounded eager for whatever was coming next.

"I was thinking vultures at a carcass," Starr whispered back.

Mav snickered, then snorted and then there was a thumping sound, as if he'd fallen out of his chair. Fiona ground her teeth. Charles had been so well-behaved all these years. Dependable. Steadfast. Boring, but at least reliable. Starr, that irritant who couldn't take a hint and quit already, was corrupting him.

Well, she'd get hers.

Fiona determined to ignore them both. The Hairies and Makeup Fairies Room was her sanctuary, and she would not let them steal that from her. A shrine to beauty—or at least a simulacrum of beauty—the room was full of enormous mirrors set off by oversized Wills and packed with racks of wigs, thousands of miniature cans of paint and brushes and uncountable hair tools, including several that could transform human locks into any conceivable shape. Every application would hold fast until the charms or spells wore off. Fiona might have enticed the creatures to attend her in her dressing room, but she did so love having a reason to swoop in, be cared for and catch up with Mav or Nora or even one of the recurring actors.

But since Starr's arrival, every day had become a battleground, every decision she made a tactical move. The Starr project would not fail. Could not fail. That disastrous first day on the set should have been the end of it, but somehow the rookie had turned things around. Starr had also wised up to Fiona's nonsense 'acting' lessons from a few weeks ago and had unfortunately begun spending time with Jason to gain advice and tips.

That meant Fiona had to move on to the next level in her plotting—level three. If necessary, Fiona had plans all the way to level ten, though actual annihilation would hopefully not be required. Best if it looked as if Starr chose to leave on her own. It all had to seem natural; TPTB might not forgive another rash decision on Fiona's part.

"Oh, dear." Fiona sat up in her chair, paging through the script. She made an audible *tsk*.

Starr's gaze was laser sharp on Fiona, awareness instantly heightened.

Perfect. The oaf loved to help, so she would give her a project. "Starr, darling—could you be a love and fetch Cris for me? These new scenes are beastly, and I worry I won't be able to handle them."

Mav cleared his throat.

Fiona ignored him.

"What, isn't Bookender available?" Starr was swaying back and forth in her chair, only half of her face currently enchanted with makeup. She looked like a before-and-after picture—perfectly foolish.

All to the better. "Alas, Bookender is occupied with other tasks." Fiona kept her voice soft and weary. "So many words to transcribe." She leaned to Starr and the Fae scattered. "Can't you help a little? You're so young and strong, and I worry I may be growing too old for this."

Mav made another rumbling sound.

"Do you require a cough drop, Charles?" Fiona shot him a look.

The smile ran from his face. "Nope, nope. Just enjoying the show."

Starr looked between them. She seemed to almost guess that this was a trap, yet wasn't quite bright enough to understand how. Fiona was very pleased with herself. "Guess I wasn't getting finished here any time soon." Starr slid from her chair, curling a script in one hand. "Any idea where—"

"His office." Fiona fluttered her fingers in the air. "He was last seen heading into his office." She turned away. "Would someone be a dear and hand me my tea?"

Several hairies scattered from her scalp and airlifted a mug to her hand. Fiona caught Starr standing at the door, dithering. "Off with you, my dear. Time waits for no mythic."

The door closed behind her, and Fiona's smile broadened. *Stage three deployed. And that should be that.*

STARR WASN'T STUPID.

She knew Fiona didn't really need help in fetching Cris; this was an excuse to get her out of the hair and makeup room. But Starr was relieved to have that excuse. The rumors of Amelia had gotten to her. A 'lost' actor was tantalizing. But then Nora had made it sound as if Amelia hadn't quit, which tipped things into terrifying. Why would someone voluntarily depart from fairyland? Or whatever this 'other side of the Veil' was? The longer Starr remained on this nutty show, the less she could imagine working anyplace else. She would discover Amelia's fate and sidestep it.

There's survival of the fittest, and survival of the most-attentive, she thought. *Cris will know things and probably have no issues with sharing them.* He'd been with the show far longer than thirty years and appeared to love breaking rules.

Plus, Starr was curious about the glamour in Cris' office.

The memory of coming to in Jason's personal space, surrounded by trees and a purple sky, sat like a warm jewel in her heart. Cris, she imagined, probably had dozens of shelves stacked with his favorite drink—rum—and a humidor for all those smokes. Plus, a private area with a heart-shaped bed for trysts with Dakota. Maybe a poster of Kama Sutra positions.

Starr paused outside Cris' door, recalling her etiquette from the Guide: *Always knock first. Mythics take gates, portals and doorways seriously. Never enter a new place without permission or appropriate access spells.*

With a brief nod, Starr knocked against what looked like a very ordinary door. Dark wood, solid. But there was no answer.

She knocked again.

It hadn't occurred to her that Fiona might be lying about Cris' presence in his office. Shrugging, Starr reached for the doorknob. Perhaps if it swung open, she could confirm whether he was there.

At her touch, the knob disintegrated into sand. Starr jumped back and the door transformed, morphing into smaller and smaller pieces while retaining its general barrier shape: fist-sized, diamond-sized, crystal-sized... and then, sand. The sand door stood in place, swinging inward slowly, then collapsed.

Coughing as sand engulfed her feet and dusted her face, Starr glanced up. The door was gone. Beyond lay... trees.

"Whoops," she said.

Perhaps this was how a pombero said, 'Come in'?

She took a tentative step inside, immediately surrounded by skyscraper-sized trees, vines as thick and tangled as Medusa's hair, and unseen, cawing birds. She trod along a dirt path that cut through the forest office and opened into a small clearing filled with a collection of boulders that vaguely resembled a desk and chairs. The ground was charred in several places, indicating either Cris had lost his temper a few times, or just didn't care where he built a firepit. The burble of a stream winding through the clearing caught her ear first, then her nose—it smelled like molasses and butterscotch. The whole place was humid, leafy and dim; barely any light penetrated the canopy above.

It was a freaking rainforest.

Starr spun around, trying to take it all in.

"Cris?" she called out. "Fiona wants to chat. But first—" She cut herself off, wondering if maybe she was talking to nobody but the unseen birds. Did mythics leave the glamour on when they weren't in like somebody forgetting to turn out the lights?

Thirsty, she bent down and scooped up stream water into her hand. "I was hoping to ask you about this actor who was here before me. Maybe you remember Amelia Beckenridge?" She tilted the water into her mouth and gagged—it was sweet and burned like alcohol.

Because it was alcohol. The creek was made of *rum*.

A giant hand clamped over her face, and she breathed in tobacco and sugar as she was dragged down the path. Struggling, she tried to remember that free Krav Maga class she'd taken six years ago but left halfway through—but with every flail the mysterious grip tightened. She could barely catch a breath, much less scream for help, and whoever it was, was not talking. When they reached the boulder desk, her captor flung her away and she stumbled against the rocks. "Who—" she gasped.

Cris stood before her, stark naked, fists on his hips.

Starr's eyebrows lifted. *That's impressive. So are those. And so is—* She shook her head, trying not to gawk at his sculpted, enormous body. He was like one of those god statues people left gifts for or insisted on caressing for good luck.

He stood about ten feet tall.

"You failed to knock," Cris boomed, and it wasn't really Cris—it was the most Cris-iest Cris she'd ever met, the Über Cris or something. Like when Jason's horns appeared, how he became... someone else. A cold fear cut into Starr. The cigar in Cris' mouth—also twice as large as it ought to be—shifted to one side. "I would have heard a knock."

The voice was not so much loud as powerful, like a bass speaker had been pressed to Starr's head. "I tried—but your door—it turned into sand—"

"That is not supposed to happen!" Cris boomed.

Kind of the motto of this show, Starr thought.

The pombero reached into a pile of ferns and withdrew a pair of cargo trousers, then slid them on. His dark eyes flared. Grabbing hold of a long vine, he curled it under one arm and tugged hard. "Uninvited trespassers are to be lashed to a tree, and the fire ants administered."

Ants of retribution! Sweat broke out on Starr's forehead. Cris didn't seem to recognize her at all. "Hey! It's me!" she babbled, trying to back away. "Starr! Sam! Helping the show! Too much hair flipping!"

He staggered to her in slow, menacing steps, all while wrapping more vines around his massive arm, eyes blazing.

Run, thought Starr. *How does a person run again?*

"Once the fire ants have consumed your flesh your bones shall be added to the—"

Unable to flee, Starr used the only thing she carried as a weapon: her script. Curling it tighter, she lashed out and bopped a pectoral muscle the size of her head.

Cris glanced down at the script, then at Starr. She grinned once, then threw the script at him. It bounced off his chest and fell into the rum stream, carried away to an unknown destination.

Crap on waffles. Starr was sweating harder, beginning to shake.

"Sugar Ears?" A small female voice called from the trees. "Dear?" Dakota's head peeped from around a mahogany tree, her lustrous auburn hair coursing down bare shoulders. "I said, 'Ready or not, here I come,' but you didn't even try to hide, you silly—"

Cris clapped a hand over his face with an enormous sigh. The fire drained from his eyes.

"I think my dress fell in the water—oh!" Dakota noticed Starr for the first time. "What are you doing here?"

"Hoping to avoid being a snack for fire ants." Starr was breathing hard, sweat pouring from her scalp.

Dakota cocked her head. "Your makeup is... um, interesting."

"I'm not done yet." Starr remembered how weird she must look.

"How did you get in here again?"

"The door—disintegrated."

Cris shoved aside trees, which split under his grip. "Doble hijueputa," he swore. "I am to be protected in my chamber. That is not supposed to happen."

"Fiona sent me," Starr rushed on.

"I heard that part." Cris tossed his collected vines aside. "I also heard the other part." He removed the cigar and used it to point. "First answer is: Fiona Ballantine can come find me when she's ready. Because she knows how to *knock on a mythic portal*." He leaned in closer and now the sugar scent reminded her of a campfire. The second part is none of your business. You hear anything about an Amelia or a Joseph, and you erase it from your tiny skull. That's ancient history. This show has moved on. Completely."

Clearly. Starr was still trying to get her legs to move again. But that second name—Joseph—she'd heard it from Cris before. Another person who was no longer here. Who had *moseyed.*

Joseph's work is off-limits. For eternity.

Cris had said that in the diner. When the leaves fell off the plant.

"Starr." Dakota gave a little wave, still hiding behind the mahogany tree. "I think you're marvelous and I promise to clear that interview with Helena any day now. But I really must ask that you leave this instant. We are in the middle of our—exercise."

"Read you loud and clear." Starr was still intending to flee—but managed to take one step toward Cris. He'd been gradually reducing in size, along with his pants and the cigar, and now loomed just over six feet. He didn't move out of her way, and she held her ground even though her hands were sweating. Swallowing, she asked what she most wanted to know: "But come on. Who are they?"

"If you have so much free time," Cris ran a hand down his bristly face, "I will have to chat with Emma. Perhaps she is not giving you enough to do."

Starr smiled awkwardly. "That would be"—she stepped to one side—"amazing, of course." She began backing toward where the door had been, nearly tripping over a fallen branch. "But honestly"—she reached for a knob that wasn't there—"not necessary. I'm doing great. *Super* busy." Her hand closed around something smooth and cold that was not a doorknob, and she flung it into the room.

Cris caught the small yellow snake in one hand and set it on the boulders. "Go," he boomed, waving at the trees, revealing a hallway behind her. "Drop this thing about Amelia. It is not your concern. And remember, I do have fire ants, if need be."

Starr swallowed and jumped into the hallway. Her heels clattered on familiar linoleum, and she felt a wave of relief. "No need. Of course. By the way, you have a really nice office." She fled into the lobby without glancing back.

Roused mythics were terrifying people.

HEAD POUNDING, HEART doing a drum solo, Starr hurtled into the cavernous lobby. It was empty except for Nico and Phil, who were chatting away over mugs of something. Coffee probably for Nico, sriracha for Phil.

Head down, keep moving. Starr tried to blot out everything that had just happened in Cris' office. *I have makeup and hair and lines and—no script.*

Nico intercepted her with a step to the side. "Hey, hey." He smelled of rosewater and cardamom. "Got a bee in your bonnet?"

Starr blinked up at him and thought *fire ants, not bees*—and burst into tears. Her legs felt soft. Her heart was still racing. Nico reached for her arm but she pulled away. A linen cloth the size of a bedsheet landed on her head. She could make out an embroidered red 'P' on one corner. Sliding it off, she glanced up at Phil.

"Or do you need security?" Phil asked hopefully.

Starr blew her nose on one corner of the handkerchief and wiped her face with another.

"Tell us what happened," Nico insisted. "I'll punch it if I can. If not, Phil will eat it."

The dragon cleared his throat. "As I have explained many times in the past—"

"Fine, Phil will grill it to perfection." Nico's comforting hand on her shoulder made Starr feel silly about having gotten so emotional. But this was her first encounter with a ten-foot pissed-off pombero threatening a gruesome death, so she forgave herself. Nico had become much more tolerable since he started leaving the sunglasses and Roland persona on the set, and she appreciated his solicitousness. He still could seem sketchy as anything— but he appeared to know how to be a decent person. And he couldn't help being handsome.

Maybe he was growing on her.

"I met a pombero," she said. "He was not happy to see me."

"Ah." Nico's gaze flicked over her shoulder, back toward Cris' office. "Let me guess: black mamba landing on your head from a tree? Or fire ants crawling up your leg?"

"Threatened fire ants. Retributive kind."

He nodded. "That's a bit of extra angry from Cris."

"Your good friend sent me in there." Starr glared at him. "She knew he'd be in there with D—"

Nico held up his hands. "Exnay on the AkotaDay, there." He faltered and turned to Phil. "What the hell is pig Latin for 'Cristian del Noche?'"

"I only know serpent Latin," said Phil. "Has a lot of esses in it."

Nico waved him off. "My point is, you never know when AsonJay will come by, and we really don't want him to know about them. He could turn up at any time, and he's a stickler for protocol."

Starr frowned; Nico had dodged the central element of her fury. "Well, Iona-Fay was the reason I was there in the first place."

Nico took a long beat before answering. "Fiona is… Fiona. Try to bear with her. Our relationship is complicated." He propped an elbow on the reception desk and leaned forward. "Of course, we could go into more detail on this topic over dinner sometime."

Roland was back. Well, kind of. He wasn't waggling his eyebrows. He wasn't acting like some kind of lounge lizard. He seemed sincere. Starr nearly rejected the idea out of hand—then had an idea: if Cris wouldn't cough up details, perhaps a few bats of her eyelashes might winkle the truth about Amelia, or Joseph, out of Nico.

And maybe he'd get more than a few bats, if he behaved himself.

Starr closed the gap between them, intrigued by the halos in his caramel-colored eyes. "I could look at my schedule."

"Tonight."

"Jeez, you don't waste time. I'll miss the Gate. It's Friday, so I'd be stuck here all weekend."

"I usually miss the Gate. Tonight. Here."

"Dinner in the lobby?"

"I'm an excellent cook." Phil breathed loudly.

Starr had almost forgotten he was there. *A person would have to be pretty bewitching to make you forget a dragon in the room*, she thought. "You're not using some kind of charisma prize, are you, Nico? Right now?"

He set a hand on his chest. "That's adorable. We'll meet here. But let's just say I have ways of spiriting us elsewhere." He withdrew a small marble from his pocket.

Inside the glass orb a white stripe swirled, dipped and circled around like a trapped dream. "This can take us to some very special places."

"Are you offering me drugs, Nico Reddy?"

He laughed. "It's just a MARBLE. Haven't you consulted your Guide yet on MARBLEs?"

"Yes. No." Her memory raced. The Guide had been incredibly helpful on any number of topics, but it kept updating itself and expanding and contracting every day. It was impossible to finish, much less know everything. Figuring out what those little glass spheres she occasionally saw actors pull from their pockets barely made the top ten of her list of questions. "Maybe."

Heels clicking on linoleum broke the moment as Dakota arrived in the lobby. Everyone turned; instead of her usual Junior League look, she wore a belt holding up an oversized pair of trousers, topped by an equally oversized man's blouse with the sleeves rolled up.

"Classy," said Nico. "The pumps are an extra-nice touch."

She sniffed at him and sailed over to Starr, kissing her on both cheeks. "You are the soul of discretion."

"That's me," said Starr. "A soul who needs to understand portals better."

"That never happened before," Dakota whispered, as if Nico weren't there. "Cris and Jason are going to have a meeting about it." She straightened. "You haven't seen my dress, have you?"

Starr shook her head. "Nor my script."

Dakota coughed into a fist. "I'm so late. Fiona says she has a column for me to pick up." Brightening, she turned on a big smile and spoke to the room. "Good news, though! I will be interviewing Starr for the upcoming

WaterWorlds!"

Starr grinned, delighted.

But for some reason, Nico only looked distressed.

CHAPTER 15
Starr Rising

JASON HOISTED HIMSELF up on Phil's desk and broke open a bag of hot peppers whose odor alone was enough to crisp his nose hairs. Without emotion, he nibbled on one, then tossed a second down Phil's gullet.

"Mmm," said the dragon, rosy-pink smoke drifting from his nostrils. "Thank Gorgon it's Friday?"

Jason signed dramatically. "I suppose. I'm halfway between doom and despair." He eyed the milling mass of show extras and guest actors who'd gathered in the lobby, waiting for the Gate to appear. Soon, they'd be gone for the weekend and he'd be left with a half-finished episode.

Part of him wanted nothing more than to be the actors' usual cheerleader, waving them off with aplomb so he could shuck off his boots and clothing and take off on a glorious gallop through the open fields and shady glens of his office glamour. Like sharing outrageously hot peppers with Phil at the end of every week's shift, his run was meant to be sacrosanct. He could burn off his excess energy for an hour before swooping in to rescue Cris' 'director's cut' version of the show, which varied in quality and comprehensibility. Cris was an efficient director who basically scared all his performers into getting the job done—but he was a terrible editor.

"I am, as the mortals say, avant-garde," Cris once told him. "An auteur. Do not mess with my process." Cris had spent a few years in France in the 1960s making movies with mortals, then returned with big ideas and phrases that meant little to Jason. It had taken until just last year to get him to stop wearing a beret all the time. Alas, all that attention to how humans told stories did not translate into an episodic reality show. Once, Cris had tried to send TPTB an 'uncut, raw' episode that had zero editing at all; another time, he'd included a segment that was eight minutes of nothing but reaction shots.

Jason told him to wise up: audiences wanted one hour of three arcs and a little cliffhanger at the end. "Simple," he'd said. "Don't overthink it."

"Your 'simple' is my 'boring' and maybe we need a little more overthinking," Cris had snapped. But the fact was this: putting out five hours of so-called human 'reality' every week to an audience that ate it up was both joyful and grueling. Jason had to pick up a lot of slack, and it was starting to wear on him.

"So," said Phil now, chewing on his pepper. "It's a Carolina Reaper week."

The strength of the pepper choice was dependent on how Jason's last few days had gone; a true barn-buster of a five-day cycle meant peppers that had to be eaten wearing goggles and handled with asbestos gloves. Reapers were the strongest hotties humans could produce—but only fair to middling in the mythic universe.

Jason's mood was also fair to middling at the moment. So many little problems kept cropping up: doorknobs and doors turning to sand. Every pen transforming into a lit candle. Then this afternoon a script and a red dress had clogged up Cris' septic system, causing the studio's water supply to be replaced by incredibly powerful rum—and the eternally thirsty cameradryads had gotten so drunk their bark had begun to peel.

Shooting had ended early for the day.

At first, Jason had worried that all the small issues with the show had been another sign of their waning viewership. But after Celtis stumbled by, rum-punch-drunk, Jason had put two and two together and got... sex. That dress belonged to Dakota and had fallen into Cris' rumspring for a reason. He was going to have words with the pombero later about dallying with the press—and it would not be pretty.

But the bigger problem was that they barely had a show to send to TPTB. Jason had managed to shoot perhaps three scenes before the cameradryads lost all their senses. Now, Jason was so mopey that even hot peppers couldn't light a fire under his mood. He took everything personally: *Tune in Tomorrow* was a work of art in his mind, on a par with Stonehenge, fairy pools and crop circles. He'd spent decades shaping it and making it live and breathe. He'd always felt he had a right to be proud.

Not so much these days. No matter what he did, nothing was getting better. This morning he'd discovered twelve new grey hairs on his head and lower legs. Sure, he'd get them charmed out at some point, but the notion that he could even go grey was enough to make a faun... go grey.

He glanced up. The Gate was now three minutes late. Yet another sign of failure.

Jason lobbed another pepper at Phil, who snapped it from the air and gurgled with delight.

"Ah, pepper time." Nico arrived at the desk, brimming with the cheer Jason lacked. "We have lived to tell the tale for another week." He glanced around the room. "What's up with all the malingerers?"

"Gate's late." Phil dabbled in terrible rhymes. "No debate."

"You're not heading out into the world, are you?" Jason tilted his head. He couldn't remember the last time Nico—or Mav, or Fiona, for that matter—had actually left. Nora and Starr had obligations on the other side, but not most of his long-term players.

"Nope." Nico shone like a penny. "Meeting a lady about a dinner."

"Fiona's not done with Emma." That was another source of worry for Jason. He'd sent the Grande Dame in for a much-delayed discussion with his head writer about how Valéncia's story had to be altered, now that Sam's was expanding. That had been three hours ago. The werepanther could hold her own, even in the face of a provoked diva known for randomly lobbing spells—but still. Emma probably had her own grey patches of fur by now.

"Not my circus tonight." Nico shrugged. "Hoping to see someone else." His face lit up as Starr strolled into the lobby, makeup de-enchanted but still glowing. "Ah, delightful. Precisely the woman I was seeking."

Starr beamed, setting her hand in the crook of his arm. "I'm all ready."

Jason ground his teeth in fury. Did no one listen to him anymore? First, Dakota and Cris. Now—Nico and Starr? His Starr? He'd thought she was smarter than that. And Nico had been specifically warned! "A date," he said flatly.

"A discussion," Starr assured him. "Dinner may be

involved. We're not going far."

"Such remains to be seen." Nico brandished a MARBLE. "My dear, have you ever had shachihoko caviar on the shores of Atlantis?"

That did it. Jason held out his hand. "Nico, you know better. No MARBLEs for recreational purposes."

"You presume, mon capitaine," said Nico. "This is a business dinner."

Jason jiggled his palm and Starr's expression sank. He wondered why it was so important to her to spend this evening with Nico—but only for a moment.

"C'mon, boss," Nico protested. "I know late Gates make you cranky. But you're just going to give us MARBLEs anyway. I mean, it's not like you want us around *working* all weekend." He chuckled.

Jason raised an eyebrow and straightened.

Nico stopped chuckling.

Jason glanced at the Gate that wasn't there yet. *One day. We really could use one more day. Or two! Two would be perfect.* "Nicodemus Reddy, you are a genius." Jason whisked the MARBLE from his fingers.

"Wait—no, what did I say?"

Jason clambered atop Phil's desk, towering over the rest of the room, and let out a piercing whistle. Silence fell as the actors turned to him. "The Gate is canceled," he said. Best to let them think this was his plan all along. "I am instituting Rule 4203B from page twelve of your Guide." The rule didn't exist at the moment, but he would ensure tonight's update included it. "If the Gate is more than five minutes late, and the show we shot is less than five scenes long, we have the right to detain you for more filming."

"There's no such rule, you fraudulent faun," Nora called from across the room.

"Am I dispersing MARBLEs?" Phil asked hopefully. He guarded the large jar of the teleport spells in his cave, alongside many other valuables. On nights when the Gate hiccupped, the actors were permitted to take one for a temporary jaunt to a prearranged safe mythic world space for the night. A weekend Gate anomaly meant they could visit wonderland for up to two days.

Jason raised his hands to quiet the buzz of irritated actors. "We can all thank Nico for this genius idea, which means—"

"Don't give *me* credit!" Nico yelped.

"—we all lose our MARBLEs this weekend," Jason finished.

"Probably not what he meant," Starr said under her breath.

"Everyone will receive a temporary MARBLE just for tonight," Jason continued. "Tomorrow morning, we begin afresh!" He applauded once, but aside from a few sickly claps, no one joined him. He lowered himself back to the desk.

The room was full of confusion, and some shaking of fists at Nico. Phil pulled out the oversized glass jar and breathed on a clawful of MARBLEs, activating them and handing one out to each actor. One by one those actors placed their MARBLEs in a palm—and winked out of the lobby. Quickly, the noise level diminished, and the room fell silent.

"I'll take mine back, then," Nico told Jason in a thin, flat voice.

"As you wish." Jason swapped his old orb for a new temporary one. "But Ms. Weatherby is not coming with you."

"Why the hell not?"

"Yeah." Starr fixed her hands on her hips. "What'd I

do?"

Jason shoved the bag of jalapenos at Phil. He was on a roll. He could do anything. This was his show, by Hera's hairnet, and he was a mythic. If the show needed help, it was up to him to do what needed to be done.

"Because Starr has a meeting with me tonight," he said. The look of envy on Nico's face was delicious. The look of annoyance on Starr's, not so much.

"You might've at least asked me," she told Jason.

"But I thought—" He had been very clear on this: Starr loved hanging out with him. He loaned her books, and she'd taken him shopping on the other side of the Gate once or twice. Maybe he'd been mistaken. Well, too bad. She was a human, and he was the boss here. "Starr, this is part of the job. Sometimes, there is overtime."

"But you could have *asked*," she said, folding her arms.

Jason rolled his eyes at the ceiling, then set his hands on her shoulders and faced her. "Starr Weatherby, will you forgo an evening with Nicodemus to help me with the show?"

Starr grinned as if she'd won a prize. "Hell, yeah."

Nico grumbled and stalked off.

"So, what's on offer, Mr. Valentine?" Starr's glow had amped up several degrees.

Leaping from the desk, Jason nearly said, "a brainstorming chat with Emma," but instead gave her a saucy look. Putting an arm around Starr's shoulders, he guided her out of the lobby. "Let's just say that we have special plans for you... and Sam."

CHAPTER 16
Starr Quality

"WHAT'S A MARBLE for?" Starr asked as Jason guided her down the hallway. "Nobody tells me anything."

"Nobody will," said Jason, withdrawing the object he'd taken from Nico and holding it to the light. "Read your Guide."

"The Guide is a new book every day and it's a little hard to keep up with. And last I checked, there's nothing about MARBLEs in there."

Jason raised an eyebrow, threw the orb into the air and caught it on the back of his hand, where he let it roll into one sleeve, across his shoulders and out the other until it landed in his opposite palm. "The Guide refers to these items as Matter and Reality Bilocation Leaving Elementals."

"MARBLEs."

"Exactly." He touched her nose with his finger. It was so delightful to share their little secrets with trustworthy newcomers, but Starr was getting him off track. He couldn't understand it: five minutes in her company left him at more loose ends than if he'd been playing Chase the Yarn with Emma. "Sometimes, it is best to set your hand on top of your Guide and ask the question. It will find the answer for you within its pages."

"Has nobody here ever heard of the internet?"

Jason cocked his head.

"The, uh, information superhighway. The world wide web. The thing that connects humans."

"Oh, of course!" He tossed the MARBLE in the air again and it landed on top of his upraised finger. "Arachne spins the web for mythics; she connects us on both social and anti-social threads."

Starr perked up. "Why am I only now hearing about this? How do I get an account? I could go on as Sam and talk to the viewers and send pictures and—"

Jason held up a hand. "Jan is the expert in all things Arachne and web-related. Mortals rarely dabble there; if nothing else, you are far too busy to fritter your time away in our social networks."

"But if you want to get people—er, mythics—excited about the show—"

Jason's head spun with possibility, but he tamped it down. They had a show to finish first, before more of Starr's big ideas captured him again. He scooped up her cheeks in his hands and held them tight. "Focus, my dear Starr. A charged MARBLE can whisk you and anyone you're in contact with to a predetermined location. It then vanishes. A second MARBLE brings you back. But when a MARBLE is not charged, it chooses your destination randomly, and not always to your benefit."

In fact, Jason knew an uncharged MARBLE was more weapon than device, which was why they were stored in Phil's cave. Nothing got out of there without the dragon's permission, and those who attempted to infiltrate risked incineration. Phil was a very different beast if his precious items were under threat.

"Random destination? Sounds like a fun date night."

Jason raised an eyebrow. "Perhaps if you're open to 'anywhere' being the River Styx. Or Kyöpelinvuori, where you'll hang out with dead women. Or Summerland. The MARBLE chooses." He swished it back into a side pocket, then came to a halt. "I hope you aren't too bothered by my interference with your plans tonight."

Starr's smile was brilliant. "I couldn't be less bothered. Where are we headed?"

"Ahem." Jason blushed. He never could resist a flash of her white, flat incisors. He almost felt sorry he was about to disappoint her. "We're already here."

Starr discovered they were outside Emma's closed writer's room door. Jan sat in their cubicle just outside, reading a book.

"I see," said Starr.

"Still in there." Jan didn't glance up.

Jason shook his head. "Emma must be cataleptic by now."

Jan refused to rise to the bait. They tossed the book on a desk and folded their arms.

"Hi!"

Everyone started at the sudden appearance of Oleander. She was bouncing on her toes, tapping her fingers together. "Mx. Janus, I see you have a book and it is not currently being read."

"I literally just put it down, bro," said Jan, exasperated.

"Brownies can read?" Jason felt a crick in his neck.

"Bookender can," Starr reminded him. "And I might have, you know, shown Oleander the alphabet one afternoon. And left a dictionary lying around. Plus some reading materials." She held up her hands. "What?"

Jason didn't mind, per se, but any change he hadn't personally instituted on the show left him feeling like he was dangling over an open pit. There probably wasn't any harm to brownies reading—but to what end? Bookender only needed to be literate so he could type up Fiona's dictated *WaterWorlds* columns.

Oleander was sneaking Jan's copy of *The Jungle* from the desk. Jason made a small gesture and Jan whipped around. "Put that back, you purloiner. I know property ownership is totally bougie, but you brownies are raiding—"

"Borrowing!" Oleander tucked the book into her pocket. "We have read all Mx. Janus' library, from *Das Kapital* to the book about motorcycles to the book by Mr. Studs Terkel and the book by Ms. Barbara Ehrenreich—" She took a breath. "And now we believe in collective ownership and sharing!" Oleander raced down the hallway with her book. "Whee!"

"Excuse me," said Jan, giving chase.

Jason had hoped to find out more about this teaching thing but was interrupted by muffled noises from inside the writer's room. Screeching. Yowling. Hissing. And a thump. The door yanked open and Fiona—makeup de-enchanted, hair bound in a tight purple turban—stormed out. The fire in her eyes would have impressed Phil. Her cheeks were two apples of high color. Leaning on her lion's head cane, she glared at Jason.

"I am deeply disappointed in you, Mr. Valentine." She pivoted her narrow-eyed gaze to Starr. "And I see the chosen one is on time for her preferential treatment. All that candy you've been bringing him seems to have paid off."

Jason's horns sharpened. It was true that he had an

unhealthy attachment to licorice, and it was further true that Starr had been keeping him stocked with high-quality Red Vines from Dylan's Candy Store, but the implication ...

Starr smiled as if she'd received a compliment. "Ms. Ballantine. You seem tired. Long days can be so stressful for... older actors. Would you like assistance in finding your way back to your dressing room?"

Jason covered his face.

The Grande Dame straightened, fingers twitching on the cane. "I am in perfect health, Ms. Weatherby, and in possession of all my faculties. But as you bring up the notion of dressing rooms"—she lifted her chin briefly, then ducked it down—"good luck finding your own." She stalked down the hallway, cane clicking.

Jason sighed.

"What happened?" Starr's sanguine look had vanished.

Emma landed in the doorway as if from a height before Jason could answer, claws raking the frame. Her fur stood on end and her eyes were unnaturally pink. Behind her, pillow feathers and black fur drifted around the room.

"Are you all right?" Jason patted her handpaw. "I know that was ugly."

"One day, that woman will set me off during the full moon." Emma glared down the hallway. "I cannot be held accountable then." She slipped her tail under Jason's chin and tickled, then led them inside.

"That doesn't seem to have gone well," Starr noted.

"Not to worry," said Emma. "Fiona sees you as the source of all her problems now, which will ease things off the rest of us, and make your life more interesting."

"Oh, great. What did she do out there? It felt like she did something."

"She disappeared your dressing room." Jason was still marveling at the skill with which Fiona had pulled it off. She was as good at subtle spellcasting as a mythic. Almost. Maybe a low-level one. "As you know, she can."

"Disappear small places for limited periods of time," Starr realized slowly. "So, wait, it's... not there?"

"Naught but a blank spot on the wall." Emma padded onto her pillows. "One must be circumspect with Fiona. She wields an absurd amount of power for a mortal. I had to set wards in this chamber for her visit."

"And hid the catnip plants, I presume," Jason said.

"Naturally. Experience has taught us that one does not introduce a new concept to Fiona, one wears her down into it. Telling her that Valéncia must take a back seat is the same as telling Fiona she is of lesser importance and that can get... messy. But the hard part's over now, and we can begin to build Sam Draper more firmly into Shadow Oak."

Starr was distracted. "When does it come back? My room, I mean."

"Twelve hours, give or take," said Emma. "I am certain Jason can find you a spare dressing room. Or you may curl up here for the night." She gestured at her pillow-packed office. She kept a fancy cardboard box in one corner and oversized scratching post in another. When she'd first joined the show, Jason had gifted her a small cabinet and a grow-Will to help with her catnip crop, while Cris' present had been a pair of breeding rats called Trentren Vilu and Caicai Vilu, after two deities he'd known for a few millennia. They provided regular live snacks that helped facilitate the werepanther's creative process.

Emma rubbed up against Jason like a cat on a chair leg, and he stroked her back. Each treated the other like a beloved pet, but there had never been romance between them. She wasn't his type, for one thing; for another, Jason adhered strictly to the TPTB-instituted rule of no interoffice relations. Jason was a firm believer in the human aphorism, 'No defecation where one finds nourishment.' Or, in the case of Emma, 'No dipping your pen in the company ink.'

In any case, he had a number of locations on his side of the Veil to get his kicks as the desire arose.

"Do please tread carefully with Fiona," Emma urged Starr. "Those who trifle with her find she trifles back twice as hard." She glanced at Jason. "Are we finished, then?"

"Wait," said Starr. "This is the big special thing?"

"Never discount the pleasures that come from keeping Emma interested." Jason wagged a finger. "She has all sorts of ideas to bounce off you."

"And you?" Emma winked at him.

"Oh, I have a show to prepare to shoot in the morning. That's the news: I have declared the weekend null and void. We will finish the show we could not complete today in the morning, and we will need a fresh script for the day after. We will be ahead of ourselves for once!"

Emma's tail fluffed out. "To think I once considered you like a littermate."

Starr and Emma were both staring at Jason with long, disappointed faces, which made him feel long and disappointed, too. But there was nothing to do but brazen it out. The show had to go on. They needed scripts. Emma was their source. He opened the door again. "Brainstorm well, my loves!"

A pillow struck him in the rear as he trotted to the door and he half-turned, but Emma was already breaking a stem from her catnip plant. "For you, my dear?" She offered half to Starr.

"Er, thanks, another time. Any chance you've got some wine?"

Jason opened the door and slid out, just as Emma was saying, "An excellent suggestion. Indeed I do. Let us get tipsy, skunked, blotto. Only then can we properly imagine, conceptualize, dream. Tell me... how do you feel about working more closely with Maverick?"

As WINE O'CLOCK began down the hallway, Fiona neared her dressing room, fuming over the discussion with the werepanther.

"How can I miss you if you never go away?" the yowling lump of fur had said to her.

Oh, I'll go away, she thought now. *I'll go away in your dreams.*

Lady Marlborough had appeared in every episode of *Tune in Tomorrow* for over a century. Viewers loved her. But now they were taking her spotlight away—and giving it to that smartass Starr.

This would not stand.

Fiona passed the kitchenette and paused. Dakota was slumped in a chair, face pasted against the orange Formica table. She wore a damp red dress. Fiona poked her with the lion's head cane.

"Later, Sugar Ears," the reporter mumbled, clutching the stick.

This was not optimal: Dakota should be on the other side of the Gate now, giving Helena the usual manila envelope. She jerked back the cane, and the reporter started awake.

"Oh!" she cried, wiping hair from her face. "What time is it?"

"Too late, that's what time it is. You've missed the Gate."

The reporter's face crumpled. "Have you seen Cris?"

"Certainly not."

The crumpling was getting closer to crying, and Fiona didn't have the patience. She supposed Cris might come looking for his lover eventually, but she didn't like the idea of leaving this wet creature cooling her heels in the open. Fiona understood what it felt like to be kept waiting.

"Come," she gestured, and the bedraggled reporter staggered after her.

Alas, once they were ensconced in Fiona's dressing room, Dakota proved to be a nonstop yammerer at a time when Fiona would have much preferred to vent about the injustices perpetrated on her own person. Dakota moaned and sobbed about having to do a walk of shame across the lobby until the beginnings of a monster headache crept up on Fiona.

She's here. Make use of her.

As always, Valéncia had the best ideas.

"Dear," Fiona cut Dakota off mid-stream, "I understand you are planning to interview our little Starr."

Dakota nodded. "Helena says the Arach-Web is practically twanging from all the fan talk. Never underestimate the appeal of a new face."

"Then your being stranded here this weekend thanks to that persnickety Gate is a golden opportunity. Perhaps you can use this spare time to speak with her. To come up with... what do you call it in your business, 'color'?"

"I do need to impress Helena," mused Dakota. "She's a tough nut."

"Allow me to offer you a brownie," Fiona continued. "I can make one available to memorize your conversation. Bookender would be delighted to transcribe it afterward."

"I would?" Bookender queried, then read Fiona's expression. "Oh, yes. I would."

"Fiona, you are the soul of kindness."

"And I would further be delighted to help you shape the piece."

"Er." A worry line crossed Dakota's face again. Fiona waited for her to object but knew she wouldn't. Dakota was in too deep with Fiona's little schemes to ever tell her *no* about anything.

"Excellent!" Fiona clapped her hands together and ordered Bookender to prepare a pot of tea made from Wolfgang Pitcher's ashes. That particular brownie was a notorious bore. "Then it's settled. You do the interview, then turn the entire thing over to Bookender and me. I will ensure the piece gets to Helena once it is ready. Agreed?"

"Yes?" Dakota shifted uncomfortably. "I mean, no. That's my job."

Fiona let her face fall. "If you don't trust me, Dakota—"

"Oh! Of course I do, it's just, er—you're busy, Fiona."

"Never so busy I can't help a friend." Fiona leaned forward and the silence in the room grew thick.

Bookender bustled in with the tea and poured a big cup for Dakota. "Well—" Dakota's eyes darted around the room as if looking for the exit. "I suppose."

Fiona smiled broadly, ignoring her own tea. "Then it's all settled. Drink up, my dear. Wolfgang is a very *particular* sort of brownie. We'll both feel better after you have some."

It was true: Fiona felt terrific minutes later when the tea put Dakota out like a drug. The sacked-out reporter collapsed against the Chesterfield, gently snoring.

Stage four in motion, thought Fiona.

But Dakota's article would take weeks to complete and publish. Fiona needed a way to push harder on Starr *now*. She had the brownies arrange a circle of her glowing, pulsing awards on the throw rug, and took a seat in the center of the aura. Then she settled deep into her mind, finding Valéncia there.

You need help, suggested her alter ego.

They don't do therapists over here. And you're one to talk.

No, I mean you need to enlist help in solving our problem.

What do you think I've been doing?

You're doing it all wrong.

Fiona wasn't sure what more Valéncia expected from her. Of course she did not plan to spend the next century sparring with Starr Weatherby, but slow and steady was wearing her down—and not driving the girl away. In just a few short months, the twit had become comfortable enough to be snide around her betters. It was too much.

Mythics love to think they can help us, Valéncia told her. *Think of all the low-hanging fruit around the set. Some of these immortals go unappreciated for decades. Use all your resources.*

Fiona felt the glow of her awards fill her, and a slow smile spread across her face. "Bookender," she announced. "Procure for me a list of our crew. I plan to call upon some old... acquaintances."

CHAPTER 17

Starrs in Her Eyes

STARR WOKE TO the sound of voices, a faint rise and fall drifting in through a crack in Emma's not-entirely-shut writer's room door. She peeled her eyes open and spotted the wordcat curled up in her large cardboard box, snoring gently.

The last few hours had been a whirlwind, and the beginnings of a hangover were already creeping in. The wordcat and Starr had gotten, as advertised, tipsy, sloshed and blotto in approximately that order, thanks to a bottomless bottle of wine. With each pour their shared ideas for Sam had flown higher and higher as Emma scribbled furiously, all four limbs and tail mere blurs. With a twitch of her nose the finished pages duplicated. Triplicated. Quadruplicated—until there were enough copies for all relevant cast members. Starr had watched the magic with bleary eyes and then—

She didn't remember much after that. Except that here she was, watching the ceiling spin gently, resting against the floor pillows.

The voices in the hall neared and became clearer. "It's

late." Jason, sounding tense. Starr's heart leaped: he was back! "We can talk about this later."

Emma's tail twitched, but she did not stir.

"We can talk now." Cris' voice, flat and unyielding. "What is up your backside lately?"

"I'm stuck on how Dakota's dress ended up blocking our pipes and getting our cameradryads drunk."

"Glitches, no doubt. Your golden girl isn't pulling in eyeballs. Caca happens."

"You might have a different take on that if you ever read the SCN reports. Or rested your ear on Arachne-Web. The hum is tremendous since she joined us. No. This is not about Starr. Besides, a bit of human *clothing* ending up in the pipes is not how this show 'glitches.'"

Starr smelled cigar smoke and imagined Cris' stogie turning colors. "Skip to the chase, Valentine."

Only Cris didn't say 'Valentine' or 'Jason.' He uttered a combination of sounds that made Starr's nostrils begin to bend. Startled and in pain, Starr clamped her fingers over her nose to pinch them back in place. By the time she had a nose she could breathe through again, she'd missed a few lines.

"—stick up your goaty culo," Cris was saying.

"That's not what this is about," Jason hissed. "Thanks to you we *must* shoot this weekend. This show nearly died after the last on-set relationship disaster. Whatever is going on between you and Dakota is not *permitted*."

"She's not a cast member."

"The point remains. You can have anyone. Stop messing around. The Seelie are not going to tolerate another Joseph-Fiona-Amelia debacle."

Starr's eyebrows nearly touched her hairline. Joseph and Amelia and Fiona! Though really, should she be surprised that the Grande Dame was involved in... whatever this was? Starr crept to the edge of the door, listening.

"Look at you," said Cris. "Being all caring. If you'd cared a little more when 'Melia started up with Joseph, or even been paying attention to his scripts—"

Starr clapped her hands over her mouth. The fantastical, unfashionable scripts had been Joseph's. And he'd had an affair with Amelia. Then he'd also moseyed.

"This is not about me." Jason sounded as worn and angry as Starr had ever heard. All that bravado and flair he carried around—she remembered his playing with the MARBLE earlier, and how her heart had skipped a beat at his grace—was gone. "Either be here and help the show or leave and take that human with you. Not like you do any useful work around here, anyway."

Cris' voice was dark and smoky. "Say that again—"

Once again, he didn't say 'Jason' or 'Valentine,' and Starr grabbed her nose, catching the nostrils in mid-flare. She'd have been more terrified if she hadn't been so thrilled by the conversation.

"Or what?" Pause. "What's that—oh, you are not spelling me, pombero." A clattering of hooves and a crunching, crackling sound like paper. "Hey! That was my horn!"

"Carajo, I missed. I was aiming for your face."

"You leave me no choice," said Jason. More stomping. "Here."

"What's this? Wait, you're not—"

Air whooshed, followed by a gentle pop.

"Enjoy Atlantis, you Polevik pitchfork."

Starr's eyes widened. Jason had MARBLEd him. She wondered what that even meant but barely had time to come up with half a thought before the door swung inward abruptly, smashing into her head. Starr bounced against the plaster wall, tumbling into the thick floor pillows.

Jason loomed over her. One of his horns glowed, sending off green smoke. It smelled like newly mown grass. Seeing Starr, the anger in his face leached away and he shook his head, sighed, and closed the door again behind him.

CHAPTER 18
Starr Dust

THE NEXT MORNING, they steamed through their new pages. Sam signed on with Mav at the Eye 2 Eye Detective Agency, they went on the hunt for his errant brother Duncan, and Sam revealed she knew how to locate some important plans for Valéncia.

Then Mav and Sam had gotten locked overnight inside the walk-in refrigerator of Shadow Oak's pre-eminent creamery.

"Mav," Sam shivered beneath a blanket, teeth chattering. She perched on an upturned bucket of Chocolate Gravel Ice Cream, and her breath visible as if it were truly cold, rather than a small spell concocted by Phil. "How much air does a walk-in creamery fridge have?"

Starr was forcing herself to stay in Sam's head, but it was tough: her wine hangover was still raging and she'd gotten about three hours of sleep the night before. But looking at Mav helped: he was utterly dashing in a peacoat and scarf. In character, he helped Sam up and wrapped his arms around her. Starr was dying to relax into that bear hug, but Sam wasn't into it, so she jerked away—as per Emma's script.

"Everything'll work out, Sam," Mav soothed. Starr

admired how he was virtually the same person on camera or off. "Beatrice—"

"Will never find us in time!"

On cue, the refrigerator door rattled. "It's Beatrice!" Nora called from the other side. "Your fiancée, Mav!"

Thanks, Ms. Narrative Exposition, Starr thought briefly, but squashed it. She would not consider criticizing Emma's writing, especially now that the wordcat had beefed up Sam's role so considerably.

"We're saved!" Mav and Sam locked gazes as the scene drew to a close. Jason held the camera shot without calling for a cut. He'd seen this in several shows years before and went one step further: most of his scenes 'ended' with a ten-second hold as characters did nothing but stare at one another. As a result, Starr had memorized every line and blemish on Mav's face. Today, the hue of his eyes was somewhere between French toast and caramel.

"Cut!" Jason cried at last. "Position three, dryads! Going again in two."

Jason was all business today, and his outfit showed it: a black ensemble of ribbed turtleneck, leather jacket and jeans—plus blue spangled cowboy boots. He'd had to take over for Cris, who was declared 'off-site,' and was blasting through scene after scene, in case of further Gate glitches. Yet Starr sensed a spark missing in him today. He kept pulling Red Vine licorice whips out and tossing them over his shoulder, rather than consuming them. He'd been like this since his conversation with Cris, never even coming back to find Starr a place to sleep for the night. Without options, she'd crashed in Emma's office.

Not that Starr had done much sleeping after he left. She was too busy mentally chewing on the newly discovered Amelia/Joseph/Fiona connection. Her current working theory: Amelia and Joseph had run away together. Backup theory: Fiona had them both fired. Further backup theory: Amelia had died, somehow. None of which explained why she was considered 'misplaced,' though the Amelia Is Dead theory was enough to clench Starr's gut.

Maybe she should let it all go, though. She had a good thing going here with this job. She didn't have to stick her nose into all the weirdness. But every time she considered that, Nora's words came back to her: *what happened to her can happen to you.*

Firing would be bad.

Dead would be worse.

Starr didn't want either to happen. Clearly, she needed more information. Starr felt in her pocket for the note Oleander had delivered that morning, which read: *Lobby. 7pm. No fauns. N.*

Nico would be a font of useful information.

"You lost in there?" Mav leaned over, startling her.

"Thinking," said Starr.

"Knew I smelled wood burning," he half-grinned. "I can tell when you're cookin' up something. Don't go making trouble."

Starr kicked at another one of the weird ice cream flavor buckets, this time Raspberry Brickle and Mortar. "I don't make trouble. Trouble finds me."

Mav leaned on a set of shelves. "Well, tell it to scram. I'm kind of getting used to having you around."

All this time, Fiona had been sitting quietly in her chair, adjusting her hairdo in a mirror held aloft by Bookender. Now, she scanned Mav and Starr, shot a glance at Nora, and slid from her chair. "My dear Starr." She sidled between them. "A word of advice—"

"Not needed." Starr ground her teeth.

"Turn down the emphasis on your 'shivers.' You're cold, not experiencing a stroke."

This was the first thing Fiona had said to her all day and Starr wanted to retort, but knew the diva well enough by now: this was a preliminary to something. "Thanks, Ms. Ballantine." She clenched her jaw. "Any other diagnoses?"

Fiona's face split in a grin. "Goodness, yes! Thank you for reminding me." She snapped her fingers at Nora, and Bookender presented the actor with a small plastic bottle.

"What's this?" Nora curled her hands around the gift.

"Something I've been told you need." Fiona gave an ostentatious wink to Starr, and Nora's face hardened in annoyance. "One can never be too careful when one is..." she lowered her voice, "enceinte."

Mav stiffened.

"Hold the phone," Starr began—but Nora had already unfurled her fingers to reveal a bottle of prenatal pills. Her face went from hard to furious. She picked up an ice cream bucket—Scotch and Soda Pop flavor—and hurled it at Starr. It was empty and her aim was terrible, so it barely brushed Starr in the behind before bouncing away.

"Hey!" Starr shouted. "Get a grip, lady!"

"I trusted you!" Nora scrabbled for another projectile, seizing a large bag of nuts—the kind usually found in a hardware store.

Fiona had clasped her hands against her mouth in delight. "My goodness, I had no idea this was such a sensitive subject! I suppose all those hormones raging makes a person reckless. Nora, think of the child!"

Mav ran over to Nora and caught her arm in the air. "Darby! Have some sense. You think she ran off and told Fiona *anything*?"

"I think—" Nora gasped but was cut off.

A tremendous thud silenced everyone. They turned to the sound. Jason's horns had extended several inches and his eyes flashed molten gold. He'd stomped so hard he'd made a dent in the floor with his boot. Small puffs of smoke swirled from his heel.

"Mav. Starr. Nora. In my office," he growled. "Now."

Not Fiona, I note. Starr's hands curled into fists. But she turned to the exit door with the others. Meanwhile, Fiona settled into her chair and gestured for Bookender to raise the mirror once more. She seemed positively smug.

JASON'S OFFICE WAS naked.

Or so it appeared; Starr had only ever seen it briefly without glamour. As the actors sat waiting in uncomfortable swivel chairs in front of a pressboard laminated desk, Jason stalked around his grey, windowless box. Then he kicked at a wall, digging a hole with his boot, which stuck. When he yanked it out, he brought a chunk of plaster with him.

"What in the goat's foot was *that*?" he demanded.

Starr felt like she'd been summoned to the principal's office, yet she wanted to stand and give this particular principal a reassuring hug. "No big deal. A little disagreement."

Nora gnawed on her cuticles.

"Try again," Jason snapped. "Mav?"

The actor shook his head. "Beats me. One second Fee's chattin' with Starr here and the next Nora's gone nuclear and so I got in the middle." He held up a hand. "Got a paper cut out of the whole mess."

Nora grumbled unintelligibly.

"Enough," Jason growled and for the moment it was like being in the room with Cris. It was easy to forget that not only was he the boss, he had inhuman powers that could be exercised at any time. "Nora, nothing's ever your fault. Why are you beating up on my actors?"

Nora's face was streaked with tears. "Everyone's out to get me!"

"That's horse hockey," said Mav. "I'm not. Starr's not. Or Jason. We're all friends here."

"Well," said Starr, but Mav shot her daggers.

"Enough is enough." He turned back to Nora. "'Fess up."

Nora blinked at him, then over to Jason. "I'm—I'm gonna have a baby. And y'all are gonna cut me out of the show like I was never even here." She glared at Starr. "And this one thought it'd be hilarious to blab it to the world."

Starr folded her arms and stared at a corner.

Jason sat on the edge of his desk. "Oh! That is news. What does one say?"

"'Congratulations,' usually," said Mav.

"'Mazel tov' is also acceptable," added Starr.

"Well, mazelations," said Jason with a genuine smile. "But when were you going to make this public?"

"I wasn't," Nora admitted.

"Makes no sense, gal." Mav rocked in his chair. "You're just a slip of a thing. You can't get the leprecostumers to dress you in muumuus forever."

"And Nora, I have no idea why Fiona gave you those vitamins." Starr turned to Jason. "That's who you really should be talking to. Fiona instigated everything."

Jason's tail twitched. Starr could imagine him with a cigar and glass of rum. He ran his hands through his hair and gave them a pleading look. "Darlings. I need you all to pull together. This show has to work. We've got the fan convention coming up, and you know what a headache that is."

Starr did not, but sat on her hands. Now was not the time to ask.

"I have a surprise or two planned for that event," he continued. "But if everyone stops watching before then, TPTB will pull our plug. This has to be a team effort. Please try not to wound, maim, or kill one another."

"But *Fiona*," Starr tried to redirect the conversation. "She's—"

Jason grabbed her face and squeezed her cheeks together. Starr gulped. "Fiona is Fiona. You must find a way to work with her, and not against her. Part of the reason I brought you here is that I am certain you can figure that out. You invent things on the fly. You don't have to like her, but she is not only senior, she's the grenade pin of our show."

"Lchpn," Starr garbled, lips still mashed together. Jason released her. "Linchpin."

Jason waved the correction away. "In any case, without her, we are not just struggling, we are drowning."

"Gee, thanks," Nora sniped.

"Great pep talk, boss," added Mav. "Problem is, she knows that's how you feel. And she's taking advantage."

Jason rested a head on his hand. "I will see what can be done, if you all promise to get along with her."

Starr sighed, twisting her mouth ruefully. "I'll try. For you."

"Dear Starr." His smile made her heart race.

"So, Nora's pregnancy isn't a problem on the show?" Mav asked.

Jason rubbed his nose beneath his glasses. "You know how this works, Nora, my love. We must keep audiences, not turn them away. The Guide is explicit that little humans or the suggestion of them have caused too many issues over the years. You may choose how you wish to take a rest, but we'll need you out of commission."

"Not yet!" Nora yelped. "We need—I need—"

The attention, Starr thought. *Nora needs the attention.*

"Coma it is, then," nodded Jason. "I'll speak with Emma."

"Ugh," Mav sighed as Nora covered her face with her hands. "I got bedsores that one time you had me laid up, Valentine. Nothing else you can do?"

Starr looked at Nora, then at her billowing dress. Sometimes, you had to go with the flow and not fight the tide. "I might have an idea," she began. "It's not a solution but it's better than being stuck in bed all day." She raised an eyebrow. "How far can we go with costumes?"

CHAPTER 19
Starr Crossed

FIONA SAT IN a lotus position on a tatami mat in the back of her dimmed dressing room, painted by the glow of several dozen awards. Their filaments shifted like grasses in a breeze as she inhaled long, slow breaths and released even longer, slower exhalations. She was like a filament herself, relaxed and bending with the moment. Even Valéncia had shut up for a while.

Creating an outer circle beyond the perimeter of the awards, eight brownies stood speaking in even, flat tones. Brownies had perfect word recall, and they were sharing with her everything they'd heard in the past day. Nearby, Bookender clacked away on the Underwood, back hunched as he balanced atop his stack of books. He was recording everything for posterity.

Of Fiona's one hundred and twenty-eight prizes, perhaps seven were of any true use. Most of the awards were like throwaway parlor tricks of little earthly—or unearthly—value. But one of the best was Waking Dream. Fully relaxed, Fiona could absorb her surroundings so that they became part of her own memories. The brownies reported to her so that she could remember things she'd never witnessed. Bookender put everything down into black and white for later reference. As such, Fiona was an all-seeing eye in the studio, and the most prepared actor on the show.

How else could she have known of Nora's pregnancy, and of her shared confidence with Starr? Her control of the brownies was unprecedented, and critical. Currently, she was hearing a mélange of the last twelve hours, from Emma's brainstorming with Starr to Jason's scolding of the actors for nearly coming to blows, to...

"They're not going to tolerate another Joseph-Fiona-Amelia debacle," murmured one brownie.

The mention of Joseph and the former interloper shocked Fiona out of Waking Dream. Valéncia went on alert.

Knock-knock. Knock. "Cookie? They're about to call everyone to set."

Fiona swore softly; the bros were just getting to the good part. She made a slicing motion at her throat, and they silenced; a twirl of her wrist and they were stacking the awards back on the shelves; a further gesture and most slipped back into the walls, though two remained to help her unbend from her lotus and rub her calves to get the blood circulating again.

At last, she stood and plucked at her hair, nodding at Bookender. The brownie opened the door to let Nico in, and Fiona gave him a series of quick kisses on opposite cheeks. "Darling, how good of you to come fetch me."

Nico was tilting his head. "Cookie," he said, taking a seat on the Chesterfield, "what have you done to your face?"

"Don't you like?" This afternoon, Valéncia, Mav and Sam were all breaking into a warehouse whose owner had been stealing Lady Marlborough's trade secrets. To be convincing, Fiona had dressed in head-to-toe black, then asked the fairies to cover her face in special makeup.

"Well, camouflage is a better look than your original take," he allowed.

"I know olive isn't my color, but I have been informed that an all-black look is not *done* anymore," she sighed.

"Not for about a century," he admitted.

"Honestly, it was all the rage in *my* time."

"Yeah, well, your time—and my time—have long since passed."

"Mythics don't care."

"But some of us do."

Fiona growled. "I suppose that is a reference to Starr. You're like a broken photograph record with that girl."

"She's been in the real world more recently than we have. And you did ask me to keep tabs on her."

"You have given astoundingly little, beyond *makeup* tips. Here I thought you were going to dine with her last night."

"Jason took my MARBLE and my date."

Fiona rolled her eyes. "I expected you to be more... resilient than this, Nico."

"I'm not made of stone. She's soft in all the right places, and she smells like the beach." He paused. "And it's annoying that my usual shtick doesn't play with her. She actually seems to *prefer* when I'm not Roland."

Fiona frowned. Nico appeared to be experiencing some form of Stockholm syndrome. Starr-holm syndrome, even. She had to nip this in the bud; a distracted Nico was useless to her.

"'Course, if you think I'm not the man for the job, I'll turn my spy credentials in now." He fished a bottle of Tums from a pocket. "Duplicity is giving me ulcers."

Fiona experienced a strange lightheadedness. It took a moment to realize she was second-guessing herself.

"Fee," Nico took her hands. "I owe you a couple times over. We both know that. The award you gifted me—I can't pay that back. But ..."

"But 'anything' has its limitations?"

His smile was rueful. "What can I say? It may be withered and unused to sunlight, but I do have a conscience."

For a moment, Fiona almost released him. She wanted to tell him to keep the award if he still required it. After all, she controlled a small brownie army. But Valéncia wouldn't hear of it. Reawakened, Fiona's alter ego seemed to be growing, crowding the Grande Dame's own withered and unused conscience to the side.

Never squander resources, Valéncia insisted. *Nico is your best resource. And your second-best is the fact that he* has *been your little spy. That is a weapon you could deploy at any time. Amelia gets* nothing.

You mean Starr.

They're the same thing.

So Fiona kept her mouth shut. In any case, if her latest plan worked as she'd hoped, it would mean Starr would exit the moment the next Gate appeared.

"You OK there, Fee?"

She waved Nico off, reeling from the force of Valéncia's malice. Not for the first time, Fiona imagined herself in the front car of a roller coaster ride, ascending a steep incline. The gears were turning. It was too late to disembark. She had to see things through.

"I am well," she said. "But I have one further request of you. Something you can do without twitching a muscle."

* * *

JASON FISHED A Red Vine loop from a jacket pocket, twirling it on one finger. It was his last: he'd have to ask Starr to ferry more over soon. Delighting in the awful artificial cherryness of the candy, he scanned the set. Mav. Starr. Celtis and the other cameradryads. Wills in place. Even Griz, who was rarely seen outside his props department, was lurking nearby. Apparently, the ogre had spent a lot of time finishing up this set for the afternoon, personally maneuvering an oversized wardrobe into the warehouse office.

"Fits," had been the only explanation he'd given, while securing it to one of the walls with a rope. Jason let the mystery stand. The ogre was their prop master and set designer—who was he to say it looked out of place?

Jason continued scanning: Fiona was missing in action. As was Nora. They had only two more scenes to film today, and then he could call it quits. But everything seemed ready to defeat him; nothing was on time, the actors were fractious, the sets fragile and wobbly. He envied Cris in that moment. Lucky pombero was probably still taking it easy in Atlantis. Sure, he'd been MARBLEd there without consent—an impulsive move Jason now regretted—but it was hardly a banishment. Perfect blue waters surrounded the hidden land, full of merfolk ready for the frolicking.

Running the show without him was not as easy as Jason had anticipated.

The stage doors swung open, and someone lumbered through with the grace of a Taurus. The Wills swiveled to light the way for Nora in her new costume—a suit packed with inflatables designed to more than double her girth. Her angular face remained all Nora, but the rest of her looked like someone had tried to duplicate Beatrice and pack them both into the same set of coveralls.

"You're radiant." Jason took her hand and led her to the set.

"I'm as big as Griz!" she moaned. "I'm hot and this is all about wanting to humiliate me!"

"Not everyone thinks a few extra pounds are humiliating," Starr fired back.

"Some of us rather like it," Mav nodded.

"Enough." Jason squeezed Nora's hand. "Does this mean I'm hearing the magical words, 'Put me in a coma, Jason'?"

"Argh!" Nora threw her hands in the air. "Fine! I'll pretend this is a totally normal human reaction to a *bee sting*."

"Must've been a bee the size of a longhorn," noted Mav.

The idea had been Starr's, and initially had seemed to placate Nora—a rare enough happening—plus, it required hardly any rewrites from Emma. It would sideline Nora a bit, but not as much as the alternatives. Her belly could grow within the so-called 'allergic reaction,' and they could reduce the number of inflatables over the next couple of months. Or however long it took humans to gestate.

"Take your mark," said Jason, and Nora shuffled away slowly. He sighed. Jason hated not loving his job. He wanted to get excited again about what he could wear to show off around the set, outfits that would earn him admiration and curious questions. He wanted to be intrigued by Emma's beautiful stories. He even wanted to bicker with Cris again. But he was—to turn a mortal phrase—fried. His focus now was how in less than two hours he would get this last scene done, then go off for the longest, farthest, most exhaustive run his office glamour had ever managed.

"Et voila!" Fiona sashayed onto the stage, trailed by brownies. One handed her the lion's head cane, while another fitted a black feather boa over one shoulder.

"Nice makeup," Starr noted.

"It is, my dear, possible for even I to accept constructive criticism," said the Grande Dame, whose face looked like she'd joined a military force, all speckled in greens and tans. "Jason, darling, we may begin."

"Really, Fiona?" Jason rested his hands over his heart. "May we?"

"Mais oui!" She pinched his cheek. "Let the festivities begin!"

"Right!" Jason clapped his hands. "Let's walk through this scene, my dears. There are a few... moving parts."

Fiona snickered.

Starr shot her a look, then snapped to attention. *Ignore her. Get along.* She had promised Jason she would do better. And she did need to know what he wanted from her in this scene: blocking had been dispensed with this weekend. Jason took Fiona, Mav and Starr—Nora was due up next sequence—around a cozy office set, meant to be situated on the third floor of Shadow Oak's industrial warehouse district. Components: metal desk, dinged file cabinets and, to Starr's surprise, a giant half-dresser, half-wardrobe that had no business being there.

"Um, are we sure this is in the right place?" she whispered to Mav.

He raised an eyebrow. "Must hold all the widgets this company makes."

"Widgets?" But Starr waved the question away. She needed to let the mythics do their jobs. If Griz and Jason wanted a giant honking wardrobe full of whatever widgets were, they would get it and she would make it work. She was making a genuine effort not to be a pain in the ass.

"You three will have broken into the offices of ABC, Inc.," Jason was explaining. "Valéncia's chief rival in the fiercely competitive world of—"

"Widgets," said Starr.

"Indeed." Jason beamed at her. "You have been paying attention."

He gestured around the room, and she tried seeing it through Sam's eyes. It was rough, with unfinished wooden walls and exposed pipes shooting out steam. The office had a single window leading out into—well, nowhere, but theoretically an airshaft Mav, Fiona and Sam would have scaled. Starr appreciated the change from all the over-decorated mansion sets, but it was a stellar example of Emma's writing being a little... basic.

Joseph had been a writer. He'd written tales that sent characters out on spaceships. She wished she'd been able to brainstorm with him. All those ideas, those worlds, packed into one great mind: writers could be sexy beasts. Starr glanced into the darkened stage area and met Nico's eyes. She wasn't even sure why he was there—he was done shooting his scenes today—but he gave her a small wave, and a wink.

Starr nodded back and patted a pocket that contained his note.

"Starr, please." Jason's voice pulled her back to reality, and she leaned against the wardrobe so he could pass by. The furniture rocked just a bit behind her but held in place. She peered around the side: a reassuring rope secured it to the wall.

"All good?" Jason clapped his hands once more. "Places!"

Mav shoved his sides into one of the wardrobe's drawers and they took their marks next to the window leading out to the airshaft.

The slate snapped.

"I wish I knew why you two dragged me here," Valéncia said, waving her cane around the room. "I have far better things to do than ruin my complexion and spotless arrest record by breaking and entering into my competitor's headquarters."

"Well, Bea can't be here," said Mav. "On account of her terrible allergic reaction."

"She said the widget recipes were in the office," Sam explained, and Starr ad-libbed: "Apparently it's a *hive* for stolen ideas."

Valéncia—or was it Fiona?—stiffened, which was not called for in the script.

Mav suppressed something between a laugh and a groan at the bee pun. "Let's get searchin'," he managed in a strained voice. "I got the file cabinet."

"I shall begin here." Valéncia settled in the swivel chair behind the desk.

Starr took a beat: according to the script, Valéncia was supposed to help them search the room, not a particular piece of furniture. But if Fiona was in the mood to wing it, Starr could *yes, and* her all afternoon. There was only one other searchable item—the wardrobe—so Starr turned. "And I'll go through the executive's drawers."

Nico's muffled laughter filtered over from off-camera. Starr blushed. "Or something like that."

Sam reached for a drawer, consciously avoiding the one Mav had tucked his sides into, and gave it a tug. It stuck fast. She tried another, but—no movement. "Having a little difficulty here," she ad-libbed.

"Try harder!" Valéncia barked. "Where's your moxie, girl?"

Another made-up line. Starr put Sam on full blast and lifted a booted foot, pressing against the dresser. Using both hands, she pulled hard on a drawer handle, which gave about a quarter inch. Another tug and another quarter inch.

The entire cabinet tottered, like a tooth gone loose in its socket.

The Wills fluttered, strobing.

The cabinet rocked on its legs.

The Wills went dark.

The entire stage fell into blackness.

"Hey," Starr began, but many things happened all at once. A large, heavy object thudded squarely on her chest, buckling her knees. *The dresser! Falling! But—it's tethered!*

A scent of lavender and linden tree drifted nearby.

"Oh, my!" Nora's twang, strangely close to Starr's ear, surprised her. How had she moved so quickly to the stage in that outfit? She wasn't even in this scene. "Look out!"

Starr shoved hard against the dresser, trying to slide out from under its angle, but her jacket caught on a handle. A wardrobe door smacked against her head. A drawer slid out and thudded onto her boot, sending bolts of pain up her ankle.

A high, metallic clang rang out, followed by a muffled *thwack* and a dull, sawing sound.

Move, her brain screeched, but while one foot was on fire from the drawer, the other seemed glued to the floor. She was losing ground with the dresser, which bore down against her outstretched arms. It would flatten her in a matter of seconds.

Come on, she imagined Sam telling her. Sam, her old self, her old name, surging up in this moment of desperation. *Mango time.*

Starr yanked with all her might, hearing the jacket rip. One foot landed in the fallen drawer, which skidded. She lost her balance and pinwheeled, still attached to the dresser, which was about to crush her. Everything seemed inevitable now. She couldn't help herself anymore.

And where the heck was everyone?

"Help!" she tried to say one last time, thudding her fist on the wooden dresser. The sound was thin and raspy with fear. "Hel—"

But the world collapsed then, squeezing the breath from her, replacing all sound with an enormous splintering crash. The darkness got darker. She couldn't take in a breath. She was under the wardrobe. Under the world. It was like being buried alive.

Just before she lost consciousness, she thought, *Being the mango might not be enough to save you.*

CHAPTER 20

Starr Wars

"TWENTY-SEVEN HOURS without me and this show falls apart!"

Starr could smell Cris before she opened her eyes; even when he wasn't smoking, he carried a scent of autumn and cloves wherever he went. Right now, she was also getting a whiff of salt brine.

Cracking her lids open a smidge, she caught Cris pacing across a hospital room floor. He was hunched over, hands clasped behind his back like an expectant father, heading in one direction. Jason, horns extended and tail fluffed, was headed the opposite way.

"Goose eyelashes, she'll be out of commission for a week! At least!" Jason worried his well-manicured fingernails. "Maybe a year!"

"Don't get your fur in knot."

"Hair!"

"It's a few measly bruised ribs." Cris paused his pacing and pulled a cigar from a pocket of his Hawaiian shirt, gripping it like a magic wand. "Mortals bounce."

Jason trotted faster, cowboy boots clacking on the tiled floor. "The convention! The rewrites!"

"Tame your tail already," Cris insisted. "I could have been back in ten minutes. I knew this place would circle the drain if I wasn't around."

"You look like you had a nice time."

Cris held out his arms; he was darker than ever. "How's that for a tan? 'Course, calling Atlantis 'lost' is a big lie. It was full of mortals and there were water slides and bars everywhere. I went snorkeling twice and they got pissy because I kept eating the fish on the reef. And have you checked out a human bikini lately?"

"Why bother coming back?"

"They have 'no smoking' signs everywhere!" Cris made a disgusted noise. "Do you have any idea how hard it is to light a cigar under water?"

That doesn't sound like the mythic Atlantis, Starr thought. *I think he ended up at the Bahamas resort.*

Even that much thinking, though, gave her a pounding headache. The last thing Starr remembered was the lights going out, Nora's voice—and not being able to breathe. Passing out. She opened her eyes wider, noting she was now wearing a white, nearly transparent linen gown. She tugged on the neckline, glimpsing bandages encircling her chest and a bruise of some size that ran like spilled wine up to her shoulder. A machine to her left went "boop" every few seconds.

"Practically a scratch," Cris noted, puffing on the newly lit stogie.

Jason folded his arms. "And when was the last time *you* sustained an injury?"

Cris gestured with the cigar. "When I was—well, no. During the war with the elves—OK, not then, either. There was that time the siren caught me with her sister—" He grinned at the ceiling. "Fine, you got me, Smarty Goat.

Never broken a thing. But neither have you."

Flashbulbs of memory went off in Starr's head. Darkness, followed by metal ringing. A particular scent. Nora's voice again. Being lifted and carried and—more darkness.

"You MARBLEd me to a hospital?" she croaked.

The mythics stopped pacing.

A mug with a straw poking from it appeared under her chin, and she drank deeply. "Howdy, little lady," said Mav, the holder of the mug. "Good to see those peepers open."

Starr swallowed. Mav's forehead was creased with concern, but his eyes—chestnut now, with flecks of gold—shone. And hearing that twang was like being covered with a warm blanket.

"You came, too?"

"Everybody did." He gestured with an arm. "Well, most everybody."

Starr squinted into the distance, discovering the hotel room had only three walls. Where the fourth should be stood a de-costumed Nora; a clutch of brownies, each holding a lit vigil candle; Wills hovering in the air; Phil's enormous eyes blinking in the far distance; Jan looking extremely hip in a pair of sunglasses and oversized bag; Dakota bouncing on her toes, eyes sliding from Cris to Starr and back again; Emma, padding in the background, and Nico, paler than she'd ever seen him. No Fiona. No Griz.

The brownies bounced up and down, cheering.

"I'm still at the *show*?" Starr sat up too fast and saw stars. She fell against the raised back of the bed. "On the hospital set? Who undressed me? Who—" She tried to shift and a shockwave of needles pierced her. She gasped, trying to breathe.

"Settle." Mav gestured. "You're doing fine. Loads of

bruises. Cracked rib, probably, or some such. You owe Nora some thanks."

Nora raised her hand. "Beatrice was a nurse for a few years when she first arrived in Shadow Oak. I did research back then. I ripped up the costume to make those bandages."

Great, Nora's sweaty fabric is holding my chest together. Still, it sounded like Starr had been lucky to have her around. She gave the actor a strained smile. But Nora's voice—something came back to her—Nora had said something. Right before the dresser fell.

"Look out!"

Why would she have said that? It was dark; no one could have seen anything, including that dresser crashing down. Starr shook her head. It was too hard to think right now. Instead, she glared at Jason. "What does a person have to do to actually leave this place when there's no Gate? Sever a limb?"

"Sweetie, this has never happened before." Jason leaned over her exposed blue socks. "This is not a usual thing."

"So, in the eight hundred years this show has been going on—"

"Approximately," muttered Cris.

"Not one person has been injured?"

"Try not to get so worked up." Jason shifted around the side of the bed and smoothed her hair. "You're still covered in electricity."

"Shock!" shouted Nora. "Shock! Maybe. And since she's functioning, I'm off to tell the leprecostumers they need to make me new inflatables." She and several onlookers waved, or swirled, into the darkness of the stages. Oleander and a few brownies raced over, candles doused, and deposited flowers on her bed. Oleander shooed the others away and raised her eyebrows.

"Does Starr need anything else?" she queried.

"I think I'm in good hands, Oleander," said Starr, patting her hands. "You can scamper."

The bro darted into the dark, leaving Nico as the only one remaining offstage. He'd been lurking in the shadows, rubbing at his neck, and now approached the bed. "I just—I can't—" he stammered. He set his hand over hers and looked like he might cry. "It's untenable what happened to you."

"What did happen?"

"Wardrobe fell." Jason raised and lowered his forearm in a demonstration. "Came off its moorings."

"Tell it straight, Valentine." Mav refilled Starr's mug. "Danged tether was cut. That's intent. Establishes a modus operandi." He winked at Starr. "Got my detective lingo down pat."

Jason's tail swished. "Perhaps it broke on its own. I am looking into it. Everything is on film."

"Except for the critical part in the pitch dark." Cris puffed his cigar.

"I plan to have a deep and meaningful conversation with our set designer, who was responsible for installing it on the set and securing it."

"Good luck, interrogating an ogre," Cris snickered.

"Well, Griz didn't dump it on her." Nico shifted on the bed. "I was standing next to him when the lights went out."

"The Wills," nodded Mav. "Talk to the Wills."

"They won't know anything," said Nico. "They don't have a mean bone in their bodies."

"They don't have bones," noted Jason.

Starr was silently steaming. They were pointing fingers

at everyone except the most obvious candidate: Fiona. Yet—though she had many powers and talents, so far as Starr knew, physical strength wasn't one of them. Nor was carrying around something that could easily cut through a securing rope. Still, someone had to say the obvious. "Someone told them to turn off the lights," she said thinly. "Someone they'd listen to. Someone who has influence."

Silence fell. The "boop" machine went "boop" a few times. No one spoke.

"Fiona!" she finally barked. "Fiona! Come on, already!"

Jason cleared his throat. "Certainly, everyone on set will be questioned."

Starr tried to fold her arms and discovered it hurt too much, so she balled her fists on the sheets. "Really? That's all I get here?"

Nico seemed even paler now. Even Mav wasn't looking at her.

Quit now, Sam suggested inside Starr. *Get out while you can, before she kills you. It's the smartest move.*

Starr wasn't sure she wanted to be smart, though. She wanted to be right. She glanced around, but no one was budging. A wave of weariness washed over her; she suspected her electricity—her shock—was asserting itself.

"So..." Jason traced a circle on the bed sheet. "How long before you heal?"

"Better ask how *short* she needs," growled Cris. "We've got a schedule to maintain."

"There's no spell you can give me to just—make it all better?"

Mav shook his head. "Not that simple. Cuts are doable. Bones are trickier, and you'll want 'em to mend right. Which means time."

"Monday," said Starr. "I'll be ready to go on Monday."

She knew she wouldn't be a hundred percent, but Starr wasn't going to slack off. That was what Fiona—or whoever was behind this—was counting on.

"Sure?" Mav leaned in.

"I don't need time off." Starr sat up again, ignoring the stabbing pains in her chest. She gave a clenched-teeth smile. "Work the injury into the script. I mean, it's reality, right? Use the footage. Tell the story."

"It's gold," admitted Cris. "You bet your sweet bandages we will."

"Viewers'll eat it up," nodded Jason, eyes bright.

"And that's all that matters," Mav nodded. "How many folks tune in."

Cris craned over Starr's legs to get into Mav's face. "Ding, ding, mortal. You win the prize. Only took you, what, eighty years to figure that out?"

"I knew it a long while back." Mav half-stood, leaning back. "Sometimes, though, I like to pretend we're more than an eyeball-generating machine for mythies."

Starr cleared her throat. She was a bit closer to Cris' armpit than she cared to be; it smelled like a campfire. "Wounded warrior here."

Cris glanced at his cigar, which had fired up green. "That's mythics, human. Don't go being racist."

"All right." Jason held up his hands. "Dial it down. And don't smoke in a hospital, Cris. It's bad luck or something."

"We're not in a hospital!" cried Starr.

Cris puffed thoughtfully. "Thank the gods I returned. I'll take charge tomorrow, Valentine. You go do your"—he waved his cigar—"ogre kaffeeklatsch or whatever and I'll see the scenes get shot."

"Thank goddess," Jason sighed.

The pombero chuckled. "C'mon. We were in the middle of a fight when I was so rudely teleported out." He threw an arm around the faun's shoulders and the pair sauntered from the set. "Don't go trying that again. I'm now armed with my own MARBLE and it's not charged."

Starr was left with Mav in a chair on one side of her and Nico perched on the bed. An awkward silence fell. Mav gave Nico a nod, indicating he should move along, but Nico didn't budge. The theme from *The Good, the Bad and the Ugly* started up in Starr's head. She finished her water with a noisy slurp.

"Right." Mav stood. "Time for a refill. You all right for a few there, gal?"

This was her moment to tell him he didn't have to return. But to her surprise, she didn't want that. Having him here made her feel secure. Just a minute ago, having Jason, Nico, Mav and Cris all surrounding her had been like being warmed by the strength of several suns. Almost worth getting nearly killed by a murderous wardrobe.

Almost.

"Sure." She smiled at him. He was such a gentleman around her, acting like she might break if he didn't keep an eye out. Mav backed away and left the set.

"Is it past seven now?" she asked Nico.

He chuckled softly. "We can't seem to catch a break."

"Part of me wants to say there's an infinite number of other chances," she said. "Part of me says I've shot my last scene." Starr hadn't made any final decisions, but having spoken the words aloud, they had a certain ring of truth. This show was a parade of red flags, and she should listen.

Nico's expression was stony.

"You have something you want to say?" she asked,

as gently as possible. She'd just accused his best friend of trying to smash her, yet he hadn't exactly rushed to Fiona's defense.

He shook his head, staring at the blankets. "I don't have an answer for you, Starr. I saw what you saw, which is nothing."

"But when I said 'Fiona,' you didn't tell me I was crazy."

Nico sighed, worry and pain knotting together in his expression. It was a familiar look to Starr, who'd seen it in Mama's face right before she poured herself another cup of 'medicine.' But he didn't speak.

"I am thinking of quitting." Her insides curled at those words. Could she really do it?

"Ma cheri," he lifted her hand and put on his Roland voice. "I would throw myself into the infinite pit of despair if I thought the marvelous Samantha Draper could be felled by a mere piece of bedroom furniture." He raised an eyebrow. "Shall we sacrifice ourselves together?"

"That would make Fiona happy."

"Who is this... Fiona?"

"Stop it." Starr pulled her hand back. "If you can't be serious with me—if you can't be *Nico* with me—then you ought to go."

Roland disappeared from his demeanor, and Nico immediately began drumming his fingers on the bedsheet. "You're such a strange duck, Starr Weatherby. Why would you prefer a nervous wreck like me to a character I've spent decades sculpting?"

"Maybe I just like being able to tell the difference between real and glamour." She blinked at him and there was a long silence. "You can't fake real, even if you're making a reality TV show."

Nico nodded. "Are you seriously considering tucking tail

and running?"

"What would you do?" She toyed with the sheet. "Somebody does not want me here." Her throat tightened. The more she put into words the idea of not coming back here, of not seeing the faces that had become so dear to her, of voluntarily abandoning the one place that ever made her feel good about doing what she loved—the more it felt like lopping off an arm.

Damnit, she realized. *I'm in love. With this place.*

"You know what happens if you take off before the first year's up."

"The Guide says I lose pretty much every penny I'm supposed to get. But if I'm dead, I won't care much about my checking account balance, will I?"

In fact, what the Guide explained in excruciating detail was the nature of fairy gold: it had to acclimate to the world behind the Veil, so while her bank account would positively overflow each month, only eight percent of those funds would become 'real' money each month. Withdrawing more than that sum every four weeks would lead to those funds evaporating the moment she walked out of the financial institution, which was referred to as a Leprechaun Storage Facility in the Guide. If she quit, or was fired, only eight percent total would remain. Why eight? Why ask for any form of logic from this side of the Veil?

"Starr, no one wants to kill you."

"Evidence to the contrary." An odd thought occurred to her then: Amelia might not be misplaced at all. Amelia might be dead.

Footfalls in the darkness neared as Mav approached with a fresh mug and straw, plus a pitcher of water. A thick sheaf of papers stuck out from under one arm.

"This won't happen again," said Nico.

"You can't guarantee that." Starr gave him a hard stare. "Not unless you know what caused it in the first place."

He set a hand over his heart. "I solemnly swear this will never happen to you again." He withdrew a green MARBLE from his pocket and set it on the side table. A blue swirl danced inside. "Use this tomorrow, if you're up for it. One o'clock."

That would be tricky timing; Dakota was expecting her in the lobby at three. Starr decided she'd make it work. "Where are we going?"

"Outside." He raised an eyebrow. "Mythic outside."

"And here we are." Mav set the pitcher down and handed over the mug, then dropped a stack of scripts on the side of the bed. "Well?"

Nico rose. "Tomorrow, then." He hurried away from the set. A moment later, the doors closed.

"Something I said?" Mav slid back into his seat, taking some of the scripts onto his lap. "Hope I wasn't interrupting anything."

Starr raised an eyebrow; this was the most disingenuous she'd ever seen him be. "Mav—do you love this place?"

He leaned back in his chair. "Never thought 'bout it. What's the mumbo-jumbo? I'm in a co-dependent relationship."

"How so?"

"The longer you're here, the less you want to leave. And then the less you can leave. This place has a way of erasing what's important on the other side of the Veil."

Starr nodded. Already much of what made up her daily life on the other side paled in comparison to what she was doing every day at *Tune in Tomorrow*. Her apartment was just a place she slept, and sometimes, not even that. Her friends were wondering when they would get to see her again and asked all the time about her secret project. What was that like after decades? "So why stay? How do you make it work?"

He rubbed his face, then got up and walked around the set. "I'm not the fella to ask. I've just been limping along for a bunch of decades. See, I was married when they first hired me. You try and tell your wife—who knows you're an actor all the way through—that you've got this job you can't talk about. And no, she can't visit the set. And no, you can't even bring her pictures of it. Further, she can't see the finished deal. Stephanie thought I was working blue."

"Blue?"

He glanced away. "Nudies."

"Oh!" Starr sat up straight and her side jolted with pain. "Ow. You mean porn."

"That's not what polite folks called it in my day." He returned to sit on the edge of the bed. "Maybe that's what split us in the end. Or maybe it was how I kept lookin' like the far edge of thirty, and she didn't—not after twenty years. Steph was a real linear thinker. So I did bring her here once. Showed her around. Introduced her to everybody. And of course, like I knew they would, they wiped her memory of it the minute she stepped through the Gate. I came back the next day, same as usual and had this flash: everybody was in costume, and we were just a bunch of children playing dress up. But I did stay. I picked the place, not the woman. She left me a year later."

"I'm sorry, Mav." Starr rested her hand on his. He stared at the contact, then back into her face. "Thing is, I don't want to quit. I want to fight for my job."

Face it, Sam piped up. *You're not going anywhere.*

Sam was right. But this wasn't about Jason. Or Nico.

Or Mav. It was all of it—all of them. She wasn't going to throw away this chance.

Mav turned his hand around and gave hers a squeeze back. The soft press of his fingers calmed her. "Thing is," he said, "it's kind of fun to keep play-acting. Maybe it's not so bad, being a bunch of children telling stories after all."

Starr's resolve felt renewed. Mav was here. He'd stayed when everyone else left. He was a good man. "Hand over my pages, please," she instructed. "Let's read some lines."

CHAPTER 21

We Are All in the Gutter, But Some of Us Are Looking at the Starrs

Starr held the green MARBLE Nico had given her up to the lobby light. The blue swirl inside reacted, creating a tiny tornado of excitement inside. "How does it work?" she asked Phil.

The dragon took a slurp from his gallon of sriracha—which Starr had hauled through the Gate from a warehouse in Queens a week ago—and burped the scent of barbecue grill. "Something to do with your hands," he said. "I don't think you swallow it."

"No, I'm pretty sure it's hands," she said. "Can you tell where it goes?"

Phil squinted at the tiny bauble. "Pretty little patch of green. Might even look familiar. If you run into Kyle, tell him I said his mare smells of elderberries."

Starr raised an eyebrow, then palmed the MARBLE. It was time to go. She downed the rest of the special tea Oleander had been making for her each morning since the wardrobe incident—it masked most of the soreness of her healing ribs—and took a breath. "Now, don't forget about the message for—"

214

"Dakota." He gave her a talon-up and went back to slurping.

Starr thought she had things under control: Nico now, Dakota two hours later. Both at the same MARBLEd green patch. She was certain Dakota would be grateful to escape the sterile confines of the studio after nearly three days; Starr herself was feeling like a shut-in. She'd had to take things carefully: her bruised ribs hurt if she breathed too hard, and she walked with the speed of an old lady. But the call of the outdoors—particularly mythic outdoors—was a siren in her ears.

She stared at the MARBLE one last time, curling her fingers around it as she'd seen the other actors do. "So, you just close your hand and—"

"—WHOA."

Starr appeared instantaneously on a rambling, grassy knoll that was far beyond a 'patch.' Her insides jolted, like she was in a plane that had lost altitude. A cotton candy-scented breeze ruffled her hair, and she shaded her eyes from the bright sun above. In the distance, a spire and crenellated fortifications poked from a stand of trees. Nearby, a pond surface sparkled with reflected sunlight.

She knew this place.

Central Park? It certainly looked like it. Or... maybe a heightened version of the legendary New York green space. *Mythic Central Park.* And only a dragon could consider it 'little.'

The expansive grass was perfect, every soft blade an unblemished shade of green. They shifted colors when she brushed her hands over the tips. Starr gazed into the cloudless azure sky, which was broken by two swirling, dancing wyverns. They were singing.

"Dashing through the snow," cawed one.

"In a one-horse open sleigh," the other picked up the line.

"O'er the fields we go?" Starr couldn't help but fill in the next part and giggled. Wyverns singing holiday carols. Well, Nico had promised something special.

Speaking of which, how did one find a Nico in a haystack in this Central Parkiest of Central Parks?

As if in answer, the earth rumbled. Shook. Did some jazzy moves. Starr stumbled, and nearly fell: it was like a ten-horse open sleigh was coming her way. Pounding hooves closed in from all sides. Just a few yards away, a gang of shirtless men astride enormous steeds crested a hill and came bounding in her direction. Their long, flowing hair billowed behind and down their backs, joining neatly with their mounts' bodies—

Centaurs!

Very, very *near* centaurs!

Starr waved her hands. "I'm walkin' here!" she shouted, but the din of the hooves and cries of the herd drowned her out. Her legs felt rooted to the spot, so she crouched down, covering her head and braced to be run over.

Silence, followed by soft snorts. A whicker, then a gruff nicker.

Starr released her arms and stared up into the shadows. She'd been encircled by a pack of seven centaurs staring down at her, breathing heavily, sweating. Their bodies were the size of Clydesdales, all sleek and varying shades of chestnut, black and patchy pinto; their male halves came in equally as many shades, and each was toned and buffed to a high, shiny gloss. They smelled like a combination of grass and Axe body spray.

"Hi?" She carefully raised a hand.

"Do you think the small mortal has it?" asked one with short-cropped greying hair and glasses.

"Let's find out!" cried a second, his deeply tanned skin perfectly blending with his horsehair shade, blond mane-hair a striking contrast. He wore glasses, but the lenses had no frames. He lurched forward and grabbed Starr's ankle.

The next thing she knew she was upside down, trying to press her skirt over her thighs, so as not to show off her pale blue underthings to the entire mythic world. "Stop that!" she shouted. "Hey! No manhandling—or horsehandling!"

"I don't see it," said a third centaur in a high, thin voice. A mustached face appeared beneath Starr's, and she had to stop squirming; it was hurting her chest. "Not sure where she'd hide the flag anyway."

"Those fillies are totally kicking our hindquarters," sighed one of the smaller centaurs, folding his arms over a magnificent chest. "Again. We are never gonna win Capture the Flag at this rate."

"I am not hiding anything," Starr barked, about one percent more angry than she was terrified. "Including a flag! And if you don't put me down I will summon my security dragon and he will send you all off to the glue factory!"

Blond mane and glasses appeared beneath her. "You know Phil?"

Starr's eyes widened. "Kyle?"

The world upended again, so that she was right-side up, head spinning. Kyle held her shoulders, then set her gently on the ground. Indignant, she stomped one foot and brushed her skirt.

"You know Phil," he repeated, then gasped. "Wait!" Kyle gazed around the circle. The centaur's eyes were saucer-sized. "I KNOW WHO YOU ARE!"

Kyle's voice boomed so forcefully the circling wyverns paused in their carol. Starr felt her hair wilt.

"YOU ARE SAMANTHANA DRAPER! WE LOVE YOU AND EVERYONE FROM SHADOW OAK!"

Legs flew. Several centaurs reared up. One got so excited he defecated, and everyone had to shift a few yards away. Starr considered trying to escape, but there was that whole moving like an old lady thing. She settled for slowly edging away from the centaurs, who had transformed from considering her a mere 'small mortal' who might be trafficking in game flags to her Biggest Fans Ever. And they were very, very big.

The centaurs hardly noticed she was trying to get away and kept trotting after her. "Sam Draper! What are you doing here?" Kyle asked, clasping his hands in front of his chest. "Is this a Very Special Episode? Are you going to invite us to Shadow Oak, Sam? Are we going to be on the show? Where are all your friends?"

The correction was out before she could think about it: "Actually, my name is Starr Weatherby."

Silence. Blank faces. Twitching tails. Then the grey-haired one grinned. "Of course it is!" He winked. "It's your CODE NAME. You're UNDERCOVER!"

Another round of excited whinnies and snorts, but fortunately no bowel evacuations. Starr opened her mouth to protest—this wasn't on the show, they had to know that—but closed it again. They kept referring to a VSE—the Very Special Episode—the kind of thing she knew only happened once each year, at a convention. But even there, reality was the watchword. Reality kept the show going; Jason was insistent on this point. The viewers had to believe it was totally happening, in one-hour bursts five days a week.

"Riiiight," she said at last. "Undercover."

"On a SUPER IMPORTANT MISSION," the centaur with the high voice added.

"And a VSE!" cried a third.

"Sure," she nodded, the *yes, and*-ing kicking in. "It's part of the VSE." She felt Sam step into her like putting on an inner costume. "Thank goodness I found you all." Starr gazed around at the eager, grinning herd. They'd completely abandoned their game and were now doing the equivalent of live-action roleplaying with her. Part of Starr wanted to forget Nico and Dakota and have adventures with centaurs for the rest of the day. Or week. Or lifetime. But every time she took a breath, she was reminded of why she'd agreed to meet Nico out here in the first place.

Not that she knew where he was—though the centaurs might have ideas. "Shhh! You are brilliant for having figured this out! But this is an Incredibly Secret Mission. Coded 007."

The centaurs quieted, and a few looked over their shoulders with worried glances.

"It is urgent that I find Nic—er, Roland," she continued. "I don't suppose—"

"YES!" boomed Kyle, turning to the others. "I TOLD YOU I SAW HIM. YOU NEVER BELIEVE ME." He lowered his voice when Starr winced.

"So maybe you can point out where he is?" She batted her eyelashes.

"I can do better than that," Kyle grinned.

* * *

"YOU SURE KNOW how to make an entrance," said Nico, fists on his hips, marveling.

Kyle slowed from a canter to a trot, then turned around and knelt so Starr could slide from his broad, sweaty back. She patted the centaur's side and grinned at Nico, positive she was glowing, too. Riding astride a centaur's back had been nothing like riding a horse—there was no bouncing, no jostling, no sense that she could fall off. Her ribs hadn't twinged in the slightest. It had been as if they flew across the field and into this shady glade next to the sparkling pond.

"Kyle, meet Roland. His code name is Nico."

Nico's eyes widened.

Kyle did a little hoof dance, then craned his head to Starr. "I won't tell ANYBODY about the Incredibly Secret 007 Mission," he stage-whispered behind a hand. "Especially not the FILLIES."

Starr suspected that wherever the herd of centauresses was—probably still looking to capture a flag someplace—they'd know everything within fifteen minutes. "Thank you, my brave and trusty steed."

Kyle handed her a small whistle made of an oak branch. "When you need to get back, just use it. You know how to whistle, don't you?"

"I sure do." Nico waggled his eyebrows, Roland-style. "You just put your lips together and—"

"Good! Then you can show her!" Kyle gave both of their heads a small pat and squealed, "Away with me!" And he galloped back into the park.

"Well, that's an interesting way to thread the needle," said Nico. He looked every inch the Romeo, in spotless white trousers and a periwinkle chambray shirt. "Centaurs are not known for offering themselves as transportation."

"Well, he didn't give *Starr* a ride. He gave one to *Sam*."

"Who's, what, undercover as Starr?"

"Exactly."

"Well played. Though it might give Jason a conniption if he knew you'd been talking to the fans."

"You were the one who brought me here! You had to know that was a risk."

He shrugged. "Best to throw you into the deep end. If you failed, we could always say Sam was having a brain aneurysm or something. A dissociative moment. There are all kinds of Band-Aids to cover a bit of awkwardness. You'll see a lot more of that at the convention."

Starr tried to wrap her head around that and gave up. "So, is this Central Park, or *Centaur* Park?"

"Both." Nico gestured her toward the pond, and they stared out over the waters. "Our different worlds stack like a club sandwich and while every version is different, there are a few nexus points, like Central Park. Here, centaurs rule the place." He took her hands. "Close your eyes."

Starr swallowed, the warmth in his touch almost like another centaur ride. The world darkened. A moment later came the rumbling of movement deep underground, like being on the sidewalk when the A train rushed beneath. She opened her eyes. "What's that?"

"Worlds, turning." They resumed their stroll down the path. "Cogs and gears and time and space." He turned. "I'm so pleased you came with me today, Starr. A person can go a little stir-crazy spending all their time in the studio."

Starr wasn't concerned about her mental state—until this weekend, she'd returned home each night and slept in her own bed. But as the months progressed, she wondered why she bothered. Emails? Laundry? Bad TV? Posting on social media when she couldn't even talk about the most important things? (She had tried, but any comments about the show vanished seconds after she posted them.) Who wanted any of those things when you could hang out with brownies?

"I never see you leave," she noted.

"Seven decades in, and there's nothing for me to leave for." He toyed with a leaf. "The world you live in? Your time? Not mine. Everyone I ever knew is either doddering or dead. I visit places like this instead. Maybe you'll let me show you some of the others. When you're a long-timer, most of what we have is time."

Starr hadn't thought about all of that before, what it was like to have infinite time and endless MARBLEs. It all came down to Temporal Arrest, as explained in chapter sixteen of the Guide. From the moment an actor won his or her first Endless Award, they ceased to age for the duration of their employment with the show. Once they left—quitting or being fired—the clock started again. To Starr, immortality was one of those thought experiments you get into with people during all-night drinking sessions. But as she was starting to understand, having the chance to stand still in time didn't prevent the rest of the universe from going on dancing without you. It actually put you out of step.

"You're a time traveler," she realized.

"If so, I'm a terrible one. I travel very, very slowly. You'll see." It was a promise, not a threat. His eyes twinkled.

"Not if furniture keeps dropping on me."

Nico slowed, gesturing at a park bench. "Let's sit." Seated, he clasped and unclasped his hands before looking at her again. "That situation won't happen again. I told you that."

"Other situations might," she said. "Other situations

have. Like... Amelia. Am I wrong?"

"I heard you'd been asking about 'Melia." He stretched his arm across the bench's backrest.

Head airy, nerves jangling, Starr tried to mentally shove away Nico's charms. But it was so much more fun—and tingly in the stomach—to imagine sliding toward him, nestling into his side like they were on a real date. Clenching her fists hard enough to let her nails bite into the meat of her palms, she held steady.

He shrugged. "Tell me what you think you already know."

Starr explained: Joseph the writer. Fiona a likely partner. Amelia, ambitious and young, coming between them. Exit Joseph, exit Amelia. "Only, Amelia was 'misplaced,' I hear," she said. "Which is not the same as 'fired' or 'quit.' And Nora hinted that could happen to me, too. Cris said it was a 'debacle.' Well, I don't want to be Debacle Deux."

Nico leaned in. The scent of olives and sage made her tipsy and hungry. "You've got no reason to believe me, Starr, but I'm trying to balance a few interests here. You're a different soul than we've had around for many moons—including before Amelia. I don't plan to let that slip away so fast." He paused. "Not from the show, and not from me."

Starr searched for the Roland in what he was saying. It was strange to be around him; like the other actors he was part himself, part role all the time. But Nico used Roland like a shield more than everyone else, as if he preferred to hide behind the smooth, charming persona. She swallowed; it had gotten very warm in this shady glen. "Then give me something to go on," she whispered. "Show me I can trust you."

"Nope," he said, and brought his lips to hers. Starr melted instantly, stomach doing somersaults, and she kissed him back. He pressed against her with gentle firmness, insistent yet welcoming, the kiss of a practiced expert. There was no Roland in this gesture, no artifice. That was frightening: if Starr believed for a hot second that Nico really had feelings for her, she might combust. He was too much of a wild card. It was easier to understand and ignore Roland, who was in it for the chase, not the long run. And yet—she was enjoying every second of this. Was that wrong?

When they pulled back, he shook his head a little. "All right," he sighed. "I can feel your wheels turning even when I'm kissing you. I give up—for now. I'll tell you something." He took a deep breath. "Joseph was no saint. His days were always numbered."

"Why?"

Nico crooked his finger and she inched closer. They kissed again and her body turned over, an engine warming up. An A train racing beneath the skin of the city. "Read some of his old scripts," he continued. "Phil knows where they are. You'll see."

"You might just *tell* me."

Nico touched her chin. "You need to find out for yourself first. Then, I'll fill in the gaps. But before you learn anything else about us here, you should learn about Fiona."

Starr pulled away and folded her arms; that was the cold splash of water she needed. "I have a hard time imagining she gets to be a hero in this tale."

"And yet," said Nico, who'd pinked in his cheeks. "Here's the short version."

He explained that Fiona had found him in a bad

place—early 1950s, on the verge of being jailed because he wouldn't fight overseas. A few years earlier he'd had a great gig as a radio personality, which went into the trash after his politics got out. He'd started drinking. He drank some more. He'd been in a bar getting pelted by slurs and beer coasters when Fiona wandered in for a pack of matches. Nico had a lighter, and Fiona had a side-eye that could scatter men twice her size.

Starr understood that part intimately.

"Long story short, once I was on this side of the Veil, I was safe from the draft and local racists." He chuckled. "Canada was an option. I was ready to run there—poutine is a weakness—but Fiona happened first. And once I was here…" He held up his hands.

She wanted to believe his story, even if it put Fiona in a new light. And he told it beautifully, with that rolling, not-quite-affected accent of his. She could listen to his voice for hours.

"Problem was, being over here didn't stop me from wanting—needing—a drink." Nico explained he'd leave on weekends and get blitzed. Then it was weekends and Mondays. Then Fridays and weekends and Mondays. He'd wake up someplace with no idea how he'd gotten there, and once that someplace was Indiana. After he'd skipped an entire week of work, the show was on the verge of booting him for good. Fiona ventured through the Gate and tracked Nico down to a flophouse on the Bowery. A few adventures later, they had him back on this side of the Veil, and Fiona received permission to take a radical step: she gave him one of her prizes.

"Or rather, she loaned it," he said. "Kept the trophy but said I could use the prize. Going Clear, they called it. Anything that might get me high—alcohol, pills, you name it—has no effect while it's mine. I could drink a whole liquor store and still walk a tightrope."

Starr took a deep breath, digesting. Mama could've used a big dose of Going Clear when Starr was growing up, but this was one instance where science was starting to catch up with magic: Mama had been taking some kind of pill for the last few years that apparently quieted the need for alcohol. She wondered if Nico even knew it was an option.

"The downside is if I ever need medicine, she has to take it back," says Nico. "I can't get knocked out chemically. So as long as I'm with the show, I'm sober. It's a... better choice. And I do owe her everything."

Starr crossed her arms. He still hadn't told her about Amelia. "How long?"

"How long what?"

"How long do you owe her?"

Nico curdled slightly.

She pushed. "Like you were saying before. Effective immortality changes things. If someone saves you from yourself—well, that's huge. But do you then owe them back for eternity? Are you ever... discharged from obligation? There should be a statute of limitations."

He remained silent, hazel eyes fixed on her face. Then his gaze flicked over her shoulder. The charming smile faded, and it was like the sun slipping behind a cloud.

Starr shot a look into the distance, then turned back. "What happened? What's going on?"

"Here." He pressed a MARBLE into her hand. "This'll take you back to the lobby." He gave her a quick, hard kiss on the forehead. "Give it a squeeze now. Don't follow me."

He jumped off the bench and jogged down the path,

back the way Starr had come a few moments earlier, and turned a corner.

Bewildered, Starr stared after him, then at the marble, then back down the path. Nico was the damnedest man she'd ever met. And she was *still* in the dark about Amelia! Why was everyone protecting her? Or the memory of her? And why had Nico started his 'long story short' by telling her about Fiona first?

Starr jumped up. There really was a connection, that's why. She had to find out what it was, and soon: Fiona was advancing fast through a playbook of ever-more-dangerous intimidation, culminating with the wardrobe incident. She obviously wanted Starr to volunteer to quit the show, because then it wouldn't be Fiona's fault. But... why? Could she still be so threatened by a newcomer that she'd take drastic steps like...

A second light bulb went off in Starr. This Grande Dame—who Starr had taken to thinking of as the Grande Damn—took decisive action for even perceived slights. If Amelia and Joseph had gotten entangled, Fiona wouldn't do something as simple as drop furniture on the interloper.

Her arms prickled. Maybe Amelia hadn't moseyed after all. Maybe she hadn't been 'misplaced' or quit. Maybe she really was dead, after all. There was nothing about an Amelia Beckenridge, actor, on the internet; Starr had checked. Well, nothing except a review of a performance in *A Midsummer Night's Dream* in a tiny East Village theater in 1988. That was it. Finding one thing was almost worse than finding nothing; it proved she'd been in the world, up to a particular year. Now she was a ghost.

Was ghosthood in Starr's future, too?

Just then, a high, patrician voice rang out. "Nicodemus Reddy, I shall walk where I wish to walk, and I appreciate your not interfering!"

As if thinking about her had conjured her up, Starr was hearing Fiona's voice filtering through the trees—back where Nico had just gone—and growing closer. She was the last person Starr wanted to see right now.

She had a MARBLE. She could use it. But Starr didn't want to run away from Fiona. She wanted answers. She remained next to the bench and fixed her jaw.

Fiona rounded the corner, dressed in every inch like a Gilded Age lady out for a stroll, complete with lion's head cane and wide-brimmed hat. Her red lips parted in an amused smile, eyes burning with carrion.

"Greetings, Ms. Weatherby," said the Grande Damn. "This is quite the coincidence."

CHAPTER 22
Shooting Starr

"*COINCIDENCE*"? STARR'S HANDS began shaking, and she clasped them behind her back. *Coincidence has nothing to do with this.*

Fiona had an uncanny knack for showing up at key moments—and for knowing when to make herself scarce. The diva had been the only regular cast member not to stop by Starr's bed a few nights ago, not even to murmur an insincere 'get well soon' wish. Now here she was, right at the moment Nico and Starr were starting to get close. When Starr was about to hear a few secrets.

"Man, this park is crowded," Starr muttered. The sight of Fiona was making her feel cold. The sight of Nico trotting along behind Fiona just made her tired.

"I am surprised to see you out and about after yesterday's excitement," said Fiona, strolling closer. So that's why Nico had run off so fast: he'd been trying unsuccessfully to head her off at the pass.

"Ah, the bench." Fiona's gaze fell on the seat Starr had just been sharing with Nico. She brushed her gloved hand against the seat and winked at him. "You are so regular with your assignations, my dear."

Starr flushed. Of course Nico invited women out to meet him in the park. Told them his story. Got them all softened up. She was no different. "Hmph, the wood's old and crumbling," she told Fiona, while staring at Nico. "Totally rotten."

He was shaking his head. "You should go," he said to Starr, voice a thin cord stretched too tightly.

"Yes, you should go." Fiona waved airily. "I have so many questions for Nico, you see. I was hoping he would tell me what was so urgent the other night when he came pounding at my dressing room door." She fluttered her eyelashes. "I am terribly sorry Bookender turned you away. He knows better."

Nico paled.

Starr flashed back to her hospital stay. Nico, racing off the set after promising her that Fiona had nothing to do with cascading furniture. He'd run to her dressing room? Why? Then Starr understood. "That wasn't Nora's voice I heard," she told him slowly. "That was *you* on set, warning me to look out. You *knew* she was going to make that wardrobe fall on me."

He let out a long, slow breath. "Yes and no. In that order."

Starr staggered, reaching for the back of the bench, but her fingers slid off the wood and she sank to the ground. Kyle's wooden whistle tumbled from her pocket, rolling into the grass.

"This is precious." Fiona tapped the end of her walking cane on the path in delight. "I love seeing you figure things out, Starr. It's like watching an ape learn sign language."

Starr narrowed her eyes at them both. "So, which of you two cut the rope? I heard it. That sound—like a sword."

Fiona's smile was a mask. "I certainly hope you aren't accusing me. I don't walk around armed for a *duel*."

Nico started to speak, then bit down on it. "You swore no one would get hurt."

"Ms. Weatherby seems unharmed to me. Also, I have no idea what you are babbling about."

As Roland, Nico knew how to regulate his emotions, but as Nico he was a terrible actor. He paced back and forth, then ran his hands through his hair. "I'm such a fool."

The word is 'patsy,' Starr thought, digging her fingers into the soft, muddy ground. Somehow, whenever she thought Fiona had scraped bottom, there was always another level. Right now, she felt like hurling something at the Grande Damn: mud, a rock, a tree. Someone had to show her there were boundaries. Starr's muddy fingers brushed against the whistle Kyle had given her.

"Perhaps," said Fiona. "But you're my fool, Nicodemus."

That did it. Fiona was starting to make her feel sorry for Nico, and all Starr wanted right now was to chew on her fury. Leaping up, Starr jammed Nico's MARBLE and Kyle's whistle in her pocket, then strode to Fiona.

Go on, Fiona seemed to dare her.

Starr smacked her on the cheek. Her hand left a long dirty smudge, and the actor's head rocked back. Growling, Fiona raised her cane to strike, but Nico leaped between them. "Stop," he whispered.

Starr smacked him, too. He clutched his cheek in surprise.

"How dare you," Fiona hissed, dabbing at her face with a handkerchief. "When we get back to the studio, you are *done*. Section eighty-nine of the Guide deals with physical assaults on cast members. And I have a witness!"

For a moment, Starr felt a cold icicle of fear. Had she just gotten herself fired? Or was that an empty threat? Section eighty-nine—what was that? Starr could never get to the end of the Guide. *In for a penny*, she decided. Brushing off her knees, she squared her shoulders. "Go suck eggs, you harpy." And she stuck the whistle between her teeth and blew.

Nothing happened.

She tried again; still no sound. Her face felt hot. *Jeez Louise,* she thought. *Centaur technology sucks.*

"What are you doing, you muttonhead?" Fiona had raised a handkerchief to her cheek. "What is that thing?"

"A stick, apparently." Starr stared at the whistle, wondering what she'd done wrong. Then the earth shifted. Did a little jazz move. Not cogs beneath the earth turning, but the sensation of being in a mass migration. Tree branches rattled. Leaves fell. Birds took to the air. The rumbling grew closer and was even louder than she'd experienced an hour ago.

"What the—" Fiona began, raising a quivering finger to point just beyond Starr.

Nico had an odd, manic look on his face.

Starr turned to find the equivalent of the Kentucky Derby bearing down on her, the herd of centaurs now expanded with the inclusion of multiple centauresses. The fillies resembled their male counterparts, though much of their torsos were encased in leather plates and straps. Several had braided hair-manes that flicked from side to side like living whips.

"SAM DRAPER—I MEAN STARR WEATHERBY— WE ARE SUMMONED!" shouted Kyle, two seconds after they came to an impressive group halt. "HOW GOES THE SECRET MISSION?" He pushed his glasses up on his nose, gaping at Nico and Fiona. "OH, MY SAINTED DAM, ARE ROLAND AND VALÉNCIA HELPING YOU?"

Starr wanted to do a little dance. For the first time in a while, she felt a surge of power. "Outside voice, please, Kyle," she said firmly. "To answer your questions: not so well and not at all."

The herd glanced at one another, parsing those answers. Neither Fiona nor Nico spoke; a quick glance over her shoulder told Starr they'd been stunned into silence. That was delicious all on its own.

"I see no imminent distress," said one red-haired centauress, pawing at the ground. "For what reason have we been diverted from our diversions?"

"I need some... assistance," Starr admitted. Part of her wanted to MARBLE out of here and curl up in her nice, sane dressing room. But running away wouldn't get her satisfaction, not for having a wardrobe dumped on her by her castmates. She had to show Fiona she could make trouble, too. It was time to brazen things out. Be the mango. *Yes, and* them all the way home. "I have to make you all part of the Incredibly Secret 007 Mission."

And there was joy and prancing in Centaur Park. When the herd calmed, Starr pointed over her shoulder. "Back there—see them?"

Two of the centaurs waved at Fiona and Nico, who were starting to come to their senses. "HELLO ROLAND! HELLO VALÉNCIA!" the centaurs shouted.

Gingerly, Fiona waved back with a dirty handkerchief. "Hello, you... all." She turned to Nico and whispered loudly enough for Starr to hear: "I am in no fit state to deal with *fans* right now. I have just been struck!"

"They're not *fans*," Nico stage-whispered at her. "They're part of the story now. Roll with it!"

Fiona pasted a grin on that looked like a rictus. Starr began to panic: she had to seize this narrative *now*. "They look like Roland and Valéncia," she told the centaurs. "But they have been possessed by demons!"

"Demons?" One chestnut centaur folded his arms. "Do *demons* exist in the mortal world?"

"Of *course* they do, you donkey." Kyle swished his tail. "Don't you remember Gregory Blanchard, the heart surgeon? It was only fifty winters ago. Gregory was *elevating* and they called that former 'corcist on him."

Exorcist, I think he means, Starr thought, and nearly broke character. "Precisely!" she cried. "Well, these demons are back. They're inside Valéncia and Roland, calling themselves FIONA and NICODEMUS."

"Now, wait a minute—" Nico cringed as each of the centaurs took three steps forward, providing a protective wall around Starr.

"See here now, my good equines." Fiona's voice trembled. "You can't possibly believe anything this whippersnapper—"

"And they're after me!" Starr raised her voice over the diva's. "They want to eat my brains!"

That'll fix their wagons.

Every pair of centaur eyes widened simultaneously. Anxious murmured whinnies erupted. "Valéncia!" the red-haired centaur stomped a hoof. "She's been such a bad mortal since she dumped Martinique for Zachary!"

"Hush, you don't even remember that," Kyle snapped. "That was before you were even foaled. Anyway, it's not their fault if they're possessed by demons! We will just have to perform our own 'corcism!"

Nico and Fiona were now taking small, careful steps back down the path.

Starr pointed. "They're running away! Very slowly! And they're covered in *mud*!"

"Nothing wrong with a bit of mud," argued one sleek chestnut centauress wearing white socks—actual socks—on her forelegs. She looked like she'd been interrupted during an aerobics class.

Starr gulped. She was losing them. And then she remembered she didn't have to make everything up. Unbuttoning her dress top, she rolled down one side to reveal the bandages covering her chest and abdomen. "This is Valéncia's fault!" she projected "And Ni—I mean, Roland assisted!"

Kyle's eyebrows shot up so high Starr thought they might fly off his head. Behind him, the rest of the herd pawed long brown tracks in the perfect grass, which grew back immediately. "WHEN WAS THIS EPISODE?"

"Er, you'll find out soon. Tune in tomorrow and all that. But meanwhile—"

The centaurs bent forward in a huddle over her head, resting their hands on each other's backs. They whinnied softly, nickering between each other, with the occasional English word. At last, with a satisfying slap of hands, they straightened and faced the actors, who'd nearly vanished around a bend in the path.

"Run!" Nico told Fiona, and their reverse gait became full-on flight.

"Ha!" Kyle pointed, and the centaurs pounded away in hot pursuit. Starr coughed at the dust stirred up in their wake, then discovered Kyle had remained behind. He kneeled. "Climb aboard again. I shall whisk you to safety while my herdmates take care of this."

Feeling a dizzying sense of power, Starr clambered above his broad back, grasping his mane. It was the softest hair she'd ever caressed on another creature, and she bent her face into it. The humans she'd hung out with today had all been monstrous. But the mythics had been some of the best people ever.

"We ride!" cried Kyle, launching into a gallop. Starr raised her head and let out a whoop as they flew over the ground, the ride once again impossibly smooth. After a few moments, Kyle rounded a hill and scrambled to the top of a rock formation where they could overlook a grassy expanse. The centaur herd had caught up to their prey and was slowly encircling them, bows and arrows at the ready. Starr couldn't hear Fiona, but she did see her waving her cane around.

Meanwhile, the altercation had drawn the attention of several groups of mythics Starr had noticed earlier while flying across the park astride Kyle: book-reading gryphons, sunbathing elves, foraging trolls. Now, they hurried toward the herd, curious.

Starr liked to imagine that Fiona and Nico were reconsidering every decision they'd made in their over-long lives. She wanted to see them feel some of the fear she had while trapped under that wardrobe. To know what it was like on a daily basis to not know which tripwire was going to knock her over next.

But there were other emotions roiling in her, too. As angry as she was at Nico, and as much as she hated the Grande Damn, she did not want them killed, or even seriously injured. How to maintain the illusion of the show while teaching them a lesson? She hugged Kyle's withers, trying to sort it all out.

"Are you troubled, Starr-Sam?" Kyle had craned around.

She sighed. She felt guilty for lying to his face. It was one thing to make a TV show everyone thought was reality—and another to continue the artifice in person, with someone who truly believed.

"Kyle," she admitted, "I have a confession to make."

"None is required, Starr-Sam. You are safe."

"But—"

He held up a hand. "The Veil is a fragile thing. Almost as fragile as mortals. It takes constant vigilance, and constant belief, to keep it from turning into nothing more than cold dragon smoke. There's no need to dispel it further."

Starr gaped. "So… you know?"

"What is there to know?"

"That—I mean—" She swallowed. Jason would kill her if she spilled. The show might crumble. If nothing else, she'd be out of the greatest job she would ever have.

A soft hand rested on her lowered neck. "Centaurs love games," said Kyle. "We play Capture the Flag every day." He turned toward the field. "We also love the games mortals play, and *Tune in Tomorrow* is the greatest game of them all."

Starr sat up. Had she heard him right? Did they know it was all made up? Could she risk asking? "What if it's not real, though?"

"It is real *enough*," he said. "Of course, some mythics take it too seriously. There is an entire morning devotion among trolls dedicated to Valéncia and her enduring… well, Valéncia-ness. A small cult of Russian Kikimora relocated to real-world Oklahoma because it is Mav's homeland. But do I not understand correctly? Do you mortals not spend most of your waking hours making this real-not-real show?" He raised an eyebrow. "It is your reality. And so, it is real enough to us."

Starr wondered at him, trying to process. The centaurs were fans not of Emma's stories per se, but of the fact that the show *existed*. That human stories, like mythic lives, could be made to last forever. She'd underestimated the depth of thought a horse-man could have.

"Fiona actually did hurt me. That's real-real."

"Then she will pay."

"They won't be killed, though, will they?"

"Nothing to fear." His mouth quirked up. "I will ensure they are released after a thorough… rumpling."

THUS FAR, STARR had not witnessed much in the way of talent when it came to Dakota Gardener, other than having very shiny hair and the ability to lose track of her clothing in the presence of a pombero. But Dakota turned out to have two specific skills after all.

One, interviewing her subjects. Two, getting those subjects drunk.

Or maybe she put in a special effort for Starr, whose mind was spinning with everything she'd seen that afternoon, and who sorely needed a good slug of something alcoholic by the time Kyle deposited her next to a red-and-white checked picnic blanket where Dakota sat.

"You—a centaur—riding—" Dakota gawped as Starr slid from the creature's broad back.

"That about sums it up," said Starr, offering Kyle a friendly wave as he galloped away. "Please tell me you brought wine."

Approximately an hour later, Starr's head was spinning in a new direction, and Dakota had clearly joined her. They lay flat on the blanket, staring up at the wyvern-speckled sky, drunk as yaks.

"Do yaks get drunk?" Starr giggled. It was an amusing notion.

Dakota swept her arm to the air, upsetting a plate of cookies. "If they don't, they should. It's fun." She pointed at a cloud. "That one looks like Fiona's face."

"Ugh." Starr cringed. "Don't go spoiling the sky." She paused. "And that's off the record."

"Of course."

Meanwhile, Alligash—introduced to Starr as the Bro of Record for the interview, meaning that he would memorize everything said during their conversation for later transcription—scurried around the edges of the blanket. He picked up the now-emptied food containers Dakota had brought for high tea: crustless sandwiches, sweet lavender-scented shortbread, crispy rainbow-colored macarons and a basket of warm scones. He asked if either of them would like brownie tea, to offset the wine.

Starr nearly told him to open another bottle but paused. If tea was over and the sky was starting to darken, how long had they been here? With mere minutes before they were to wrap up, all she could imagine was the reporter's pretty face nodding along eagerly with every grand statement Starr had made. That afternoon, Starr had felt very sure of what she was telling Dakota—but the wine mixed with her pain medication, paired with the loopy encounter with Fiona, Nico and a centaur herd was apparently inducing temporary amnesia.

Clearly, I've been quite marvelous, she decided, then slurred something to the same effect. Wyverns spun overhead, and she closed her eyes.

"Indeed you are," Dakota agreed. "This interview is marvelous. Wine is marvelous."

"You two are marvelously out of your heads." Alligash tucked away the empty bottles. "Humans are such

239

lightweights."

A shadow passed across the sun and stayed there. Starr opened her eyes and flinched: the Grande Damn loomed over her, looking as if she'd passed through an ivy-covered wind tunnel in a convertible at autobahn speeds. "We have a visitor," she whispered, feeling extremely vulnerable and unmarvelous all at once.

Dakota, who'd begun to drift off, jerked to attention and bolted up. Starr tried to rise on her elbows, but the world swam.

"Oh, don't stand for me, Ms. Gardener." Fiona scowled, scratching her wrists. "I wouldn't wish to interrupt your little soiree."

"It's for the magazine," Dakota spluttered. "The one we talked about?"

"Hush, you simpering nitwit," said Fiona.

Dakota quailed. "I should go," she squeaked, and grabbed Alligash's hand, closing her fist around a MARBLE—then vanished from the park with a soft 'pop.'

Starr couldn't suppress a wicked grin. "Did you have fun with the mythics, Fiona?"

Nico staggered into view, as disheveled as Fiona. A twig stuck up from his curls. His periwinkle shirt had torn at the sleeve, and he had no shoes on. "Do you have any idea what they put us through?" he screeched. "We were tied up with poison ivy vines!"

"Fortunately, Nico talked sense into those crazed beasts." Fiona tugged at her cuffs, trying to hide the red blisters that had already formed. "It was wise of him to suggest we could be 'cured' of our apparent 'madness' at Shadow Oak General Hospital."

"Pretty smart for a fool," blurted Starr.

Nico's outrage turned to genuine anger. "We were

supposed to be on set twenty minutes ago! Don't you think they might be wondering where we've gone?"

"The minute you freed yourselves you probably could have MARBLEd back," Starr observed. "But it must have been much more satisfying to march over here to berate me."

Still, something he'd said snagged in her like the twigs in his curls. *Jason would wonder where his actors had gone. This misplacing actors is probably very bad form.*

Amelia had been misplaced.

And in that moment, Starr knew with the conviction of a drunk yak that it was definitely Fiona who'd done the 'misplacing.' And not just misplacing: Fiona had killed Amelia, then disappeared her body. It was the only explanation. That meant Starr no longer had to worry about whether she'd lose her job if she continued to antagonize the diva. It meant she might lose her *life*.

Swallowing, Starr struggled to her feet. As much as she hated doing it, she held out her hand to Fiona. This was her only card left to play. "Truce?"

Fiona's face twisted. "After what you did to me? Ha! I will end you, missy!"

"Enough." The anger was gone from Nico, and he only looked tired. "Shake her hand."

"Traitor," Fiona growled. "You've always been weak for—"

"Cookie," he said, the nickname a bludgeon. "Take. Her. Hand."

Starr waited. She had nothing else to offer. The last thing Jason needed on top of everything he was trying to do for the show was to have two of his actors approaching him with outlandish tales of centaur kidnappings and sabotaged furniture. He might take action against Fiona, but he probably wouldn't. He couldn't risk penalizing her—she was too powerful, and too important to the show. She was worshipped by trolls, for goodness' sake. It stuck in Starr's craw to do this, but she kept her hand outstretched.

Not that she was done investigating the Amelia matter, of course. Even on this side of the Gate, murder had to be a one-way ticket to a pink slip. But she couldn't get anything accomplished if she was constantly monitoring whatever Fiona had up her sleeve next, beyond poison ivy.

"Truce," Starr repeated.

A gentle squaring of her shoulders, a lift of the chin, and Fiona became Valéncia. Months ago, Starr wouldn't have noticed a difference, but now she knew better what it meant to truly become a character—or have the character become you. "I see," said Valéncia. "We shall call this... a draw."

"Sure." She jiggled her hand. "No tricks. Working together. Cooperation."

Valéncia's mouth spread into a thin smile, but her eyes remained cold. She squeezed Starr's hand tightly. "Accepted."

"And I'm the witness," said Nico. "Again."

There was a long, heavy pause in which parts of Starr relaxed for the first time in months. The trees looked sharper. The sound of wyverns singing in the heavens was purer.

"With that sorted," said Nico, "anyone have a plan for how to get back to the studio?"

"Nicodemus, did you neglect to bring a return orb?" Fiona raised an eyebrow.

"Must've fallen out of my pocket. You know, when I

was being dragged through the grass." He fixed his gaze on Starr.

She reached in her pocket, prepared to reveal the MARBLE he had given her, then thought again. "Guess I lost mine, too." She kept her eyes wide and face blank. "Centaur riding and all."

Fiona sighed with a grand, put-upon sound. "Very well, then." She revealed a MARBLE from a small shirt pocket. "I shall transport us all. Hold on to a hand. Or a shoulder. Or don't." She gave Starr a superior look. "I always carry a spare, you know. For just such emergencies."

For once, Starr thought that was a very smart idea indeed.

CHAPTER 23
Diamond Starr Halo

EIGHT SEELIE—UN- and original Recipe—ringed the SCN conference room, relaxing on body-conforming clouds surrounding a frosted glass table shaped in undulating waves. A constantly looping waterfall made a gentle shushing on one of the otherwise blank, off-white walls. It was the largest gathering of Seelie Court Network Executive Vice-Vice-Vices—known colloquially as The Powers That Be—that Jason had ever faced.

This meeting is Seeliously serious, he decided.

Slowly, he removed his sunglasses and squinted. Protection was usually a necessity in the presence of the Fae creatures, who glowed like LEDs: a harsh, cold light that was as blinding as it was attractive. In a few moments, his vision adjusted, and he could make out an array of skin and hair colors around the room, all of which were, as ever, sheer perfection. Not a strand of hair blew out of position, no one had an asymmetrical feature or body part.

Gods, were they boring.

Not that Jason would even hint at such heresy. He

knew spending time among beautifully imperfect humans would warp his perception over time, and he had learned to prefer the random dings and imbalances that decorated mortals. Seelie uniformity was tiresome, and they were all fruit from the same fairy family tree.

A single Seelie rolled forward in an elevated chair. "Céad míle fáilte," she wished him graciously, clasping her hands with his. A folder of charts and numbers Jason was clutching tumbled to the floor, and as he stooped to pick it back up, he caught a glimpse of shapely, iridescent scaled legs. Perhaps this Seelie was more accustomed to water than land.

"I am"—here she offered her own True Name, a combination of bubble sounds and vibrating gill slits— "and I am the Supra-Executive-Vice-Vice-Vice President of Mortal-Based Entertainments, Programming Division of Reality Series, Modern." Most creatures would need to take a deep breath after such a pronouncement; this one could inhale through those gills and speak simultaneously. "Pleased to make your acquaintance."

"Likewise." Jason glanced around the room; as usual, he recognized no one. SCN heads changed positions nearly as frequently as they changed the weather. Fae liked being in charge and collected titles as a hobby but had little patience for work.

"I hear there was a bit of an… incident in the lobby on your way in," said the SEVVVP.

Jason stretched his smile a little wider. He'd erred by not confirming the latest fashion trend before arrival; it had turned out that last year's au naturel trend had given way to head-to-toe diamonds that made everyone look like giant prismatic disco balls. They'd made him change into a fluffy white bathrobe embedded with thousands of gems, the weight of which made Jason sag. He shrugged with effort. "All's well that ends."

"Well," the SEVVVP said.

"Well, what?" Jason wasn't sure what she meant.

"Well. Ends well."

"Are we playing a game?"

Rolling her eyes, the Seelie spun around in her chair and wheeled to the far end of the extended conference table, around which no fewer than twenty other SCN execs floated. A cloud emerged to cradle Jason's backside, and he braced himself. "We've had quite a year at *Tune in Tomorrow*," he began. That much was true: ratings spiked in the weeks after 'Sam' had been temporarily smushed by a falling wardrobe, but overall eyeball numbers rose and dipped as frequently as Nora's mood swings. Last year, the SCN Vices had been clear: shape up, or they might start turning off the Wills.

The SEVVVP held up a delicate hand before he could get any further. "We have parsed the optics and examined the evolution of methodology behind your narrative arcs and collective decisions, and have arrived at the conclusion that your project is in serious need of JOI."

Seelie Corporatespeak was a dialect Jason had never gotten a handle on. "More *joy* on the show?"

"J-O-I," said an Unseelie with silver hair and gold skin. "Jolt Of Imagination."

"Hold on." This was already going poorly. "Emma has been—"

The SEVVVP clicked her tongue. She'd settled back in her chair and was resting her hands in two small bowls of water. "Our personnel records indicate there have been fractious interpersonal interactions among your humans, and after taking a deep dive into your EEC it became clear you are no longer a good ROI."

Jason's blood sank into his heels. They couldn't be pulling the plug on his show; they wouldn't have invited him all this way to do that. They'd just send a couple of jokers to break everything down magically and whisk it away—that was what cancellation looked like. That was not this. But something was definitely up: EEC meant Expected Eyeball Count, and if the EEC was down the show was not a good return on magical investment. "Darlings," he began, and cringed; one did not call TPTB that. "We are on the case. I have big plans for something special at the convention, and—"

"Yes, yes," said the SEVVVP. "But first, please explain this development." She fluttered the fingers of one hand, spraying droplets around the table. "This Bee-Roll was taken some weeks ago."

The Seelie's gesture conjured up two dozen small, soundless images in the waterfall-screen. The pictures wove and hovered like disorganized security camera footage. Jason recognized Centaur Park, then a grassy field, then—Starr, surrounded by a herd of centaurs. His eyebrows rose, as did his horns.

"Do pay close attention," the SEVVVP continued. "This is a high-level view of the occurrence, as Project Drone has only proved partially efficacious. Bees are terribly hard workers but having some of the smaller members of our clan equip each of them with miniature cameras has proven somewhat off-piste and we may need to go back to the drawing board. The silly things never remember to turn them on, and there's a gratuitous amount of inner flower footage. Audio is also proving tricky. Now, if your cameradryads had been on site ..." She trailed off, twiddling her fingers again.

In the frames, which switched viewpoints and angles randomly, Starr was speaking with mythics, though nothing could be heard. Then she was astride a centaur and all but flying across the park. Jason stood up. "She's riding a centaur!" he blurted, then winced. "I mean— she's riding a centaur. Naturally."

"Indeed," said the SEVVVP. "Quite extraordinary."

A new angle: Fiona and Nico being carted away ungracefully by elves and gryphons, then dragged into a grotto behind a rock outcropping and thoroughly rumpled for an extended period. Perspiration began to mat Jason's hair. A new angle showed Starr looking out over the tableau from the top of a boulder, still astride the centaur. Jason felt funny in his gut, and also very hungry.

With a wave of the SEVVVP's fingers—and another spray of water drops—the images vanished.

Jason sat down slowly, body thrumming, and stared hard into the frosted glass of the table. He had no idea what to say, a fact that had only happened to him three times in his life before now. What he knew for sure was this: he'd lost the show. There was no coming back from this—his mortals and those mythics mingling like it happened every day. Which it did not. Except for conventions and special protected MARBLE locations, he kept the actors out of the mythic milieu. Their reality, to mythics, was only supposed to take place on the show. It was a disaster.

"I can't explain," he began. "It happened... organically."

"Of course it did!" The SEVVP slapped her hands on the table, and was so overexcited she had to be misted by a nearby assistant. To Jason's surprise, the other Seelie were grinning. "What we have witnessed here in this footage—which, to be clear, has only been seen by all of us in this room—is a true example of TOTB!"

"TOTB?"

"Thinking Outside the Box," whispered a feathery green Fae to his left.

"It's a brilliant step toward the future," the executive continued. "Immersive action with your audience. Allowing them to help choose the adventure they wish to participate in. Guiding them toward that adventure— by their favorite mortals! We appreciate your innovative experimentation and declare it a tentative success that requires more exploration. Well done—" Here, she spoke Jason's True Name.

The room burst into applause, a sound that generated rainbows on the wall.

Jason felt drunk. The intense need to find out what had happened in the park warred with his desire to lap up the approval, but was overridden by the realization that no, they were not taking the show from him. He hadn't lost it—at least, not to the network. *I might, though, have lost it to Starr.* That would have to be remedied, immediately. But what had happened? Obviously, Starr had MARBLEd to the nexus and made some friends. Had she kept the façade of the reality show alive simultaneously? He thought of the extraordinary gesture that centaur had made by allowing Starr to ride it and suspected she had. His latest human acquisition continued to surprise him, and he thought of seeing her on that stage again as a mango. Then he recalled the magical concept of what she had called *yes, and.*

Well, if a human could do it, so could he. "Yes," he said. "And."

"And? There is more?"

Jason's mind scampered. Emma was the one who came

up with the good ideas; he put them into practice. "And."
He paused again. "And this was just a—test gallop."
He searched for more. "We have more ideas like this
to put into play. One doesn't want to make them too
commonplace. They might lose their... zing."

"Zing indeed!" the SEVVVP cheered. "Which brings us
to the most critical juncture of this meeting."

Flushed with success, Jason leaned forward. *Bring it on!*

"At your upcoming convention, we wish you to film
just such a sequence."

Jason held steady, gripping the table. True, they usually
filmed a full episode while there; it was known as a
VSE, a Very Special Episode. It was a tricky balancing
act to keep the show in reality with the actors running
around the hotel, having adventures and pretending not
to see any mythics they came across. Any mythics who
ended up on camera were carefully edited out of the final
version, which then aired at the winter solstice. It was a
laborious process, but paid off exponentially in eyeballs;
the audience loved seeing their favorites in fresh spaces
and always hoped they *might* have made it into one of the
human escapades.

"We already have a story set up for the convention,"
he said carefully. "There are some explosive revelations
prepared. I am on top of this."

"Naturally," the Seelie nodded. "This is a win-win
proposition. We are merely asking you to TOTB and
include some mythics this time. Dress them up as mortals
if you like but *include* them."

Jason's eyes widened. "But no mythics are supposed—"

"We know the dictum. We invented it. And we are
considering that perhaps it has outlived its usefulness.
But as your hotel VSE always ends up as a dream, or

hallucination, or head injury and so doesn't 'count' toward the show's canonical structure, we have concluded that this is the optimum space for further experimentation."

There was no option. Jason swallowed and nodded.

"*However*"—the SEVVVP leaned across the table—"be advised: your situation with *Tune in Tomorrow* is at a critical juncture. No, perhaps I misspoke. The *show's* situation is at a critical juncture. You need a win here."

"So you want to experiment on a show that you already say is in trouble," he said.

"TOTB," nodded the SEVVVP.

"TOTB," agreed the rest of the conference room.

"To that end, this Central Park Nexus event has given us a further Grand Idea," continued the SEVVVP.

Jason's smile froze. No producer ever wanted to hear that an executive had been attempting to be creative. *Gods save us from network heads with Grand Ideas of Their Own.*

Still, how bad could it be?

CHAPTER 24
Guest Starr

ON THE SURFACE, Phil made sense as a security guard. He was a proper, enormous dragon, theoretically full of fire in the belly and leftover meat in the teeth.

But so far as Starr had seen, Phil was a receptionist. For one thing, his belly fire was mostly a small, flickering flame. "My therapist says I got lack of confidence," he'd muttered to Starr some weeks back in his tractor trailer-sized voice. "I got issues."

One of which was that flame—which meant he'd be more likely to smoke things than scorch them—and the fact that he'd never consumed a human. "Yet," he always made sure to add, third eyelid nictitating over one lightning-bolt pupil. It was meant to be a threatening gesture, but mostly it made him seem like he was winking at Starr.

His 'issues' left him with a smaller skillset and fewer job prospects than most dragons of his size, which meant he put extra effort into guarding the contents of his cave, a jagged rocky opening that burst from the wall behind the reception desk like an explosion and emitted damp breezes.

Starr hadn't expected pushback when she asked if she could go through the archived scripts he held back there. Much had happened in the Central Park/Centaur Park Nexus, but the action item that had stuck with her was Nico's advice to read Joseph's old scripts. She knew they were kept in the cave.

For weeks, Phil had refused her entry. "It's a mess back there," he said. "I don't get visitors."

He hadn't budged when she promised to leave any gold or jewelry alone either; the mere mention of precious valuables had made the spikes on his back rise up, piercing his grey shirt. Sparks had shot from a corner of his mouth.

Starr went back to the drawing board, refusing to give up. The scripts were the one tidbit of useful intel she'd gleaned from that bonkers afternoon in the nexus, and she held onto that thread with both hands as the weeks dragged by. There was no section in the Guide about how to deal with dragons, and back home on her side of the Veil the internet was so chock full of dragon lore as to be virtually useless. She wasn't going to stab him with a lance, and Oleander had no tea that would knock out a creature of that size. Besides, someone would notice an unconscious security dragon if they did that.

One idea with potential came from a web-based cooking show about historical recipes, in which she learned that some dragons could be felled with huge servings of Yorkshire parkin. She made eight trays of the sticky gingerbread cake and hauled them in—and they disappeared down Phil's expansive gullet in less than a minute. He belched and left a smoky stain on the far wall, then went back to being intractable.

Starr was getting desperate. Cessation of hostilities with Fiona had been fresh when she'd first approached

Phil, and they couldn't last forever. She was going to have to find a misdirection that had staying power. Maybe offering Phil something he found irresistible.

All of this assumed Nico hadn't been having her on, providing Starr with her own misdirection. Ugh, *Nico*. He wouldn't come within a few feet of her, except on set— and his sole communication since Central Park had been to send loud, gaudy flowers daily to her dressing room. The card always read the same: *Forgive me.*

Nope, Starr thought each time, handing them over to Oleander to share with other brownies, who ate them with relish, then picked their teeth with the stems. Watching Nico wear his hair shirt was satisfying, and Starr was doing just fine in the silence. She had a new project in Phil.

"Mortals steal from me." Phil slurped sriracha from his mug. "If my possessions are under threat, I can't help myself. It's in the blood. Even if I let you in, I'd *feel* you in there rooting around. And you'd end up mangled or maimed or smoked and I'd end up fired and my therapist would have to see me *four* times a week, instead of three."

Starr shivered. It was like talking to Hannibal Lecter about his favorite recipes.

Phil ran his long tongue around the inside of his cup, lapping up the final drops of the hot sauce. "Sigh. There's never enough."

A small explosion lit Starr up. That was it. Sriracha was going to save the day.

Over the past months, Starr had observed a few interesting facts about the effect of sriracha on Phil the dragon. For one thing, he could sip it by the gallon. For another, it sent him into a blissful, meditative state that reminded her of her brother Bill getting stoned on the couch in their basement back in Maryland. She'd brought in bottles of the stuff from time to time as a gift—but now, she was going to give him more than he could handle. The next day, she cleaned out the Costco warehouse of their supply of the condiment and began importing five-gallon jugs of Señor Sriracha through the portal, stacking them in her dressing room. Three days later, the room had filled with fourteen containers, and Oleander had questions.

"Glad you asked," said Starr. "Because I'm going to need your help."

Oleander clapped her hands in delight until Starr revealed how close she was going to have to come to the dragon. "All you have to do is make sure he keeps drinking," said Starr. She had brought along a series of PVC pipes linked together in a looping, swirling shape to serve as a crazy straw that would slow the draw on Phil's slurping ability. Based on observing the dragon, Starr guessed he'd go through five gallons every two minutes—which would give her nearly half an hour to get in, search, and get out.

"Oleander is not on board with this at all," said the brownie. "Must Ms. Starr do this?"

"Starr must," she said, giving the brownie a hug. "But if you don't want to help, I'll ask—"

"No!" Oleander stood firm. "Of course Oleander is there to help. But Starr must be quick and careful. Yes?"

"Hell, yes," Starr nodded. "I'll be faster than I've ever been before."

With that, they wheeled out the containers in a cart and unveiled them in front of the dragon. "For you," said Starr, waving her hand over the containers like a presenter on a game show.

Phil smoked appreciatively and dropped his magazine.

"For *me*?"

"For... putting up with my endless questions," said Starr. "I even got you a special straw."

Delighted, Phil snatched up the PVC pipe construction in his recently painted talons, stared into it, and began to bounce with excitement. The entire lobby shook. Oleander peered from behind Starr. "Oleander is here to help with the containers," said the brownie, voice weak but steady. "No eating brownies, yes?"

Phil's eyes were wide. He could barely focus on anything other than the bounty of containers in the shopping carts. "No brownie eating. Got it," he muttered. "Sriracha me!"

Starr had plotted this out as best she could. Secrecy was optimal: she didn't want to provoke questions or have someone in charge tell her she couldn't do this. Cris was directing that afternoon, which meant they were bound to start late. Jason was out at a network meeting all morning. She'd convinced the hairies and makeup Fae to do her up early, getting her hair pinned back and held in place, and slid into costume before bringing Phil the goodies. She patted the pockets of her bomber jacket and nodded.

"Don't go." Oleander grabbed onto Sam's jacket. "Too much danger."

"Not if you help." Starr hugged the brownie and took a deep breath, imagining Sam—fearless, game for anything. She shot a quick glance at Phil, who was settling against the outer wall of the cave, eyes fluttering closed as he slid into sriracha bliss.

Her heart was pounding. Time to do this thing. She flattened herself against the cave entrance and tiptoed in like a ninja. Her phone's flashlight app illuminated the dim cave interior, a cool breeze caressing her cheeks. A thigh-high brown shag rug swallowed up her legs and she felt like she was wading through very tall grasses. Though she tried to move quickly, the shag dragged on her. As she passed through Phil's living quarters, she noted a stereo system with speakers the size of refrigerators, a lava lamp with what looked like real molten rock inside, and giant posters pasted on the rough walls for films like *Firestarter*, *The Towering Inferno* and *Lair of the White Worm*.

Abruptly, the sea of shag ended, and the room broke open into a space even more vast and imposing than the lobby she'd left behind. A deep pile of gold coins obscured the floor, illuminating the room with a warm glow. *Fairy gold*, she thought. *Guess they have to store it somewhere.* Starr leaned down to pick up a coin, but jerked back. No point in prematurely waking the beast from his bliss.

On entering the cave, she ran out of plan. She had no idea what it would look like inside, and so had no idea how to start looking for scripts. But that turned out to be the easy part: amid the piles of gold and shining gems stood a series of battered and rusting file cabinets. Some were as tall as Starr; others loomed over two stories high. Drawers hung open here and there, coughing up loose pages and stapled-together script-sized sheaves. It was as daunting as a look from Fiona and Starr sighed, grasping the task at hand. There wasn't enough sriracha in New York City to give her the time she'd need to properly investigate in here. Phil would die of an overdose before she could even make a dent.

A light film of sweat broke out on her forehead. *Well, if it wasn't for dumb luck I'd have no luck at all*, she thought, and began clambering over the coins. Reaching her first file cabinet, she dug through an open drawer randomly. She tossed aside scripts written on parchment paper as too ancient; ditto to those mimeographed in purple ink.

Every so often she pushed her injury a bit too far and had to pause, sipping long, shallow breaths. Oleander's pain-relieving tea was a godsend, but not a cure-all. All along, her heart pounded, and every small sound made her jump.

"Five!" the brownie called down the throat of the cave, alerting her to the dragon's progress. It was the one alert they thought they could get away with while Phil disappeared in his hot sauce fugue. But if he was already on five of fourteen, Starr knew time was running short.

Gritting her teeth, Starr came across plain black typewritten scripts, assuming they were more modern and potentially Joseph's. Each script was its own treasure trove of words and characters long forgotten by writers just as unremembered. She would have loved to read them, but there was no time. She was just looking for one byline.

Nothing, nothing and nothing.

Backing away from the cabinets, Starr tried to assess. Random search was useless. She could have used an extra pair of hands—like, say, Nico's. But they weren't talking. Mav would have been an excellent choice; since the wardrobe incident, he'd been a bright light for her. They spent hours rehearsing in her dressing room, and on set they were plugged into one another's wavelength. If she missed a line, he guided her back; when he picked up the wrong prop once, she'd cued him to the correct one. Mav had become a real friend.

Sometimes, she wished he'd be a little less hands-off. Once or twice she'd nearly suggested they MARBLE somewhere interesting for dinner one night. Talk about anything except the show, like regular mortals. If Mav were here right now, he'd have something sensible to suggest.

Darlin', he'd say, *the thing you want's in the last place you look*. And his eyes would crinkle up at the sides.

The cabinets still loomed, all more or less alike—except one. At the farthest, deepest, back corner of the cave one stood over twenty drawers high. She'd ignored it for now, as it was the last place she wanted to go.

The last place you look.

Well, then. The drawer on this highest of high cabinets, at the tippiest of tops, had a padlock that glinted in the coinlight. It practically screamed: *Don't you dare come over here.*

Starr dared.

Far away, but not far enough away, she thought she could make out the sound of slurping. Of a straw scraping around the inside of a container. A pause and then... slurp. Slurp. SLURP.

"Eight!"

Oleander's voice carried like a clear bell from outside of the cave and spurred her into action. Stumbling across the coins, occasionally wincing, Starr grappled onto the second file cabinet's handle and hoisted herself up. And up. And up. One foot on each drawer handle, five, six, seven drawers. Ten. Fifteen. Glancing down from the top, the floor seemed to fall away from her.

Grabbing on to the top drawer's handle, she gave the padlock a firm twist—and it held fast. "Rats and cats," she muttered. The whole cabinet might have looked eighty years old, but the lock was naturally the most secure part about it. Her back was damp with sweat, and her chest felt like someone had stepped on it. *Focus.* What to do about the padlock? She needed a saw. A set of pliers. A lockpick, at the very least.

Aha!

For her latest escapade as Sam, the hairies had begun

binding her hair back, holding it in place with spells. But Starr preferred to keep a few old-fashioned bobby pins and clips in her jacket pockets, in case she had to adjust on the fly. Reaching into one pocket now, she rooted around. Her fingers brushed the MARBLE Nico had given her in the park—she was taking a cue from Fiona and holding onto it for an emergency—and landed on one of the bent pins. She'd never picked a lock with one before... but it worked in the movies. And surely this place was as fantastical as the movies.

Jamming it into the padlock, she wiggled the metal bit around and around, bending and twisting... and then it snapped in two. Tossing the pin into the coin pile far, far below she reached into her pocket again for a second. Same result. Third time, she grabbed the pin... and the MARBLE fell out.

"No!" Starr shouted, watching the small white orb fall nearly two stories, landing on a fallen script and rolling over the title page. Well, at least it wasn't lost. Staring at her third and final bobby pin, she willed it to behave and eased it into the lock. The half in her hand bent downward into an angle, which gave her a bit more control over the adjustment. A rivulet of sweat traveled down the side of her face. And then—the pin slid home. She turned it and the shackle fell away from the lock body. Tossing the padlock away, she clambered to the top of the cabinet and jerked the drawer open with satisfaction.

Reaching inside, her fingers fell on thick sheaves of papers. Scripts. She pulled one out.

Written by Joseph Abernathy.

Starr ran her fingers over the typewritten indentations like a talisman. She grabbed a second script, then a third and fourth. Joseph's name was on every one of them.

"Twelve!" Oleander's voice was tinged with panic.

Starr's head shot up. Twelve was not good. Swallowing, she stuffed several scripts into her bomber jacket and zipped it closed. Now all she had to do was get down and out before Oleander reached "fourteen."

It was going to be tight. But she could make it.

Just then, the file cabinet rocked. Then it shimmied. The entrance to the cave, some several stories down and many yards away, filled with darkness.

Fourteen! What happened to fourteen?

A low, threatening growl trickled through the neck of the cave.

Thud. THUD. Thud. THUD.

The room quaked. The cabinet was now actively swaying. Small bits of rock and dust tumbled from the ceiling into her hair, and she sneezed. Nico! This was his doing. He sent her in here. Had he and Fiona planned this together? Were they hoping she wouldn't emerge—

Phil came into the cavern. Yet that wasn't sufficient, to say he merely 'came' into the cavern. Phil *stormed* into the room. Phil *occupied* the room. Phil *owned* the room. The enormous space fit him like tailored pants. The problem was, it wasn't Phil at all. His eyes were a bright, hard gold, an unseeing mania plain in those lightning bolt pupils. His lips snarled. His tail swished from side to side, stirring up coins and overturning chests. Smoke poured from his nostrils. The room temperature had increased by at least ten degrees.

Starr was out of time. This was an emergency. But her pocket was empty: not only was she fresh out of bobby pins, she was also fresh out of MARBLEs. Swallowing, she scanned the ground, but all the swaying and quaking and rocking and shimmying had shifted the fallen orb—and it had vanished.

Phil opened his mouth. Smoke poured out. "HEARTS. TIME. POWER TOOLS."

His deep voice reverberated in the chamber. Starr felt her insides shift with the sound. If she'd had any questions left about the Phil-ness of the monster now occupying the cave, it vanished: this was a genuine, fifteen-foot, red-scaled *dragon*. And his gaze was trained on Starr with the heat of a sun lamp as he slowly made his way forward.

"IDENTITY. JEWELS. YOUR LIFE."

Could a dragon babble? What was he saying? Did it even matter? She searched her memory frantically for things dragons did, or liked, and came up with nothing. Ogres and giants liked rhyming, centaurs liked games, and dragons—did they like riddles? Was that what this was?

A light above her head suddenly turned on, and at the same time, Starr understood: everything Phil was saying was connected. Like Mama's favorite game show, *$100,000 Pyramid*: one person listed the words, the other had to guess what they had in common.

"Things that can be stolen!" she shouted back.

Phil stopped. Smoke trickled from his nose. His stomach glowed. But he wasn't moving. It was as if he'd been stunned, though Starr wasn't sure how long this might last.

The glow that had been illuminating her cut out, and something landed on the file cabinet next to Starr. A soft scurrying of feet made her flinch, and she dared to spend a millisecond glancing away from the dragon. "Oleander?"

The brownie latched on to Starr's jacket. "At—your—service," she breathed, teeth chattering.

"How did you get here? Why aren't you out *there*?"

"St-St-arr Weath-weather-by n-needs h-help so Oleander is h-here."

"But where did you *come* from?"

Oleander pointed at the ceiling.

A brownie door? In the cave? Starr didn't know what to make of it, and didn't have time to find out.

THUD. THUMP. THUD. Phil—no, the *dragon*—was on the move. "BONNIE. CLYDE. FORTY," he bellowed, closing the distance between them.

Starr grabbed Oleander's hand. "Why didn't you pull me *out* of here?"

Oleander's face paled and she squeezed Starr's hand. "Too *high*, Starr Weatherby!" she wailed. And she was right; the ceiling was a good ten feet higher than Starr's head. Still, a rope might have been more useful than a suicide mission.

"I appreciate your willingness to be eaten along with me," said Starr. "Because we're both about to find out what happens when you royally piss off a dragon."

"JESSE JAMES. BUSTER. ROBIN HOOD." Phil's sulfurous breath made Starr think of tacos. He was so much closer now; she could almost see herself reflected in the black of his eyes.

Figure it out! Sam shouted inside her, and Starr put the words together like a puzzle. "Thieves!" she cried, then wilted. This emerging theme was not soothing.

Phil halted again, steaming, tail raised in mid-twitch.

"Starr!" Oleander tugged on her sleeve. "Starr, MARBLE! We can both go if I hold on! I put it in your pocket every morning. Go *now*!"

Starr pointed at the floor. "The stupid thing is down *there*. It dropped. I'll never find it in time."

Without hesitation, Oleander took two steps back, then leaped from the top of the file cabinet. Astonished, Starr leaned forward as her brave brownie landed on bent legs, then rolled onto the pile of jewels, coins, and scripts. Standing, Oleander took a deep breath, clasped her hands together as if in prayer, and literally dove into the mess. Starr clapped a hand over her mouth.

"GUILLOTINE! HANGING! ELECTROCUTION!" Phil was at it again, stomping forward. The room was heating up further and smelled like burned things. Every *THUD* and *THUMP* made Starr cringe, not just because it meant Phil was getting closer, but because Oleander might be squashed beneath his heavy tread at any second.

"FIRING SQUAD! GAS CHAMBER! CRUSHED BY ELEPHANT!"

This time, the theme was enough to make every hair on Starr's arms stand on end. Down on the ground, a small hand burst through the pile of paper and gold, clutching a tiny white orb. Oleander's head popped up immediately afterward, and the flash of movement caught Phil's eyes. He turned his sun lamp gaze on the brownie, who offered a sickly grin. Raising a giant foot, he made as if to slam it on top of Oleander.

"Wait!" Starr stood on top of the file cabinet, waving her arms. Phil turned to her. She hollered as loud as she could, "Methods of execution!"

And Phil froze.

In that second, Oleander scurried from the shadow of Phil's enormous taloned toes and began ascending the cabinet. Starr started climbing down. It was much harder going down than up; she had to feel around with her toes for the handle of the cabinet. Everything was happening too fast. The chamber was now so hot the metal of the cabinets was searing into her hand.

Fingers closed over her ankle.

She slipped—and dangled, attached to the eighth

cabinet's handle now by a single hand. Oleander climbed up Starr, pausing at her waist, and thrust the MARBLE at her. Behind them, Phil's foot came down hard. The file cabinet wobbled. Then it toppled. Starr and Oleander were falling.

"STEALING! SAMANTHA! SCRIPTS!"

I'm the theme this time, Starr thought, and clasped her hand over Oleander's, giving the MARBLE a huge squeeze. Behind her, a belch of fiery heat reached out to envelop her. Phil had finally found the fire in his belly.

But Starr—and Oleander—were gone.

A SLIGHT 'POP,' and Starr was elsewhere.

She was hot. Seriously, sweat-drippingly, hot—as if she'd been swallowed by a dragon. But that wasn't possible; she didn't even feel mildly mangled.

Starr opened her eyes. She was in the lobby, stretched out on the floor behind the waiting area couch. The heat of Phil's final roar had come with her, along with the strong smell of smoke. It was as if she'd taken a bath in charcoal, then ducked into a sauna.

But she was intact—as were the scripts in her jacket.

Well, Nico had said the MARBLE would bring me to the lobby. He didn't say where *in the lobby, I guess.*

Oleander was sitting on her stomach.

The brownie grinned. "We landed!"

We survived, thought Starr, and wrapped her arms around the brownie for a moment. "Oleander, you saved my bacon."

"Saved *all* of Ms. Starr," grinned the brownie. "And my bacon, too."

"You all have a door to the roof of the *cave*?" So far as

Starr knew, brownies lived in the walls. They had access to all the rooms with actors in them. The end. But a dragon's cave?

Oleander became skittish. "Mr. Phil is not the show's *first* security dragon." Her eyes darted around the room. "Other one had a brownie helper. Other one got… hungry."

A few degrees of heat drained from Starr. "Oh, Oleander. I'm sorry."

"No brownies for security guards again. Ever, ever. Brownies locked the door forever. Until—"

"Until today. Until me."

Silence fell between them. *You could have told me about it*, she thought, but bit down on the idea. This had been *her* big plan. Oleander owed her nothing, particularly access through a door with such horrible memories. She gave the brownie a mighty hug. "Thank you for saving me from myself."

Oleander practically vibrated in her arms. "Tea!" she insisted. "Teas all around for—"

The lobby shook. The lobby trembled. An enormous wave of heat reached Starr seconds before a THUMP landed mere feet from where she lay hidden behind the sofa. Starr's eyes went wide: Phil had followed her here. She peered over the edge of the sofa, Oleander mimicking her movement, and bit her lip.

Phil now lay flat on his back in the center of the enormous room. His belly was distended from consuming approximately seventy gallons of sriracha. His grey security shirt lay in ruins. His legs and arms were flailing. He was making great, gasping sobs and small gouts of fire jetted from the corners of his eyes. He looked like the world's biggest two-year-old having a tantrum.

Nico and Nora stood at a careful distance nearby, holding their script sides, bewildered.

"Gone!" cried Phil. "At the moment I rediscover my *glorious* fire I am *ruined*. I have consumed a *human*!"

"A human?" Nora paled. "Fiona?"

Nico elbowed her. "Phil! That can't be."

"It isn't." Starr rose carefully on still-wobbly legs. "I'm right here."

Phil sat up so fast he knocked his head on an overhead lamp. It swung outward and came back to clock him a second time. "*Starr Weatherby!*"

Her name was getting shouted a lot. "That's me."

Phil shot out a short arm and scooped her up, hugging her to his hot, searing chest. "I am *pure!*" he cried. "I have not consumed living flesh!"

"No, but you're burning mine," Starr said, and he set her on the floor. She reached a hand to her cheek: hot, but not actually seared.

"For gods' sakes." Nico ran over and paused just shy of embracing her. "You went *in* there?"

Starr bit her lip. "You told me to!"

"You're crazier than a soup sandwich." Nora sank into one of the chairs in the waiting area.

Phil leaned down, glaring at Starr. "You came into my cave. You *took* things."

Starr swallowed. He wasn't wrong. She had to fix this. "I did. I'm sorry." She paused. The mission had blinded her to how Phil might feel, and the dragon had always been a friend. "Phil, do you have paper and a pen?"

"Starr, maybe this isn't the time to play games—" Nico began, and she shot him a look.

Phil reached behind his desk and emerged with a pad of paper the size of a truck's flatbed, and a pencil as long as Starr's leg. "Um," she said. "OK, *you* write this: 'Starr owes Phil five scripts.'"

"You went in there for *scripts*?" Nora was screeching.

"Hush," Nico said.

Phil finished and stared at the paper.

"So, see," Starr gestured. "It's not stealing. It's borrowing… uh, without prior permission. And with a promise to return."

"Borrowing." Phil squinted at the oversized sheet. "Well. Borrowing." His voice was a low growl. "All right. But tomorrow you will return my treasure. And you will *always* ask permission in the future." He gave Starr a pat on the head, then lumbered around the desk to file the IOU away.

Starr staggered with relief.

Cigar smoke and the scent of rum filled the air. Everyone turned to find Cris standing at the stage door entrance, fists on his hips, chewing a cigar. Behind him, Mav and a few of the day players lingered in the doorway, holding scripts. "Are we done playing with giant lizards?"

Still sweating, Starr nodded. She had no idea how much he'd heard.

"I couldn't be more thrilled. Then let's start shooting this maldito show already, shall we?"

Then Jason MARBLEd into the lobby with a soft pop and a clatter of hooves.

* * *

JASON APPEARED TO have spent the afternoon at an extremely ritzy spa. Outfitted in an oversized terrycloth robe encrusted with what Starr had to assume were crystals, he was bare-hooved—a sight that might have thrown Starr off-balance if she hadn't been minutes from potentially being consumed by a dragon—and appeared both disoriented and discontented.

"Nice duds, Valentine," said Cris.

"Are those... gems?" Sticking his head back out of the cave, Phil extended a tentative talon.

"Back off, dragon," Jason snapped. His eyes were hard and green, and when they landed on Starr they only got harder and greener.

Starr cowered. In this moment, Jason scared her more than Phil ever had.

With a grand leap, Jason summited Phil's reception desk, towering over the rest of the room. His horns had overflowed his head and now curved past his hairline, heading down his back. His hooves were shiny and dark. His eyes burned, their pupils contorting.

"Do you see these?" He gestured at his horns.

The actors all nodded. Cris chewed on his cigar.

"What do they say?"

"They don't say anything." Mav sauntered into the room. "They're horns."

"Wrong!" Jason pointed. "They say that I am the immortal in charge here! Does anyone question that?"

The extras cringed and ducked behind the cameradryads.

"Good!" Jason cried. "I have come from a meeting with TPTB. And they had *footage* of Starr riding a centaur! Of Fiona and Nico being tied up by elves!"

Starr swallowed. She'd had no idea they were being filmed in Central Park, and based on the look on Nico's face, he didn't, either. "Well, ah—" she began.

"They *loved* it," Jason continued. "They want more like that."

"Yay?" Starr asked tentatively.

Mav hurried to her side. "A centaur? Really?"

Starr swiped her finger over her heart and followed it

with a boy scout on-my-honor hand sign.

"All of which means we're doing something Extra Super Special at the fan convention this year, I've now been informed." Jason's voice rang around the lobby interior. "Something which, if we fail to do it right, means we are all *finished*."

"Don't keep us in suspense, Il Duce," Nico called out.

Jason sputtered. Paced around the desk. After a long pause, he faced the actors. "We will be doing... a show at the convention."

Nora crossed her arms. "We always do a show there. Y'all know that already. We shoot all over the hotel and then y'all spend a couple days editing out all the mythics and it's like the folks of Shadow Oak hit the road and then one of us wakes up with a concussion and it was all a dream."

"This time," said Jason, "we're leaving the mythics in."

A general gasp went around the room.

"And," he continued, "it'll be streamed *live*."

Cris swore something so dark and ugly the cameradryads began to wilt. "That's two weeks from now, Valentine!"

Jason deflated and took a seat. Starr set a hand on his arm, the terrycloth robe's gems scratching at her hand.

Holy fried mackerel, those are real diamonds.

"We're going to lose the show." Jason tore at the robe's belt, and several gems clattered to the floor. A talon stole forward and scraped them behind the desk. "I can't do it. I can't."

"You won't be alone." Starr waited until he met her gaze. "We'll do whatever it takes."

"What she said," agreed Mav.

"Thirded," said Nico.

Nora threw up her hands. "Whatever."

Cris leaned up against the desk and smacked Jason's leg once, hard, then re-lit his cigar by looking at it. "Kumbaya," he said, glancing around the room.

And then he began laughing.

CHAPTER 25
Starr Trek

FIONA NEVER ARRIVED fashionably late. She arrived fashionably, intentionally, last.

The diva of *Tune in Tomorrow* popped into the wide atrium of the waterfront hotel precisely seven minutes after the rest of the show's cast had MARBLEd over. She tossed her head and began assessing the room.

We're here! Valéncia squealed. *Let's get this party started.*

Pipe down, you, Fiona shushed her. The persona she once thought had abandoned her had rallied to the cause of defeating Starr Weatherby so thoroughly that Fiona now feared she was starting to take over the whole operation. It took more and more effort lately to shove Valéncia aside, and her alter ego had even fewer scruples than Fiona did.

Accepting a 'truce' with Starr had made things worse.

You're caving? Valéncia screamed at her nightly, so loud that Fiona had begun taking the same sleep draught she once gave to Dakota. *To the Blonde Blob? The Interloper? Sheer Wannabe?*

Wheels are in motion, Fiona always assured her, which for a time had been enough to mollify Valéncia. Now that they were at the annual convention, though, Fiona would have to shift into a higher gear. If she didn't, Valéncia threatened to hop permanently into the driver's seat.

I refuse to go insane over Starr Weatherby, she thought. *But I also refuse to be defeated by her.* Fiona twitched involuntarily, thinking of the treatment she'd received in Centaur Park; the scent of rampaging beasts still filled her nose.

Jason sauntered to the middle of the gathered group of actors and held up his hands for calm. They'd ported in nearly a dozen performers, from fan favorite non-regular players to extras to the usual cast. Nora, big as a house even without the inflatables, rested on a couch. Mav and Starr whispered to one another like they were old pals. Nico stood next to a tall non-cameradryad plant, checking out his bitten fingernails. Fiona had kept him at arm's length since the Centaur Park mess, but it was time to let him back into her good graces. She'd need him to put in motion the next step in her Starr Eradication plan, and he'd be desperate to help by now.

Later, the mythics would arrive, then Dakota; the reporter would gather quotes all weekend for a summary story to appear in *WaterWorlds*. But Fiona anticipated her arrival for another reason: Dakota would bring the latest issue of the magazine—one with a cover story that would set the stage for much mayhem.

"As most of you know," Jason began, "this weekend will include up-close contact with thousands of your most devoted fans." He outlined some of the highlights: a signing event, a Q&A session, and panels featuring both actors and fans discussing weighty topics.

Fiona shrugged off her yeti-fur coat, dumping it on top of Bookender. His arm shot out from beneath the fabric to hand her a program booklet, which she began to flip through. The panel listings included topics ranging from the quotidian ("Ask a Human: Personal Hygiene in Shadow Oak") to character-specific how-tos ("Scarf-Tying the Lady Marlborough Way") to wish-fulfillment ("Imagining Characters as Mythics"). There was even a private service Sunday afternoon at 4:37 designed for trolls to worship Valéncia.

She tossed the book aside and gazed around the familiar interior of the hotel. It was tastefully done, with an open-air restaurant, escalators leading up to a mezzanine and down to the ballrooms. It was snowing on the other side of the multi-story glass entrance, and a water feature cascaded down a granite wall.

Over the years, Fiona had participated in thirty-nine fan conventions, the last ten in this very building, and each provided a welcome break from the usual routine. They would have almost three days of nonstop adoration, applause and the occasional annoying—if easily deflected— love spell. The location was one of Jason's whims, as he opted every year to base it in the human side of the Veil.

"We run a reality show," he had told the actors once. "It's more fun for the viewers to enter 'our' world for even a short time."

Fiona also suspected it was an aesthetic choice—no matter how fastidiously a poltergeist set might be designed, nothing could fully approximate a real lived-in human space. The convention occupied the entire hotel, with all outside humans aside from staff warded away with spells, and at the end of every event Jason sent a team of glawakuses—known for their memory-erasing gaze—to meet with hotel staff and gently reshape their recall of the gathering. Post-convention, all the staff would remember was that they had provided hospitality to an enthusiastic group of role-playing, costumed attendees, which wasn't so far from the truth.

Jason paused and turned serious. "Finally—and I can't emphasize this enough—you must be in character at all times. Think of this hotel as the latest and greatest stage set, and if you interact with mythics, it *must* be as the human they know and love, not *yourself.* Capiche?"

Starr had her hand up. "And the live show on Sunday? That's in the Grand Ballroom?"

Fiona smiled. The live VSE: a place for her to shine, and for Starr to fall. It would be delicious. Over the past two weeks, they had all put in extra hours to rehearse the 'live' experience—a first for the show. Jason and Emma's big plan was to cordon off a large ballroom in which the entire show would take place and invite special VIMs—Very Important Mythics—who could behave themselves around their favorite stars, to interact as part of a 'cocktail party.'

"Precisely." Jason gestured at the lobby water feature. "And that is where everyone *not* participating in the live show will be able to watch it. In real time."

Fiona nodded along quietly, organizing her own thoughts. She had a different game plan for that night, one that would fix her Starr problem once and for all. The trick would be to make sure it didn't upend the show simultaneously.

While Jason wittered on with further hotel details, she began strolling the lobby. Nico watched her intently, but did not approach, and she passed him by with nothing more than a small smile.

"What're we doing in a Boston hotel in the middle of winter?" Starr was wondering to Mav as Fiona approached. "It's not exactly magical here."

"Au contraire," Fiona settled a hand on Starr's shoulder.

She loved watching the conflicting emotions flicker across the young woman's face; she obviously had many things she wanted to say to Fiona but was biting down on them for the sake of the 'truce.' "This is a highly magical locale."

"Grindylows," Mav said. "Water mythies live in the harbor. They keep the hotel a protected area."

"Far from a complete answer, Charles." Fiona gestured at the tall glass panels of the lobby entrance. "Irish presence in this area has made pockets of the city clear for mythics for centuries—everything from sídhe to fear dearg roam the common. Their soirees are delightful if one can wrangle an invite." Fiona herself had attended several under-the-hill gatherings, but after one too many uisce beatha drinks she'd ended up in a swan boat in the public garden, painted head-to-toe in blue. "The subway is protected by a local human-hybrid creature, the endless rider they call Charlie of the MTA."

"That's a silly old song," Mav said. "Don't think that falls into mythic territory, Fee."

"You know best," she said with a smile that indicated otherwise. "In any case, to consider Boston unmagical is sheer ignorance. We are quite safe here and have been so for a decade. The humans will barely remember we've even been here, until we show up again next year."

"What, they think everyone's in costume?" Starr raised her eyebrows.

"Nailed it," said Mav. "It's not a bug, it's a feature."

"Or it's a mythic bug *and* a feature," Starr grinned.

Mav chuckled.

She's after him now, Valéncia sniped.

Patience, Fiona shut her down. *They'll all be singing a different tune by this time tomorrow.*

Yet, Fiona was also nervous about the live show. It could

not be 'attempted.' It had to succeed. That was the only thing TPTB would accept; she knew that in her heart. That was why she had insisted on the full complement of brownies attending the event. All hands needed to be on deck, with multiple hands for her personally. Only Phil and Emma had remained back at the studio, and the werepanther was taking a few days off to hunt during her monthly cycle. The dragon wasn't invited: he'd become mythic non grata at the con since the year he'd carried off a taco truck, consumed all the guacamole and hot sauce, then abandoned it on the roof of the building next door. His flatulence that night had forced everyone in the hotel to wear masks.

"And that about wraps things up," said Jason, passing out key cards from an envelope. "Your bags are in your rooms; as usual, you have exclusive access to the top floor block of suites and roof deck. There's one hitch, though—"

"Hey," Nora held up her card. "We're sharing rooms?"

"There was a plumbing... incident," said Jason. "Half of our usual floor got flooded. And the live show's been so popular the rest of the hotel is sold out. So... everybody's got a roommate. But I've added something special to each of your domiciles that I promise will make up for it." Silence from the actors. "Trust me, loves!"

"Of course," cooed Fiona. She never worried about her own room—she always stayed in the presidential suite, which had better not have been waterlogged. That was her special spot, solo occupancy. Well, with Bookender, who didn't count.

Though this year, there would in fact be someone else in the room: Valéncia.

We'll have so much fun, her alter ego chuckled demonically.

For once, Fiona saw no reason to hush her up.

CHAPTER 26

Double Starred

Piercing shrieks streamed down the hallway, reaching Starr all the way at the twelfth floor elevators. Tired though she was from a long day of rehearsals, she barreled down the hall, dodging a maid's cart along the way and found they were coming from the room she was sharing with Nora. Praying her roomie's water hadn't broken, Starr tapped her keycard and shouldered open the door.

An object the size of an infant flew straight for her head.

"Crap!" Starr ducked back into the hallway, slamming the door. Whatever it was thumped against the other side.

Nora's screeching continued.

For a moment, Starr wondered if Nora had given birth— to a projectile—and shook her head. That hadn't been a thrown object; it had been a flying one. Also, definitely not an actual baby.

She scanned the hallway. Mav and Nico would be in the shared room at the opposite end, but summoning Mav for help would require going through Nico, and that was definitely not happening. Starr snagged a vacuum hose extender from the cleaning lady's cart and lifted it high.

If exploring a dragon's cave had taught her anything, it was that she shouldn't enter strange spaces unarmed. She raised her key again to tap.

"Yoo-hoo! Starr!" Dakota waved from the elevator bank, trotting over on her high heels. "What good luck to run into—"

"Not now, Dakota." Starr gritted her teeth. "We've got a situation." She pushed into the room. Something came at her again and she swung for the fences. The vacuum extender clipped it with a hollow thunk and it fell to the floor, unmoving.

The creature resembled a beautiful, elfin doll. Its hair shimmered from violet to teal to royal blue and back again, and its nearly transparent wings fluttered, then stilled. Starr bit her lip, squatting next to the creature, which snarled, revealing tiny, pointed teeth.

"*Eech!*" Starr fell backward.

"Starr?" Dakota poked her head in the room. "What's that—oh, boy. You've got bugs."

"What the hell is that?" Starr pointed.

"Manic pixie," said the reporter. "Big one."

Nora's brownie Quintuple leaped from one of the beds, holding another of the creatures by its heel. He doffed his top hat. "Deee-lightful," he crowed. "Well done, Ms. Weatherby. Ms. Gardener—please restrain that one; it's merely stunned."

Dakota upended her messenger bag, dumping manila folders, makeup accessories and a compact onto the carpet. Then she scooped up the creature in the bag, securing the fasteners. "And so!" she said with a flourish. "Not just a pretty face, after all." She helped Starr up. "No hotel room is safe unless you do a sweep."

"Which you were supposed to do, Quintuple!" Nora

lowered herself to the bed, where she'd been standing. She set a hand over her heart, breathing heavily.

"It was on my agenda, but the bros have been mightily occupied today," said Quintuple.

"Like we weren't?" Nora barked. "Starr and me've been stuck rehearsing our guts out all afternoon and you can't even bother to—"

"Yo!" Starr interrupted. "Problem at hand, first." She gestured at Dakota's bag, which had started to wriggle. The creature Quintuple still held onto was trying to swing forward and bite him.

"Entirely sensible." Quintuple gestured at the balcony. "If you would be so kind as to unlatch the door."

Starr dragged the balcony door to the side. Frigid air rushed inside the room, and Quintuple stepped out, arcing his arm back.

"Wait!" She held up a hand. "Shouldn't we see what they want?"

"Little sneaks," Nora groused from inside the room. "Want our memories. Want our time. Want our toothbrushes. They'd steal everything if we let them stay."

Quintuple nodded. "They are impossible to avoid entirely; humans call them—" He snapped his fingers.

"Groupies," said Dakota.

"Indeed. A pernicious, persistent version of the more common 'fan.'"

Taking advantage of its captor's momentary distraction, the manic pixie in his grip made a dash for the skies, beating its wings so hard it sounded like a giant bee. The force dragged Quintuple off his feet, and Starr launched herself at the brownie, holding him in place. He released the pixie's ankle, and the creature soared into the night. Dakota opened her bag to the skies, and the second mythic escaped with a buzz, turning backward once to give them all the finger.

"This room is clean." Quintuple slid the door back in place. He dusted off his top hat and tapped it back on his head. "I shall take my leave."

"How about grabbing us some dinner, first?" Nora demanded.

"Perhaps room service?" Quintuple opened a small door near the air vent that Starr was certain did not exist in classy hotels when brownies weren't around. "We bros are on... hiatus until morning."

"Hiatus?" Nora, Starr and Dakota spoke the same word, in the same tone, simultaneously.

But the brownie had already slid through the door, which shut behind him.

Starr flopped on her bed, exhausted. It had been a long, nutty day. They'd shot regular scenes that morning before MARBLEing to the hotel, then spent the last three hours walking through the live show again. Part of her wanted to do nothing but sleep. The other part was her stomach, which growled. "Want to join us for dinner, Dakota?" she asked, rolling over.

"No, indeed," said the reporter, who'd refilled her messenger bag with the items she'd dumped on the floor. She cradled a thick manila envelope. "I have a meeting of my own."

Nora raised an eyebrow. "You mean you and Cris' are bunkin' together."

Dakota flushed and turned away. She gestured at a dimmer switch on the wall Starr hadn't seen before; a note card dangled from the dial. "Look at this," she said. "'This Room Glamourized for Your Enjoyment.' Wonder what it does?"

"C'mon," Starr prodded. "Even Jason knows about you two."

Dakota patted her hair. The heroic quality on display from a moment ago was gone, replaced by an arch formality. "Be that as it may, the reason I'm really here is"—she handed Starr the manila envelope—"this. Well, also Fiona's column pickup. She's punctual, even on the road."

"You're bringing revisions?" Starr opened the envelope and peered inside. "Oh, my. You're not." She pulled out a thick, glossy magazine that read *WaterWorlds* on the cover, the words partially obscured by a beautifully rendered watercolor painting of the cover model—herself. In the artwork, Starr was Sam, wearing a wasp-waisted beige trench coat, with a revealing décolletage, and a matching fedora cocked over one eye. Her heels were higher than either Starr or Sam had ever worn.

I always dreamed of being Lauren Bacall. Starr's heart pounded. *Wish I looked this good in real life.*

"We timed it so all the convention attendees would have a copy," Dakota explained. "Helena was most insistent. Alligash is delivering copies to everyone tomorrow morning, but I thought you'd like a sneak peek. The expression on a first-time cover actor's face when I hand over her copy makes my heart go pitter-pat."

Starr jumped from the bed and pulled Dakota into a hug. Stiff at first, the reporter relaxed into the embrace, then pulled away.

"Can't wait to see what you think," said Dakota. "Your quotes were sheer gold, after all." And with a flutter of her fingers, Dakota saw herself out.

Nora eyed the magazine cover. "Well, congrats, roomie. I'll borrow that later. What'll you have for dinner?"

Starr thought about what Dakota had said, how her eyes had glittered. "Sheer gold," she'd said. The problem was, Starr still couldn't remember much of their chat.

All at once, she was no longer hungry, and stared at the magazine as if it might explode. Something about it scared her more than the manic pixies.

OVER DINNER, NORA became civil. Friendly, even. First, they investigated the dimmer switch Dakota had pointed out, and discovered that pressing it put the room into Glamour Mode. "Ah," noted Nora. "Jason's 'something special.'" A turn of the dial flipped the room through a number of illusions, and after spinning through a nebula galaxy (too dark, Nora insisted) and a crystal castle (too transparent, said Starr), they settled on a verdant mountainside with purple skies.

Once settled, Nora began talking, as though she hadn't had a simmering distaste for Starr all this time. At first, Starr joined in cautiously between bites of salad, but once she decided Nora was genuine, she shared her own stories about Mama, Bill, trading one of the quieter parts of Maryland for one of the noisiest places in the world—and of being discovered in a diner by Jason.

I could talk to her about the scripts, Starr thought. *She knows I went into the cave.* No one had asked her about that particular escapade. She'd survived a dragon, thanks to some resourceful brownies, and now had her hands on old scripts by the mysterious Joseph—yet it was as if it hadn't happened at all.

Maybe it had been eclipsed by Jason's live show news. Maybe no one was asking her about it for a reason. The closer she got to the whole Joseph script issue, which then appeared to dovetail with the Amelia disappearance issue, the less anybody had to say on the topic. It was like a conspiracy of silence.

The scripts were something she wanted to talk about, though. Joseph Abernathy had been a revelation. She had only five of his episodes and had read each multiple times in her apartment. Each had been more fantastical, imaginative and weirder than anything she'd played so far on *Tune in Tomorrow,* and she wished she was in *those* stories, not Emma's.

But after parsing them more closely, Starr had discovered problems. Two had taken place aboard the Supership Starprise, on which Roland had been a swaggering, smooth-talking captain who romanced the ladies and made planets more amenable to conquering. He'd had a key romance with Wilhelmina, played by Amelia. Two other scripts had featured a flying blue Toyota that dashed through space and time, with a trench coated, scarf-wearing Valéncia piloting the vehicle, which was larger on the inside than the outside. Maverick was often her co-pilot, helping her out of scrapes. The final script had sent the entire cast down a volcano to the core of the earth, where they found oversized lizards.

Having read all three, Starr had poured a big mug of wine and drank to the sheer audacity of it all: Joseph Abernathy had been a hack. A plagiarist. In the space of five scripts, he'd ripped off *Star Trek*, *Doctor Who* and Jules Verne. That said, was it plagiarism if no one on this side of the Veil had heard of Captain Kirk, the Doctor or *Journey to the Center of the Earth*? Did mythics care about copyright?

As promised, Starr had handed them back the next day to Phil, along with another jug of sriracha. But she'd kept their secrets to herself.

Was it time to share them yet? Well, Nora was on a roll, and she had quite a tale to tell. She'd grown up in rural North Carolina, playing in a forest behind their house. "Parents didn't believe in TV—we didn't have one and I barely even watch it today," she said. "We ran wild all over the neighborhood, and in the forest nearby."

That was where she'd seen Jason for the first time. Trying to get some peace away from her older brothers, Nora had taken to writing in her journals while in the forest, leaving them in a Tupperware, then tucking that container into the trunk of a tree. While she wrote, she occasionally looked up and saw a flash of hairy legs passing through the trees. They never spoke and she told no one—a man-goat in the forest was the sort of thing her religious mother would have labeled the devil's work.

She'd decided to be a writer after her journals turned into wish-fulfillment, with stories about romances with some other girls in her school filling up the pages. But that made the need to hide them even greater. "Nobody ever talked about 'coming out' in my part of the world, not back then," she said. "I don't think Mama believed women like me existed."

When she was nineteen and trying to figure out how to save enough money to move to the city, Jason showed up on the family doorstep. He'd been dressed in a funky bowler hat with a high red feather, rainbow suspenders and pinstriped pants, with shoes of purple crushed velvet. Nora hadn't recognized him until he asked why she hadn't been hanging around in the forest lately.

"I have a unique opportunity for a woman of your talents," he'd said formally, handing her a card with a script that pulsed. "Your stories are delightful."

"How—" But she knew. Once, she'd opened a journal

to find a smear of berry juice on a page. "But I have no talent."

"I firmly disagree," he'd said. "Your stories are delicious and pair beautifully with blackberry wine. And you are a magnificent human specimen."

Nora had been desperate, or she'd never have listened. But her world had been closing in on her—secretarial school was a slog, and it was getting harder to explain to her parents why she didn't date. She had no money of her own, and no prospects. She'd left with Jason the next day.

"And I'm still here." Nora licked the last dregs of ice cream from the spoon.

That was a lot to take in. "But you and Nico were married once. You told me that."

She shrugged. "I was a kid and I experimented. Anyhow, nobody says it's against the law to keep your options open. He is a handsome brute, you gotta give him that. For me, doin' the wrong thing showed me just how right the *real* thing is."

"So, you've got the real thing now... on the other side of the Gate?"

She nodded. "That's why I go home every night. She's my world, not this show."

"Don't you age then, every night?"

"Yup. Prizes don't work on the other side of the Veil, not unless you're in a protected place like this hotel. But it makes it kind of hard to tell how old I am now. I usually guess around thirty-two."

"How do you do it?" Mav's marriage had imploded over the long hours and show secrecy, but Nora seemed to have struck a balance. "You tell her you're with the CIA?"

Nora chuckled. "She was on the show for a bit. She

understands."

"Her memories didn't get erased when she quit?"

Nora took a long time to answer. "That one is a puzzler. We figure it has something to do with her seein' me every night. Like, the thread never snapped. Or maybe it works if you love somebody."

Numbers whirled in Starr's head. Nico had told her once that they'd hired new actors once every five or ten years, usually—until Amelia came on board. She imagined how old Amelia would have been by now—Mama's age, maybe a bit more. A child of... the television era. Born with the television on. That wouldn't have been true of Mav or Nico or Fiona, and Nora was an exception—TV wasn't part of her world.

But a child of television would know TV. Would have heard of *Star Trek* and *Doctor Who*.

The penny dropped. Starr got it, now. Joseph, the story thief, had met Amelia, the child of television, thirty years ago. And now she doubted they'd had a love affair.

Rather, Amelia had known he was a fraud.

CHAPTER 27
Rock Starr

STARR WAS BEING poked. Something pushed against her forehead. Her shoulder. Her back. She awoke with a start and sat up, a page from *WaterWorlds* plastered to her face, where she'd fallen asleep on it.

"Morning!" Oleander chirped, withdrawing her poking finger. "Convention time!"

Starr peeled the magazine from her face and dropped it on the bed. She had no memory of falling asleep, only starting to read the article about herself and then— darkness. She guessed she'd only managed to read a sentence before collapsing from the long day.

Rubbing sleep from her eyes, Starr noted that Quintuple was also doing the Brownie Wakeup Poke on her snoring roommate. "What time—" Starr muttered.

"There's a seven and a three and a two on the clock," Oleander reported.

Might be a good idea to teach them how to tell time, Starr thought. Last night they'd learned they were first on the call sheet for hair and makeup, which was certainly Fiona's doing. Starr and Nora now had less than half an hour to get down the hall to the Hairies and Makeup Fairies Room, but what she wanted most right now was—

Oleander held up a mug. "For the waking."

Starr eyed the brownish-mauve swirling mixture and took a tentative sip. It went down buttery and kicked every cell she had into high alert. "Whoa," she gasped, shaking her head and glancing at the magazine.

Samantha Draper is a most unusual young woman, the article began. *When I sat down—*

"Ms. Starr!" The brownie beckoned, and she slid to the floor so they could be on the same eye level, tossing the magazine behind her. She desperately wanted to read it and also to have read it already, so she'd know what those 'sheer gold' quotes were. It was probably nothing more than a glowing puff piece, but if there was anything inside that might make her cringe, maybe she should wait until she didn't have a full day of fan interaction ahead of her.

She finished the drink and raised her eyebrows at Oleander.

The brownie took a deep breath. "You know we bros like you. You taught us letters so we could read books."

"And you read a *lot*, if I understand right."

"Yes! Mx. Jan gives us good books! And Mx. Jan meets with us."

"Like a book club?" Starr had a vague recollection of signing something Jan had put under her nose, some kind of permission slip for a gathering.

"There was a petition Mx. Jan helped us write up, with many asks," Oleander continued. "Many brownies agreed and signed, too. But—TPTB turned the pages to cinders."

Nora's snoring cut out abruptly. "Quintuple, get your finger out of my nose!" she barked.

"I'm sorry to hear that, Oleander." Starr wondered what this had to do with her.

"So, bros need plan Bs. But brownies have small ideas. Jan has big ones. Ideas. Should we use big or small plan Bs, Starr Weatherby?"

Starr shook her head. Even with the drink this line of questioning was coming too early in the morning. "What kind of plan?"

"A plan to be heard! To make changes!"

Petitions. Jan. *The Jungle*. Their *Impeach Everybody* pin. It was all starting to come together. "Well, do you know what you really want?"

Oleander nodded with enthusiasm.

"There's this phrase I like: 'Go big or go home.' I once had to sing a song while pretending to be a mango. I thought it was my low point, but Jason saw me—and that's what made him want me on the show. So, sometimes I think about being the mango again. You know, going for it."

"Be the mango," Oleander committed the concept to memory. "Go be a big mango."

"Something like that." Starr grinned. "Mango it up, girl."

Oleander gestured at the small door near the vent. "Come, Starr Weatherby. Tell others."

It was a ridiculous notion. "Oleander, even if I had time I wouldn't fit."

The brownie opened the door, pressing her hands around the frame, and pushed. The frame gave way as if the wall was made of rubber. The door grew taller and wider. Starr marveled at the elastic qualities of magic drywall. "Come!"

"Where are we supposed to go?"

Oleander touched the side of her nose. "Surprise."

Most of Starr wanted to dive right in. Adventure ahead! But then Nora turned on the shower. "I'm not even dressed, Oleander. I have some appointments. Maybe later?"

The brownie thought a moment. "Later!" She ducked through the doorframe, which slowly returned to its original dimensions. "Yes, very much later!"

And she was gone.

THE CROWD GOES *wild* was a hoary cliché Starr had heard dozens of times, perhaps nowhere more often than when her brother Bill was doing basketball layups in the driveway.

Witnessing it was a whole other thing.

Starr peered around the curtain that divided the backstage wings from the packed ballroom, bouncing on her toes as each of the actors went out onto the stage. Cris gave a short introduction, the announced actor walked out and waved, then took a seat in a director's chair. This was the combination opening ceremony and Q&A session that kicked off the convention.

"Next up, she's the loveable scamp who stumbled into our hearts with a serving tray—but now works to dig up all the mysteries of Shadow Oak at the Eye 2 Eye agency... it's Samantha Draper!" Cris turned and held out one of his arms.

Everything moved in slow motion as Starr crossed the stage. Feet, claws, hooves all thumped on the carpeted floor; wings, antennae, arms and mandibles waved, clicked, shook and flapped; howls, screeches, whistles, moans and cries of excitement filled the room. More than one member of the audience was dressed up in human garb—some in Sam's bomber jacket replicas, some with boas to emulate Valéncia.

Ahead of Starr's entrance, Mav had given the room an 'aw, shucks' shrug, wave and smile before sitting down, but the tumult transfixed Starr on her way to the chair. *Deer, meet headlights*, she thought. It was like staring across the ocean and hearing the waves call to you. Some mythics covered their eyes, others blew what might have been kisses. A sign covered in glittery letters caught her eye: *No Wardrobe Malfunctions!*

Eyes pricking with tears, Starr clasped her hands over her heart. She could have stood there forever, drinking in the glow of this form of love. It washed over and through her, an embrace from the entire room. It was better than kissing Nico.

It was a drug.

I'd do anything to have this forever.

Just like Fiona, she realized.

That made many things clearer. Starr had never thought of acting in this way, but it had been a long search for this moment, when a roomful of very strange strangers declared that she mattered. That she'd moved them. No one else cared like they did.

"STARR!" someone shouted from the audience, followed by a muffled thud of hooves on the carpet. From far back in the room, a man's hand waved, and a whiff of Axe body spray filtered forward.

Starr froze, then squinted. *Kyle?* A second centaur swatted Kyle on the hindquarters, and they conferred. Kyle glanced up again, abashed.

"I MEAN, A STAR—IS ON THE STAGE!" shouted Kyle, then sat down, giving her a wink. "THAT IS ALL

I MEANT."

Starr sent back a weak thumbs-up, until a tap on her shoulder reminded her she was still in the middle of the stage. "OK, Ms. America," Mav whispered in her ear. "We've got a whole weekend to be the most important people in the world." He took her hand and Starr stumbled behind him, drunk from all the affection.

"Holy moly." She slid into her seat, clipping a lavalier microphone to her dress.

"It was beautiful to watch you take it in," he said, covering his own microphone. "But don't love it back. It's fickle stuff, the love of the crowd."

Starr held his gaze, thinking of all the times they'd stared at one another in front of the camera, then quickly looked away, face heating up.

Mav patted her hand.

Then it began.

FANS ASKED EVERYTHING; no detail was too small. Beatrice's shoe size? Sam's preference on fresh-killed meat for breakfast, or scrambled eggs? Had Mav ever slept in a cave, instead of on top of a mattress? Would Valéncia consider sanctifying a harpy mating ritual?

Dakota was in charge of the two-hour Q&A, interviewing actors from her own chair at far stage left. About half of the session was curated with special questions pre-approved by Jason and Cris—and the other was devoted to fielding questions from the audience. This part was the trickier bit, and Starr—despite now having most of a year under her belt with the show—was still trying to parse out the exact level of knowledge mythics had about the series. On the one hand, they knew they weren't watching the adventures of Shadow Oak 24/7. They were only seeing a small wedge of the story, which meant there were hours and hours of things the Shadow Oakians, in theory, were doing outside of the viewers' knowledge.

Yet the range of understanding about this 'reality' show covered a broad spectrum. The centaurs were very wink-wink, nudge-nudge about the whole thing, yet instantly knew how to jump into the game of it all. Trolls, on the other hand, were incredibly serious about every aspect of the production, down to an accounting of the shoes Valéncia owned. (They kept spreadsheets.) Elves seemed to believe it was one hundred percent real, and the only reason the actors were on stage now is they had been whisked away by mythic powers for this brief weekend. Still others—usually flying beasts like hippogriffs, zizes and winged fairies—who had a lot of questions about writing fanfic—yearned to believe it was true, even if logically they knew otherwise. All of which meant answering questions wasn't as easy as either telling the truth or improvising.

"Yes, you can embellish, gild, enhance your answers," Emma had told them all before they'd MARBLEd to the hotel. She'd fixed a narrow gaze on Starr. "But don't get *too* fancy. Having to back fill anything in my scripts with 'story' you add on is a pain in my whiskers."

Starr got the message. Be creative but watch your step.

Nora fielded questions on her size, which were not always the most polite. A Slender Man was particularly pointed on the topic and even wondered if Beatrice was expecting. "What can I say?" she said, long robes flowing over her distended belly and inflatables. "I like fairy cakes."

The Fae gasped.

"They're *not* made of fairies," Nora growled, then more

quietly added, "you ninnies."

"How come there aren't any human offspring in town?" asked a roc. "It's my understanding that mortals must propagate the species."

At this, a handful of mythics bounced up and down in their seats with excitement—the La Llorona, the Baba Yaga, the El Cuco and a series of changelings. "Yes! Children! Children! Delicious children!" several chanted.

"Well," said Dakota. "I think that answers the question. As you all know, Shadow Oak is a *special* town, with residents who live far longer than your average human. They do not *need* to replace one another. As the saying goes, 'Never work with children or animals.' Now, moving on…"

Dakota did know how to interview, Starr had to give her that—she moved from topic to topic with the grace of a ballerina.

Then the spotlight turned on Starr, with seemingly endless questions for Sam. She'd tried to prepare for this but had a slower reaction time than the others for questions like where Sam had been 'whelped' and about others in her 'litter' (this from a werewolf, standing on his hind legs). She tried to be creative, but vague. During the live show, Emma had prepped them for two big reveals: Sam was about to become the long-lost daughter Valéncia had apparently forgotten she'd given birth to. The wordcat was certainly getting clever, but Starr had been secretly disappointed. She'd been sure Emma had been leading up to a romance between Sam and Mav. Then the other shoe dropped: Mav would turn out not to be Valéncia's son. Problem created, problem solved, everything thrown in the air.

But those twists couldn't come out *yet*.

So, when asked about any future storyline, Starr deflected

with a classic feint: "That's an excellent question." She used the mythics' names, when she could read them on their convention badges. She looked directly at them as she answered. "I'm a mystery," she said. "I mean, I know where I came from—at least, I think I do. But I'm thinking it's time to do some investigating on myself!"

Starr shot a glance at her fellow actors, most of whom wore curious smiles. That seemed to be a go-ahead, and Starr turned on the tap. In her story she was from Maryland (true), but left at the doorstep of an orphanage (false, but fit in with Emma's DNA reveal), with a note attached in a language no one could decipher (whole cloth). Her co-stars effortlessly picked it up, embellished a bit, and spun it back to her. It was like playing catch with an invisible ball, one they scrupulously kept out of Fiona's hands.

That turned out to be a mistake. After some time of this story invention, Fiona cleared her throat. The room went silent, and she sauntered to center stage. When she'd entered the room earlier, Starr had discovered that the enthusiastic reception that had overwhelmed her was only the tip of the adoration iceberg for Fiona. They might love Sam, but they worshipped Valéncia, and Fiona milked it expertly. She'd shaken hands, paws, claws and fins, blown kisses, then held her arms aloft and flapped her hands while backing into her chair.

That's how you do it, peon, her glance had told Starr.

Until that moment, Starr hadn't fully grasped the wall she'd been beating her head against. Fiona *was* the show. Without her, the small collapses they'd been experiencing in the past weeks would become catastrophic. No wonder they let her get away with so much. Even proving that she'd turned Amelia into tea sachets might not be sufficient to uproot her from the show. This had never been a competition Starr could win.

Now, Fiona took center stage and spread her arms so wide that her yeti fur blocked most of Starr's view of the audience. "Darlings," she drawled. "Our Sam is the most wonderful, is she not? It's such a shame she won't be with us for very long."

Starr sat up in her seat. It wasn't true, but even if it was—could Fiona *say* that?

A low buzz filled the room.

"Now, Valéncia," Mav jumped in. "You just ain't warmed up to her yet. She might turn out to be closer to you than you imagine."

When Emma had told them that Sam would turn out to be related to Valéncia, there had been two reactions: one, in Starr's head, that sounded like, '*Eech.*' A second, which Fiona had made verbally, was, "Over my dead body."

Emma had hissed at her

Fiona had lifted her chin defiantly. "All right. Then over *her* dead body."

Jason had pulled Fiona to one side, and Starr had not overheard that conversation. But when they'd returned, Fiona had been approximately thirty percent more accommodating. "It certainly sounds interesting," she'd told Emma. "I am curious to see where this goes."

Well, Starr had wanted creativity from the wordcat— now she was getting it. What she didn't want was creativity from Fiona, onstage in front of the entire audience. While the exchange wasn't being captured by cameradryads, many of the audience members had activated personal inscribing spells and would undoubtedly share their thoughts on Arachne's web later. No streaming video was permitted, but words traveled like lightning across the threads of their social media.

"I'm not going anywhere," Starr said now, jumping from her chair.

Mav grabbed her hand, shaking his head. Covering his mic, he whispered, "This is exactly what she wants."

Starr shrugged free and ducked under Fiona's extended arm. "Really, I'm not," she said, waving. "Take everything from Valéncia with a grain of salt. She recently had a visit to Shadow Oak General Hospital that we couldn't feature in an episode." She tapped her temple. "A little unsteadiness in the brain."

The trolls in the audience gasped. Behind her, Nico cleared his throat. "I was there," he called out. "I myself was battling some delusions."

Fiona whipped around with a *you are dead to me* gaze, then returned to the crowd. "Stuff and nonsense."

Starr shrugged, cupping a hand over her eyes. "Kyle?"

A delighted whinny rang out, and Starr's centaur hero trotted into the aisle. "HERE FOR YOU, SAM DRAPER!"

"Inside voice, Kyle." Starr grinned at him, then turned to the crowd. "I know you all didn't get to see it, but Kyle helped me out of a life-threatening situation the other day."

"VALÉNCIA WANTED TO—" Kyle caught himself and turned down the volume, "eat Sam!"

Gasps.

"Why wasn't this on the show?" called out a witch. "This is the best story *ever*!"

"Actually, why do *centaurs* get to be part of the show?" sniped a merman, swimming in a large tank at the back. "I want my close up!"

"Same here!" twittered a series of fairies. "We want to

visit Shadow Oak now!"

"Let's invade!" cried two Chimera. "Someone find Shadow Oak on the map!"

The room erupted in chaos. Mythics shouted over one another, pointing and accusing. Kyle's eyes widened, and he pawed the ground anxiously. Starr flushed; Mav had been right, of course, she should have kept her trap shut. The volume in the room rose, and rose some more until—

WHAM. WHAM. WHAM.

Fiona slammed the base of her lion's head cane onto the stage. With the first crash the sound cut out by half. With the second, the room had gone quiet. And by the third, the mythics had all returned to their seats. She raised an eyebrow and set a hand on Starr's head. "Poor Sam," she said, digging her fingers into Starr's curls and holding her in place. "She's new to our world. She doesn't understand, and may never. None of that happened, of course. It was just a little... game she was playing. Isn't that so?"

Starr looked up at her, then out at Kyle. She had no choice. "Yeah," said Starr, totally deflated. "I was just making things up."

Kyle's jaw had dropped. "I was only playing along," he muttered, tail drooping. He retreated down the aisle and slipped through the back doors.

Starr's heart hurt for reasons she couldn't even explain.

"Well, then," said Valéncia, releasing Starr. "You see why we must be so careful with our newest town resident. She can be so... fragile with her perceptions. Perhaps she will need her own visit to Shadow Oak General in the near future."

Applause surged from the audience, then rose. Fiona lifted her arms as if to capture it in a hug. Starr took a step back, then another, until she was seated again.

"Nice try." Nico leaned over to Starr, covering his microphone. "But you never had a chance. She's the master at this."

Now they were chanting Valéncia's name. The diva backed away again, returning to the chairs. A long, slow smile drew across her face like a blade, and on her way to her seat she paused in front of Starr's chair.

Muffling her mic, she leaned forward, smelling of linden tree and lavender. "I hope you enjoyed your spotlight," she whispered. "You'll want to remember that warmth when the world grows cold. Which for you, I imagine, should happen... any minute now."

CHAPTER 28

A Starr is Torn

THE MOMENT DAKOTA declared the endless Q&A over, Starr raced off the stage, down the hallway and through a set of double doors, exploding onto an empty, snow-covered terrace outside the hotel.

And she screamed. Threw her voice to the heavens, picturing the sídhe busking on Boston Common stumbling over a note while hearing it, or Jason pausing mid-gallop during his daily run along the Charles River. She wished she sounded so fierce that even the grindylows in the waters beneath the hotel would dive deeper. She wanted to be heard.

Screaming wasn't enough, though, so she kicked out at a potted evergreen shrub, which toppled over. "Ow," she muttered, hopping on one foot.

"Whoa, lady." Mav pushed through the same set of double doors. "Trees are our friends."

Starr whirled away from him, breath puffing in hot, angry gusts. Of course Mav knew she'd be furious after Fiona's antics on the stage. He always understood. Starr didn't deserve him.

"Lemme guess," he said. "The burr in your saddle starts with an F and ends with an I-O-N-A."

"She's *done* something." The circles she paced in the snow grew smaller. "I don't know what. But it's going to turn all those mythics against me."

"No chance. Nobody as fresh as you ever got that kind of reception at their first con. They love you."

"They don't know me. They love Sam."

"Who is part of you. Anyhow, why do you keep taking Fiona's bait?"

Starr flared. "Better question: why do you all let her get away with that shit? Grandstanding. Threats."

"Why do you?" Mav folded his arms. "Not like you ever tattled about who dropped that wardrobe. Not even to me."

She shook her head. "I've got no proof. Fiona and I had an understanding that's over now. And I didn't want to bother Jason."

"And there you are. Nobody wants to bother Jason. But there's never a time he's not wrapped around some axle. That's part of the thrill for him." He leaned on the wall. "Be smart, will ya? She knows how to press on your soft parts, 'cause you always fall for it. Bullies only retreat when you fight back. If she knows she can't push you around anymore, she'll look for other quarry."

Starr thought about what had happened on the stage and how Mav had tried to prevent her from facing off with Fiona. "You're no help. You tell me to stand up to her, but the minute I do, you say, 'Don't give her the satisfaction.' At least Nico supported me up there."

Mav let out a long breath. "That Nico. Mr. Helpful."

Behind them, several guest actors pushed open the doors and huddled off to one side to light up. Nico passed by on the other side of the glass and waved. Starr fluttered her fingers briefly, not sure whose side he was on.

"I can't concentrate when Fiona gets that way," she said. "My mind gets all… squirrely. She reminds me of dealing with my mother. And I don't want to fight. I want to do my job."

There was a long pause between them, and Starr realized she could barely feel her toes.

"I'm popping back in before I become an icicle." Mav stepped toward her. "Panels're going to start up in a couple minutes. I came out here to tell you we'll all be 'round the firepit on the rooftop tonight, near nine. Just mortals, no fans. It's a tradition. Might even be marshmallows, and I'll have my guitar. Sometimes, we sing."

Starr gnawed the inside of her cheek. "And Fiona?"

"She's invited, but it's been at least eight years since she put in an appearance. Everyone's happier that way. She sounds like a dying badger when she lets loose with a tune."

Starr nearly smiled. Mav lifted her chin with the side of his finger. "It's your life, partner. You going to let her cheat you out of it, or are you going to take those reins yourself? Don't let her have that power, too, on top of everything else she has."

You wanted to be heard? Mav hears you. He cares.

In the hospital, she'd vowed to fight for this job. For this life. It was time to start doing just that. She'd taken charge in Centaur Park—and she could do it again. "I'll be there," she insisted. It was as much a promise to Mav as herself.

HOURS LATER STARR stumbled into her hotel room, exhausted. Following the endless Q&A Session from hell, she'd sat on three panels of an hour each: Best Meals Never Eaten (on why nobody consumed food on the show, just let it steam in front of them); Mapping Shadow Oak (things had gotten heated over the nonsensical geography of the town); and Woo! Let the Ghosts Out (exploring why mortals who died on the show never returned in non-corporeal forms).

She hadn't been back to her room since first thing that morning, and as she pushed inside Starr had two plans: nap, then head up to the roof for some carousing, marshmallows and a song or two. Dragging herself to bed, she was preparing to face-plant when a rustle of paper startled her.

Nora was sitting on her own bed, holding up the *Water Worlds* with Starr on the cover. She rustled it again to make sure she had Starr's attention.

Starr had perhaps, willfully forgotten about it. When Dakota had delivered the magazine the night before she'd been wary; now, after one of the more draining days of her life, she didn't have the fortitude to dive into *sheer gold*-ness.

But here was Nora, resting the magazine on her distended belly. Her face was like a fist.

When the world grows cold.

A twisting cyclone of anxiety stirred in Starr's gut. This was old, vindictive, mean Nora—not the woman she'd finally been getting to know and like. Nora had been a team player on the stage a few hours earlier. Now she had the magazine.

"That bad?" Starr screwed up her face.

Nora hurled the magazine at her, and it bounced off the side of the bed. She slid forward, ungainly. "Here I was, starting to warm to you," she hissed. "That's done now, cutie pie." She pointed at the closet. "Find yourself another roomie, 'cause there's no way I'm sleeping in the same room with a dirty snake like you." She stood, tottered and grabbed her coat. "Be gone when I get back."

Dazed, Starr felt like she'd been hit with wooden plank. "Wait—I haven't even—Nora!"

The door slammed shut.

Starr stared at the bent and twisted magazine on the floor. This was going to be bad. Bits of that afternoon floated in a hazy soup toward her, but mostly all she remembered were the generous pours of wine Dakota gave her during their chat.

What the hell did I say?

Starr sat on the edge of the bed, gathered up the magazine and her courage, and flipped to the center spread.

Then she read about herself.

THE ACTRESS, WHOSE *soft curls form a halo around her winsome face, throws back a third slug of wine and gulps noisily.*

"Where I come from, mortals don't live as long as most people in Shadow Oak," says Sam. "Everyone here is really holding back the years. A few look a little decrepit, and yeah, some of them are like talking to ancient elders. But I'm catching up fast. I can't wait until I'm as old and wise as the others in town!"

Starr lowered the magazine and glanced around, looking for a hidden cameradryad. Could she really have *said* those things? She didn't even *think* those things!

Sam also hints that there's all sorts of shenanigans

that go on when the cameras aren't running, though she gleefully dodges naming names. "Let's say that what you see on the show is only the tiniest amount of the weirdness that goes on with us. If we had the cameras on all the time, you'd be stunned. I once saw a mythic and a human... getting naked in an office!"

The actress shoves another éclair into her mouth, and when she's almost finished chewing, winks. "We're not even allowed to show you the best stuff. The thought is that the audience probably couldn't handle it."

Halfway through the piece, Starr's mouth hurt she was grimacing so hard. This didn't sound like her. Dakota could take all the 'ums' and 'likes' out—that was polite. But these were *not* things she'd have said. The article was designed to do one thing: make her look like a total blabbermouth creep. And... *wait a minute.* Starr scanned back: *"I once saw a mythic and a human... getting naked in an office!"*

Now she knew something was up. On the one hand, Starr had seen that happen. But it had been between Cris and Dakota. Dakota, the author of this very article. She would *never* have put that quote in, no matter how much *sheer gold* it constituted.

Starr's heart was pounding, and perspiration beaded her forehead. She felt like she was back in Phil's cave, with the dragon on the rampage. The article was beautiful to look at. There were sketches of show scenes—no photos were allowed—of Sam with Roland, with Mav, with Valéncia. In each, she appeared daring and darling. None of that matched the words. The article made her seem like a child who mainlined pastries and couldn't keep her trap shut.

Gritting her teeth, she forced herself to read on.

Still, Sam admits she feels trepidation about the future. The longer she stays in Shadow Oak, the harder it will be for her to venture out into the rest of the world. The place is so special, she says, it changes the rest of the mortal realm.

"We spend a lot of time working, and with each other," she says. *"It's a magical atmosphere. But anything outside Shadow Oak can be... a problem. Mav told me he'd been married before he came to town, and how she didn't understand his work. They had to break up. That's why he's so sad and lonely all the time. I pity him."*

At that, her mind blanked. Her stomach lurched. Starr raced into the bathroom and vomited her lunch into the toilet, then sank onto the cold tiles. Her mind raced.

"Dakota, you bitch," Starr gasped. "You are *toast*."

She burst into tears.

STARR DIDN'T PASS out from her weeping, but she lost about twenty minutes, dragging herself to the bed and flopping onto it. The crying jag fed on itself—each time she felt the storm was passing, she remembered what had been so upsetting, and the whole thing started over.

Assuming Alligash had done his job, everyone in the hotel now had a copy of *WaterWorlds*, including the cast. Dakota couldn't have shafted Starr better. Only... why *would* Dakota shaft her? Had the reporter felt blackmailed because of what Starr knew about her and Cris? Maybe? But that was all in the open now, wasn't it?

Starr shook her head. Some of the quotes were real, which was what had made it so diabolical: Mav had told Starr about his broken marriage—but they'd been alone on that hospital set when he confided in her. Every dressing room, the stages, the bathrooms even would have to be bugged for all those conversations to be recorded. Starr was reasonably confident Dakota had neither the resources nor the will to undertake such a project.

But Fiona did.

Starr lifted her head from the duvet, turning to stare out the sliding glass doors at the darkening sky.

Oleander stared back.

"Yah!" Starr jerked away so fast she threw herself off the side of the bed. "Oof." Rising up on her knees, she faced the brownie across the bed. "Oleander, please start wearing bells on your shoes or something?"

"Of course, Ms. Starr." The brownie handed over a box of tissues and a steaming mug of brown and purple liquid. "You were busy with tears."

Starr honked into one tissue. "I take it back, don't actually wear bells."

Oleander nodded.

A sip from the mug calmed Starr down almost immediately, soothing her aching chest. The brownie dabbed at the corner of her eyes. No makeup came off on the tissue; Starr would look perfect, if red-eyed, up on the roof later.

I can't go up there. Everyone will have the magazine.

The thing was, she didn't care about everyone. To her surprise, the only person whose opinion mattered was Mav. He'd told her things in private, and there they were, splashed on the page alongside outright lies. She didn't *pity* Mav, not in the least. He wore his dignity like a cape, and it had commanded Starr's respect for months. Her heart ached to think she might have embarrassed him.

"Ms. Starr... come now?" Oleander tilted her head, gesturing at the brownie door.

Starr remembered: Oleander wanted to show her something, and it had to do with Jan, and a petition. "Oh, Oleander, I can't right now. I'm a mess."

The brownie tugged on her hand. "Bros know what we want now. And what we don't want. Need to show you a Don't Want."

Starr sighed. She couldn't be gone long: the roof beckoned. As much as she didn't want to go up there, she had to convince everyone that this article wasn't her doing. But she was so tired.

"Please?" Oleander asked again. "I look out for you with Phil. You come, look out for me."

Starr's head snapped up. The brownie had never asked for anything, other than more books. If she was calling in a chit, this must be worth seeing. "All right," she nodded. "I'm in."

Oleander clapped her hands, reshaping the brownie door this way and that, as if it were made of clay. After it was wide enough for Starr to fit, she peered inside to find darkness broken by the flicker of Wills lighting a narrow path. Searching the brownie's face, Starr thought of the small group of friends she had on the show who'd never had it out for her: Mav. Jason. Phil, mostly.

Oleander, always.

"Lay on, Macduff," she said.

"Oleander! I'm Oleander!"

"Of course you are."

They disappeared behind the door, which promptly shrank behind them.

WITHIN THE WALLS turned out to be roomier than Starr expected—though not quite roomy enough for her to stand. Or turn around. She took deep, calming breaths to force aside claustrophobia, and crawled slowly behind Oleander.

They wound through inner walls, brushing past twisting wires, hand-lettered brownie graffiti and a few mouse pellets. Wills swirled over their heads like mobile flashlights, and amid the darkness Starr felt she was moving through a blank place in space and time.

A few minutes in, her knees and back ached, yet she was impressed by the world between the walls. "Is it like this at home?" she asked as they turned a corner. She had to sit up and rotate her legs around to make the angle work, thanking her yoga exercises for making it possible.

"Better at home!" said Oleander. "Home walls have glamour. Looks like a city!" She lay a finger over her lips. "Now quiet. Nearly there."

Starr could make out the sound of overlapping voices ahead, like a cocktail party conversation. It reminded her of her first visit to the stages. Where was she being led? Was she about to hear the cast dragging her name through the mud over the article?

The brownie halted next to a small doorframe resembling the one in Starr's room. "Not my door," she whispered. "Can't change shape. Stay here. Listen. Yes?"

Starr nodded as Oleander twisted the inner doorknob slightly, pushing it into the room a few inches. The overlapping voices grew stronger, the sound of the conversations clearer. But it was a monotone chorus, without modulation or affect. Starr crept closer, getting a surprisingly good view of the room, though at floor level.

"You see?" her brownie whispered.

At first, Starr didn't. It was another hotel room, though twice the size of her own. A suite. A canopied bed dominated the back of the room, which had its own sofa and plush chairs and a row of windows offering a glittering vista of Boston beyond a balcony so large Starr's entire dressing room back at the studio could have fit into it.

And smack in the center of all this luxury was Fiona, lying on a soft recliner, face serene, eyes shut. Her long-nailed hands rested across her chest.

She's dead!

But no, under those claws Fiona's chest rose and fell softly.

None of that was the strange part, though. What was truly odd was the approximately dozen brownies encircling her, chanting. Well, not chanting. Speaking. Talking. Reciting.

"Trees are our friends."

Mav's exact words from a few hours ago—coming from his brownie, Pardner's, mouth.

"Oleander?" Starr half-turned.

The brownie shushed her and whispered. "Recitation. Every day. This is a Don't Want."

Alligash was now giving voice to Dakota's words: "You gave me *sheer gold* with those quotes."

Quotes.

Ally is a Bro of Record, Dakota had explained to Starr. *He remembers everything. So much better than a voice recorder. Fiona let me borrow him.*

Starr sat back, nauseated. Oleander pulled the door closed. "You all can do that, can't you?"

The brownie saluted. "Bro Network! Tell Fiona everything, every day. Bookender transcribes." She re-opened the door a crack and gestured at a desk near the sofa, where Fiona's brownie was typing away furiously.

"So many pages."

"Where do they go?"

"Fiona has personal archives."

"Every single conversation in this place, every day, she saves in some kind of *vault*?" Starr couldn't fathom it. Oleander nodded. "Let me guess: nobody knows they're being eavesdropped on."

"Just we, you and Fiona."

"Not... Nico?"

"Mr. Nico said many years ago to Ms. Fiona, 'Stop.' He said, 'This isn't worthy of you.' And Ms. Fiona said, 'For you, I will.' And she did stop! But then Ms. Amelia and—" She clapped her hands over her mouth, trembling.

Starr shook her head at the scope of it all. Fiona hadn't needed to bug anyone. She'd brownied them. All these brownies, eager and happy to do the errands humans were too lazy or busy to take care of—also burdened with reporting every conversation back to Fiona at the end of the day. What a waste of time and effort, all in service of a woman whose greatest fear was irrelevance. Who then turned the words into weapons, deploying private thoughts like poison blow darts.

Her weapons. Her brownies. Oleander had been *reporting* on her. "I had no idea the Stasi was serving my tea every day."

"What is Estasy?"

"Government spies," Starr said, furious. "How could you?"

"We must! Or she sends us home!" The brownie was quaking again. "Gets new helpers. We don't want to do this anymore. Bros want to help but this is too much. Mx. Jan says make a list of Don't Wants to give to Jason."

"What else is on the list?"

"No more glitter." Oleander raised her finger. "We throw it away. Also, some days to leave the show. Not forever. To see friends. Family."

The petition: that's what this was about. The thing TPTB had turned to cinder. Jan was organizing the brownies. Jason was going to love this.

"And we don't have to go home if we do this right, Mx. Jan says!"

"Great plan," said Starr. "You've got my support." But she was losing her focus. Quotes. The magazine article. Alligash, on loan from Fiona. No doubt he'd given her the transcript of Starr's interview. Dakota must have let her write the article, and her good pal Helena, editor-in-chief, had blessed it into existence. This had been a group project.

Starr wanted to burst through this wall and strangle that horrible woman with her own scarf. Then, mid-murderous impulse, she heard a thudding through the low hum of voices.

Someone was knocking at Fiona's door.

CHAPTER 29

Don't Let's Ask for the Moon. We Have the Starrs

DEEP INSIDE HER Waking Dream trance, Fiona recognized, then ignored, the pounding at her door. The bro voices were soothing and empowering. She would awaken with their words in her head, as if she had been present at every one of those conversations. Though there were gaps—Oleander hadn't reported in yet today. She'd have to look into that.

The thudding continued and distracted her. Waking Dream paused, then disappeared, the spell broken. She rose slowly from that deep, dark mental place, irritated. The Bro Network had nearly completed its summary. If a maid was on the other side of that door, she'd have her fired.

Fiona fluttered her fingers and the overlapping conversations ceased. A second gesture had the bro lift her seat into a raised position. Still a third bro stepped forward to present a warm, moist towelette. Without opening her eyes, she plucked at the cloth and dabbed at her face.

Still more pounding.

This had been quite a day, one which still held so much promise. The article on 'Sam' would cause a mass outcry, she was certain. Did hotels keep a supply of tar and feathers these days? Perhaps the noise at her door was Starr herself, blind with fury. Fiona rubbed her hands in anticipation and rose from her chair. Patting her turban, she flicked her hands at the bros, who scampered to their little door at the back of the room.

The pounding ceased. Then: *Knock-knock. Knock.*
Nico?

It was their agreed-upon signal. Had the first outraged visitor departed and Nico taken their place? Or had Nico forgotten himself altogether? He'd been such a trial since the Centaur Park debacle. He needed serious reining in, but Fiona's energies had been turned Starr-ward—and toward the encroaching, insistent Valéncia voice inside.

"Answer please, Bookender."

Her assistant hopped from his desk chair where he'd been transcribing, wiping his glasses with a linen cloth before opening the suite's double-door entry.

"Evening, Mr. Reddy," he said. "Ms. Fiona is not—sir!"

Nico pushed past Bookender into the suite's living area. His hair was awry, his shirt untucked, and he wore a grey fleece coat far too warm for the room. He brandished a rolled-up *WaterWorlds* like a club, then tossed it on the coffee table. "That," he said, "is an outrage."

Fiona peered at the magazine as if seeing it for the first time. "Oh dear." She rested a hand on her chest. "Have they published the wrong column of mine again? They do love repeating that classic one about crafting dragon feathers into a boa. It's the first in a series, though, and—"

Nico drove his fists onto his hips. "Stop that. You know what I mean."

"Bookender." Fiona waved at the bro, who had finished hoisting himself back into his chair. "Tea, please. Calming. Mr. Reddy appears somewhat… exercised." She turned to Nico. "Perhaps you should shed your coat, dear. You are perspiring excessively."

He flung the fleece to the floor. "Well? What do you have to say?"

"Nico, I do wish you'd speak your mind. I enjoy your visits, but the hour is late."

"The cover story. About Starr."

"About *Sam*, my dear."

He frowned. "Same thing in this case."

"Is it? What poor writing." She cocked her head at the magazine again. "You're right, that photo does her far too much justice. In any case, I have yet to read it. Ms. Weatherby is so persistently present that I wonder if I need to read anything further about her."

"That story has your fingerprints all over it."

"Oh? What is the source of such an accusation?"

"There's no way Starr gave that interview, and there's no way that article gets published without someone pulling strings with Helena. The most controversial thing that rag ever printed was about the time Griz walked behind a window while filming and nobody cut it from the edit, which meant we had to explain a rogue ogre in Shadow Oak." He took a deep breath. "That magazine is embarrassingly on our side. They airbrush the hell out of us and the show, which gives them *access* to the show. So you want me to believe they changed decades of precedent for this one piece?"

"Oh, Nico!" Fiona clapped her hands in delight. "You gave a speech."

His face darkened.

Bookender tapped Fiona's hip. "Brownie door—stuck," he said. "Tea is... delayed."

"Well, pull harder," she said absently. "Don't brownies have unusual strength?"

Bookender bowed, racing back to the door.

Nico was pacing.

"Where were we?" Fiona wondered. "Oh, yes. Has Starr been bending your ear with complaints?"

He slowed, running a hand along the back of a chair. "Starr no longer speaks to me."

"Delightful!" Fiona rose and lay her hands on the room's paltry coffee and tea service. "Never mind, Bookender, we have what we need here." She passed the tray to her assistant, who retreated to get hot water from the bathroom sink.

"My point"—Nico began stalking the room again—"is it's clearly your handiwork. What I don't get is how— oh." He paused behind the sofa and pointed. "Fiona Ballantine. Get your ass over here."

Fiona folded her arms. "I don't appreciate such language—" but she followed his pointing finger. "Good gracious. What are they doing here?"

A huddled group of brownies lurked behind the sofa. A dozen pairs of eyes turned to the mortals. "Door's stuck, mistress," said one.

"Please tell me this isn't what it looks like." Nico's words were thin and hard.

"I couldn't possibly say what it looks like," Fiona retorted. "You aren't suggesting I'm having an affair with a dozen brownies?"

"You activated it again."

"Tea!" Bookender announced, setting the tray on the coffee table. "Mundane Earl Grey, but I had a few herbs and spices at hand to make it—" He glanced at Fiona. "Mistress?"

"Get them out of here *now*." Fiona swung her foot at the pile of brownies, striking one. A howl rose. "Out by the front door if you must, but out. Now."

The brownie door swung wide. The bros flooded toward freedom, spinning Nico around and nearly knocking Fiona over. In three blinks, the bros had all passed into the walls.

"Anything more, mistress?" Bookender pulled the door closed.

"Why was that door stuck, Bookender?"

He shrugged, decanting two cups of tea. "I could not say, mistress. It is a new phenomenon. Shall I pause in my transcription to investigate further?"

"Send him out," said Nico.

"Absolutely not." Fiona sipped her tea. "Bookender has work to complete."

"Bookender." Nico crouched down, jerking his thumb at the door. "Out. Now."

The brownie looked at Fiona, who shrugged. "Very well. So much drama, Nicodemus. Bookender, please adjourn for a moment."

With a brief bow, the brownie followed his companions out the door. Once it shut, Fiona set down her teacup. "Nicodemus, we have been friends far too long for you to be peremptory with me. If you wish to have a reasonable discussion—"

Nico was no longer pacing, or sweating. His face was set in a hard, unreadable expression. "Tell me this: you have the Bro Network up and running again. Yes or no."

Fiona sighed. Nico was best handled like a large, domesticated pet. Feed him, stroke his ego and throw him a treat every so often so he wouldn't question the universe. For decades he had sailed along in semi-immortality, satisfying himself with whatever pretty thing happened to be on set that week or MARBLEing off to the more exotic corners of the Fae universe. Now he was a dog with a bone and could not be fobbed off with easy words or promises. He would have to face the reality of the situation.

Such terrible irony, Valéncia's voice dripped with sarcasm. *Nico is unimportant. Cut him out if he's become an obstacle.*

Icicles ran through Fiona at the thought. Nico was her champion, her Greek chorus. "I was under genuine threat." She poked a finger at his chest. "Action was required."

His face sagged. "You invented that threat out of whole cloth. It's all in your head!"

He's right! Valéncia cackled. *I'm all in your head! But I can fix that!*

Fiona envisioned the roller coaster again, creeping up the track. She fought to silence Valéncia, but it was much more difficult now. Part of her didn't want this djinn to go back in the bottle, but part of her lived in fear of it.

"I put up with this for a long time," said Nico. "The way you see every person they hire on this show as a personal threat. I also ignored you belittling my concerns. But this… this was a promise you made to me. You've broken a promise to me about using the brownies this way. Even after what happened last time, you haven't learned. It was over nothing then, and it's over nothing now."

Anger surged and bubbled over. "It was not nothing!" Fiona/Valéncia shrieked. "It was never about nothing!"

* * *

THE BRO NETWORK was not new. A few years after Bookender was awarded to Fiona, he began inviting his fellow brownies to help out at the show. Fiona became den mother to a group of fans who were thrilled to do whatever she asked. So, she gave them tasks—keep her dressing room neat, organize her wardrobe, serve her tea, color-code her feather boas. More brownies showed up, so she'd sent them to help the other actors.

One day, quite by accident, she'd discovered they had the ability to recite from memory anything they'd heard, indefinitely. Fiona asked them to tell her things they'd overheard. That knowledge was too delicious not to use for her own benefit, and over time they became her intelligence system. Then she'd erred by sharing the Bro Network secret with Nico.

"It's like McCarthyism," he had said, making some topical reference to his own time that meant nothing to Fiona. "You're like Big Brother. Also, it's morally wrong."

Back in those days, Nico had been far more concerned with ethics, and was a much more tedious man. Reluctantly, Fiona promised she would end the project and released the brownies from their duty to report daily.

Though she did check in here and there.

Decades passed. Joseph Abernathy became the writer's room and churned out fantastical stories—at that time, TPTB weren't as concerned with reflecting mortal reality—that dazzled Fiona. They fell in love. He gave her all the best parts. So what if some of them had the ring of the familiar? Making a show every day meant they churned through so much narrative she barely had time to read books or take in any human-centered entertainments. Did she suspect some of the tales weren't fully Joe's? Perhaps. But they had never discussed it.

Then Amelia Beckenridge was hired, and in a matter of weeks began making comments about some of Joe's story arcs. As Joe told Fiona later, the newcomer threatened him with exposure if he didn't start giving *her* the biggest, meatiest parts. Fiona swore to Joe that the mythics wouldn't care if his stories had been copied from the mortal realm—but by then, TPTB had started shifting their desires to make the show more 'real' and less about spaceships and alternate realities and journeys into the center of the earth.

Joe had no idea how to pivot. He lost his spirit for the adventure. Faced with his own fraudulence and impending irrelevance, he broke. Lashed out at the brownies, then Fiona. Horrified with what he was becoming, he left the show through the Gate one afternoon—and never came back. Quitting the show meant one thing: within a day or two, his memories of ever having been beyond the Veil would be scrubbed. Fiona had chased after him, frantic, searching through the bizarre and frightening modern New York City every night and weekend for months.

In the end, she'd tracked him down to a subway station corridor. He was typing out poems for commuters at five dollars a pop. "Tell me about the person you want to dedicate this poem to," he'd said to her when she approached, no recognition in his eye.

Fiona opened her heart. For twenty minutes she expounded about Joseph Abernathy, the only man she'd loved without reservation. Who was not necessarily tall, dark or handsome, but who had gentled her in a way no one ever had before. Who saw the weirdest parts of Fiona Ballantine and channeled them into the right stories to showcase her brilliance. Had he lifted them from more talented writers? Certainly. But they'd been his gifts to her, like hearts torn from living beings, presented on a plate for consumption. They'd had eight good years together.

This was the poem Joseph wrote in that subway corridor:

Oh! Joe!
Where did you go?
I'll never know.
You seemed a swell man
What had been your plan?
You wrote words for my heart
But now we're apart.
Joe, now you're gone
But not forgott-on.

Joseph, as it turned out, was not a good writer. But he'd been a very good plagiarist, and an even better lover. Fiona kept that poem framed on the wall in her office, and never went looking for him again. Whatever they'd once had was lost with his memories.

With Joseph gone, Fiona had reactivated the Bro Network. She could have helped him ward off Amelia if she'd been alerted early enough. She'd have heard all those awful things that vicious woman had threatened him with. Information was power—Fiona knew that now. Lack of information was weakness. She'd been too late to save Joseph, but she hadn't been too late to give Amelia what she deserved.

And using what she knew from the bros, she'd done what needed doing.

Afterward, Nico had insisted she pull the plug again. He'd made her swear on their friendship. She'd been good for a time.

But then Starr had arrived.

NICO SANK INTO a plush chair, the wind knocked from him. "Jesus, Fee. You swore to me. You swore on *us*." He blinked. "You know, mythics don't really like people who break promises."

Fiona towered over him. There was a quaking in her now, something she almost didn't recognize as fury. It was clean, pure and simple—something she'd been ignoring for a long time.

Joseph, Joseph, Joseph. I'm so bored with Joseph, Valéncia taunted her inside. *Just another weak man who couldn't hack it. Good riddance.*

Fiona fought to maintain control. The Starr disaster was nearly over. So long as Nico kept his mouth shut, Starr would find being on *Tune in Tomorrow* intolerable. She would quit. Lose her memories. Be erased from the mythic world.

"You will not speak of this with anyone," she said.

"I'll damn well speak about it if I damn well want to," Nico shot back. "You don't seem to understand the depths of what you've done here."

"I confess to doing nothing. Watch yourself, Nicodemus." Her eyes were hot and prickly.

He leaned forward. "You aimed at Starr. You wanted her to look like an idiot. Congratulations, that worked. In the process, you burned everybody. You put Cris and Dakota's thing in there. You made Jason look like he had no idea about what's going on in his own show. And you did that at the exact moment the SCN is considering giving all of us the heave-ho. We're on life support, and you turned off the juice. All because you think Starr is out to get you."

"It's Amelia's fault." Pieces of Fiona were crumbling inside. "I mean, Starr's fault. She's a useless speck of nothing and we'll be well rid of her."

Nico leapt to his feet. "It isn't true, and you make me sad to hear it. Sad for you, Fiona. I used to think this kind of thing was beneath you."

Valéncia couldn't take it anymore. Roaring forward, she shoved Fiona down like laundry in a hamper and took over. The crumbling feeling vanished. "How dare you pity me," she roared at full stage volume, hurling her teacup against the wall. The crash and splash was deeply satisfying. "Who are *you* to tell me anything? You're nothing but a worthless drunk Fiona picked up out of the gutter. And she can drop you back down in a heartbeat."

Nico's face had lost all its color, and he seemed strangely old. "OK, we've gone to a weird, hurtful place here. This isn't my Cookie saying this."

"Fiona is having a little break," Valéncia growled. "She's as sick of you as I am, but now you're hearing *me* for once: Lady Valéncia Marlborough. You are unimportant, Nicodemus Reddy—you're not even that good an actor. Until now it has been convenient to have you around. Do not give Fiona any reason to alter her beliefs in this matter."

Nico blinked several times, speechless.

"Fiona wishes that you not speak of this 'network' with anyone. As you appear determined to ignore her, I shall have to rescind her 'gift' from years ago. It always was a loan, after all." Fiona/Valéncia closed her eyes a moment, then opened them again. "There. Rescinded. You shall not have it back until we are satisfied you are willing to toe the line."

Running his hands through his hair, Nico circled the chair. "That's it. I—" He paused, seeming to remember something. "I discharge myself. Whether it's Valéncia or Fiona hearing this, as of this minute, the debt is paid."

Nico turned on his heel and headed to the door.

"And where are you off to?" Valéncia sneered. "Is the bar open?"

He paused, hand on the doorknob. "None of your business, 'Valéncia.' I'm going to find Starr. But if I feel like getting shitfaced for the first time in thirty years after that, you can't stop me. Tell that to Fiona... when she comes back."

He shut the door gently behind him.

Bookender ventured through the brownie door several moments later, but Fiona hadn't moved an inch. She stood in the middle of the room, the now-retreated Valéncia's words echoing in her mind. *Who spoke to him like that? Valéncia? Or the unvarnished me?* Fiona no longer knew. She ached to undo what had happened. To un-rescind the award she'd given him.

Do that and I will give you no peace, Valéncia sneered. *We're in this together. For all time.*

Bookender held up a linen handkerchief. "Mistress?"

"I do not require that," she sniffed at him, though actually, she did.

CHAPTER 30
Starry, Starry Night

HEARING NICO MAKE clear that he knew the *Water Worlds* article had been tampered with, a rush of relief and affection washed over Starr as she hid in the walls with Oleander. Nico had seen the article's fakery and gone to its source. He was defending Starr, not Fiona! Maybe she should reconsider her policy.

Oleander pulled the brownie door shut. "No more Estasy."

"C'mon," Starr pouted. "It was just getting good."

Muffled, raised voices permeated the wall and Starr wanted desperately to claw the door open again, but Oleander refused. The door's knob rattled, and the brownie wedged a bit of wood into the frame to delay the opening. "Bros come!" she cried. "No room in here for bros and Starrs!"

Oleander leaped over Starr's bent legs and hurried down the inner corridor. Starr scrambled to catch up as the Wills swirled over their heads. A few moments of awkward scrambling later, Oleander drew open the frame of the door to allow Starr back into her hotel room.

The brownie remained in the walls. "Tomorrow!" she chirped—and shut the door.

Starr hauled herself up on the bed, cringing at the hated magazine with its grinning, lying cover gleaming up at her. She flipped it over. Beneath the magazine lay a manila envelope that must have been dropped off in her absence, and she peered inside: dark pink-colored pages that smelled of cherry. Rewrites for tomorrow's live show. She rested the envelope on her lap, knowing she'd have more strength to read them later.

Mav. Dakota. Jason.

She needed to speak to all of them. Mav, to assure him about the article. Jason, to ensure she wasn't getting in serious trouble for the article. And Dakota, who she planned to stuff down the hotel's laundry chute. Starr ran her hands over the envelope, and the answer came. Mav first.

I can say we should run lines, see what he knows before breaking the bad news. Assuming he doesn't know already.

Gripping the envelope, she raced to the elevators. Just beyond them lay the staircase to the roof, one flight up. Adrenaline surged through her like a raging river.

Bong!

Up ahead, an elevator door slid open, and someone exited at top speed, just as Starr arrived at the elevator bank. The impact between them was hard and immediate, and spun them both around. "Oof!" cried Starr.

"Ow!" cried the other.

They both crashed to the carpet. Starr rolled over to discover Dakota just a few feet away.

Mav can wait, she thought, and launched herself at the conduit—if not the source—of her current misery.

Wrenching Dakota's lapels, she shook the reporter and hauled back a hand to deliver a slap on that serene, composed face. But Dakota was neither serene nor composed. Long streaks of unmagical mascara ran down her cheeks, tears flowing from puffed red eyes.

Dakota took long, shuddering gasps of air. "He—he—he—"

Is she laughing?

Dakota hiccupped.

OK, she's crying.

"He dumped me!" Dakota wailed. "Crissy threw me out!"

Starr released her and sagged back to the carpet. "Oh."

Dakota's shoulders hitched. "You're going to... hit me?"

Starr was still furious, but she couldn't hit a woman while she was down. Glancing at the mess of envelopes, makeup and hairbrushes scattered on the floor from Dakota's messenger bag, which had emptied on impact, Starr shook her head.

"No," she growled, scrambling to her feet and grabbing a manila envelope from the pile. "But get your shit together, lady. We need to talk."

DAKOTA SANK ONTO Starr's bed like a deflating balloon, burying her messy face into the pillow. Starr tossed their belongings aside, then summoned Oleander for tea. Less crying, more talking was what she wanted from Dakota right now. When Oleander failed to materialize, she dampened a facecloth and returned to the reporter's side of the bed. "Hey."

Dakota turned, and Starr dabbed at the mascara

rivulets, offering a tissue box. Three giant goose sounds later, Dakota had reached a quieter level of grief, though the hiccups remained.

"He—he—"

"Dumped you." Starr nodded. "I'm caught up there. My condolences. Any idea why?"

Her body shuddered from hiccups. "He started y-yelling at me. Said he thought I knew how to do my job. And he threatened—"

"To tie you to a tree and release fire ants?"

"Killer bees."

"Wow. He's super-pissed." Starr slid the issue of *WaterWorlds* over. She had a pretty good idea why Cris would axe Dakota from his life; she just found it odd that the reporter hadn't perceived the consequences of her *sheer gold* actions. "Did he happen to mention if it was related to your article?"

Dakota eyed the magazine like it was a tarantula. "He did! He said there were damaging quotes in there, but that doesn't make sense. You didn't say anything *really* off-color, just a little silly. But he said they made the show look bad. That Jason was going to talk to you l-later but *he* was talking to me *now* and it was like we were strangers." Her lip quivered.

Starr cocked her head. Surely Dakota was in on this. *Or was she like Nico? A patsy?* "When did you last read the cover story?"

Dakota flushed. "Right before Helena got it for sign-off. But, see—Fiona asked for a favor. They're friends. So she got the final, final look."

Starr flopped against the bed and grabbed the magazine. "Here. Read it, you hack."

Dakota flinched at the word, then paged open to the

article. "This isn't my story."

"Keep going. It gets better. And by that, I mean it gets worse."

Ten minutes later, after racing through the piece, Dakota's jaw had dropped. She pointed at the line about Starr pitying Mav. "You did *not* say that," she gasped. "If I included a quote like that in a story, Helena would put my head in a sling."

Starr stared at her. If this was Dakota lying, she was due an Endless Award of her own.

"Crissy! He has to know! We need to tell him!" Dakota started to stand.

"Yeah?" Starr asked. "He's going to listen to you telling him his star performer sabotaged the article?"

"Helena will confirm—"

"Sure she will. Come on, Dakota, who's the low woman on the totem pole? Who do you really think those two will sell out in the end?"

For the first time, anger crept into the reporter's face. Then, a little hurt. "Bitches."

"Breaking news," said Starr. "Meanwhile, I'm even lower down than you are: I'm the blabbermouth piece of gluttonous trash." Saying it aloud made seeing Mav even more urgent. She had to resolve this before the night was out. "I gotta go."

"Where?"

"I need to see a man about a lie."

STARR SHOVED OPEN the penthouse rooftop access door, stepping into a night so chill it made her eyes water. She burrowed into her parka and cocked her head, listening for music, laughter, carousing. It was supposed to be a party, right?

Nothing reached her but eerie silence and the faint noise of traffic some thirteen stories down. Starr crossed the rubber tiles leading to the elevated deck as a musky, burning scent tweaked her nose and the sound of soft guitar strumming drifted her way. Up on the deck, chairs and benches filled with her fellow castmates surrounded the firepit, in which a large blaze danced.

Copies of *WaterWorlds* lay strewn around the deck. Some actors were nose-deep in the story; others had the magazine laying across their laps. Nora was staring off into the night skies, while Mav played the guitar softly, gazing into the flames.

Starr swallowed. This was bad. She'd hoped to get up here before anyone had seen the article, armed with Dakota as backup. But Dakota had sacked out in bed after reading the article, exhausted and tear-stained, so Starr had left her back in the hotel room. Probably for the best.

Starr partly blamed herself. She could have made everyone else's life easier by just kissing up to Fiona. She was an actress. She could have acted it out. Yet, that felt wrong. If the price of admission to the show was sucking up to Fiona and ignoring her petty insults and the occasional knocked-over furniture, Starr knew she'd come to hate the place. She'd tried mollifying her mother as a kid—one of her earliest roles had been to play Perfect Daughter. She'd spend a few days getting on Mama's good side by making dinner, shoving the junk in her room under the bed, or mowing the lawn.

"Whatcha really want?" Mama would spit after a day or two of the farce. "Ya making me nervous."

That had convinced Starr she needed to learn how to

act properly.

Now, she paused on the roof deck for a moment before Nora turned her way. She was radiant, big and powerful, her belly almost too big for her coat. "Well, well, well," she said, rising awkwardly. "Look what the weasel dragged in."

Here we go. Starr offered a hesitant wave.

At first, she didn't know what she heard coming from all the day players, the guests, and even some of her regular castmates. It started as a low, sibilant hiss, then rose in volume and became true 'oooing'. Or, rather, 'booing.' A balled-up piece of the magazine arced in her direction, falling far short of where she stood. That began a flurry of torn-page missiles, and finally the actors tossed their magazines into the firepit. The flames turned bright green and blue briefly, and a sharp scent of frying ink replaced the cozy earthiness of the fire.

Starr staggered. This was the opposite of the applause she'd felt hours earlier. It sapped her strength, and she shrank under Nora's gaze. It was as if all hope was leaching from the world; maybe she would throw herself from the balcony, it wouldn't hurt but for a few seconds—

But wait. That was Nora's key magic. Knowing her roommate was using her award to make her feel worse helped a tiny bit. "Quit it," she ordered, words a croak. "There's an explanation."

No one cared to hear. Still making low, grumbling noises, the actors shambled in her direction like pissed-off zombies and she flinched. They streamed around her with ugly looks; one muttered, "Thanks for nothing, idiot," while another hissed, "So much for this gig." As they passed into the hotel and tromped down the staircase, the booing was replaced by grumbling and threats until the noises faded altogether.

Only Mav and Nora remained. She waddled Starr's way. "All I can say is I'm thrilled I didn't open a vein with you until after your gossip session with that rat reporter," she growled. "Congrats, lady, for killing a beautiful night under the stars. And maybe the whole danged show."

Mav had stopped playing and was taking a long sip from a flask.

"That article—it isn't the whole story," she tried again. "There are things you need to know."

"Not certain there's much you could say," said Mav at last. "Not sure a'tall. And truth? Not sure I care to hear it anyway." He laid the guitar in its case and snapped the latches closed. "We're all a little tired. And I'm a little lit. There's a whole passel of new pages to go over for tomorrow and"—he looked at Starr for the first time— "I'm not so sure I've got patience for fun and games."

"Do I look like I'm enjoying this?" Starr threw one of the balled-up pages at her feet into the fire, which popped and sizzled. "I don't give a crap what anyone else on this show thinks about me except you, Mav."

"Hmph," Nora muttered.

"That's why I came up here. I said I'd come. I knew you'd be here. I'm here to tell you that I didn't *do* this."

Mav rose and stumbled a step, then righted himself. Starr hurried over to help, but he warded her off. "Look," he said. "I got caught up. Read me some signals wrong. Best to let this one set."

"Which is exactly what Fiona wants."

He dropped the guitar case down angrily. "You are not gonna lay this one on her." He did seem tired, but also deeply furious and hurt.

"Fiona, Fiona, Fiona," Nora sniped. "You're a broken

record, Starr. She's a witch-and-a-half, no question, but you're obsessed. What, she spiked your drink? She made you say those things?"

Starr remained focused on Mav, who looked as if he wanted to run but couldn't make himself move. "Do you have that low an opinion of me?" she asked him. "Does everyone?"

Behind them, the door blew open. Nico staggered out, flushed and wide-eyed and without a jacket. He carried with him a bottle of rum, holding it by the neck. He still looked like someone who'd fallen out of bed, but the dishevelment Starr remembered from spying on Fiona's room was now marinating in alcohol.

Wait, she thought. *He isn't affected by alcohol.*

Unless something had changed.

Nico raised his arms and lurched to the roof deck. "The gang's all here!" he shouted, glancing around. Raising his arms again, he clarified, "The gang's mostly gone!"

"Jesus, Nico." Nora pushed past Starr and caught him before he toppled over. "What have you gone and done, you silly fool?"

"Did a little experiment," he said, brandishing the bottle, which was about a third gone. "Took a few nips. For... for science." His face briefly pulled into an unhappy grimace, which then disappeared. "See, Fee and I had this fight and I wanted to see if she really could take back that little prize she loaned me. Guess what?"

Guilt, then anger and sadness washed over Starr. "She took it back?"

"That's three decades down the drain," said Mav.

"It's not!" Nico set the bottle down. "I only wanted to *see* if she would really do it. Tastes like watery *shit*. But 'pparently, she is that vindicious."

"Vindictive," said Nora.

"Vicious," said Mav.

"What I said," said Nico, glancing at the bottle, then dragging his gaze away from it.

"C'mon, Reddy," said Mav. "Let's get you some hot coffee and a cold shower."

"Oh, no." Nico shrugged off Nora and held Mav back. "I've got a little show-and-tell. After I realized I could get drunky all over again, I went and found some friends." He stepped aside and beckoned at the door, which was being held open by a few small hands. Brownies began filing onto the roof—Alligash, Oleander, Pardner, Quintuple, Silverjacket and Respectable Windlight, every bro Starr knew by name except Bookender. Her heart raced.

"Why are we on the roof, Mr. Reddy?" Silverjacket asked.

"We're not," said Mav, grabbing the guitar case again. "We're on our way out."

Nico pressed a hand into his chest. "Hold those horses, cowboy. You want to hear this."

"No, I don't." Mav was openly angry.

His bro Pardner stepped forward and began to speak in a monotone. "'Steph was a real linear thinker. So I did bring her here once. Showed her around. Introduced her to everybody. And of course, like I knew they would, they wiped her memory of it the minute she stepped through the Gate. I came back the next day, same as usual and had this flash: everybody was in costume, and we were just a bunch of children playing dress up. But I did stay. I picked the place, not the woman. She left me a year later.'"

"Pardner?" Mav dropped the guitar case again,

crouching down. "What the hell?"

"I can do more!" Pardner said cheerily. "Pick a day, any day since you and me was paired up. Seventy-two years, four months and three days ago. First thing you said was"—he dropped into that tone again—"'Well, pardner, you're a slip of a thing.'" She returned to her own proud, excited voice. "Then you gave me a hat and started calling me 'Pardner.' Wanna hear something else?"

Mav shook his head, looking away.

Nico pointed at Nora. "You are gonna love this."

Quintuple cleared his throat by coughing into his fist and said, "'They'll put her—I mean, me—into a coma or make me hide behind plants and furniture for the next six months or maybe even write me out.'" He made a small bow, then rejoined the group.

Nora gasped at hearing her words from the bathroom conversation with Starr. "What is this voodoo?"

"Meet the Brownie Network," said Starr, hands laid over her heart. "They're in our walls and our shadows... and they report to Fiona daily."

"We were spies!" said Pardner cheerfully.

"Estasy," corrected Oleander, giving her a dirty look.

Pardner stopped smiling. "But not anymore."

"Now we're organized," Oleander announced. "Starting tomorrow."

"Even if that made sense, how did it get from *me* to the pages of *WaterWorlds* if Starr didn't tell it to Dakota—" Mav cut himself off. "Wait. You guys tell Fiona everything?"

"They did," said Starr. "And in this case, it's a straight line from Helena to Fiona, who got the last pass on this story, Dakota tells me. Probably took no effort at all to make up a few extra quotes or take a few from

Bookender's transcripts. He types everything up and it goes into her personal vault."

Mav whirled on Nico. "And you knew about this?"

Nico beamed, then tried to become serious. He was drunk and didn't want to be, Starr suspected. "Hell, no," he said. "Well, once I did. The lady said she was dunzo with it, forever and for all time. Swore it to me. Then guess what?" He paused dramatically. "She lied!"

A long silence. Then: "My goodness, the bonfire soiree proceeds apace! And me without my marshmallows!"

Every head turned to Fiona as she sashayed onto the roof deck, swaddled in the white furry depths of her yeti coat. Bookender trailed behind like a familiar. She swung her lion's head cane in front of her to clear a path, and the brownies shrank away. Once seated in the best chair before the fire, she warmed her hands.

"Funny," said Mav. "I was about to pay you a call, Fiona."

"Then I'm pleased to have saved you the effort." Fiona gestured at Bookender. "Thank you again for alerting me to these rooftop events," she told the brownie. "Please escort your friends downstairs. I am considering a purge. Perhaps it is time to do a mass replacement of our helpers."

"Can she do that?" Starr asked.

"Of course I can," said Fiona. "It is a privilege of being me. Now, Bookender, remove them from the rooftop. I have had quite enough rebellion for one day."

A small pair of arms wrapped around Starr from behind, and she turned. Oleander was bouncing on her toes. "It'll be fine," she told the brownie. "I'll fix this. I swear."

Oleander released her. "Hugs are good, Starr Weatherby. Words are good. But bros—we will fix this ourselves."

That sounded ominous. "How?"

"Tune in tomorrow." The brownie winked, then scampered down the stairs behind the others, pulling the door closed.

Fiona became the focus of everyone left on the deck. "Explain yourself," Nora ordered.

"Perhaps you can be more specific." Fiona stood up, tall and sturdy as a statue.

Mav closed in. "Starr's informed us that you've had our brownie assistants report back to you. Private things, said behind closed doors. That so?"

"Goodness, Charles, you sound as if you're testifying." Fiona half-shrugged. "Of course it's so. It has been so on and off for decades. I'm astounded this is news to anyone other than"—she waved her hand at Starr—"this one."

"But *why*?" Mav pressed.

"I owe none of you an explanation. But I will say that during my tenure on this show it has become clear that being aware of all secret things is critical for me to function. I have been injured when I trusted blindly. I have lost things important to me." She sniffed once, then regained her composure. "In this case, I have decided that Ms. Weatherby is no longer a good fit in our family. It was my error to believe she could be molded to our style."

"That's not your decision to make," said Mav. "What do you think Cris and Jason are gonna say when they find out about your... Bro Network?"

Gotcha, Starr thought.

But the Grande Damn laughed. "Charles, you are a treasure. What makes you believe they would care?"

"Only one way to find out," said Starr.

"I believe I hear a gnat buzzing." Fiona stared at her gloves. "Am I the only one who understands that our petty grievances are mere distractions to mythics? We are like dolls in a playhouse to them. I mean, one of us could utterly vanish from the set, never to return—and they would only be concerned about how to rewrite the story."

Nora covered her mouth.

"Amelia," Starr whispered.

Fiona's smile was full of jagged edges. "Do go explain things to our overlords. In fact, allow Starr to handle this... revelation. Perhaps I shall receive a slap on the wrist. Meanwhile, I plan to read my lines, do my job and preserve the show. That is the only thing they actually want us to do."

"It won't be just Starr," said Mav. "Darby will back her up. So will I. We all heard the brownies tonight."

"Count me in, too." Nico lay down on a bench, pointing at the sky.

Fiona brushed her fur and straightened her hat. "What none of you seem to comprehend is your outrage is meaningless. This show is a hobby to the mythics. They keep us on their string by doling out tiny pieces of junk magic to poor, undeserving, stupid humans. And we trade our lives for these trinkets. We trade the lives of people we love."

Fiona's ability to jerk the rug out from under them was perhaps the greatest trick of all. But her vitriol struck a nerve in Starr. "Shame on you. You work in an actual fantasy land. We get to tell stories to mythical creatures." She paced the deck, breathing hard. "Yeah, Mav once said we were all like children for sticking around here. That's not necessarily a bad thing. We're in a shared dream world. It could be the best place ever. But just because you'd prefer to live in a paranoid nightmare doesn't mean the rest of us have to follow along."

The corner of Mav's mouth quirked up.

"If you hate it here so much, why don't you leave?" Starr asked, truly wanting to know.

The Grande Damn set a clawed hand on Starr's shoulder. "My dear, your naiveté is priceless. There is no place for me to go. The world has moved on, and I am here, trapped in amber. Long ago, I chose this bed and now I lie in it. But I've never fooled myself into believing we're doing anything important." She squeezed Starr's shoulder so hard it felt like the bone would break.

"As for the rest of you"—Fiona glanced around the deck—"as you have witnessed today, the audience loves me. If I want to turn this show into a sequel to *Lord of the Flies*, I can and I will. I have carte blanche." She chuckled. "As long as the viewers tune in, I am the one who provides us all with a tomorrow."

CHAPTER 31
Written in the Starrs

A LONG SILENCE fell across the roof in the wake of Fiona's departure, and Starr imagined the grindylows many fathoms below them, stirring in the harbor. They echoed the wild, angry beat of her heart. She kicked at the fire, which was dying.

"Well, I'm chillier than a brass toilet seat in the Arctic," Nora announced. "I'm goin' back inside to scream into my pillow."

"'Tis the witching hour." Nico sat up and clutched at his head. "Yet the witch has departed."

Mav helped him to his feet, and they all slouched down the steps to the twelfth floor, pausing in front of Nora and Starr's room. Starr decided not to ask if she was still evicted, and furthermore decided she would not leave even if she was. "You know," Mav began, "maybe we oughta... give those new lines a quick read. This live thing we're doing tomorrow... I'd be lying if I said I was A-OK with it all."

Starr perked up. "I can get coffee going. We'll share scripts."

"Woo!" Nico cried, and everyone shushed him. "Hoo," he whispered.

Dakota yelped as they entered; she'd burrowed under Starr's sheets and was sitting up, flipping channels. "Sorry!" she said. "I don't have any place else to crash. Crissy threw me out."

Nico snickered. "Crissy? Crissy."

"We're going to rehearse," said Starr. "New pages." She gestured at the manila folder she'd carried up to the roof.

"So much for the spontaneity of being 'live,'" Dakota muttered.

"And that's why you're not an actor," said Mav.

Everyone sat on the beds, staring at one another as the coffee percolated, a burbling happy sound that clashed with the mood in the room. No one made a move for Nora and Starr's envelopes.

After a few minutes, Starr couldn't take it anymore. "I don't know about all of you, but I can't let this go. I can't work with a despotic queen who has no consequences." She felt like she'd swallowed a cannonball. "I'm going to have to quit." She looked at Mav. "For real this time."

"Oh, don't," Nico pleaded. "The whole losing-most-of-your-earnings part aside, you take off and she'll be worse. There's got to be a way through this."

"Fact is, she's done it before and she'll do it again if we don't call a halt." Mav filled mugs for everyone and sat next to Starr on the bed. "We can't go pulling an Amelia every time to keep her happy."

Nora made a strangled yelping sound.

"Mav, ix-nay," Nico muttered.

"C'mon, Darby." Mav held up his mug. "You think Starr hasn't figured most of this out already?"

Nora stared at Starr. Starr stared at Mav. "Um, I don't

think I have," she said.

"Sure y'have." Mav took a sip. "I heard you up there, muttering 'Amelia' when Fee made that crack about folks disappearing. I'm the one who told you about Joseph—"

"And I told you about his scripts," Nico nodded.

Mav gaped. "So you're why she went into the cave?"

Starr held out her hands. "That's a side story. Distraction. Don't get off track here."

"Well, point is, you never let it go," said Mav.

"But I don't have a full picture," Starr said. Something new was forming in her mind, and she turned to Nora. "You're the one who started this, you know. You told me what happened to Amelia could happen to me. And at the time, it felt like you wanted it to happen to me."

"Criminy," said Nora. "I was trying to scare you off. Nothing personal."

"Instead, you scared her into becoming a detective," said Nico.

"So, what am I missing?" Starr wondered. "Did Fiona kill Amelia, or what?"

Nora's eyes widened, and she burst out laughing. The bed bounced both her and Nico in undulating waves.

"Whoa there, you." Nico grabbed the sheets. "You'll make me seasick."

Nora dropped her smile, her face going stony. "I'm not sure about this."

"Tell her," said Mav. "Or I will."

Nora sighed. "Fiona wanted to kill her. Amelia. But she didn't. She just... thinks she did."

Dakota gasped and they all remembered she was in the room.

"Off the record!" Nico cried.

"Sure, sure," said Dakota. "But this is better than the

show, you know that, right?"

Starr threw up her hands. "Will someone stop doing the two-step and explain things already?"

"May I?" Mav asked, and Nora nodded. He was sitting so close to Starr she could smell the smoke from the firepit on his clothing. His face was windburned and his eyes glowed like burnt honey. "See, 'Melia was even more of a thorn in Fee's side than you've been. First, she was doing fine. But then she started asking about the scripts. Lots of questions. Got all cozy with Joseph. That got Fiona suspicious, then riled up. She thought they were—well, you know."

"Which was hilarious," said Nora. "If you ever saw Joe, he wasn't a guy women fight over. 'Melia and I got friendly, and she asked *me* about the stories. Said they sounded like TV shows she'd been watching on the other side of the Gates. I told her I was an ignoramus about TV. Never caught the bug. Anyhow, we started hanging out more. And, well, then we did more than hang out. Kept it hush-hush 'cause we didn't want the mythies to tell us to stop."

Starr sat bolt upright. "Wait. You were with Amelia?"

"Still am."

"She's who you go home to?"

Nora rested her hands on her belly and grinned.

"Amelia started hanging out with Joe for the same reason we all like hanging out with whoever's leading the writer's room," Mav picked it up. "Better characters. Better storylines. I mean, they say it's reality and in some tiny way it is but… it's all about story. People's real lives are too boring. If the mythies ever really followed us around to the bank or the grocery or while we sat there and read books, this show would've been gone years ago. You gotta give people, and mythics, something to grab onto. Anyhow, Fee had been Joe's main muse for years, but with Amelia around, suddenly things shifted. And then 'Melia got nosy. Like you. She went home and did some research and confirmed that Joe'd been lifting stories from other people for years."

"That's what I thought!" Starr said. "I read through some of his old scripts and—I mean, come on. *Supership Starprise*?"

"We didn't catch it," said Nora. "She did. And thing is, 'Melia has this righteous streak. She thought it was pretty lousy that he was considered a genius for ripping off great works. He was winning awards, getting prizes. And I agreed with her."

Mav made a grumpy sound. "Still. She didn't have to blackmail him, Nora. That was a rotten move."

"You can start that debate with her again next time you hang out," said Nora, and her tone suggested that didn't happen often. "We don't walk in lockstep."

"And I guess Fiona didn't like being sidelined," Starr continued.

"She did not," said Mav. "She made his life hell. Basically told him to tone it down with Amelia. And if he didn't, then she'd out him and the mythics—"

Starr thought about what Fiona had said on the roof. "Would they have cared?"

Silence in the room.

"You know, probably not," said Nico. "It was a hollow threat. But—the damage was done. Amelia had made Joe into a joke among the cast. And you can do a lot to a man, but laughing at him... that kills something you don't get back. He lost his oomph."

"So he quit."

"He walked out," said Mav. "Could've done it right, but instead he just… walked. With him gone, Fiona went haywire. Amelia was her target. She used every tool in her arsenal. 'Melia was going to quit, too—but we were pretty sure Fiona would take this one past the Gate if she had to. So we set it up: we made Fiona think she'd gotten rid of Amelia by shoving her into the bottomless pit."

"I gave her a spare MARBLE," Nora explained. "While she was falling, she MARBLEd right back into my dressing room and we dressed her up like a day player and sneaked her out the Gate that night. Nobody pays attention to those randos. And nobody knew except—well, except us. Four on a secret was too many, but we knew: Fiona wouldn't let it rest if she knew the truth. She was ruthless."

"Is ruthless." Starr's voice sounded far away in her ears.

"We made a pact not to talk about her," said Mav. "Warned our bros there'd be trouble if they so much as spoke her name. Told them—and this was a lie, but it was all in a good cause—that they'd start crumbling if they discussed it. See, we knew we were being overheard a long time ago, but we didn't know how. Then you showed up and started asking questions."

This was so convoluted and extensive Starr knew it had to be the truth. Yet it was almost a letdown: there was no true mystery, just a lot of secrets. Everyone held in check by an off-balance Grande Damn. "So where's Amelia now?"

Nora touched her belly. "At home. We married once it got to be legal. We're both gonna be a mom to this little one." She grinned at Mav. "She's been sorry about Joseph all these years. She still misses the show."

"And she remembers it?"

Nora nodded. "We're not sure why. We think it's 'cause

she went through the Gate as a day player—they don't get zapped with a full memory wipe, just a couple of hours."

"We miss her, too." Mav set his hand over Starr's, and she let it linger there, warm and soft as the first day they met. "We can't stop you from quitting, Starr. But—I'm open to other ideas. Pretty much any other idea."

Starr drank the rest of her coffee. Something had to be done, especially now that she knew the truth. Fiona needed to be outed, the way Joseph had been—only this time, as publicly as possible. Clearly Fiona had something she could hold over Helena, so a new article wouldn't fix things… but there was Arachne and her mythic discussion web. Starr had never done more than scan it for references to Sam, but if it operated like social media on her side of the Gate, that might be the way to reach the right audience.

"Let me work on it," she said. "But first, we should run these lines, don't you think? Then I can sleep on how to handle a problem like Fiona." She gestured at the manila envelope she'd been carrying, still wrinkled from the crash with Dakota near the elevators. For the first time, she noticed it had a red 'H' in one corner. "Hand that over, will you, Mav?"

Envelope in hand, Starr flipped open the flap and reached inside. No cherry scent drifted from the pages. Pulling them into the light, she discovered she was holding neither sides nor script. "How to Knit a Dragon Feather Boa While Recovering From Third-Degree Burns, Part 2," she read the typewritten headline aloud. Below that, Fiona's byline.

Dakota vaulted across the bed, trying to snatch the envelope away. "Gimme that!"

"Gimme my lines and this one's all yours." Starr recoiled. "Obviously we swapped envelopes when we banged into each other."

Nico plucked the envelope from Starr's hands, holding it away from Dakota's twitching fingers. The reporter settled, rummaging in her own messenger bag. She pulled out a second manila envelope and opened it; the sweet cherry odor of revisions drifted out. "Guess I picked up yours by mistake. Here."

But Starr wasn't paying attention to her. Nico was dangling the envelope holding Fiona's column and eyeing it. "Feels like there's more than an article in here." He upended the envelope over the bed and out slid three currency-strapped packets of twenty-dollar bills; likely thousands of dollars, all told. A note in Fiona's familiar, looping handwriting fluttered out last.

Nico caught it. "'Thanks for all your help, Helena,'" he read slowly, regretfully. "'Enclosed find my usual "thank you." Let's keep that Endless Award streak going!'"

"A bribe," Nora stated. "She's *bribing* that magazine."

"But how?" Starr asked. She looked at Dakota, who'd turned pink. "Is Helena the only person who picks the prizes?"

"Of course not," Dakota said primly. "Our viewers *vote*. Our editors vote. It's all very democratic—"

"But let me guess"—Nora raised an eyebrow—"Helena gets the final look-see on the ballots."

Dakota opened, then closed her mouth, and nodded.

It's just like the article, Starr thought. *Doesn't matter what anyone else writes or thinks, if Helena and Fiona decide to put a thumb on the scales.* "So, if Fiona wants to amass even more—what did she call them, 'junk magic' prizes—all she has to do is pass along a few bucks," she said.

"That looks to be the size of things," said Mav.

Starr turned to Dakota. "And every week the envelope's stuffed like this?"

"I guess?" The reporter was sinking into the sheets. "I'm not allowed to look."

"But it weighs about the same, don't it?" said Mav.

Dakota gave him a sickly look.

"No wonder Helena will publish whatever Fiona wants her to," said Nico. "All that fairy gold she's got stockpiled. Now I know where it's going."

"Son of a beeswax," Mav swore.

But Starr's grin was almost as big as the one she'd worn while riding a centaur. "Well, then. Things just got a lot more interesting."

AN HOUR LATER, the jolt from the coffee had worn off, and they were all frayed and exhausted. The revelations about Fiona had fueled a considerable amount of outrage, drinking and disbelief. Mav had nearly worn a groove in the carpet from all his pacing.

At last, he stopped and faced everyone. "I call for table." He stuck the note and money back in the envelope, leaving it by the television. "As in, we table this until after the live show." He turned to Dakota, who'd been staring quietly out the window and hugging a pillow like a teddy bear. "I also call for a complete embargo from your corner."

Dakota was glassy-eyed as she turned. "Like anyone would believe I didn't know I was a bagman for Helena. Trust me, I don't want to get fired. Nobody may read me in my world, but I have an actual career on this side of the Gate. I'm not going to blow it all up for nothing."

"Good," said Mav. "We try sinking Fiona now, the live show will tank."

Starr folded her arms. She wanted to act, and act now. Storm over to Fiona's room, blast her with what they knew. But if she'd learned anything from the scene on the rooftop, it was that Fiona was not easily cowed.

"Gonna kill that woman," Nora muttered. "Should've done it years ago."

"Get in line," said Starr. "And we were calling Joseph the fraud."

"I get it." Mav set a warm hand on her shoulder. "You're like a rocket right now. You want to take aim. We all do. But—after the show."

Worn out, Starr agreed. She needed a plan, and marching to Fiona was a losing one. This level of ammunition required a defter hand. Fiona might be correct that Jason and Cris would overlook an intra-show spy ring but buying her awards and magic... that had to get TPTB into a genuine snit. And if the audience found out, well, that was the last thing Fiona would want.

An electric tingle ran through Starr. That was an idea, actually.

Nico met her gaze. As if he could read her mind, he shook his head.

She gave him the tiniest of shrugs and tapped the manila envelope Dakota had pulled from her messenger bag in the scrum earlier—Starr's revisions. "I'll keep mum," she said. "But since we're all here, let's check out these lines at least once before we pass out."

They finished around three in the morning. Nico staggered out first, still slightly tipsy, throwing off any offers of assistance from Mav. "I've been walking a long time," he said, heading unsteadily off to his room.

Starr saw Mav out, joining him in the hallway.

"You're doing the right thing," he insisted. "Show first. Always. Without it—"

"I know. We sink. Or tank. Or are out on our behinds."

"It's a nice behind." He winked, then straightened. "Er, I don't know why I said that."

Starr blushed a little. "When you're right, you're right." Caught up in the moment, she wondered if he would kiss her. It was so late that it was early and anything was possible. Not that she had to wait—she'd taken the bull by the horns before—but she held back, and the moment passed.

"Best get some sleep," he said. "Got a big day tomorrow." He gave her hand a squeeze and kissed her.

On the forehead.

Then he was gone down the hallway, carrying his guitar case.

Starr stamped her foot. *The forehead!*

But she brushed the space where his lips had made contact and thought, *Maybe I just got tabled, too.*

CHAPTER 32

Lucky Starr

STARR RACED INTO the conference room the next morning, landing in her seat seconds before doors opened to the fans. Gulping down a glass of water, she steadied her breath and checked her appearance in her cell phone camera: one eye was painted in green eyeshadow, the other in violet sparkle. She had no lipstick on, and her hair was half curls, half frizz.

Starr shook her head. *Focus.* Yes, she was a mess, but so were her fellow actors. Not one had received a brownie wake-up call that morning. The creatures were AWOL across the board. That meant everyone had converged on the frazzled hairies and makeup fairies en masse. The poor Fae had been so stressed they'd perspired, filling the makeshift makeup room with the scent of burned cinnamon and overcooked doughnuts.

Glancing around the room now, Starr noted that everyone else seemed out of sorts, half-made up and bleary... except Fiona. The diva had her hair spiked and perfect, makeup expertly applied. She twiddled her fingers at Starr, tilting her head.

Then the fans streamed in, and for an hour Starr was too distracted to dwell on the night before, from the discovery of Fiona's bribery to that 'kiss' she got from Mav. Nor could she wonder too much about the missing brownies, either. Mythics commanded her attention as they lined up in front of all the actors, and she had to be present for a quick smile, an autograph or chat—whatever they wanted, within reason.

Starr smiled a lot, even when she wasn't sure whether she was being smiled at: mythics with beaks, muzzles or no mouths at all made facial interpretation a challenge. She braced for the first fan to come at her about the *Water Worlds* article, but there was no criticism—instead, fans loved the quotes. They thought Sam was particularly feisty. They'd never read a story like it. Starr relaxed a hair and concentrated on chatting with the fans that specifically came over to see her.

"You're much bigger in person!" a gnome cried.

"They shrink me to fit in the camera," she told him.

She admired the look of a cockatrice, who'd padded to her table wearing a leather jacket and dark sunglasses. "You're like a rock star," she said.

"My gaze kills humans at twenty paces." He rustled his feathers. "And Roc music is old-fashioned. I prefer EDM."

A trembling dryad rattled her branches, trying to convey how much the wardrobe collapse had upset her. "I was so scared I went into premature autumn!" she cried.

Eventually, the crowds waned, and Starr let out a sigh of relief. She was about to turn to speak with Nora when the doors to the conference room blew open. Cris stood in the open space, fists on hips, rolling his cigar around his teeth. He burned a stare at the remaining fans in the room, who bowed their heads and scampered out.

"Right," he addressed the room. "Three hours before the live 'cocktail party.'"

"Why is there a cocktail party at two in the afternoon?" Nora asked.

"Because Emma *wrote* it that way!" he bellowed. "Anyhow, it's a 'soiree' now, so apparently that makes more sense. Revisions in your rooms."

The actors groaned. Starr's foot began tapping from nerves.

"I'm trying something new today," Cris continued, extending an arm to introduce three cameradryads. They shuffled into the room, roots whisking on the indoor carpet. Each wore a brace around their trunks, which attached to a camera mounted on a pole. Celtis struck a pose as if she were modeling on a catwalk.

"We're freeing the cameras to follow you wherever you go." He fixed his gaze on Starr. "So, if you do feel the need to 'wing it,' these fine ladies will tail you anywhere and everywhere. Celtis, remind me of the order of the day."

"Keep your eyes on the actors' balls," she chirped.

Cris grimaced. "Ugh, *plants*. That's keep your camera's eye on the ball," he enunciated. "Follow the ball. The actors are the ball. You never take your eyes off the ball."

Mav raised a hand. "This thing's been orchestrated down to the second, Cris. When're we supposed to 'wing it'?"

"It's my experience that some of you mortals wander a little off the path." Again, he stared at Starr. "I'm preparing for eventualities."

"Jason wanted it," said Nico.

"Yeah, and Jason wanted it."

"Where is he?" Starr asked.

"Far, far away from any copies of *Water Worlds* magazine, let's just say that. He'll be here for the show." Cris' cigar glowed. "Look. You all have three hours to eat, rest up, hit makeup and hair—and some of you *really* need to hit makeup and hair—and get in costume. The brownies are missing, which is a different nightmare, so *set your alarms*. Do not wait until the last minute or I will personally—"

"Tie us up and pour red ants down our shirts?"

Cris pointed the lit end of his cigar at Starr. "You are on my last nerve, female. Strike one was that maneuver in my office. Strike two, that article. Don't let me get to strike three."

Fiona cleared her throat, poorly stifling a grin.

Starr wanted to speak out now, but bit down on her reaction. Everything would become clear in time. The important people knew the article wasn't her doing. Cris and Jason would learn the truth and her reputation would be restored. Still, restraint was *hard*.

"That's the sound I like to hear. Silence." Cris was back to chewing his cigar. "Meet you all in—"

"The Grand Ballroom," they intoned.

"Red hot. Three hours. You ain't there on time, don't bother MARBLEing back." He marched out of the conference room.

Nico stretched. "That is a man who knows how to light up a room and leave." He slid down the row to Starr. "Literally."

Cris' words jangled in Starr's head. Not because she was intimidated, but something he'd said about baseball. Strikes. "Oh!" She jumped out of her chair and spun, colliding with Nico.

He cocked his head. "Got a couple minutes?"

"No. I have to find the brownies."

There was no time to explain. She slipped around him and out to the mezzanine. There were three hours to the show, and she had to stop the brownies from setting their big idea in motion. Mango time would have to wait.

NOT THAT SHE had any idea where to start. Should she knock on the brownie door in her hotel room? Should she seek out Bookender? After all, he must have woken up Fiona on time. But no, that was a terrible idea.

Muffled voices drew her attention. She leaned on the mezzanine's glass railing and peered down at the level below. The lobby looked normal, with usual mythic traffic visiting the Starbucks and check-in counter, bar and restaurant. Down in the lobby a few day players were setting up pillows and chairs to view the live streamed show on the hotel's water wall. But the voices she'd been hearing were gone.

"Don't jump." Nico appeared next to her. "We need you for the show."

"Do you hear voices?"

He shook his head and leaned on the railing. "How's the hand?"

She flexed her fingers. "Went numb halfway through the session."

"Gimme." He held out a palm.

Starr hesitated. Yesterday at this time, she was not even speaking with Nico, who was either too gullible to know when Fiona was using him or as bad as she was for helping her out. But he'd come to her defense. Whatever he'd said in that suite to Fiona had been enough for her to revoke his sobriety prize. Perhaps he'd seen the error of his ways. But Starr had been wrong before.

"All right," he said. "Now I know. You haven't forgiven me. It was worth a try."

Biting her lip, Starr slid her hand into his. Nico pressed softly on the knuckles, then waved the wrist back and forth. Jolted by his touch, Starr sensed an invisible thread pulling them together, just like in the park. There were advantages to the attentions of a man like Nico. He knew where all the sensitive places were and how to make them sing. You just couldn't take him too seriously.

"Thanks." She reclaimed her hand, and it did feel better. More awake and alive. What was Nico up to? Could he be trusted? And did that matter, especially if she was starting to have feelings for Mav?

Who kissed me on the forehead last night, like I was some disappointing date. Or a kid.

And yet, she was a child, in a way. Chronologically, in real human time, all her co-stars were at least as old as her mother, if not her grandparents. They probably found *her* hard to take seriously. But the visuals hid the truth: none of them looked much older than thirty, and with makeup they could appear even younger. Their ages were where they'd been temporally arrested, but their minds—their experiences—were much older. So where did that leave her?

"I wondered if I could talk with you," he said. "I want to clear a few things up."

"We're talking now."

"In private."

Starr looked around. The other actors were filing out behind them. Mav paused briefly as if he wanted to say something, then moved on. "This is private."

Nico didn't seem convinced, but shrugged. "You were magnificent on the roof last night."

Her cheeks burned. "I took a friend's advice about standing up to bullies."

"Despite everything, Fiona's not evil."

Starr narrowed her eyes. "She shoved Amelia into a bottomless pit, Nico."

"It's not like she's still there, Starr. 'Melia transported out. She's safe."

"Does that make a difference—to Fiona?"

The voices started up again, and Starr remembered why she was here. Brownies! Nico was a terrible distraction.

"Confession," he continued. "I went back to Fiona's suite last night after we all went our separate ways. She... she agreed to loan me the award again. I'm forcibly sober once more."

"Oh," said Starr. "I'd been thinking it was a good thing to rip that bandage off, but I guess... I'm not the one with the problem." Then she thought of Fiona. "What'd you give her in exchange?"

"Nothing of any importance."

Starr waited, staring at him.

He shifted uncomfortably. "Jesus, Starr, how do you do that?"

"I'm not doing anything." Except, she was. She'd been around both Roland and Nico too often to not know the difference now. One, she had to work with. The other one, when he showed himself, had an unexpected, endearing shyness to him. Roland could get away with anything, but despite decades of acting, Nico wasn't as good at hiding things.

"She wants to see you, Starr. Before the show. Wants to... talk."

"Ha!" The dismissal burst out of her. "So you get your protection back if you hand me over to the wolf."

"It's not like that. She's not up to anything—we've all got a show to do today. She just wants to explain why she's had such a hard time accepting you."

"Did you tell her? That we know about the bribes?"

He shook his head. "I have some limits. I am on your side. I'm on the show's side. Fiona needs reining in. But you get more bees with honey than with vinegar. It's worth a shot." He blinked. "You've given me more than one chance."

She took a long, deep breath. She wanted to believe him. If she believed him, she could give in to what she was feeling inside. What she'd been feeling since she'd met him that first day, but couldn't trust. Yet if Starr knew one thing about herself it was that she had a hard time being halfway with her heart. She *loved* this show. She *loved* this life. She did not love Nico, and wasn't sure she could risk getting close to him. He was trouble, even when he wasn't being Roland.

Nico pressed her hand between both of his own. "It's been a long, long while since I've met anyone like you, Starr. That's a cliché, but it's not a line. And by long, I mean decades. Maybe my whole strange extended lifetime. For some reason, you prefer me to be... me. Not Roland."

"No. Yes. I mean ..." Her voice was husky. This was a good play, if it was a play. She was starting not to care whether he was on the level or not.

"When I was speaking with Fiona just now," he said in a low tone, "it wasn't only about getting her loaned prize back. I told her my obligation to her was over. I have discharged myself. And that's thanks to you."

Warmth flowed across Starr's face, and down her body. "Oh. Oh."

"Indeed. Look, I'm pretty worked up about today. Last time I did anything live it was on the radio. Aren't you even a bit nervous?"

"I'm nothing but nerves," she admitted. "Closer we get to the live part the more my insides feel like they're chasing each other around." Though in this exact moment, she wasn't sure how much was the live show—and how much was Nico Reddy holding her hand. Her heart thrummed as if a hummingbird was trapped inside.

Stop playing around, Sam piped up inside. *Go with him. It doesn't have to be a* thing, *it can just be an afternoon.*

"I'm familiar with a terrific way to relieve stress." His half-smile was as bright as a movie marquee.

Starr raised an eyebrow. "Really? So am I."

"Then what are we waiting for?"

They ran for the elevators together.

CHAPTER 33
Starrs and Stripes

JASON SPENT HIS morning before the live show savoring the swell of honey yellows and rosy pinks streaking across the horizon as the sun rose over the ice plains of Niflheim—he'd switched the default setting on his office glamour—while sipping from a tankard of energy tea distilled from the ashes of the hundred most frenetic brownies.

He'd unplugged from the show on purpose. The stress from the past weeks of trying to get the live event ready to shoot had made him so anxious his horns weren't even growing out evenly. He'd purposefully not checked in and not sent messages to the hotel since the convention began. He'd told his brownie, Respectable Windlight, to get lost. But Emma was in touch. She'd joined him in the wee hours of the night before, blood still on her paw from last night's hunt. They'd curled together as fire-buddies and that—plus the tea—left him ready to take on anything.

Pulling open his sequoia wardrobe, he admired the outfit he planned to wear while overseeing the biggest show of his life: a high-necked, white paisley satin blouse to be worn beneath a glorious white suit pinstriped in aquamarine, made of wool from the Vegetable Lamb of Tartary. It smelled mildly of carrots.

Dressed, he made his final shoe selection: iridescent white boots lined in bedazzled buckles and three-inch solid rubber platforms, for maximum spring in his step.

"You are going to dazzle and amaze with this show." He psyched himself up before a sheet of reflective cave ice, tweaking the jacket cuffs.

Emma opened one yellow eye, twitching her whiskers. She was nearly back to her usual retro-dress-wearing wordcat self, but still had a day or two to go in werepanther mode. "You are a picture, my catnip," she purred. "I could eat you up."

"Please, don't." He smoothed the high collar. "You will be watching today?"

"If I'm not seized by the need to prowl. The revisions are all with the players, and my work here is done." She twitched her tail around one of his boots. "Break a neck. Or whatever the mortals say."

Jason glanced at his desk. The light on his ice block phone was flashing. He knew he should listen to the message. Find out what was so urgent. For a moment he hovered a hand over the ice block—then retracted it. He'd find out soon enough.

"You'll be late, wooly legs."

"Hairy!" He swatted at her, laughing. "*You.*" Psyched and ready to take on multiple worlds, Jason blew Emma a kiss and touched the MARBLE in his jacket pocket—

—arriving in the hotel lobby with a small 'pop.'

Voices chanted, heading his way. *Cheers! For me! How delightful!* But then he heard the words.

"What do we want?"

"No glitter!"

"When do we want it?"

A pause.

"Never? Never!"

Jason nearly tripped over his giant boots as he turned to stare at the far end of the galleria. A horde of brownies was streaming up the escalator into the lobby, shouting in unison.

"Bread for all! And primroses, too!"

"Don't need the boss! Boss needs us!"

Every brownie was dressed in jeans and a white T-shirt; many held signs mounted on yardsticks and broom handles. Most of the words were outlined in glitter. Every sign included one word: *Strike*.

Strike? Jason wondered. *Who are they planning to hit?*

Janus materialized next to Jason, clasping their hands tightly. "Aren't they beautiful?"

Jason frowned. "Are they preparing to perform a dance number?"

"Hardly." Janus tossed back a thick twist of hair. "The rights of brownies have been ignored for far too long. Today, you learn what it means to have no brownie help at all."

"Wait, what?"

"Your brownies are on strike, you guileless goat," Janus said. "They ain't gonna work for you no more."

Jason felt faint. "Can we schedule this for—Tuesday?"

"'The revolution is not an apple that falls when it is ripe. You have to make it fall,'" quoted Jan. "Che Guevara."

"Shay who? And what are *you* doing here?"

The brownies were filling the lobby, signs bobbing up and down. They flowed around Jan and Jason and sat, occupying much of the available floor space—including all the seats in front of the streaming waterfall. A few mythic fans stood in clumps on the edge of the protest, pointing and talking.

"I am their mentor," they said. "Starr taught them letters, I gave them books. They shall not be enslaved by The Man anymore."

"I'm not The Man! I'm The Faun!"

Jan rolled their eyes.

"And they're not *enslaved*! They can leave any time! They get paid!"

"In *glitter*," growled Janus. "The most obnoxious material in the world. Which is useless to them."

"They made pretty signs with it," Jason noted.

Janus ignored him. "Glitter was Fiona's idea. It was insulting then, and it's worse now."

Respectable Windlight strode up to Jason and tugged on his white jacket. "Afternoon, Mr. Jason." He held up a five-page document written in green Sharpie. "Our demands." He paused as if chewing on something. "Please agree to them. We want to help again!"

All the beautiful energy Jason had summoned with his dawn rise, tea and show-stopping suit drained away. No brownies meant no help behind the scenes. No help behind the scenes made the live show a potential disaster. Or at least, extremely complicated. And they had less than two hours to solve this.

"Like I said, beautiful," Jan sighed, gazing at the chanting protestors.

Jason did not want to be angry. Angry ran contrary to his suit. But this useless display threatened to upend his plans and potentially ruin the show. A ruined show today meant the end of the entire series. On his watch. It would kill him. Or at least make him feel really bad for a few weeks. Anger unfurled in Jason, and he lost the ability to control his horns, which shot out of his carefully combed hair and curled down his back. His tail whipped back and forth, grazing Respectable Windlight, and he crumpled the document in one hand.

Then he stomped.

A faun has only a few mid-level magics. Jason deployed his rarely. But sometimes, a bit of showmanship was necessary. With one great boot he lifted his hoof and slammed it against the floor so hard the tile broke. The shock wave rippled out and made anyone standing in the lobby stumble, except himself and Janus.

The hotel staff retreated into a luggage holding room next to the check-in desk. The chanting cut off mid-word.

"This is not happening today." Jason had never been so severe. It hurt, a little. "If you want me to even glance at this"—he held up the wrinkled document—"you will return to your duties at once."

There. That'll hold 'em.

"Put a lid on it, Valentine," said Jan. "You don't scare anyone."

Respectable Windlight raised his hand. "I'm scared."

Jason didn't understand it. He'd shown horns. He'd stomped. Was it the boots? How could anyfaun know he'd have needed the black patent Docs for today—

"Look," said Jan, strolling among the brownies. Their leather jacket had recently been oiled and reflected the winter sun streaming through the windows. "I know this show is your little... project. That's cool. Everybody needs a hobby. I signed on 'cause I get a lot of reading done and otherwise can kick back, and you get to have me call you boss." They clapped a hand on Jason's shoulder. "But never forget: I am a manifestation of a *god*, and you are a pipe-playing hairy *spirit*. If I want the brownies to take a day off, they get a day off. And if the SCN takes issue, they can take it up with me—on the battlefield if necessary."

Jason paled. The world was upside down. Crumbling, literally, beneath his hooves. "Do I need to remind you what happens if this show flops? They end us. And you won't have time to kick back and... read." That did sound weak. "Or foment revolutions!"

Jan shrugged. "Nothing lasts forever. Gotta keep things interesting." They gestured at the brownies to stand again. "Now! Where were we?"

CHAPTER 34
Starr Bright

STARR FLEW. HIGHER than the ceiling, or where the ceiling ought to be. She soared among the clouds in an endless azure sky, then descended into the springiest, softest cloud ever created. Flexing her knees, she bounced again, hair flapping, arms akimbo.

The other night, when Nora had scrolled through possible room glamours, she'd stumbled across one that left them in mid-air—everything turned blue except for the furniture, which became clouds. Nora claimed vertigo and shut it off immediately, and they'd flipped to hammocks and the mountainside glade.

But Starr wanted to fly. And so she did. It was so wonderful, she almost forgot Nico was standing in the sky next to her, arms folded across his chest.

"This wasn't quite what I had in mind when I said I knew a great stress-reliever," he said.

"This is exactly what I had in mind." *Sort of.* She slowed and offered a hand. "C'mon."

"I am not going to jump up and down on the bed with you. I'm not five."

"Right, you're a million years old. Maybe it's time to try again." She flapped her hand. "Also, it's a cloud. Not a bed."

"Ahem." He coughed. "I reckon I'm about ninety-two, not a million." But after another moment of hesitation, he allowed her to hoist him into the cloud.

"It's like a trampoline," she said. "Just bend your knees and go!"

"I do know what bouncing is."

So they flew together, leaping without effort into the skies. His curls haloed around his head and with each leap he appeared to grow younger, until he was smiling unabashedly. Nico shone, and the hummingbird in Starr's chest took wing.

Then, without saying a word, they were jumping less, and less. They stood on the cloud and held hands. It had been so easy to fly, but now Starr was warm and breathless and grounded. Something inevitable was happening here, and she no longer wanted to hold it back.

Just a little fun, she thought. *An afternoon, not a thing.*

"OK," she said. "Now, show me what you had in mind."

LATER, STARR STIRRED in Nico's arms and snuggled into him. What they'd done was the opposite of relaxing, yet here she was, blissed out and free of nerves.

"Never did that on a cloud before." He spoke into the crook of her neck. It tickled.

"What have you done on a cloud, exactly?"

"Er—" He thought a moment. "Bounced?"

Starr rubbed his hair and sat up. "That was fun." She'd expected nothing less. Naturally Nico would be good at lovemaking; he'd had a lot of experience. Still, she hadn't expected that level of enthusiasm. The important part was not to make a big deal of it. They'd bounced, they'd landed, and she was not *falling* for anything.

Starr swung her legs over the cloud, experiencing the momentary vertigo Nora had referred to. Her head insisted she was about to leap into the air without a parachute. *Without even a bra*, she thought, noting how their clothes had landed on various puffery around the room.

"Fun?" Nico sat up, pressing a hand to his chest. It was admirably hairy and well-developed; she'd liked running her hands over it. "You wound me, madam. Are there no stronger adjectives in your fevered brain?"

Starr raised an eyebrow. "Dial it back a smidge there, Roland."

"Roland? I know not this man of whom you speak."

Starr slipped off the cloud and landed on the sky. "Well, I'd say the earth moved but there's no earth. Hey, it's an hour to the show. We better get moving."

"Starr."

She turned.

"This doesn't have to be a one-time stress reliever."

"Oh—" The hummingbird opened its eye. "Maybe it should." She collected her clothes, forcing herself to remain cool. "People around set talk and—"

"And your interests lie elsewhere."

She gaped. Had it been that obvious about Mav?

"Jason isn't your type," he said. "Female species aren't his type in general. Also, trust me, mythic-ness is no small stumbling block."

Starr hadn't thought of it that way before; she'd figured everyone was Jason's type. That was disappointing on some level; Jason was like this distant light she hoped someday she might reach. But she was relieved Nico didn't suspect about Mav, who clearly was not interested in her. "Can we not make a decision right now?"

Nico slid across the cloud, patting the space next to him. Starr sat, admiring him in a way she hadn't had a chance to earlier.

"Allow me to give you something to think about." He smoothed her hair down. "Assuming this show survives, assuming you get your first award, you will have all the time in the world. Have you thought about that?"

"I—"

He shushed her. "I've had a lot of years to parse that, and it didn't truly hit until after the first couple of decades. I didn't age. I didn't go grey or develop lines or a pot belly or wattle. I didn't even have to work out and I stayed, well—" He gestured at his taut chest and abs.

"Watch it there, Narcissus."

"Wait until you meet *him*. My point is, a person with all the time in the world doesn't have to restrict herself at life's banquet. 'Ever after' only really means something when there's an end date. Sampling the banquet is a wonderful thing, and when you find something you truly care about, you can indulge. And no, this is not only about sex or relationships. It's about anything. I have a great deal of patience now."

That was both terrifying and titillating. Starr shivered. "Even with all that time available to us, the show still starts in less than an hour."

He chuckled. "You'll get it one of these years. My point is, I'm not bothered. You won't get jealousy out of me. Go ahead, chase Jason. Mav probably wouldn't mind being chased a bit by you, either. He's out of practice. But if you want to... bounce... again, I'm here." He kissed her firmly, curling one hand behind her head.

They showered and dressed hurriedly, and she tugged on his shirt to smooth it out. He fluffed her hair. They switched off the sky, returning to Hotel Blah.

A knock came at the door. It was Bookender, standing at attention in a dark maroon jacket over a soft green vest. "Good afternoon, Ms. Weatherby and Mr. Reddy. Ms. Ballantine requests Ms. Weatherby's presence in her suite, forthwith."

"Can't this wait?" Starr asked. "We've got the show."

"Ms. Ballantine says it will be brief. She and Mr. Valentine are waiting for you in her suite."

Nico frowned and Starr exchanged a puzzled look with him. Surely Jason wasn't considering firing her—not before the show, even assuming a firing was in the offing.

"I'll come along," Nico offered.

Starr shook her head. "If Jason's there, Fiona won't pull anything." She wouldn't dare: Starr still had the packet of money and the article with the note hidden in her room. "All right, I'm coming. Has to be fast, though. Nico, you go get made up. Though you do look awfully pretty already."

He kissed her once more. "Hurry up," he said. "There's a show to put on."

BOOKENDER LED STARR down the hallway, past a cleaning cart and open doorway, where two maids chattered between runs of a vacuum cleaner. He pushed open Fiona's presidential suite door and held it open for Starr.

"Ms. Ballantine will be along shortly," said the brownie, gesturing at a tray of tea and biscuits.

"And Jason?" Starr also wanted to prod him about where all the other brownies were—on strike, she had no doubt, but *where* was the question—but Bookender was too fast for her, disappearing behind his little door.

As if he were trying to… get away.

Starr stood very still in the room. There was no sign of Fiona or Jason, and the place had an oddly vacant feel to it. Everything was neat and tidy, almost untouched. An uneasy coolness stole over her, and she began wandering cautiously.

Nico's face flitted through her mind while she paced the room. She imagined his hands still on her, and the exhilaration from their exertions gave her more warm tingles. When she'd arrived at the hotel, the idea that they would end up in bed together had been as unlikely as, well, brownies being derelict in their duties. But he was as enmeshed in Fiona's web as anyone. No one should be able to hold power over someone's head to make them dance—and she never would have had all those powers without cheating.

Starr wondered what would happen when the truth came out. Would Fiona be stripped of her titles? Would it be as though they never existed? Like they'd disappeared from existence?

Disappeared.

It had been almost ten minutes since Bookender had slipped away. There was no sign of anyone. It was quiet.

Too quiet.

Starr hurried to the main double doors and pressed her ear against them. No chattering cleaning ladies on the other side. No vacuum cleaner. Not even the white noise hum that always threaded its way through walls and doors, the sound of a structure existing. Only deadness.

Blood rushing in her ears, Starr yanked open one of the double doors and saw—nothing.

Literally, nothing: a vast, empty grey blank filled the space where the hallway had been, as if the cloud she'd bounced on earlier had gobbled up the world. Gasping, Starr reached out to the emptiness, which was solid and unyielding and very, very cold. It filled the doorway and began to creep inside, wisps turning to ice crystals that spread across the carpet and crept up the walls.

Starr slammed the door, shivering.

Apparently, Fiona's power to disappear spaces was not limited to the small ones anymore.

HOLLERING AT THE top of her lungs, Starr re-opened and slammed the door again, and again. She screamed at the nothing, but it remained unchanged. Rage flooded through her in hot, sickening waves. Fiona had wanted her to do something... and she'd *done* it!

Starr wanted to slap her own face for being the fool this time.

The patsy.

She was too angry to cry. Instead, she banged her fists on the walls, rattled a post of the canopy bed until she heard a crack, and shouted until her throat hurt. Nothing changed. She was nowhere. It was as if she'd been erased, along with the room. How long would this last? Minutes? Hours?

Regardless, there was one certainty: she was going to miss the live show. They wouldn't even be able to come looking for her until it was all done. All hands and hooves were on deck for this performance.

Had Nico known?

Starr wouldn't believe that. He'd gone along with Fiona in the past, but she'd never known him to be a good liar. Fiona had likely asked him to do her a favor—so he had done it. *Like I did.*

Was there no other way out of this mess? Starr yanked back the curtains, but the windows and balcony were covered with the same misty nothing. It pressed against the glass and obscured even the balcony railing two feet away. Besides, she was on the twelfth floor. What did she think she could do, jump?

If only there was another exit.

There was: Bookender had taken it.

Starr fell to her knees and crawled to the small door that led into the walls of the hotel. She'd been in there once, and knew it connected to every room a brownie could access. And it was malleable. Did it have blank nothingness on the other side, too?

She jiggled the knob, but it wouldn't budge. Pulling harder got her nowhere. Frustrated, she ran her hands through her hair and tugged. The Guide's advice surfaced, just as it had when she tried entering Cris' office: *Knock first.*

She knocked.

The door swung inward, revealing Bookender.

"Good afternoon, Ms. Weatherby," said the brownie, bowing slightly. His glasses hung low on his nose, and he held a book in one hand.

"Bookender, are you aware of what's happened?"

"I am."

"Why did you do this to me?"

He sighed. "I do as I am bid. I am the only one of my lot currently providing assistance to any mortal, now that my compatriots have betrayed everything it means to be a brownie. They are 'on strike,' as if that means anything. We live to serve. And—"

Starr held up a hand. "So they really went through with it?"

"Indeed. Mx. Janus is leading them in a chorus of 'We Shall Overcome' in the lobby and Mr. Del Noche is attempting to convince them to whisper it, as they are audible at some distance and it will interfere with the live show. In addition, they have filled the lobby and the attending fans have nowhere to sit, so they are also not being terribly quiet. Mr. Del Noche has threatened to burn down the lobby if my fellow brownies fail to comply, and the hotel manager is begging him—"

"Gotcha. Sounds exciting. Bookender, I have to get out of this room."

"Sadly, I am unable to comply." He stared at the ground. "I am bound to Mistress Ballantine, who desired to disappear her own room for a purpose. That you happened to be inside when it occurred is unfortunate, but not something I can fix."

About what I figured, Starr thought, and studied him closer. Bookender was so formal and rigid, like a regular little butler. Some of him even reminded her of Mav; they both valued their dignity. Bookender was bound by fair play and rules. She wondered how difficult that had made it to work for Fiona all these years.

"Bookender, how long have you been indentured to Fiona?"

"Ninety-three years, eleven months and twelve days," he said.

"And why aren't you with the others right now?"

"Even if I desired to be, I cannot. Per the terms of Mistress Ballantine's award, I am tied to her prize. I am, in fact, her prize. The others are here of their own volition."

"And that's OK with you?"

"It is neither for me to agree nor disagree with," he said. "The Seelie have dictated that I may not depart until she wills it."

"But you have your own honor."

"A gentlebrownie relies on custom and etiquette to keep the world spinning correctly." He adjusted his vest. "I can do no less."

Starr had hoped he'd say something like that. "Then what if I told you that your… mistress has been doing something particularly unethical for years? Something that has earned her more prizes than she would have won otherwise? What if the entire reason you were assigned to her was a lie?"

Bookender went rigid and his mouth twitched. "I should desire proof."

Starr wondered how to make that happen. She could show him the envelope with the money and the note, but that would require giving Fiona's sworn second-in-command access to the one piece of hard evidence she had. "Does this door give you access to the hotel?"

"Indeed." He nodded. "All mythic portals supersede the Room Obliterate spell."

Trusting him, Starr explained about the manila envelope in her room and what was in it, telling him to get Oleander to let him in the room. *If* he could get Oleander away from the strike, that was. "It will explain everything. Fiona has been buying her awards, Bookender. For years. She's bribed her way into who knows how many prizes. I can wait, but the faster you go to check it out, the better."

He hesitated, then reached over and peered intently into Starr's face. "You believe this to be true."

"I know it is. But ask Dakota, or Mav, or Nico or Nora.

They all know it is, too." She took a deep breath. "She's tricked everyone, including the SCN. Including you. You might have been with her falsely all this time. If you help me, I can fix that."

And I will. Forthwith. Starr knew what she had to do now—if she could get out to do it. And Cris' unspoken 'strike three' be damned.

Bookender removed his glasses and ran a white linen square from his vest pocket over them. After wiping them down with agonizing care, he set them back on his nose and ducked behind the door, shutting it tight.

Starr stared at the little door, stunned. She'd been so sure she'd gotten through to him.

Three long moments later, the door opened again. Bookender handed a black cocktail dress and heels to Starr—Sam Draper's outfit for the live show. "Ms. Weatherby," he said, "please get dressed. There is a show that requires your presence."

CHAPTER 35
A Starr is Born

"I FAIL TO see how this strike is… beneficial." Bookender held forth as he guided Starr—now outfitted for the show—through the maze of walls. She did her best not to tear, stain or otherwise ruin her dress. At least he'd been kind enough to carry her high heels.

"Not my idea," she muttered, crawling as quickly as she could.

"You are the one who brought them the literacy spell," he said. "Reading is high-level human magic."

"I just taught them letters."

"And see where this has gotten us."

Starr had no idea where he was taking her. They crawled for several minutes through near-darkness but never descended, and she imagined they were still on the twelfth floor. She'd covered the palms of her hands with her socks, but they were starting to wear through and get caught on the occasional loose screw. The darkness enfolded them like a shroud. The Wills were all down with the show, so they only had Bookender's lantern to guide them.

"I sincerely hope you are mistaken about Mistress Ballantine," he continued. "The consequences will be terrible for her if you are correct, and worse for me if you are incorrect."

"You don't have to help. I don't want you to get in trouble." Of course, if he left her alone in the dark, all she'd have was a cell phone flashlight with a low battery and no sense of where to go or how to escape.

"I choose to assist," he said. "This is from my heart, not my head. Oleander says you have brownie best interests in mind. We are so often treated like a part of the furniture. It can be easy for others to take from us."

"I think you know exactly what the strike's about, then," Starr said.

At last, Bookender halted in front of a sliver of light on the ground. "This brings you to the lobby." He lowered the lantern and adjusted the door size so she could exit. "I recommend you move with alacrity. Filming has begun. Mr. Valentine is deeply unhappy, and Mr. Del Noche's off-stage vulgarities are beginning to melt the walls. The sooner you arrive, the sooner you can set things right."

Starr gave him a hug, which Bookender tolerated. Then he gave her a gentle push out the door and closed it. The drywall creaked.

Starr stood, dusting off her knees and shaking out her hair, then sidled out from behind a ficus to find a lobby packed with seated, silent brownies and wide-eyed, excited fans. Protest signs rested on the floor, and every mythic eyeball was turned to the wall, where the water had smoothed out as flat as an ice-locked lake and now projected the show being filmed just a few yards away.

Then she realized she'd never gotten her shoes. Starr stood, barefoot and bare-legged, with the closed door behind her, and knelt to knock. "Bookender!" she whispered. This time, there was no reply. Standing, she turned to find every eye in the lobby turned to her.

Jan hurried over. "St—that is, *Sam* Draper, where in the dragon's breath have you been?"

Oleander popped up. "Sam Draper has come to protest with brownies!"

Half of the room shushed them, and the other half shushed the shushers.

"Er, no," Starr told the room. "I was... unavoidably detained upstairs." Oleander looked so downcast her heart hurt. "I would be with you if I didn't have this... um, soiree to attend." She raised her fist. "Er, power to the brownies?"

"Good enough," muttered Jan. "Now get out of here." They waved at the fans. "Make a path, you gawpers."

A wide lane opened across the linoleum, pushing mythics to the side whether they chose to move or not, and Starr dashed down it, the tiled floor cold beneath her toes. She reached the escalator down to the ballroom and hesitated—bare feet on escalator stairs seemed like danger incarnate—and instead threw herself onto the rubber handhold, balancing as it carried her all the way down. Once there, she found another hallway, packed with mythics. They all sat in front of a portable fountain, which shot up a fan of smooth water that streamed a simulcast of the live show.

Drawn to the screen closest to her, Starr recognized the scene: Beatrice, Valéncia and Mav were strolling around the well-appointed ballroom as if attending a party, chatting among themselves. A fireplace had been set on the far side of the room, flames crackling in its hearth. The rest of the guests at the soiree, all of whom chatted quietly in small groups so the main actors could be heard, were either guest actors or costumed mythics. Starr spotted a Cyclops in a suit and tie with an additional fake googly eye pasted on the side of its head; a mermaid in a long, flowing dress and giant red wig whizzing around in a bedazzled wheelchair; and at least one unicorn in a mask and tuxedo, a top hat disguising its horn. They looked nothing like humans, but not a single fan in the hallway rebelled against this so-called intrusion on reality.

"They're our VIMs," Jason had explained to the cast. "Tested and vetted by the EVVVs at SCN, they are able to handle themselves in human situations."

"What happened to this whole 'reality' thing?" Mav had asked. "I know *we've* been in on the joke for years, but are you really gonna risk everybody else figuring out?"

"They want to be in on it," said Starr. "It means they're on TV. Or whatever you want to call a wall of water. It's magic, and it's reality, and they don't necessarily care about the difference, as long as we play along."

Jason had given her a nervous smile. "I hope you're right, Starr Weatherby."

A fluttering in the distance caught her attention. A centaur was picking his way through the group, waving a linen cloth that read *SAM DRAPER!*

Kyle, of course. He stopped in front of Starr, the audience following him to gape at the newcomer, just as the others had upstairs. The centaur gave the cloth a shake, and now it read, *Using my inside voice.*

He's textiling me, Starr realized.

Another shake, and the words changed again: *They said you were delayed in traffic. But there is no traffic in the hotel! Plus, I knew Sam wouldn't let traffic stop her! Not with the DAN tests about to arrive!*

He means DNA tests, Starr recalled, and reached over to hug him. "I'm sorry," she whispered.

For what? his cloth read.

"For not playing by the rules," she whispered. "You might not want to watch this next part."

Rules change, the cloth read. *The question is, are we having fun?* Kyle turned the cloth to the audience. Hands, hooves, fins and other appendages raised and shook. They were politely avoiding noise that could interrupt the recording in the ballroom.

Starr gave everyone two enthusiastic thumbs-up and followed Kyle as he carved a path to the most distant ballroom doorway. Above it hovered a bright red light and a sign like the one Starr had seen on her first day at the studio:

SOIRÉE ENTRANCE
DO NOT ENTER WHEN RED LIGHT IS ON
UNDER PAIN OF BANISHMENT

The red light was on.

Starr patted Kyle's withers. "Screw banishment," she said, and stepped through the door.

THE NONDESCRIPT BALLROOM they'd rehearsed in the day before had been transformed by the poltergeists into a grand, opulent... well, ballroom. Mahogany walls accented with golden light sconces now framed a shining parquet floor covered in small round cocktail tables. Broad French doors lay open on one side of the room, with the illusion of a starry night outside on a patio.

Guests clustered, holding bubbly drinks and small hors d'oeuvres. Cameradryads shifted around the room, making gentle shushing noises as their roots traversed the ground. Starr decided they were too focused on the work to think twice about the fact that the floor and walls were made of hardwood.

Meanwhile, in the short time since Starr had arrived from the lobby and this exact moment, the guests had all pulled back, giving Valéncia a space by the fireplace for her lines, while Mav and Beatrice stood off to one side. Jason constantly lingered just out of camera, gesturing and shaking his head, but Nico—who had no lines for another couple of scenes—was nowhere in sight.

Celtis sidled up to Starr and began filming her.

"Sam is forever missing out," Valéncia was saying. "I had warned her about her car being useless. I have been informed she has a flat tire, a broken headlight *and* the tailpipe fell off. Does anyone have the mail?"

"Maybe we should be attending to the guests," said Mav, but he handed her the prop letters as rehearsed. One of the other cameradryads zoomed in on the envelopes. They were part of Emma's big twist, the one that would re-order the Marlborough family. Everyone was about to learn that Sam—not Mav—was Valéncia's offspring. "Or we could wait until Sam gets here."

Valéncia snicked the envelope from his fingers as some of the VIM guests closed in, curious. "There is no point in waiting. Sam may learn the truth after she arrives." She paused. "If she arrives." She slit the envelope open with a nail and withdrew the paper inside. "Goddess." Valéncia sank into a chair next to the fireplace. Her cane clattered to the floor. "Maverick! You have some explaining to do!"

The prop paper had some words on it, to keep things realistic. But Fiona was going off-script. Starr took several steps forward, winding through the crowd, aware of being disheveled and without her shoes. Mav glanced off camera at Jason, who waved at him to stick with it.

Yes, and-ing during the live show? Starr wasn't sure where any of this was going. All she knew was she had to get to someone—Jason, Mav, anyone—and find a way to turn everything around. Things were finally going to get real.

"It says—" Mav picked up the prop letter. "Well, this is something."

"It certainly is!" said Valéncia. "It says here that Sam is your *daughter*, Mav."

Beatrice billowed in, long loose dress nearly flowing into the fireplace. "That can't be right."

Mango time! thought Starr, and strode forward. "Phew!" she breathed hard. "Goddess love Kyle's Tow Truck Agency!"

Beyond the door she heard a soft whinny, then a thud. Kyle had probably fainted.

Valéncia nearly fell out of her chair.

Mav dropped a poker he'd been carrying to adjust the fire.

Beatrice... moaned.

Jason wrung his horns.

Celtis kept her focus directly on Starr.

"That letter is a *fraud*," Starr said, whipping it from Mav's hand and tossing it into the lit hearth. As it crisped nicely, she turned to her co-stars. "That lab was completely compromised. The results were falsified!" She pulled out her cell phone and held it aloft. "I have received a special"—*oh, yeah, right, no cell phones here.*

Well, go big or go home—"textile message that confirms the truth. Mav... will you read this special note?"

She handed him her phone, poking it awake and pulling up a text message from several weeks ago from one of her roommates.

Mav met her gaze. She gave him a nod. This wasn't so much a *yes and* as it was a way to put the train back on the rails. "With pleasure," he said, turning the phone around a few times. "Well, this can't be true either. It says I'm not Valéncia's son, and *you*, Sam Draper, are her daughter!"

A collective gasp swept through the VIMs and resonated with the audience outdoors.

"Noooo!" Valéncia swooned.

"Yes!" Starr drove her elbow down and made a fist. The train was back on track, but it was her track now. She folded her arms and strode over to Valéncia—while speaking to Fiona. "Guess who falsified the original results? The one woman who'll do anything to make the world turn her way. Anything. Am I right... *Mother*?"

Valéncia sprang to her feet, and Starr saw no division between her and Fiona. They were one, united, furious lady. "Watch your mouth, young lady. Say not another word, or you will regret it."

"Aw, Mom," said Starr. "I know you think you can run things like—what did you say to us the other day, like *Lord of the Rings*?"

"Flies." Mav coughed into his fist. "*Lord of the Flies*."

"Right, different story entirely." Starr paced the dance floor, waiting to be cut off, but no one ran onto the set. No one broke the fourth wall. This was her show, and she was running with it now.

"I mean, Valéncia—you're the sort of person who would

sabotage a DNA letter because you wanted a different answer," she began. "You're also the sort of person who might, oh, I don't know, bug everyone's rooms so you could hear everything being said, then use it against people. And you're also the sort of woman who would, let's say, *bribe the press* to give you the best and most important prizes. That's the sort of person Valéncia is. Or is that even the name I should use? Maybe I should say… *Fiona*? 'Cause while you're a lot like the mother I grew up with, I'm never going to call you Mama. But I will call you a liar, a cheat and a fraud."

The only sound in the room was a small, strangled noise from Jason off-camera, and the fireplace crackling. Throughout Starr's speech, Fiona had kept her shoulders squared, with the imperious look of someone about to deliver a devastating rebuttal. She had not blinked once. But now, one of her eyes twitched disconcertingly.

"I have no idea who this Fiona is you speak of," she said, gripping the lion's head of her cane. "There is no Fiona here." With a swift jerk she wrenched the head of the cane off and dropped the blunt end to the floor, revealing a six-inch dagger—a blade that rang a high and metallic note through the ballroom.

"That's the sound!" one hatted unicorn neighed, clopping around a cocktail table. "I heard that before!"

"Yeah!" cried the Cyclops with the googly eye. "Right before the furniture went falling!"

"When Sam just about got *crushed*!" a further mythic Starr couldn't see gasped.

Thanks for the confirmation—Starr started to think, but just then Fiona lunged with a snake's precision strike, driving the blade directly at Starr's throat. Dodging, Starr slammed into the fireplace and grappled for something to fight back with, but Fiona twisted with the agility of a much younger woman, pinning Starr's arm behind her. Starr tried kicking free, but the cold point of the blade pressed against her throat, and she froze. Her chest, still not fully healed from the wardrobe, throbbed.

"That escalated quickly," noted a masked Gorgon off-camera.

"Make no moves," Fiona hissed at the cast and the audience. "Sam and I are going to have a little… mother-daughter chat." The knife began to cut into Starr's jaw and Mav took a step forward.

"Do not lay hands on me, boy," said Fiona. "Or this ends quickly and in a way that will make you most unhappy."

Behind them, Beatrice staggered against a chair and let out a ragged yowl. Starr wanted to roll her eyes; there was no moment of drama that woman wouldn't try to upstage.

"Help," Beatrice gasped. Only, not Beatrice: this was Nora. "My water… it's broken."

Of course it has, Starr thought, fighting panic.

"Beatrice, your timing is impeccable." With a quick jerk on Starr's bent arm, Fiona lowered the knife and pulled a small object out of her pocket, closing her fist around it. "Adieu!" she cried.

Celtis, doing an excellent job of keeping her eyes on the ball, reached out, perhaps to get a better shot. Starr couldn't say. But in the instant Fiona's fingers closed around the object from her pocket, the cameradyrad's branch brushed Starr's arm and the three of them winked off stage—

—AND INTO THE *Tune in Tomorrow* lobby with a soft popping sound.

Dizzy from the unexpected teleportation, Starr flailed at Celtis' branches. The cameradrydad jerked away. Starr wrenched from Fiona's knife grip and raced around the reception desk, pounding on the boulder closing off Phil's cave.

"Phil!" she shouted. "Emergency! Emergen—"

The knife had returned, this time at her back. Fiona growled ferally. "Once more and you'll see blood." She whirled on Celtis. "And if you make a move, *shrub*, I start pruning."

Celtis shivered, dropping a few leaves, but kept filming.

Fiona wrenched Starr's arm again, the point of the dagger piercing cruelly between her shoulder blades. She thought about planting her feet, refusing to walk, or even faking a faint—but who knew how far Fiona would go? She already thought she'd killed one interloper, so why not go for the deuce?

"In." Fiona poked Starr through the stage doors, and they entered total darkness. "Wills!" the diva shouted. Three tiny lights swirled out from the ceiling, spinning around the trio.

"Help me," begged Starr. She was freezing and sweating at the same time, and her whole body ached: chest, neck, back, bare feet.

"Light our way," Fiona ordered. "And stay back."

"Boy, Fiona, you missed your calling as a director," said Starr. "Look, can we have another truce?"

"My name is Valéncia. Yours, for now, is *worm*. Now, march."

Starr marched, desperately searching for a way to escape being skewered, but her mind wasn't working well. Terror paralyzed her beyond basic movements, making her compliant. She hoped that by doing whatever Fiona demanded, she'd make this all stop faster. But part of her inside was screaming to take action.

She's an old lady! I can take her! Starr thought. *Well, she's an old lady with a knife who moves better than I do. And she's nuts.*

A few minutes later they rounded a corner, a blue glowing light illuminating Fiona's intended destination: the wide, round pit with water spilling into it. The bottomless pit. The pit that had swallowed Amelia—who had been given a MARBLE ahead of time. Starr had no such out. Somehow, arriving here was both unexpected and inevitable.

Fiona pressed harder and the tip of her blade pierced Starr's back. "Walk."

Starr inched toward the lip, the hole's enormous drawing power urging her forward. Icy cold water ran over her bare toes, making her feet feel like numb bricks. But she kept going: the hole was calling to her softly, urgently. It needed her. It was hungry.

"I'll leave." Her voice trembled. "I'll leave and they'll make me forget and I'll never remember you existed—"

"Too late," Fiona snapped. "You spilled *all* the beans. They know everything. You've left me with nothing, worm."

"That's not true." Nico slipped out from behind a nearby set. He was breathing hard and had a few buttons open on his shirt, as if he'd raced here mid-costume change. "I'm sorry it took me so long," he gasped at Starr, then turned to Fiona. "I also keep a spare MARBLE, Fee. And I can't let you do this."

Fiona snatched up Starr's arm again, wrenching it back, keeping the knife at the ready. "Why not? She has no place here. She's ruined everything."

"You brought this on yourself," he said. "Lower the knife, Cookie. Let's talk."

"I am not Fiona! I am not your Cookie!" Fiona screamed. "The next time someone calls me anything other than Valéncia, I will slit her throat!"

Nico, who had been advancing with one hand raised, halted.

"I am taking out the trash," Fiona growled. "This is an enormous trash bin. We can put all the stupid brainless newcomers in it we like, and they float away like bad memories."

"What do you want from me?" Starr quavered. "If you think I'm going to wave goodbye and jump in, think again, lady."

"Certainly not," said Fiona, spinning Starr around and lifting the blade into the air. "I'm here to help."

She drove the dagger down in a swiping motion and in that half-breath Starr grabbed for her wrist, gripping the blade instead. It sliced into the meat of her palm, sending a searing, blinding pain up Starr's arm. But she held on, shrieking—and leaned toward the pit.

We all go down together, Starr thought.

They fell.

RATHER, THEY FELL a short distance.

Starr released the knife as gravity took over, flailing for anything she could latch onto—for a moment, Fiona's sleeve, which slithered from her bloodied fingers. Then she was descending again until—

Her other hand hooked on the metal lip of the hole and—

She jerked to a stop, shoulder wrenching painfully as she dangled over the rushing water and held on by four fingers. Straining mightily, she reached up with her injured hand to grab the lip of the pool and ended up with a fractionally more stable grip. She panted from effort and fear. Her hand cramped as cool pit water ran over her fingers, seeping into the sleeve of her dress. She gasped with relief and surprise.

"Roooooland!" came a wail next to her.

Starr turned and groaned, frustrated that Fiona had also secured a handhold on the pit's rim a foot or so away, where she dangled, kicked, flailed and screamed. The dagger was nowhere in sight—Starr imagined it was the one victim of the pit today. Thus far.

Starr's fingers slipped; the edge of the lip was cutting into her good hand, while the bad one had begun to ache in a deep, awful way. She imagined tearing the cut open wider and wider until the skin unraveled like a glove from the hand. She shivered.

Nico's head and shoulders appeared over the edge as he flattened himself on the ground above them. "Ay-ya!" he cried. "That water is *cold*!"

"Tell me s-s-something I don't know." Starr's teeth chattered.

He extended both of his arms into the pit. Fiona snagged one, Starr the other.

"Ladies," he grunted, "I never thought I'd be a witness to such an apt metaphor of my own life, but here we are."

"Hoist me up, Roland," ordered Fiona. "You know what to do."

That woman has slid all the way into Valénciaville, Starr thought.

Nico's brows came together. "Not as easy as it looks."

"Whyever not?"

"Rumors to the contrary, I do not have the strength of ten men. Or even two."

"Then release the hussy!"

Had Starr not been sliced up, cold and terrified of falling to her death she might have found that hilarious.

"No can do." Nico shook his head.

"Where is everyone?" Starr yelped. "Is no one else coming?"

Celtis peered over the rim, aiming her camera. Waving her leaves, she dipped a root into the water and sipped.

"Extend a branch!" Starr cried.

Celtis shook her head, gesturing at the camera. She was *on duty*.

"She's useless," Nico sighed.

The cameradryad dropped an acorn on his head.

"Didn't everyone else see what happened?" Starr was somewhere between crying and laughing. Either way, hysteria was definitely a factor.

"I told the boss I got this," he admitted.

Starr gaped.

"Fine. I overreached." He blinked. "In more ways than one. Problem is, they're preoccupied right now. I mean, we're getting this particular Perils of Pauline moment just great, but there are... scenes happening back at the... soirée that include introducing the wide mythical world to the miracle of human birth." He sighed. "Poor Nor— Beatrice."

"Poor Beatrice!" Starr shouted. Part of her was astonished they were still using each other's show names. "How many warm-blooded species do they need to deliver a baby?"

"I can lift just *one* of you," he said testily.

"Sincere apologies," Celtis' leaves whispered. "My branches would not withstand the—they would break. But this is excellent streaming! Jason will be so pleased."

"You three are remarkably calm considering we are about to die in a bottomless pit!" Fiona screeched. "Make your choice, Roland, and get me out of here!"

Nico turned his head. "Choose? You mean, choose who I can pull up?"

"There should be no choice whatsoever, but *yes*!"

"Then 'fess up."

"Roland, I have no time for this. Lady Marlborough has guests to attend to and—"

"Stop it."

"And Mav and Beatrice are having some kind of incident—"

"*Stop it now*," he roared. "I can smell bullshit all over you. If you don't get straight with me—and the audience—I am letting you go for real."

Fiona gaped.

"You let Bookender take me to her room," Starr told him. Her bleeding hand was beginning to go numb, and she wondered if she'd hurt her ribs again in the fall.

"I should have come with you."

"Did you... kn-know?"

For the first time, she registered not guilt, but true hurt in Nico's expression. "Good goddess, Starr, do you think so little of me?"

Her vision swam. She was going to pass out.

Nico looked away. "Right. I can't hold you both forever and I don't think anyone's coming to help in time. Valéncia, buzz off. Fiona, apologize to Starr."

Fiona shot daggers at him and dropped the pretense. "Nicodemus Reddy, what are we? Three years old?"

"No," Starr chuckled dimly. "We are five and we bounce."

Fiona made a dismissive noise. "I apologize for nothing, aside from trying to save this show from itself. I'd do it all again, but better next time. And if you're not on my side, Nicodemus Reddy, then you are my enemy. Furthermore—"

"Adios, Fiona," he said, and released her.

A long, anguished scream of surprise trailed off as the darkness swallowed Fiona Ballantine. Her shout lasted long after she'd disappeared from sight, but eventually both the Grande Damn and her fury... vanished.

Nico swung his free arm toward Starr and she grappled with it, trying to kick her ice-block feet up to the top of the pit, but she kept slipping. "I can't," she whispered. "My arms."

"Mine, too," he said, trying to drag himself backward. "We talked too long. I'm numb. I can't pull."

"Truth." Starr's mouth was dry, despite the water all around her. "What does it mean to fall... forever?"

He made a face. "First of all, you're not going to fall. Second, it is *not* a bottomless pit. Once it was. But... we had budget cuts. It's plenty deep, though."

Starr tried to process that. "So won't Fiona be smashed?"

He bit his lip. "Depends how she lands. It's a... soft-ish fall. Think of a septic tank. That's what's down there. Plus, a lot of glitter. I hear the brownies dispose of their 'earnings' that way."

"Shit," said Starr.

"With luck, there's more glitter than waste but... yeah."

"That's disappointing."

"Well, it's mythic shit, if you prefer."

They laughed softly and her hand slipped on his wrist.

The blood and the water made everything slick, and she was losing coherence. Nico's face swam in and out of focus. "I'm—sorry," she said.

"For what?"

"Doubting you."

"I gave you good reason," he said. "More than once."

"Don't let go." Her eyes fluttered. "She'll strangle me if we end up down there together."

Nico became deeply serious. "Never. Hang on with me a little longer. I promise I'll never let go, if that's what you want."

"Never is a long time." She drifted, then returned. "Especially when you have all the time in the world."

Neither spoke for a moment, putting their energies into holding on a few more seconds, the water rushing around them. Starr knew what was going to happen. Nico probably did, too. But they weren't going to let it happen willingly.

And then—noise. Clatter. Nico perked up, glancing over a shoulder. "The cavalry!" he cried. "Over here! The pit!"

Footsteps. Many, many footsteps.

"How did you guys get here?" he shouted into the darkness.

"Brownie doors go everywhere!" Oleander called back. "*ORGANIZE!*"

Much scuffling and scraping followed, and Nico yelped in surprise. "That's my shoe! Why do I keep losing shoes? Oh—OK." He peered down at Starr. "Don't pass out yet. The bros are making a chain and pulling my leg. My legs. No joke."

"Ha, ha." Starr inched up as Nico inched back. Her bloody hand slid from his wrist, dangling. "I think… I'm going to… fall," she said.

"The hell you are," he barked and shouted over his shoulder, "pull faster!"

"Trying!" Oleander fired back. "We are mighty, but we are small!"

Nico's body jerked another few inches. Starr came with him, but her arm had turned from lead to sand. Her fingers slipped into his and they hooked together for a few seconds. He tried reaching forward but missed. "Hold on!"

"I can't," she whispered. "Just... clean me up before you get Fiona."

Her fingers slipped from his.

Starr fell. Her stomach lurched, her arms flew out wide. Whatever was coming, would come—

A long prehensile appendage arced over everyone's head, curling around her body and surrounding her in warm, ember-colored feathery scales. A dragon tail. Phil's dragon tail. It jerked Starr out of the pit and set her on the stage floor.

Nico scrambled over and scooped her head into his lap. Starr's eyes fluttered.

"I did a thing!" Phil cried. "I dreamed I heard Starr at my door but there was no Starr at my door but there were brownies—" He took a deep breath. "I finally did security!"

"You sure did." Starr reached up to Phil. "My hero."

The dragon lowered his gigantic head, accepting a gentle pat under the chin.

Starr turned to take Oleander's hand. "My other hero."

"Aww." Oleander toed the ground. "We like to help. All of us. Together!"

Starr waved at the collection of brownies just out of arm's reach.

"Ahem?" said Nico. "Up here?"

Starr gave him a pat on the chin, too. "My top mortal hero."

"I'll take it," he said, and turned to Oleander. "What news of Nora?"

"She has a girl!" Oleander clapped her hands. "Many soirée guests have headaches. One fainted and one ran into Boston and nobody knows where he is. But a unicorn donated his top hat to put the baby in. This is the best day ever!"

Starr didn't want to know how they were going to make this particular, truly *real* slice of reality penetrate into mythic brains. She was too tired. "I guess it is," she told her brownie.

Nico craned down to kiss her, aiming for the forehead and Starr grabbed his face. "My lips are down here, buddy."

They came together. He smelled like olive oil and cardamom.

"And—scene," said Celtis, turning off the camera.

CHAPTER 36

Lone Starr

STARR'S HAND THROBBED. Her chest ached. Her shoulder was singing to her. She wore Sam's damp, bloodied dress and a pair of slippers she'd never seen before.

But she was alive, and not in a bottomless pit. Instead, she was in her dressing room, having bolted awake from a deep sleep that could have lasted hours, minutes or days—she had no idea. What she did know was that she was alone.

Staring at her hand, she remembered fragments of what happened after the pit rescue: Nico carrying her into the lobby, setting her on the sofa. Oleander giving her a slug of uisce beatha, that fairy-hoarded whiskey, then covering her wound with fragrant, moistened bandages. Feeling sleepy. Starr giving Oleander the nod to return to the protest. Nico promising to return after attending to 'rescue efforts.'

Then dark, quiet rest.

Now, though, she was out of sorts and confused. Was it day or night? Where was everyone? Her windowless dressing room was dark, but a bright glow filtered in from the hallway, as if someone had parked klieg lights in the lobby. She poked open her door, squinting into the too-bright light. Locating a pair of sunglasses, she padded down the hallway toward vague noises that reminded her of construction. The light grew brighter but not hotter, and soon the sunglasses were barely enough. It wasn't just light either—a fuzziness surrounded her, like the nothing that had enveloped Fiona's disappeared hotel room.

"Hello?" she called out after reaching what should have been the lobby. "Who's there? Can you turn down the spotlights?"

Some muttering, and the illumination lowered by half, reaching the brightness of the desert on a sunny day. "Oh, my, it's a loose human," said a deep voice that came from a tall, white-clad figure, addressing a shorter version of itself. Both mythics were covered in some sort of bumpy, rocky material. "Your sweeping magics are terrible."

"Perhaps she was unconscious!" noted the second mythic in a thin, reedy voice. "Sleeping mortals register differently."

"I was asleep." Starr shielded her eyes. "And I'm a little blinded now."

The taller one thwapped the shorter in the head. "And she's unsighted, you fool! This is another fine mess you've gotten us into."

"No, I just mean you're awfully bright for me."

"Ah!" The shorter of the two made a waving gesture and the light dialed down to nearly normal indoor levels. Now Starr could make out two of the most breathtakingly beautiful beings she'd ever laid eyes on. Their coral-shaded skin had silvery undertones, and their almond-shaped black eyes were proportionately larger than their elfin features. Their hair was shimmery platinum, and their white outfits were covered in radiant, rainbow-casting diamonds.

Like Jason's robe when he got back from the SCN meeting. "You're Seelie," she realized. "And you're from the network."

The tall one glided over. Neither of them quite touched the ground, hovering an inch or two above it. "Unseelie," they said. "But you were close." Neither being suggested gender, so Starr defaulted to Jan's pronoun of choice. The taller one noted, "I am the Vice-Vice-Vice-Director and Supra-President in Charge of Dismantlement of Special Projects, Operations and Facilities, Seelie Court Network." He shivered with pleasure at being able to offer his title. "At your service. Call me... Hardy."

"That must be a challenge to fit on a business card," said Starr, dazzled.

"And I am the Vice-Vice-Vice Director and *Associate* Supra-President in Charge—" said the smaller Seelie, rolling off a similar title. "You may call me Laurel."

"You've got to be kidding me."

"We have been ingesting human comedic entertainments for centuries," smiled Laurel. "You should see us try to relocate a piano up a flight of stairs without magic sometime!"

"Maybe," she allowed. "I'm Starr—"

"Weatherby!" cried Laurel. "AKA Sam Draper AKA Samantha Wornicker." Starr cringed at hearing her non-stage name spoken aloud as they conjured a hovering notepad. With a few flicks several pages turned over. "Indeed, we'd had you as already returned to the other side of the Gate, but—"

Hardy leaned closer to Starr, examining her. A wave of pleasure descended, like a combination of being kissed by Nico and eating a large bowl of ice cream. When they pulled away, the sensation receded. "Many thanks to you,

Starr Weatherby!" they chirped. "You have given us a new project, so you have!"

For the first time, Starr noticed that the lobby was empty. The furniture had been removed, as had Phil's desk. Even Phil's cave was gone. "What sort of project?"

Laurel conjured up another screen, this one a memo handwritten in illuminated calligraphy, and read aloud: "Following a comprehensive examination of the mortal-based entertainment known as *Tune in Tomorrow*, it has been determined that Shenanigans of the First and Second Orders have taken place, rendering it non-viable."

Starr started to feel cold again. "Is this because now everyone knows it's not *real*?"

"Surprisingly, no," said Laurel. "Breaching the wall between the *real* and the *story* is the least of the problems here. However"—they returned to the floating document— "to wit: Key Performer has exchanged fungibles for magic, a prime violation; Key Performer has perpetrated violence on a second Key Performer within a protected zone. Secondarily, unsanctioned relations between mythics and humans have occurred; and a general disregard for mythic authority." Laurel flicked their fingers again and the memo vanished. "I am disappointed, however. I was a fan of the show. Still, I am thoroughly delighted to have a project to dismantle!"

"Indeed, I delight in being so occupied, but it was a reckless, foolhardy thing you did, Starr Weatherby," Hardy added. "Indirectly—"

"I killed the show."

Hardy nodded.

The chill that began at the words 'non-viable' had raced to Starr's heart as the violations were enumerated. By the time Hardy acknowledged the truth, she felt sick and broken.

"Please don't do this," she pleaded.

"Already done," said Hardy. "You are the last and will have to go. All the others have been sent forward, I believe."

"Correct," said Laurel. "Low-level mythics have been assigned or are awaiting reassignment at headquarters; higher-level ones are released on their own recognizance. One select mortal is awaiting a Seelie Court decision; all others have been released into the wild on the other side of the Gate." They nodded at Starr. "You get to go home!"

"But—no—" Starr stammered. "I was trying to help! You can't cancel a show for shenanigans! Just fire me!"

Hardy regarded her like a petri dish specimen. "Such devotion is admirable and will be noted, but we are not decision-makers. We are the un-dreamers of dreams. We dismantle. Now, it's time you were gone."

Her heart ached on every level: Jason's life work ruined, Mav cast into a world he found overwhelming, Nico stripped of protection. And on top of that: "Am I going to… forget everything?"

"In time," said Hardy. "But it won't be a sudden thing, as you're not quitting or being fired, you're being released. Over the years all of this will seem more distant. Like something that happened to another."

Laurel patted Starr's back. "Memory Erasure only matters when there is something to protect. No show—nothing to protect. All that will happen when you depart is you will remain unable to discuss this with anyone who has no connection to the show. A safety precaution for us as much as you. In less… regulated times, mortals who visited our side of the Veil rattled off far too many details about their experiences to the uninitiated."

"Terrible how much false mythos lingers," Hardy sighed. "It's nearly impossible to feed or water a visiting mortal anymore, and they never do understand about acclimatizing fairy gold. So, you see—"

"I don't see!" Starr wiped tears from her cheeks. "This has been the greatest experience of my life. I almost died—twice!"

"And your reward is not to be tried in Seelie Court," Hardy said patiently, gesturing. As they had been speaking, the Gate had materialized, a wispy grey mist trailing inside for the last time. "Now, Ms. Weatherby, we must turn off the lights. Please attend to the exit."

"I'll escort her," said Laurel, gently guiding Starr into the fog. "Perhaps you can finish the paperwork."

"Naturally," said Hardy, conjuring up their notepad. "Always with the paperwork."

Laurel paused with Starr inches from the Gate. The extraordinarily good emotions the Fae's closeness conjured clashed with the pained loneliness going on inside Starr. She turned as they neared the Gate, thinking to make a break for it. Maybe she could hide in her dressing room.

"Don't," Laurel whispered. "Wherever you may think you can run won't be there in a few breaths." They glanced over their shoulder, then blew on their fingers and pushed something into Starr's hand. "I've watched every *Tune in Tomorrow* since it began. This is my thank you gift."

Starr uncurled her fingers to find a purple piece of candy twisted in wax paper. "Laurel, this is a cough drop."

"Is it, now?" The Unseelie raised an eyebrow. "Maybe 'tis, maybe 'tisn't. Its true purpose is to hold every one of *Tune in Tomorrow*'s shows, including today's. The archive, if you will. I have saved them all and pass them to you. In the next moment, all will be lost."

"Lost!" Starr restrained herself from saying such an erasure was inhuman. Of course it was: these were not humans. "What do I do with it?"

"You will know at the appropriate time," they said, and gave Starr a gentle push.

Starr tumbled through the Gate, falling through misty greyness, clutching a purple cough drop that contained a universe—and landed on the path just below the Verrazzano Bridge. Before her, rusted and bent gates squeaked in the early morning breeze. There was no one else around.

It was tomorrow.

And *Tomorrow* was over.

CHAPTER 37

Port Out, Starrboard Home

THREE MONTHS LATER, no one was calling her 'Starr Weatherby' anymore. She was Samantha Wornicker, the name she'd been born with. Starr Weatherby had hope and goals and a future. Samantha Wornicker worked in a strip mall lingerie store, a place with a familiar routine she could sink into and not think about what she'd lost.

Samantha *had* tried to pick up the pieces after landing on that path beneath the bridge as the first streaks of daylight ventured over the horizon. She'd arrived back in the real world and resolved not to let it beat her down.

But three months later, it was World 1, Samantha 0.

Her cascade of terrible fortune started almost right away. She'd shown up at her Brooklyn apartment to find it empty; a box of personal items and papers labeled 'Starr' had been left with the superintendent. Next, she'd discovered she was broke. As the Guide had warned, by not staying in her job for a full year she lost everything except eight percent of her earnings. Her balance on the ATM screen the day after she was deposited back in the city was not all that far from what it had been the day she was hired: $287.25. Rent and general living expenses had nibbled down the eight percent she'd earned until it might never have even existed.

Starr had couch-surfed. Taken on extra shifts waitressing at a diner that was not Mike's. Secured a weekend job at a comedy club that provided stage time for its staff improv troupe. She'd hoped a spark of joy would return the moment she joined the troupe on stage, but then an audience member had given her a prompt of 'papaya' and she'd crumbled.

But the real problem wasn't the challenge of living in the city. The problem was how tightly she was trying to hold onto what was gone. It was as if the fog of the Gate had taken up residence in her head and she couldn't focus. She wanted to be elsewhere. She didn't want the forgetting process to start. She had a hole inside her in the shape of *Tune in Tomorrow* that included fauns and dragons and cloud-bouncing and a cowboy with a guitar on the roof and grindylows doing the backstroke in Boston Harbor.

After the papaya moment, she'd thrown in the towel and gone back to the one place they couldn't turn her away: home. There was no rent, her furniture was just as she'd left it, and she could mourn in relative solitude while saving money. A few months later, she'd almost managed to not think of the show every waking hour.

Then things changed, yet again.

Samantha was hanging up 'Or Bust' brand 32A bras on plastic hangers in the back room of the lingerie store one afternoon when the interim associate store manager, Anthony, stuck his head in. "Someone up front to see ya," he said.

"I've got a break in five." She didn't even pause. "They can wait."

"He's pretty cute." Anthony winked.

Samantha rolled her eyes. Bradley, most likely. Ever since she'd moved back to Maryland, her old high school flame had been sniffing around, even though he'd knocked up Melanie Chizzoli, who was due any second now. Melanie was the jerk he'd cheated on her with the summer after their senior year, and Sam could barely stand the idea of him. He also gave off a distinct odor of pepperoni.

Samantha wasn't tempted, not with Bradley, not with anyone. Her whole life was menial work, then going back home to listen to Mama, who bemoaned on a repeating loop that her daughter's life was a tragic waste. When *Wheel of Fortune* came on, Mama would pour a glass of 'medicine' and they'd watch it together, dreaming of fabulous prizes and skinny hostesses who had all the answers. Then Samantha would hide in her bedroom and force herself not to forget until work the next day.

Fridays were the one break in the action: she grabbed a beer at Yolanda's bar, fending off comments from former classmates who reveled in seeing her slink back from the big city.

Last week, she'd ordered two beers.

Samantha knew she was hiding out. In Hagerstown she could forget about soul-sucking auditions, whether she needed a new headshot or if that producer who called was a complete letch or only partly one. This was a different track of life, a simpler one that would reward her eventually with a kid or two and a guy who liked watching football all weekend and also drank more beer than he should. That, or a house of cats.

Maybe both.

While sitting in Yolanda's, sometimes Samantha would pull out the purple cough drop Laurel had claimed was the history of a show that no longer existed and set it on the bar. Once she even left it there while going to the toilet, letting the fates deal with it. After all, it was probably a Fae practical joke.

It was back in her pocket before she even reached the bathroom.

So Bradley, if that's who it was out there, could wait. Samantha was in no hurry. He could wait forever, or until she officially gave up all hope.

A few minutes later, she carried the 'Or Bust!' bras back to the 32A rack and began hanging them up.

"Last I remember, that was absolutely not the right size for Starr Weatherby," said a familiar voice.

Samantha whirled, holding the bras in front of her like a shield. Jason Valentine was lounging on top of the underpants display, head tilted to one side. "Yep." He nodded at the bra-shield. "Totally the wrong size."

Tears burned in the corners of her eyes. She wanted to hug him more than anything, but couldn't move.

Jason held up a fifty-dollar bill. "You still doing instant Shakespeare for cash? Or does Samantha Wornicker not stoop to such theatrics?"

"How—how did you find me?"

He tossed the bill behind him into the underpants. "I'd've been quicker if I had known to stop asking for 'Starr Weatherby.' Finding you was a hell of a lot harder than assisting in a human birth. Sheep ears, what a mess. But at least that was over in thirty-two minutes, which I understand is rather quick. Do you have any idea how long it's taken me to track you down?"

"Depends when you started looking. I've been waiting for months."

Jason smiled and her heart softened. "All right: three days. But I *wanted* to do it for months."

Samantha flashed back to the first day she'd spotted him in the diner booth. He'd stood out like Technicolor in a black-and-white world. Her heart sang and beat true again for the first time in many weeks.

Oh, hug him already, a voice inside her urged, so she ran over and wrapped her arms around his lean body. He smelled of fresh-mown grass and sugar. Jason hugged her back so fiercely her feet left the ground.

"I missed you," she told his chest. "Why did it take so long?"

"Complications!" He threw some underpants into the air in frustration. "The live show was the best thing ever and I had such hopes! Every mythic who could watch, did watch. Do you have any idea how many mythics that is?"

"Eleventy billion?" Samantha's mouth quirked up. Jason always made her want to play.

"Just about! But!" He slid from the display. "Not replicable. Which, thank goodness, because kidnap and murder—"

"And slicing of hands—"

"Are not easy to pull off."

"That's not quite what I thought you'd say."

He pointed at her. "The SCN hates… mistakes. Fae make so few and Fiona's antics looked like one. Your enumerating further failures in front of all the worlds didn't help—and then Nora ripped the curtain right off the dividing wall by giving *birth* in the middle of everything. I don't think many mythics had seen that before. And also, you know—"

"She wasn't supposed to be pregnant on the show."

"Bingo." Jason was quivering with the memory. "SCN wanted a bit more participation by mythics, but that was too much reality even for them. It all crashed at once. Easier to end things, in their opinion."

"That still doesn't explain why it took so many months for you to find me."

Jason pulled out a Red Vine and gnawed on it. "I was... dismayed for a time."

Samantha folded her arms.

"All right, I holed up in an ice cave and my horns fell out from the stress." He twirled a hand. "But I also ran five hours every day and my hindquarters are like rocks right now, so that's the upside."

"Then what brings you here?"

"Some of us are tracking down errant humans."

"Does everyone blame me for what happened?"

Jason rested his hands on her shoulders. "Darling. Sweetie. Of course they do! Mostly, though, they blame Fiona. Then they blame themselves for letting it get that far. There's so much blame we've officially canceled blaming anyone. Everyone's to blame, so no one is."

Samantha chewed her lip. "Again, though: why now?"

"It's Endless Awards time!" He clapped his hands together. "Helena got the boot and Dakota is in charge of this year's prizes and no one wants to miss the big awards show. It's our last hope, you see. If we win for being the best, most awesome show, we get a prize. And a prize can be... anything at all."

A strange sensation flowered in Samantha. It felt like hope. She was afraid to trust it.

"Also, we didn't get a chance to say farewell, Starr."

"Samantha." She was trying not to cry. "Jason, I don't think I can bear to see everyone again, and never after that. This broke me."

Jason took her right hand and held it out flat. Oleander's poultice and bandage had stanched the bleeding, but ultimately she'd needed eighteen stitches and still did physical therapy twice a week. No tendons had been severed, but one knuckle would be permanently askew. "Cool," he said, running his thumb over the long pale scar across her palm and fingers. "Makes you look tough."

"I'm not."

"You're much tougher than you know."

Gum popped and they glanced up to find Anthony staring at Jason the way Samantha expected she'd stared at the Unseelie. "Wow." He chewed. "You guys are really into baseball scores, I see."

Baseball? Then Samantha remembered: speaking of the show to outsiders translated into extremely mundane language. "Go Orioles," she said with a fist pump.

"Well, hello, you." Jason beamed at Anthony. "This underclothing store is full of very handsome and interesting individuals."

Anthony giggled.

"I'm Jason," the faun offered. "And you are?"

"Free," gasped Anthony. "I mean, Anthony. I mean, I'm free. For dinner."

"I appreciate a mortal who cuts through the clutter." Jason batted his lashes and adjusted his jacket. "You are terribly pretty, Anthony. But I have an errand to complete." He tilted his head at Samantha. "Any chance you can release this one early? If so, perhaps I might have time... after?"

"I need the money," said Samantha, feeling slightly wounded. "I can't leave early. Also, I'm not an errand."

"My mistake," corrected Jason. "You're not an errand, you're an adventure."

"Don't clock out then." Anthony waved at her. "I'll punch you out at normal time."

It was the kindest thing her interim associate manager had ever said to her.

Jason curled Samantha's hand around his bicep. "C'mon, you. It's only coffee. Coffee and tea and maybe some toast. Or fruit salad. Or an ice cream sundae. Whatever a person eats at whatever time this is. Also, some talking."

Samantha blinked at him. A tiny flicker inside her had always wondered if someone would show up for her. Dakota, Jason, Oleander—maybe even Mav. Nico seemed unlikely; she suspected the outside world would be hardest for him to learn to negotiate again. But whoever came, she'd worked up a way to turn them down—because as much as she hoped to one day save up enough money to flee her old bedroom and her mother's critical, undermining eye, she wasn't ready to open herself up to magic again. It was too capricious. It took your heart and held it up to the light and then, for no damn reason at all, threw it away like a pair of... well, underpants. She felt so fragile these days, and it was easier to drift than take the wheel.

But now something was happening, and it was Jason of all mythics who'd come. She was overjoyed—he'd cared enough to track her down and was not angry with her. Jason had pulled her from that diner less than a year ago and changed her life. She owed him at least a snack.

"There's a diner down the block," she suggested.

"I had noticed," said Jason.

"Have fun!" cried Anthony.

"We will." Jason gave Samantha's hand a squeeze in the crook of his arm. "Now, drop the bras, honey—and come with me." He paused. "Goose eyeliner, it's been a long time since I said *that*."

* * *

THIS IS WHERE I came in, thought Samantha as they entered the diner by the side of the highway. The restaurant was not busy, its chrome-edged stools gleaming unused in the late afternoon light, the deep booths nearly empty.

Then she spotted the trap.

"Oh, hell no." Samantha came to a hard halt.

Fiona was sitting alone in a booth by the window, swirling a spoon around in a coffee mug, her arm in a gold lame sling.

Jason caught Samantha as she tried to back out. "I know. I know! But once we knew where you were, she insisted the only way you'd come back is if you two had a sit-down."

"I am *not* sitting down with Fiona Ballantine like we're old buddies and last I checked there is nothing to come back to!" Betrayed, Samantha wondered if this was Jason's real reason for finding her—because Fiona wanted it.

"Then, don't," he said. "Sit with Ethel Smith."

"*Ethel?*"

"I understand it was a popular name back in her day. You're not the only human to have reinvented herself."

The woman in the booth was pointedly not looking at them. She was smaller than Samantha remembered, paler and older looking with makeup—clearly not magic—inexpertly applied, and barely disguising some bruising. Her fall down the not-bottomless pit had been far from a soft landing, Samantha realized.

Jason brought Samantha to the table and the women locked eyes. Samantha wrinkled her nose; there was a faint whiff of the sewer underlying an almost overpowering linden tree and lavender perfume.

"Yes, yes." Fiona waved a pair of reading glasses in

her hand. A bit of glitter drifted from her hair to the table and shone there. "I'd almost have preferred to land in *plain* shit. At least that washes out. No matter how many showers I take, I continue to sparkle. Glitter is so persistent. The smell won't be fully eliminated until the glitter is, so here we are. Greetings, Starr."

"Samantha."

"As you like it."

"Thanks, Ethel."

Fiona's icy stare almost made Samantha nostalgic. She sat at the edge of the booth, ready for flight.

"Order away, ladies," said Jason. "Check's on me."

"You're not staying?" Samantha touched his jacket sleeve.

"Even if I didn't have a date, I think you two should hash things out without a mediator." He paused. "No blood this time, please."

"Jason!" Samantha frowned. "You are the worst."

"I'm the best." His tail tickled the back of her neck, and he bowed, then hurried through the exit doors.

Fiona stirred her coffee again and Samantha shifted uneasily. Who knew what that woman had hidden under her fake fur coat?

Eventually, the waitress sauntered over. Heavily pregnant, she wore her long dark hair in a ponytail that arced down her back. She smelled a bit like pepperoni. "More coffee, ma'am? And for you, miss?"

"Melanie Chizzoli?" Samantha gasped. "Holy crap."

"Sam Wornicker?" Melanie's face lit up as if they were long-lost friends. "Wow! You look great!" She smiled at Fiona. "We went to school together!"

"You don't say," said Fiona.

Samantha wanted to shout at Melanie, *Hey, are you*

aware the boyfriend you stole from me, your baby daddy, is trying to get into my pants again? But instead, she bit down and said, "Having a business meeting right now, Mel."

"Gotcha!" she cried. "I bet it's about acting! I knew you would be a big star one of these days."

"One of these days I hope to be," said Sam. "How's Bradley?"

Melanie ran a hand over her distended belly and pushed the other forward so Sam could squint at her engagement ring. It was about the size of a grain of rice. "We're doing the deed next month!"

"It appears you have already done the 'deed,'" said Fiona. "Perhaps more than once."

Samantha turned aside, biting her lip. She was not going to let Fiona make her laugh.

Melanie twisted her mouth and lost the gossipy girl voice. "More coffee?"

"As soon as you brew something worthy of the name, yes," said Fiona.

Samantha ordered tea.

"Charming," said Fiona once Melanie had deposited a mug of hot water and a Lipton bag on the table. "Always a pleasure to see how the next generation plans to leave its mark on the world."

Samantha steeped her bag, thinking of brownies. "What do you want, Fiona?"

The actor leaned back in her booth, glancing out at the setting sun. Her face was softer, more handsome in the gloaming. She was no longer young, but her cheekbones scaffolded her face in such a way that she would never appear truly old, either.

"Are you aware of how I spent my days prior to *Tune*

in Tomorrow?" she asked. "I was a Gibson Girl. That phrase likely has no meaning to you, but I understand you can look it up on your phone device. Suffice it to say that they liked to draw my picture. I had an audience. But that fleeting moment left me hooked on the attention the way some are hooked on opium. I turned to burlesque, sometimes with light escorting on the side. Nothing prurient; the smart ones of us carried sleeping draughts for the friskier customers. But it is—and was—always about attention. You feel this, too; I saw it on you at the convention. You drank up that love from the audience like it was water and you'd just crawled from the desert."

"The water of life," Samantha murmured. "Only, it's not just about the applause, Fiona. That's the icing on the cake. The real meal is performing. Becoming someone else and telling a story that *moves* people. Or mythics. Those centaurs in the park were so excited to see Sam because I'd made them believe in the story. You had mythic creatures worshipping you because you were so incredible at being Valéncia. That's what it was really about. The applause is a bonus."

"But it can feel like the alpha and the omega." Fiona nodded. "That is the tightrope one must learn to negotiate."

Samantha felt a strange jolt. Had she and Fiona actually agreed about something?

"It took me far too long to truly understand that aspect," said Fiona. "Hanging on to that root of what performance is about is critical, because I discovered, as I aged out of being wanted for my appearance, that audiences are always changing. They want different things. Jazz came along and they desired young ladies who looked like young boys. I missed my opportunities for marriage and children, so when Jason found me—much as I found Nicodemus years later, in a bar—I married the show. Metaphorically. The world is hard for women who dare to age."

The last thing Samantha wanted was to think of Fiona as a human being. She'd been monstrous for so long, it didn't seem fair.

"This will happen to you as well, whether you continue acting or not."

"At the moment, that's a 'not.'"

"Well." She sniffed her coffee, then pushed it away. "Perhaps that will change after the awards. The Powers That Be do love a winner, Starr."

"Samantha, Ethel."

"Good gracious, I don't give a fig what you call yourself. But you do have the bug for audience approval, even if that is not your sole motivation for acting. From that first moment you stepped into my dressing room I knew two things: Jason had chosen well. Also, I could not bear to have you around. To watch another young woman fall in love with my show, and ultimately try to take it from me. It is not easy to say such a thing, mind. Temporal Arrest is the sharpest of double-edged swords: I owe everything to the show, and have nowhere to be without it. The world has moved on and I am unmoored. I erred in making the show my life, my home. Had I been wiser, when you arrived I might not have been so deluded and grasping. So fearful of... irrelevance."

You made a speech, Samantha wanted to say, but held back. The Grande Damn seemed sincere, but... "C'mon. You were the Queen of the May over there. One snap of your fingers and everyone did what you said. Not a bad life at all. Anyway, I'm surprised you haven't been hired by another of the reality shows. Or even one of those movie towns."

Fiona shook her head. More glitter tumbled out. "I have retired. After the awards, I am done."

Samantha laughed.

"I imagine it does sound ridiculous but imagine me, starting on the lowest rung possible in a new story, even if my character is given a significant role. You see, after the trial, the Seelie Court took everything away from me. Even the awards I didn't pay for."

"Good."

"So you say. But it leaves Nicodemus without any protection at all, and he hasn't been seen since he helped haul me out of that pit of shiny, stinking foulness. I'd almost wondered if he would be here with you. I worry each moment about him. Nico puts on a good show, but he is not a strong man."

That's what I liked about him, Samantha realized. Nico had always understood his weaknesses, but he was trying to get past them—at least with her. "Maybe because you were his crutch for so many years."

Fiona dabbed at her eyes. "I deserve that. But unlike Nico, you are strong, Samantha. I have known it since that first day."

Samantha's heart and stomach hurt; she ached afresh for the loss of the show, and now for Nico, too.

"The nominations for the Endless Awards arrived a few weeks ago," Fiona said briskly, sliding an invitation across the table. "You have received two nominations; I shall be receiving a Lifetime Achievement award. This is yours."

Even after all that, they still have a prize for her! Starr's cheeks flushed, but she reached for the invitation.

The moment she touched the card, it popped into three dimensions, words sparkling and swirling above the paper for a moment before settling down to form ornate, gold-leaf letters. The awards were being held in the same Boston hotel as the convention had been, on Saturday night.

Tomorrow.

She ran a finger over the pulsing, alien name on the invitation. *Starr Weatherby*. The stranger she had been, for a time.

Fiona drummed her fingers on the table. "You should attend."

"But the show is done."

"Done, but perhaps not over." Fiona raised an eyebrow. "And if by some miracle the show does come back, changes will be made. You should be there to assist. I say this not for you, or for me. We are not important. But *Tune in Tomorrow* should endure. I wed myself to it decades ago and I believe you have, too. Neither of us wishes for it to be dead forever. It needs someone like you to make it breathe again."

We could have saved ourselves a lot of trouble if you'd just talked to me like that when I came for the audition, Samantha thought. She glanced out into the diner and caught Melanie's eye. The waitress came over. "Anything else, ladies?"

"We're done here," said Samantha.

"You're all paid up," said Mel. "That cute guy took care of the tab." She hesitated, cocking one hip back. "Samantha?"

She waited.

"I think it's cool you're making things happen. Out there. Not all of us are that brave."

"It's not bravery," Samantha insisted. "It's a feeling like you don't have a choice. You have to go and do the thing." She hadn't really put this into words before. "You can say no—but you also know if you do that's the day your soul starts to… wither."

"Right." Mel toed her shoe on the ground. "I sucked in high school. I'm trying to do better. I picture you up in the city sometimes—Bradley always talks about how great you were in the school plays, which I never went to—and I wonder how everything might be if I'd picked different. I was an asshole about Bradley. But hey, look at it this way: you could be me if I hadn't come along." She looked confused. "Or something like that."

Shit. She's right. The worst moment of Samantha's teenage life, catching Bradley and Melanie in the back room of the Pizza Pad in the summer before her senior year—took on new meaning. "Thanks, Mel," she smiled. "I appreciate that. Good luck being a mom."

"Bradley's the dad. I'm gonna need it." She gave a little wave before clearing the table and walking away.

Samantha rested against the back of the booth, recalling what it had been like to be Starr Weatherby. It was like examining a familiar coat, one that came with armor and confidence and desire. All things Samantha had never believed were part of herself.

I miss you, Starr Weatherby. And you, Sam Draper.

"There's an invitation on the table," Fiona reminded her.

Samantha popped the card into her bag. "One of these days, I'm sure I'll thank you," she said. "Today isn't that day. Tomorrow probably isn't either. Goodbye, Fiona."

She approached the diner doors and stared through the glass, past the parking lot to the highway beyond. It was a thread, one that could carry her all the way back to New York if she wanted. Closing her eyes, she changed. And as she pushed her way through those doors, the cool evening air hitting her cheeks, she felt like Starr Weatherby again, head held high and sass firmly in place. A wild excitement swept through her, and she imagined her feet lifting inches above the ground, as if Jason were carrying her. She was going back. Everyone would be there. There would be glittering prizes and sparkling gowns—who knew what kind of an award show mythics threw?

All she had to do was get to Boston.

But how?

CHAPTER 38
Highway Starr

BOSTON MIGHT AS well have been the moon.

Stumbling into her cold bedroom late that night, having quaffed more than her usual beer at Yolanda's pub, Samantha left the room dark and flung herself onto her bed face-first. There was no money. Asking Mama or even her brother would be like shouting into a canyon. Samantha's paychecks had gone towards household expenses, student loans and the occasional beer and right now she had just twenty dollars socked away under her mattress. That wouldn't even get her to *Baltimore*.

All thoughts of being Starr again fled. She grabbed the duvet in her fists, sensing a crying jag coming. Her heart hurt: not just because she would miss the ceremony, but because this was the end. The show was already starting to fade from memory; soon, it would feel like something that had happened to someone else.

Which would be true.

Her desk light flipped on, and Samantha froze. Her room was a wreck, even more so than she'd left it that morning. Her CD collection lay scattered around the floor. Fear battled with confusion as she lifted her head and spotted a familiar faun sitting cross-legged on her throw rug, leaning against her desk chair. He had her old headphones over his ears, and she made out the tinny sound of pop music.

"'Bout time you got here!" Jason sat up, pulling the headphones over his neck. They were attached to her ancient Walkman. "Did you know you live in a *castle*? You have a fondue set in your kitchen! And great weasel vests, the tile in there is Harvest Gold vinyl! I want to bottle this house and take it back with me!"

Samantha sat up, wiping her eyes. "How did you get in here?"

Jason thumbed at her window, which stood wide. That explained the chill.

"Didn't you have a date?"

"Been there, done that." He pointed at the clock next to her bed and gasped. "The number! It changed! I can't stop watching!"

Samantha sighed. "It's just my old flip clock. Mama had it when she was in high school. It turns the numbers like a Rolodex."

"A rolling deck?"

"Jason, it's great to see you again, but I'm not sure I feel like being a docent for a tour of my crappy home."

"Crap my pointed horns!"

Starr shushed him. "You'll wake Mama!" But that probably wasn't true. Once she'd downed her 'medicine,' Mama was out for the night. Bill would be stoned in the basement.

Jason held up an empty CD case: Air Supply's *Greatest Hits*. He thrust it into the air. "Starr Weatherby, you are a *tastemaker*!"

"I was a fan when I was twelve. Take it."

Jason gave her a giant kiss on the lips that ended with a resonant 'smack.' Samantha flushed so hard she was certain she'd catch on fire. "You darling! I would hire you for my show, if I had a show."

"What are you doing here?" Then it occurred to her. "Are you going to take me to Boston?"

"Hmph." For the first time, he looked only ninety-nine point five percent excited. "Unlike your centaur pals, I do *not* give rides. But! I have a solution." He gestured to the window, and Samantha peered out. A car she didn't recognize sat in the driveway.

Jason waved out the open window, and a man emerged from the driver's side. Mav wore a Navy pea coat and a wry smile on his face. A night breeze ruffled his hair and a thick section tumbled over his forehead. She imagined his eyes sparkling, and was certain they were the color of toasted pecans.

"Where d'you want to go, little lady?" he asked. "Your chariot awaits."

Samantha laughed. "It's a Prius!"

"Same thing!" Jason said.

"Yeah," called Mav. "Use your imagination for once." She bounced on her toes.

"I hear tell you need some help getting up north," he continued. "Unless you'd like to continue using your immense skills to keep lacy underthings tidy?"

"Wait for me!" It was a matter of moments to throw her clothes into a duffle bag, but she got stuck over what dress to wear to the awards. As in, she had nothing: Mama had put anything that was worth anything on consignment years ago. Then she spied her prom dress hanging lonely, still in its dry cleaning plastic. She snatched it from the hanger and zipped the bag, then scribbled a note for Mama.

"Let's go!" Samantha headed to the door.

Jason caught her arm and guided her back into the room, walking to the window. "I'm not coming for the ride," he said. "I can gallop back faster. But you two"—he flicked a gaze outside—"should get some time together. Mav's missed you."

"Could've fooled me."

"Well, he's a—what do they say, a dark kelpie."

"A dark horse?"

"Just so. He's not going to fall over himself and make grand gestures, but I think he'd do most anything you'd ask."

He kissed me once. On the forehead. I got tabled. But she didn't say that. "I'll believe it when I see it."

"Then go see it." He folded her into a one-armed embrace. That was when she noticed he'd unplugged the flip clock and stuck it under an arm. "Mind?"

"My time is yours, Jason."

"Splendiferous." He sat on the windowsill. "See you soon, Starr Weatherby!"

"Samantha Wornicker," she corrected.

"Oh, I know what I said," he laughed, and fell out the window.

Samantha ran over—but he was nowhere to be seen. The clock, her cassette and the faun had vanished. "All right, Jason Valentine," she said. "You win. Starr it is."

SOME HOURS LATER, Starr awoke. She was in Mav's car, but it had stopped. Outside was dark with a faint hint of sunrise coming on. She rubbed a bit of dried sleep from the corner of one eye, wondering where her escort had gone.

Wrapping a blanket around her shoulders, she stepped out onto the dew-dampened grass. The car was in some kind of field, the road a short distance away. Not an interstate, just a small back road. The kind she'd traveled on most of her life.

Soft shushing in the grass made her turn as Mav headed back to the vehicle, tucking his shirt in. "You were out cold," he said. "Had to find a necessary. Empty cornfield's as good as any."

"Where are we?"

He pulled out his coat and another blanket from the car. "New Jersey, I reckon. Still shocked I remember how to drive. When I first signed on the show, they didn't even have interstates. Driving down here was an education. Rest stops! D'you know there's something called a Cinnabon and it's the size of a dinner plate?" He snorted softly. "Listen to me, yammering like a teenager."

Starr's throat felt tight. She'd never seen Mav nervous before. She leaned against the car's hood, which was still warm from the engine. "I missed you," she whispered. It was a little easier to say in the fading dark.

Mav was silent for a long stretch. "I should've come after you when I saw Fee with that knife. All those years, none of us knew she had a deadly weapon in that cane. That's on me. I could give you excuses—like Nora having this vise grip on my arm and saying, 'If 'Melia can't be here you gosh darned better be,' though she didn't say 'gosh' or 'darned.' But I saw Nico pull out a MARBLE and pop after you and I knew you'd be OK. He'd do anything to prove he's a good guy."

"His ways are mysterious to me."

The sky glowed with faint oranges and pinks. Samantha

wondered when she'd last seen a sunrise. "Why did Nora want you there so badly?"

Mav paused. "Well, it's been a lot of years since I became a dad."

Samantha's legs buckled. *I should have seen that coming. Wait, there's no way I could have seen that coming.* "But Nora and Amelia are—"

"I'm a family friend, 'specially since I helped 'Melia get out under Fee's nose. They wanted a kid. I said I'd help. Amazing what they can do in a lab these days. And they wanted to have the kid before 'Melia got too old to be a stay-at-home mom."

"Shame there is no show anymore," said Samantha. "They could re-hire Amelia again."

"That is a most interesting consideration, Starr."

She almost corrected him. Paused. But no: with Mav, she felt like Starr. Somewhere before the Maryland border, she'd left Samantha behind. "I guess I'm back to being myself again."

"Darned glad for it." He leaned on his elbow and turned her way. "This Samantha Wornicker is a perfectly nice person from a perfectly nice town, but she don't work on my show. We don't do 'perfectly nice' there too well."

"I think you're perfectly nice, Mav."

"Why must you insult me?"

The sun was coming up and she could read his features. She remembered the days when Jason had them hold one another's gazes for an extended pause. She knew every line in his face, every crease at his eyes and the freckle at his jaw. "Toasted pecans," she murmured.

"What's that now?" His voice was soft as the dawn.

"Your eyes are nuts." She stopped waiting, bringing her

mouth to his, coming in tentatively at first—what if she was wrong about him—but to her great joy, he pressed back. Mav rested his hand at the back of her head, pulling her close with a shuddering of air, as if he'd been given a great surprise. Then the kiss ended and Starr—she would be Starr forever, now—bent away from the car, hoping for more.

"At least it wasn't on the forehead," she said.

He chuckled. "I'm a slow mover."

Starr watched him carefully. Wondered if he had a speech for her, the way Nico had after they'd bounced just before the live show. Instead, Mav slid his hand around her waist and pulled her close. They turned toward the daylight. His voice was warm and soft, just like his kiss.

"It's gonna be a good day, Starr Weatherby."

CHAPTER 39
Starr Spangled

"Here." Amelia handed baby Wisteria over to Starr and grabbed her sewing kit. "It nearly fits, dear, but you have to hold still."

She knelt on the hotel room carpet, pinching the iridescent fabric against Nora's hip, and shrugged it down. Nora's gown resembled a metallic rainbow and contrasted strikingly against her pale skin—but it had been purchased pre-pregnancy and no longer fit around what Mama would have called the "rear and gear."

Pacing around the room with the baby, Starr marveled at how quickly things had changed. Yesterday she'd hung up overpriced bras in Maryland; today she was in Boston dandling the baby of her former co-stars while watching one of their wives do nip-and-tuck.

"What if I leak during the ceremony?" Nora fretted.

"Could happen. Probably will, these things take so long. Bring the pump." Amelia spoke through pins clenched in her teeth. "Crowd'll love it; you're the one who ushered in the Fae baby fad, after all."

Starr had only one ear on their chatter, entranced by

the miniature features of Wisteria. She looked for Nora in the baby but saw only Mav's high forehead and chin. Open, her eyes were pale blue but at this moment she slept, crepe paper-thin eyelids shifting as she dreamed.

"I hear they're allowing mortal kids in the movie towns and on other shows." Nora tossed her hair.

"Yes, dear," said Amelia. "You're a trendsetter. Now, my 'it' girl, please hold the fuck still."

Starr and Mav had arrived in New York by breakfast, picked up Nora and co. at their apartment, then continued on to Boston. Starr had to remind herself not to stare at Amelia, the disappeared woman she'd spent so much time investigating last year. She hadn't pictured a fifty-something woman with a long white braid running down her back. Her eyes were lively and quick, her face smooth and unwrinkled. She moved like a dancer but when she spoke—pure steel. Nora said her parents had emigrated from South Korea when she was just three. She and Nora were so easy together, giving off a welcoming, reflective glow to everyone around them.

Now they were making last-minute preparations for that night's awards. Mav had vanished into his own hotel room for a nap after promising to escort everyone to the ballroom later, and given Starr a brief kiss before leaving. The sensation lingered on her lips—and everywhere else.

Satisfied that Nora could pass muster at the awards, Amelia waved at Starr to reveal her prom dress. Starr handed the baby off to Nora and held up the cheap old thing, a ten-year-old ruched blue satiny fabric with long sleeves and a plunging neckline.

"Well, that's... dreadful," said Amelia.

"It was on sale."

"Nora—"

"On it." Hefting the baby onto a hip, Nora withdrew a garment bag from the closet. "Always good to have an extra. This might work for you."

Starr gaped at what emerged: a cream-colored, ethereal ankle-length dress accessorized with sparkling, candy-colored beaded shoulder straps and matching belt. The bejeweled fabric seemed drizzled in raindrops.

"Er, Nora, you've never been my size in your life. Where did this come from?"

"Old girlfriend," she shrugged. "You'll get a tour of my closet sometime."

"Nora acquires dresses like some men put notches on bedposts. Least, she used to." Amelia nodded at Starr. "Get your pants off."

Nora raised an eyebrow. "Ahem."

"Fine. Get your pants off, woman to whom I have no sexual attraction."

"Better." Nora settled Wisty into a portable carrier. A hotel-arranged sitter would watch her for the duration of the show, which meant Amelia could attend. Jason had provided wards on the room to prevent mythic baby-snatchers.

Starr wriggled into the dress, which was far too long and utterly un-zipperable in the back. She'd just hoisted the second shoulder strap when someone knocked. Nora darted over.

"You are more generous upstairs than I'd estimated," Amelia tutted.

"I'm generous all over," said Starr. "Allow me." She reached into the bust; often she could slide herself into a dress with sturdy stitching and a decent zipper if she manipulated the girls first.

"Ladies," came Nico's smooth, assured voice from the

hallway.

Starr froze, one hand in the process of lifting a breast.

"Jumpin' Jesus, Nico Reddy as I live and breathe," said Nora. "Where in tarnation have you been hiding yourself?"

"I had a few projects to complete," he said. "Am I correct in hearing that Ms. Starr Weatherby is in your party?"

Starr peered around a corner. Nico was fenced off in the hallway by Nora's outstretched arm. His hair was shorter and he'd grown a beard. He looked older, and though she imagined it impossible, more swoonworthy.

"Hello, sweetheart," he said.

Sweetheart! Starr wanted to throw a shoe at him. All the sympathy she might have had for his rough landing in the new world had evaporated after the show had been over for a month. He'd vanished. And before that, he'd chosen to help Fiona out of the pit rather than sit with her and her sliced-up hand. Starr ducked back around the other side of the wall and sank to the floor, bending her head over her knees.

Nico took a beat. "OK, then. Glad we're all present and accounted for. See you downstairs." A soft smacking sound as Nico parted with a kiss to Nora's cheek. "I am looking forward to meeting your little one."

The door closed.

Nora loomed over Starr. "Get up, you. Stop wrinkling that dress. And no crying. There are no hairies or makeup Fae for touch-ups tonight."

OUTSIDE, THE PENTHOUSE balcony was cool, the air fresh and the view unparalleled. The wind played with Starr's curls as she searched for manic pixies on the horizon.

Nora emerged in a shawl, sliding the glass door closed.

"Wife and baby down for the count. It's Miller time." She paused. "That was a feat of magic, getting a panel sewn into that dress, I must say."

"You've both been so good to me. I haven't thanked you."

"I'll take what's on offer." Nora leaned on the railing. "We both owe you some thanks for putting a crowbar under that crone and getting her to move on. Retirement's the least punishment Fiona should get after all she did." She paused. "Still ..."

"We got the tumor, but the patient died." Starr thought again of Laurel and Hardy. Of the small grape-colored cough drop.

"Let's say life support," said Nora. "Guess we get the diagnosis soon. I don't know how much hope there is; Dakota's in charge of the balloting this time, which would have been good for us before the live show, but she split with Cris so..." She shrugged. "You do know Cris is gone, right?"

Starr shook her head.

"They had a new slot for him on a reality competition show in Patagonia or Paraguay or one of those places and he took it. Never loved the show like Jason did. Better for Dakota in the long run, I guess, since she's running the magazine and Helena is out on her big ol' ass."

"I'm sure Helena will rebound," said Starr. "The bad ones always seem to."

Nora shrugged. "Folks rarely get what they deserve. It's easier to be mean and selfish. But easier ain't always better. Having Wisty puts things in a new light for me. I want her to have a clean slate, and good role models."

"Gosh, Nora, if you start being wholesome and sweet it's going to be pretty dull around here."

Nora squinted. "For you, I'll be a jerk. You like trouble."

"Not always."

"About that." Nora leaned closer. "I don't like getting involved in other people's crap. Had too many nosy parkers doing that to me when I lived back home. But I'll say this: don't play with Charlie. He's one of the good ones. If you're not sure—if you're one of those chicks who gets off on the attention—let him go now."

"Wait," said Starr. "How did you know?"

"Give me a little credit. I saw you this morning. And I saw you every day on set. I know what that glow looks like. Anyhow, I'm the only person you know who's been married to Nico. Longest three months of my life, remember?" She reached for the sliding glass door. "All I'm saying is, be as sure as you can be."

Starr remained on the balcony a while longer, chewing on everything. She thought she'd put a solid fence around her feelings during the show, but it turned out she'd been transparent all along.

Sweetheart.

Mav resonated with her. They danced the same dance. But being with Nico was a passport to everywhere, no limits.

A person with all the time in the world doesn't have to restrict herself at life's banquet.

Eventually, Starr let herself back inside. Nora and Amelia were napping in one of the two queen beds, curled around one another like commas. Like spoons.

Like love.

CHAPTER 40
Starr Fruit

AWARDS SHOWS OCCUPIED a special place in Starr's heart; they were one of the rare times she had spent in Mama's presence for multiple hours, consecutively. Together they spent every show cackling at crazy outfits or awful facial hair while eating pizza and popcorn while the winners clutched their chests and embraced peers as they hurried to the stage to cheer God and their agents (not necessarily in that order) before striding backstage to face the press.

Starr had fully expected that kind of awards show tonight.

But after passing through the hotel's ballroom doors with her castmates, plus Jason and Emma, she had no idea why she'd ever set the bar that low. The entire room was a glamour, glammed up beyond any glam she'd ever witnessed before.

"Let the party begin," said Jason, leading his cast through the doors and along a low rocky cliff overlooking a vast green meadow framed by thick walls of evergreen trees. Above, soft azure skies streaked with rose-violet clouds canopied an open field—which stretched far beyond the true footprint of the ballroom. The air smelled of jasmine, gardenia and pumpkin bread.

Mav gestured at the scene before them. "Takes your breath away, doesn't it?"

Down on the meadow proper, where Starr had expected to see a stage and rows of chairs, there was nothing of the sort. Instead, hundreds of actors and mythics spun and twirled around a small circular platform, like pilgrims on hajj worshipping Mecca's black Kaaba. The field was filled with their whirling, synchronized dance, a hypnotic kinetic sculpture that took her breath away. Leaving the cliff and joining the dancers would be like being caught in a whirlpool.

Starr paused and set a hand on Jason's arm. "Thank you for finding me. Twice."

Blushing, Jason covered her hand with his own. "Believe me, I was torn the second time. A terrible, awful part of me needed to blame someone for the loss of my show."

Starr nodded, tears in her eyes.

Jason frowned so hard that even his outfit—the exact combination of clothing he had worn on the day of the live show, from the white-and-blue striped jacket to the iridescent boots—sagged. "But Emma helped me see things clearly."

"Indeed," the werepanther purred, slinking up behind them in a Will-o'-the-Wisp-studded cobalt blue gown, whisking her tail back and forth. "I reminded him that humans are not spells. They do not 'fix' things in an instant. They come with pointy bits and curved surfaces and squishy, delicious hearts. Human creativity keeps immortality interesting. But that creativity can lead to unexpected consequences."

"I just asked some questions," said Starr. "I didn't mean to ruin everything."

"If asking questions was all it took to sink the show," said Jason, "clearly, we were halfway to being the Titanic. I've always known that hiring you was utterly brilliant on my part." He pressed a splayed hand across his chest. "I shall never doubt you, or me, again."

A fairy the size of Starr's head descended from the trees. She unveiled calla lilies from beneath her wings and handed them out to the cast, then cupped her hands together and poured a fizzy blue concoction directly from her palms into each lily. The drinks glowed in the soft twilight.

Emma raised her flower glass. "Sláinte. Skol. Gan bei! Na zdraví! Proost! Santé! Salute—"

"Yes, yes, wordcat." Jason nudged her with his shoulder. "Drink before the bubbles disappear, my dears!"

Tipping the flower into her mouth, Starr swallowed fizz and citrus, champagne without the burn. The drink raced through her body like an electric jolt and her eyes widened. Everyone else was still sipping when her lily was empty, though she'd noted Nico hadn't touched his.

"What was that?" She burped. "Whoops."

"Fermented hummingbird extract," said Jason. "Not made of actual hummingbirds. It'll keep you—"

A faint restlessness stirred in Starr's feet and began traveling up her legs. "Humming."

Mav leaned over. "Might want to slow down a bit on the next one. This is your first rodeo."

"Is this being streamed?"

Emma leaned over and shook her head. "You have the night off to both get down and/or get funky, without fear of being observed."

Jason returned to the cast. "Let the Endless begin, my honey delights! Eat, drink and be merry because after tonight—there may be no more *Tomorrow*!"

He led the actors down a set of carved stone steps onto a pebbled path, gentle sounds surrounding them with every step. Music wasn't quite the right word; Starr picked out the rhythm of a waltz, the epic soar of an opera, the earworm of a pop tune and the brutal power of a shredding guitar solo all at once. Rather than a cacophony, it was glorious. It was everything at once. Her ears wanted to weep, her eyes wanted to hear, her skin tingled as it drank in the notes. She was totally pixilated on beauty.

I must be in the dance. Right this minute.

Mav was one step ahead of her, eyes shining. "This way, little lady." He held out a hand.

Starr took it.

DAYS PASSED, OR seemed to pass. The sky remained in gloaming for an extended stretch, then the clouds parted to reveal a sky studded in white flickering stars. Wills illuminated the edges of the dancing horde as night fell, after which… twilight reappeared, replaced by another crisp, clear night sky. Starr lost track of how often this happened. No days, no sun—only eternal dusk, followed by night.

The song never finished; one could only abandon the dance for a time. At the flick of a finger a fairy would descend with another calla lily glass filled with something fizzy, fruity and colorful. With one sip, Starr felt restored. She spun in the circle with Mav, his steps confident and attentive; then Emma, accepting Starr's hands in her handpaws, ebony fur silky as mink. For a time, Starr twirled with Jason and together they seemed to float through the crowd. Later she spun with Amelia and Nora together, and sometimes with total strangers from other 'reality' shows—*After Yesterday* and *Forever Paradise*. Eventually, Mav returned to her.

Awards... happened. At random intervals the musical layers faded, then dropped to near-silence and the dancers slowed to a stop as if the machinery keeping them turning had run out of steam. The first time this happened, Jason lifted Starr's hand to point at the sky as a small, pearlescent white hot air balloon slipped through the pink-purple clouds. It was piloted by a mouse in a flat-cap that leaned over the attached basket as if searching for a place to land, directing the balloon with small bursts of hot gas. Finding its happy place, the mouse dug into a sack and tossed a cloud of maroon dust into the air that re-formed into flashing, bright words suspended above the center stage: *Most Charming Performance by an Actor in Boots*.

"That's a very specific category," Starr murmured.

"I can't wait to see those boots!" cried Jason. "Anyway, nobody knows what they're nominated for until tonight, and many of the categories shift each year. All we know is, you wait for the mouse in the balloon. Then you discover what you won, and what for."

"So, it's totally nuts."

"The human method of doling out awards is much more mundane," he said.

The mouse heaved a scroll into the crowd, which tumbled into the hands of an actor Starr had danced with earlier from *After Yesterday*. The moment the scroll touched his fingers, the words in the air changed and flashed: *Lyon Addison*.

Lyon raised a fist in the air and a cheer rose from select paused dancers. Everyone else applauded politely.

"Squirrel nut zippers, I thought Nico had that one in the bag," Jason groused. "*After Yesterday* is nothing but flash and trash."

That made Starr realize she hadn't seen Nico since they'd come down from the cliff. *Not that I really need to see him.* She was still irritated with his distance over the past months yet yearned to tell him of that irritation to his face. She wanted to hear his excuses, find out who he'd shacked up with once he didn't have all the time in the world. Because it sure hadn't been Samantha Wornicker.

Over the next several hours, the mouse returned to distribute more awards. Mav earned *Most Ingenious Use of a Flowerpot*, referring to the moment he'd clocked his wayward on-screen brother with such an item. Nora won *Outstanding Emotional Blackmail*, which Starr thought could apply to anything Beatrice ever did. Starr thought she'd have a shot with *Most Glittering Newcomer* but lost to someone else on *Forever Paradise*. Jason kissed the top of her head in condolence.

When the mouse soared away, they danced again. Whirled. Shifted partners. The sky changed. Starr closed her eyes from time to time, enjoying the sheer sensation of movement amid the fragrant air. She never tired.

At last, though, her stomach would not allow her to dance anymore. Starving, she thanked her partner and slid from the horde to one of the expansive food tables lining the edges of the meadow. Packed with every kind of canapé, sandwich, pie, cake, casserole, fruit, vegetable and meat dish possible, the tables never needed replenishing. Starr popped a vegetable puff into her mouth, savoring the creamy, sharp sensation—and another appeared in its place instantly. Further down, Jason plucked a ripe whole pineapple from a basket of fruit and chomped into it. Another perfect, unblemished pineapple sprang up to take its place. The fruit was all ripe, soft and sweet, without a pit or seed in sight. As for drinks, all Starr had to do was think of one and a fairy would appear at her shoulder.

She chose a flaky fruit tart the size of her hand and chomped into it. The sweet berries burst in her mouth with the sound of bells.

"Wonders and delights to behold," said a voice behind her and she turned, the other half of the tart in front of her face. "'Tis the evening Starr I see."

This was the moment Nico chose to come over: while her mouth was full of tart. Starr chewed uncomfortably and swallowed.

"Buzzleberry," he nodded in approval. "One of my favorites. Like a raspberry had a baby with lavender honey and your favorite song."

Starr shoved the rest of the tart under a napkin and it vanished. Parched, she wished she had something to wash it down and a fairy appeared with a filled lily. Nico waved the Fae away when she darted to him.

"I'm not—" She coughed, clearing her throat, remembering what she wished she'd said in the hotel room. "Your sweetheart."

"Noted. I'm doing quite well, thanks for asking. What a lovely series of evenings we're having, wouldn't you agree?"

His beard included several white hairs; his curls were also threaded lightly with pale lines. None of it made him less attractive, and the fluttering bird inside her heart opened an eye.

"I should get back to dancing." She swiped at her mouth with the napkin.

"There's all the time—"

"There isn't." She banged the table. "This is a farewell party, and then we all go home again to nothing special."

"Come." He gestured at a trunk near a clump of trees and took a seat, then patted the empty space to his side. She flashed on how he'd done that on the hotel room cloud and knotted her hands behind her back, not sitting.

Nico crossed his legs and waited right back.

"Fine," she said, exasperated. "And how was your vacation?"

"I wouldn't go so far as to call it that." He slipped a hand into his tuxedo vest pocket and returned with a small green coin with the number 4 on it. He flipped it her way and she caught the coin in mid-air. Not real currency, more of a symbol. Plastic, not magic.

"Everything disappeared with no warning," he said. "One second I was watching Fiona wipe glittershit from her face, and the next I was sitting on a path near a bridge. A couple of cyclists nearly ran me over. The point is, we all got dumped by the show and we all had to go through this insane mourning period and if it means anything the first thing I thought—after I avoided being mown down—was, 'Where is Starr?'"

She set her hands on her hips.

"All right, so maybe it was the third or fourth thing. I didn't even know what year it was. I was terrified they'd dumped me back into the 1950s. But once I got my act together a little, I looked into whether AA meetings still existed and went to my first one. Then a second. That's my four-month chip there."

Now his refusal of the flower drinks made sense. Her

anger receded and she took the offered seat.

"At first I did it because I could be around people who didn't judge me for being weird or asking who the president was. I did it to stop being afraid of the world, and then I did it to stop being afraid of what it meant not to lean on magic. My sponsor is a seventy-two-year-old named Bernie, and when I told him I was older than he was he laughed himself silly. We get coffee and he never asks what I do for a living, which is great, because at the moment I don't have an answer. I'm living off my acclimated fairy gold."

He took a deep breath. "Second, I did it for us, in case there actually was an us. An us in a life where we didn't have all the time in the world. Because I discovered if that was the case, I didn't want to run out my time in the real world without seeing if we had a chance."

Starr gripped his hand fiercely, then hugged him. He bent into her like a floating man grappling driftwood. After a moment, they let go, but the imprint of him against her lingered.

"I'm deeply proud and impressed by you," she said. "None of that was easy."

Nico's fingers slipped from hers. "It was a waste, wasn't it? I should have come to you."

"What you did was so awesome I can't get my brain around it." She tried to figure out what felt wrong here, and at last it came to her. "But—it's not a gift to me, Nico. You do that kind of thing for you. That's how it ought to be."

"It took time," he said. "For a while I only went out to meetings and the corner diner. Bernie said to keep things small and manageable. I couldn't look for you. I didn't have the—what do they say these days?—the spoons. I wanted to, but I wanted to have clean hands first. To not be some quivering wreck. This is my first real outing since the show ended."

Starr took his hands again. She'd known for some time that he was more than his looks. That, given the choice, he'd let go of Fiona. But she couldn't get this dark or deep right now. She was full of fizzy drink and the music was summoning her again. Tonight was not the time for decisions; it was the night for all possibilities.

She stood. "Time to join the dance again," she said, giving him a gentle tug.

Nico came. And they whirled into the circle.

UNSLEPT NIGHTS SLID by. The dance went on. Scrolls rained down. Overburdened tables remained laden. No one grew weary or footsore. Starr's dress was as glittering and fresh as the moment she put it on.

At some point, Nico kissed her as they danced and her heart exploded. Another time, Mav had his arms around her and they breathed in one another as if sharing the air.

My life has become a reality show, she thought. *Maybe more like a soap opera. It's like making a home on the tail of a dragon.*

The music slowed. A mouse descended from the heavens, hurling a paw of maroon powder that announced: *Most Splendiferous Scene-Stealer.* The pilot pulled on the little cords of its balloon, tugging this way and that until it hovered just overhead. A scroll came tumbling down, end-over-end, directly into Starr's outstretched hands.

The words in the air changed: *Starr Weatherby.*

A cheer louder than any she'd heard these nights went up through the crowd. Starr's heart swelled, and she felt made of fizz and bubbles, her smile threatening to break her face in two. Nico and Mav made their way to her, applauding and grinning. Emma's beautiful tail stroked her curls and Jason embraced her from behind. She buried herself in mythic affection, then slid a nail under the SCN seal to discover her prize.

Temporal Inhibit.

"Inhibit?" she asked.

"Inhibit?" Emma and Jason echoed together.

A small asterisk followed the last "t" in "inhibit" and the trio read the microscopic writing at the bottom of the scroll: *Due to complications unearthed during the Ballantine/Pit Incident, Temporal Arrest has been retired. 'Temporal Inhibit' shall now permit all performers—past, present and future—to age approximately one-tenth as fast as their expected human lifespan on both sides of the Veil. Consult your updated Guide for further details, terms and conditions.*

"That's the first smart thing those Seelie've done in a hundred years." Nora nodded.

"You're *in*, darling!" Jason hugged her again. "You get to stay!"

"I have to sit." Starr slipped from mythics and humans alike and beelined to the food table. She leaned against it, trying to catch her breath, eyeing a cornucopia next to her. She was grateful for any award—*Most Marvelous Pain in the Ass* would have been just as wonderful—but this was different, somehow. It signaled not just change, but hope. They wanted her to *stay*. Her hands trembled.

Meanwhile, the mouse in the small balloon soared away, though the music remained muted. A new balloon emerged from the clouds, larger and in the shape of a human head. Starr squinted as it neared, spotting a different sort of pilot in the basket—a kitsune in a blue beret, multiple tails waving crazily. The fox shot mauve fire into the balloon, steering it toward the stage.

But the fox was not alone, and the passenger's identity became clear the moment the balloon spun around to reveal the visage of... Fiona Ballantine. From the pointed hair to the impossible cheekbones and haughty expression, Fiona's head—or the image of it—had been blown up exponentially and spread across canvas to announce her arrival. The woman herself, who Starr had assumed was skipping the event, waved from the basket.

"Will metaphors never cease?" Starr muttered, gawping at the approaching craft as it set down on the stage with pinpoint accuracy.

A small gate on the side of the basket swung open and Fiona stepped out, resplendent in a Snow Queen outfit: a stark white suit closer to a tuxedo than dress, framed by a fur-trimmed white cape with collar that swooped behind her head in a half-cowl. She raised her arms, clearly expecting more applause than was being generated.

She got it from a small group on the opposite side of the stage that hooted and cheered with abandon. Among those making the most noise was one Lyon Addison, Mr. Charming Boot Wearer, whose dark handsome face glowed with adoration.

The fox tossed out a handful of green powder, which formed the words: *Multiple Lifetimes Achievement Award*. It dissolved, then re-formed to read Fiona's name.

"That woman does know how to milk a spotlight." Nico arrived next to Starr, shoving the fruit cornucopia to one side so he could lean on the table. "That's what she really should win for."

The fine hairs on Starr's arm and neck rose. She'd sat with

a wan, listless actress in a diner the day before, a woman who seemed to have embraced humility after a stint in a foul, sparkling pit. This was not that woman.

"By the way," Nico whispered as the balloon ascended and left Fiona alone on the stage, "toutes mes félicitations. Well-earned."

"Thanks." Starr's teeth were clenched. The one thing she still needed from the ceremony was for Fiona to make it official. She could enjoy the party after that. Right now, though, she dangled in purgatory.

Fiona had already greeted everyone and thanked the SCN and *WaterWorlds* team for the special award. "It caps a wonderful, harrowing, exciting, and—dare I say it—magical nine decades as Valéncia Marlborough," she projected across the crowd. "The last months have been full of challenges, for my show and me personally."

"Challenges, like how to gaslight the entire cast," Starr groused.

"There are those of you who hope I have attended this event to offer accumulated wisdom, bon mots, aphorisms," she continued. "There are others who undoubtedly expect me to beg forgiveness and exit on a note of dignity as I announce my retirement."

Starr grabbed Nico's arm.

"But while I shall always retain my innate dignity and wisdom, I have no intention of leaving this beautiful business," said Fiona. She fixed her dark gaze directly on Starr, smiling.

"Son of a bitch!" Starr spat, much more loudly than she expected, and slapped her hands over her mouth.

A buzz ran through the crowd.

Fiona ignored the interruption. "I had entertained thoughts of going out on a high note—but ultimately, I decided, along with the insightful members of the SCN, that I still had so much to give. After some soul-searching, I concluded I was not yet done with the mythic world, if that mythic world was not yet done with me."

Starr bent over, trying to breathe properly.

"For the next six months, I shall pay my penance on MSC, our favorite Mythic Shopping Channel. I embrace the challenge of tackling a show that never ends, and never changes hosts. The magic that will allow me to abstain from sleeping, eating or drinking will permit me to announce my new lines of feather boas and mythic-styled loungewear."

"Bullshit," muttered Starr.

Nico faced her. "It was never going to be more than a slap on the wrist, Starr. Seelie don't admit mistakes, and you have no idea how much dirt she's managed to sock away on particular EVVVPs over the decades. Another phrase I learned once I was back in the real world: too big to fail. That's her."

Fiona wasn't finished, though the crowd was buzzing. "After which"—she blew kisses in Lyon's direction—"I have been blessed to be hired by a cast truly worthy of my knowledge and expertise—*After Yesterday*!"

The small *After Yesterday* cast broke into wild applause again.

Jason shoved his way through the dancers and joined Starr and Nico. "I must not kill a mortal. I must not kill a mortal." He made a fist. "We're going to make a real bottomless pit next time."

"Additionally, I formally extend the show's invitation to anyone else from my late, lamented series that would care to join me on my new journey," Fiona continued at full volume. "All are welcome."

"Poacher!" Jason gasped.

Starr looked for the exit. She was going to vomit if she didn't get out of here. Everything had soured; she had to leave. Fiona knew exactly where to stick the knife, and the only time she'd ever been able to face her down had been in the park. She'd slapped her with a muddy hand. Probably should have thrown some mud *clods*. That would have been even more satisfying.

"And so"—Fiona was wrapping up at last—"here's to nine more decades!"

The rest of the *After Yesterday* cast surged to the small stage, embracing their newest acquisition like the winning football team celebrating their coach. But they were the only ones cheering; the rest of the party had gone as muted as the music, with a low hum of discontent threading through the crowd.

"Jason, I have to—" Starr turned to tell him she was leaving, noting how he'd picked up a ripe, pit-less peach and squashed it between his fingers. Pulp and juice dripped on the ground.

"Yes?" he sighed.

Light burst in Starr's head. "I have to tell you that you are a genius." She kissed him on the cheek. "Help me up."

Jason lifted her to the table effortlessly. Starr reached down into the cornucopia basket of fruit and closed her fingers around a nice, soft piece.

"Hey!" she shouted in her own stage-trained voice. "Ballantine!"

Fiona stepped forward from the knot of her new castmates and smirked.

"Have *this* for nine more decades, Ethel Smith!" Starr cried, hurling the ripe, squishy thing in her hand.

Which was, of course, a mango.

The fruit landed inches shy of Fiona's foot but exploded

on contact with the stage and sprayed her pristine trousers with yellow goo. Starr's second fruit bomb was better aimed and smacked her in the shoulder, bursting open like a sunrise. She fully expected Jason and Nico to yank her down—but no one did.

The low buzz in the audience turned to soft laughter.

"How dare you!" Fiona shouted as Starr cocked her arm back for another throw. "Don't you know who I am?"

"Of course I do!" Starr shouted. "You're the Grande Damn pain in my ass!" And she hurled a third mango. It splotched directly onto Fiona's jacket, sliding down with orange-yellow juice, and Starr grinned with satisfaction.

Another piece of fruit arced out of the crowd, followed by a series of tomatoes, all aimed at the stage. Laughter began mixing with boos. Nora and Amelia jogged to the table and Starr helped them up, whereupon all three women began hurling whatever food they could lay their hands on at the stage.

The crowd caught on and dashed for the tables. Ripe fruit and booing filled the air. Chaos erupted. Apples, bananas, passion fruits, pomegranates, avocados, more tomatoes, kumquats, jackfruits, kiwis, persimmons. All sailed at the stage like angry insects. The *After Yesterday* cast gamely tried to shield its new star and even threw a few of the lesser-exploded fruit bombs back, but they were grossly outnumbered. Lyon held up his hands for calm—and hundreds of berries barraged him.

"Retreat!" he declared, and the cast—including Fiona— dashed from the stage, zigzagging through the melee. The last Starr saw of any of them, they were disappearing into the trees.

But the food fight didn't end there. The boos transformed

into laughter. Pies and cakes joined the fracas. Sandwiches and chestnuts. Ice cream and papayas. Tarts and sandwiches, legs of lamb and waffles. Everything from the tables was fair game, and nothing on the tables ever ran out. It was a glorious, chaotic mess, as if everyone wanted a diversion from all that dancing.

"I haven't enjoyed a good food fight in six hundred years!" Jason cried at her, arcing a pudding across the stage. At some point, he and Nico had hopped up on the table next to the women to escape the fray; Mav arrived last, having been sprayed with melted chocolate across his side. After a few minutes they were all standing atop the buffet, surrounded by canapés and fruit and sandwiches, no longer hurling anything. They were like shipwreck survivors on a raft, drifting in an ocean of insanity.

Starr wiped at her hair with a sticky hand, cheeks flushed, imagining herself as tall as a pombero in the rainforest. "This is the greatest awards show of all time," she told Jason.

Amid all the madness, a small balloon emerged from the clouds, drifting over the food fight, virtually unnoticed. But the shipwreck survivors spotted it immediately. The mouse twitched its whiskers at the mess below, tugged on the gas and soared past the stage, over the cacophony of laughter, outrage and squishing. Eventually, he slowed and tossed out a pawful of crimson dust that formed the words: *Most Outstanding Show in the Universe*.

Then, as he had for many nights, the mouse tossed out a scroll that tumbled end-over-end into the one pair of peach juice-fragrant hands outstretched to receive it, the one pair of mythic appendages not currently engaged in smearing their neighbors with an infinite smorgasbord of food.

Jason's.

The dust shifted in the air to read: *Tune in Tomorrow.*

Jason clutched the scroll to his chest, squeezing his eyes shut and staring into the purple sky. Then he held it with shaking hands, pulling apart the SCN wax seal. There was one word written on it.

Renewal.

A roar of triumphant joy went up among the cast, and everyone began leaping up and down on the table, which groaned and creaked, but did not break.

Starr had never seen a mythic cry before.

But then, this truly had been a night of wonders.

CHAPTER 41

Super Starr

ALL THE AWARDS had been handed out, all the fermented hummingbird extract and buzzleberry drinks drained. The food on the tables was no longer being replenished; pieces disappeared every second. The music lowered, then stayed at half-volume. A few dancers insisted on twirling in pairs or trios. Slowly, mythics and humans alike began exiting the glamour, covered in smears of food and drink, smelling like a grocery store explosion.

The cast had scattered. Nora and Amelia slipped away first with murmurings of wanting to cuddle Wisty, but Starr sensed that the joy of renewal—and Jason's immediate request that Amelia return to the show—likely made them want some one-on-one time. Starr delayed her own return to their shared room for now, to give it to them. Jason and Emma remained sitting atop a table, picking through the vanishing fruit and cream buns, plotting future story arcs. Their arms and tails and paws wove ideas no longer constrained by human reality; Starr wondered if the Supership Starprise might make a return to Shadow Oak.

Starr lost track of Mav and Nico. Once things quieted down, she took off her shoes and found food-free patches of grass to crinkle between her toes, luxuriating in the silky softness of the greenery. Occasionally, she took her scroll out from where she'd tucked it in her bra to make sure it was real.

She returned to the round stage, sweeping away a clean spot. Setting her shoes to one side, she sat and gazed up at the purple twilight as it flipped to night stars the way a GPS in a car changed to night mode. A man in a well-cut tuxedo sauntered her way, one hand in a pocket. A man with a greying beard and a head full of curls she'd once run her fingers through. Nico pushed aside some more detritus on the stage with a cloth napkin and sat next to her, pointing.

"That's the Flamingo Nebula," he said. "And over there's the Macaroni Cluster."

"Remind me never to ask you for directions on the open sea," she said dreamily.

Nico moved closer, the olive and cardamom fragrance of him pulling her back to a shaded park and a sparkling pond. Then she vaulted to a room full of clouds, where the weight of him across her body had been the only thing keeping her from evaporating with joy.

"She asked me to go with her," he said.

Starr knew instantly who, and what, he meant. "Oh?"

"I told her no."

"Should I wonder why?"

He laughed softly. "Remember what I told you back at the not-so-bottomless pit?"

Starr shook her head. She couldn't remember a lot of that night.

"I am not letting go." He set his hands on her cheeks

and ran the pads of his thumbs under her eyes, bending inward. They kissed, and Starr's body woke almost as fully as when she'd drunk the hummingbird extract earlier. There was a bit of Roland in him, and there always would be, just like there was Sam within her. But this was Nico. They'd bounced. "You'll have to be the one to let go first."

She didn't, so he bent in to kiss her again as Jason and Emma strolled by. "Heading out," said Jason. "The show is saved. You're both good mortals."

Starr blushed.

"Don't worry too much about Fiona getting off easy," Jason added. "The minotaur who runs *After Yesterday* and I go way back. He'll give her the *worst* storylines for the next decade at least."

"I guess that's something." But Starr didn't want to think about Fiona anymore.

"See you Monday." Emma waved a handpaw. "Same Gate time, same Gate place."

Nico gave them two thumbs-up.

"And Starr—" Jason hesitated. "Come see me when you pop in. I want to proposition you."

"Jason?" Starr's eyebrows rose.

"What he means," said Emma in her smooth, proper voice, "is that with Cris no longer in place, there may be a way to expand your role with the show. Deepen. Re-think. But I reminded him that humans require more rest than we do. There are stories to invent. Scripts to write. Myths to create. We begin from the beginning on Monday."

Stories, Starr thought, and remembered. She unwound a small pouch she'd kept tied to her wrist, and opened it, then handed the purple cough drop to Jason. "I think you should have this."

Jason held it up in the moonlight, grinned, and popped it into his mouth.

Starr gasped. "What did you do?"

"Mmm," he grinned. "Tastes like history." He rolled it around on his tongue. "Oh, my, darling. Thank you yet again."

"You're sucking on the archives of *Tune in Tomorrow*!"

"And they are *delicious*," he said. "I taste that Laurel is also my benefactor. I shall send my gratitude to them immediately."

Starr shook her head. "I will never understand mythics."

"We prefer it that way." Jason waved his fingers. "Until Monday."

They headed up the steps, handpaw in foreleg, and leaped through the ballroom doors.

"One final twirl?" Nico asked, holding out a hand. "They'll flip off the glamour any minute now."

Starr's mouth quirked up. "Absolutely. But—please tell me there's still something in here to drink. I'm parched."

"Your wish, my command, etc. etc.," he said. "Don't move."

He dashed away looking for a stray fairy and Starr craned her neck to the sky again, locating the Flamingo Nebula.

A small cough. Pardner was standing on the stage, staring down at her. She wore a beautifully styled dress made of satin and gems, topped by a cowboy hat bedazzled within an inch of its life. "Where'd you come from?" Starr asked.

Pardner gestured around the lawn. "Bros had our own dance. Too big around here for us." She paused and cleared her throat into her fist. "Like all bros, I am now a free agent. We are unionified! So I do this because I

choose to. There is a message from Mav—from Charles."
She opened her hand and revealed a piece of folded paper.
"He would like you to read this. He further says you will
know where to find him if that is your choice. And he
further says, I quote, 'It's your life to live.'"

With that, Pardner tweaked the brim of her hat and
dashed into a tiny doorway in a tree trunk.

Mav was not a mysterious man, but apparently he was
not above a little drama of his own. Starr knew precisely
where he was right now without opening the note: up on
the roof, thinking about grindylows, among other things.

A soft click—and the glamour shut down. Starr was
left sitting on a stool in the middle of a hotel ballroom,
and Nico was nowhere to be seen. Her shoes, set aside on
another stool, were worn down at the heels. Her dress was
in tatters. None of this had been evident in the glamour.

I'm the last woman sitting, she thought, and unfolded
the note from Mav. It read, *Where'd you like to go, little
lady?*

It was what he'd asked her, leaning against a car in her
driveway. Reminding her of things said and unsaid. Of
decisions she was expected to make.

The next thing she knew Starr had left her worn-out
heels in the ballroom and was running barefoot through
the lobby. *Why can't I ever remember my shoes in this
hotel?* she thought, hopping into an elevator. It was the
slowest means of transportation she'd ever been on, and
the stares of guests—wondering what sort of pink-faced
creature who smelled like tropical fruit and was roaming
around with no shoes and a worn-out dress—bore into
her.

At last, she reached the top floor and shoved open the
rooftop door with her shoulder. Before she could clear

the frame, it slammed closed on her ragged dress hem. "Crap on toast," she said, bending to tug it free. A small tear—but no luck. Standing, she shaded her eyes from the oncoming sunrise. Mav was exactly where she expected he'd be, staring out into the harbor, a dark shadow against a pink-blue sky. Out here, it was not night at all; it was the start of a new day.

"Mighty dramatic for a cowboy," Starr called through cupped hands, then shivered. April in Boston was still wintry.

The shadow turned. "Come on over here and tell me that."

"I'm having wardrobe issues."

He strolled over, laughing quietly as he discovered what held her in place. "Oh, boy." He wiped tears aside. "I don't know that anybody's ever made me laugh like you do."

She tugged on the dress as he swiped the door open. "I'm not always hilarious to myself."

Mav draped her with his tuxedo jacket and offered a hand. "Check out these colors with me." They walked to the raised deck. "Glamour's good, but it can't capture a real sunrise."

"What day is it?"

"Morning after we left. Just about eight hours passed here."

"Imposs—" But she cut herself off. With mythics, nothing was impossible. She'd figure that out one of these days.

"Am I right, then? You're giving the show another try?"

"I'm in," she said. "Fiona's not on *my* show anymore." The phrase 'my show' rang a deep and clear bell inside her. She'd won. Not every part of it; nobody got the whole pie to themselves. But it was awfully damn close.

"Gratified to hear that," he said. "Once the food stopped flying, I left to get cleaned up and thought I might drop back in on the party—but the party was over. Just a few folks dancing and a few others sitting back and looking at the sky."

And kissing. He must have seen Nico showing me the stars. But Starr didn't look away. The thing was, she had all the time in the world now. Maybe not immortality, but... something very close to it. She could stay on the show for a hundred years and only age ten. The banquet of life was almost as infinite as awards show cornucopias.

"Like I had Pardner tell you, it's your life. And being with the show again, which is right and proper, means it'll be a good long life. For all of us. Already I see you're different than the gal I picked up in Maryland. The show shines out of you like you swallowed a bucket of Wills. But this part's new for me, Starr. I never did feel like I had to fight for someone I spent all day working alongside. Don't know if I like the idea of being in a soap opera."

"Too late," she said. "They might call it a reality show, but that's what we've been in all along. Our arcs, our stories, they go on and on. Anything can be possible, if we want it enough."

"Ah, that's Nico telling you things. Guess I understand. But I'm not keen on being someone's second place."

Starr understood. She'd lost Gerry and his motorcycle to a job, she'd lost Bradley to Melanie. Good riddance to both. But those were the rules on this side of the Gate. With mythics, things didn't have to be binary. "Mav, who says there's a race to be won?"

He stared out over the brightening horizon and took her hand. "So's you know where I stand."

"I do," she said. "You're standing on a roof in Boston today. On Monday, in the mythical land of Shadow Oak. But there are so many lands to visit in all our tomorrows."

Mav's squeeze against her fingers was soft and warm. "I hear you. Think we have ourselves a chance in a couple of those tomorrows?"

Starr watched the light crossing his face, replacing shadows with sun, illuminating his warm cocoa-colored eyes. She thought about seeing two sunrises in a row with him. How managing to entangle herself with two such different men as Mav and Nico was a knot she could never undo. Nor did she want to. One wasn't much for shenanigans; the other seemed made of nothing but. And the thing was, Starr loved shenanigans as much as she loved someone who could take her seriously.

Behind them, the penthouse door squealed open. Nico hung in the doorway, face wide with surprise. He carried her shoes in one hand. The wind caught his curls and tossed them around. Starr imagined him as a wild thing come to spirit her away. A mythic, taken human form.

There was a choice to make.

But who said she had to make it?

We do have all the time in the world, she thought. *And in time, all things are possible. Just like in a fairy tale. Just like in a soap opera. World without end.*

Starr closed her eyes and chose—everything.

ACKNOWLEDGEMENTS

I ALWAYS READ acknowledgements. I am a nosy parker. It's, part of the job—whether as a journalist or an author. I always wondered how someone could be brave enough to show the unfinished, unvarnished novel she'd just poured her heart into to all those names in the acknowledgements, and also how so many people would want to read it before it was complete. Part of me also wondered *why* it required so many people to get a book published.

Now I know: It's never just about putting words on a paper and sending them into the world. Writing a book is a solitary endeavor—and, for me, a largely joyous one—but finishing and perfecting a book takes a village.

It took me many years to find my village, in part because I had to become a person ready to embrace expertise, assistance and constructive criticism. Once I was ready to show my work both to people who loved me and people who didn't have an emotional investment in making me feel like the writing was any good—only then I was ready to have a book out in the world.

Writing an acknowledgements section means I've gotten there: *Tune in Tomorrow* is a book, and will be joining the many, many books of the world. But writing an acknowledgements section is also about recognizing that while a book may have one parent, it has many caring, intelligent, thoughtful and wise villagers who've helped raise it.

Here they are, my fine cast of amazing characters:

This book is dedicated to my mother Lois. She's always been my No. 1 fan, and I'm hers.

To my wonderful, handsome and brilliant husband Maury, who is a teacher in so many ways and who not only reminds me that I have wings to fly, but clears the runway for my takeoff.

To my brother Craig, who will go to all lengths to help me sell books—including making a special at his Moonie's restaurants dedicated to them. If you're in the Austin, Texas area, skip the ribs and get a Moonie's burger!

To my friends, many of whom have been hearing me talk about being a published author since we were in grade school: Rebecca Hoffman (I know you really read everything); Julia Harrington-Reddy (you make me want to be a better person, and yes, I've borrowed a couple parts of your name for this book, dear Juju); Alexis Gerard and Lynda Del Genis, you're literally two of my earliest readers and dearest friends; LJ Cohen (your warm embrace, wonderful writing instincts and precious Starfield Farm are balm to my soul); Ian Randal Strock of Fantastic Books—you gave me the courage to reach higher; Elaine Isaak (you're a visionary writer I'm proud to call a friend, and your brilliant editor's acumen was invaluable on the developmental edit of *Tune in Tomorrow*). Ellen Kushner and Delia Sherman, my fairy godmothers, I couldn't have gotten here without your enthusiasm, guidance and open hearts. Rona Gofstein, Teel James Glenn and Carol Gyzander, Sally Wiener Grotta: you are incredible friends with dazzling writing talents who are always there to boost me, and I love you for it. Writers never forget the ones who amplify the message.

To my agent, Bridget Smith of JABberwocky Literary Agency: No. 3 is the charm! You're the one who saw me through two books that didn't sell—and advised, "Maybe you should try something different." The different thing is this book. Bridget, I'm so lucky to have you in my corner.

To my publisher and editors: I can never thank Kate Coe (formerly of Rebellion Publishing, of which Solaris is an imprint) enough for taking a chance on this wacky adventure and holding tight as we all screamed through a pandemic and shutdown. You've made my dream a reality. Many more thanks to Michael Rowley—you took the edit from Kate and made the process painless. You truly have the touch! And finally, thanks for Jim Killen's brilliant cleanup in the final innings of the game. This would look very different without all of you.

A mighty hug to my friends and former writing group partners in Tabula Rasa: Sally (again!), Barbara Krasnoff, Terence Taylor, Terry McGarry and Elena Gaillard. You were so supportive of this book from its earliest iterations, and gave fuel to attain liftoff. I wouldn't have made it without your support and insights.

Ideas are born in the strangest places, and I want to single out Rebecca Slitt from the interactive game company Choice of Games. *Tune in Tomorrow* started as an idea I pitched to you but could not complete as an interactive fiction game; with your blessing I then decided to see if it could be a funny novel. I might not have ever made it to the outlining stage without you on this one.

Further deep, heartfelt thanks to early readers Zin E. Rocklyn and Meg Elison; to my 9th grade English teacher Marcy Versel—you're the first adult I wasn't related to who encouraged me to write; the writers networking group Broad Universe, where I made my first baby steps in sharing my work publicly; to my lawyer Nicholas Ranallo for his time and advice; for the Trashcan Sinatras, who for decades have crafted songs that speak to my heart—thank you for letting me use some of *your* words.

Anyone I forgot: My apologies! Remind me and I'll get you into the next book.

Finally: A hearty hug to everyone I've ever encountered as an entertainment journalist—co-worker, fellow traveler, interview subject. "No one is safe around a writer," says my husband, and he's a wise man. Still, the business of show is also the business of storytelling, and when done well, that's how you make magic.

That's how I've always discovered mine.

Randee Dawn
March 30, 2022
RandeeDawn.com

FIND US ONLINE!

www.rebellionpublishing.com

/rebellionpub   /rebellionpublishing /rebellionpublishing

SIGN UP TO OUR NEWSLETTER!

rebellionpublishing.com/newsletter

YOUR REVIEWS MATTER!

Enjoy this book? Got something to say?

Leave a review on Amazon, GoodReads or with your
favourite bookseller and let the world know!